DUE
WEST

DUE WEST

30 GREAT STORIES

FROM ALBERTA

SASKATCHEWAN

AND MANITOBA

EDITED BY WAYNE TEFS
GEOFFREY URSELL & ARITHA VAN HERK

COTEAU BOOKS, NEWEST PRESS,
TURNSTONE PRESS

This anthology celebrates twenty years of publishing for Coteau Books, NeWest Publishers, and Turnstone Press.

Cover design by Dik Campbell.
Book design and typeset by Ruth Linka.
Printed and bound in Canada.

The publishers gratefully acknowledge the financial assistance of the Alberta Foundation for the Arts, the Manitoba Arts Council, the Saskatchewan Arts Board, the Canada Council, the Department of Canadian Heritage, the City of Regina Arts Commission, the Manitoba Department of Culture, Heritage and Citizenship, and the NeWest Institute for Western Canadian Studies.

Canadian Cataloguing in Publication Data

Main entry under title:

Due west
    "20th Anniversary anthology co-published by Coteau Books, NeWest Publishers and Turnstone Press."
    ISBN 1-55050-096-1

1. Short stories, Canadian (English) – Prairie Provinces.* 2. Canadian fiction (English) – 20th century.* I. Tefs, Wayne, 1947- II. Ursell, Geoffrey. III. Van Herk, Aritha, 1954-

PS8329.5.P7D83 1996   C813'.01089712   C95-920252-8
PR9197.32.D83 1996

Coteau Books	NeWest Publishers	Turnstone Press
401-2206 Dewdney Ave	310-10359 Whyte Ave	607-100 Arthur Street
Regina, Saskatchewan	Edmonton, Alberta	Winnipeg, Manitoba
S4R 1H3	T6E 1Z9	R3B 1H3

Contents

Introduction

Welcome to *Due West* – thirty new stories mapping the territory of prairie fiction in the nineties. For each of our three presses, Turnstone, Coteau, and NeWest, it's a joyous celebration of twenty years in publishing, and a recognition of the wonderful stories being told here. I suppose it's also a tribute to cooperative ventures, something else that's thrived in Manitoba, Saskatchewan, and Alberta.

When we all began publishing in the mid-seventies, there were very few publishers on the prairies; now there are many. Over the last twenty years, the publishing and writing communities have developed and flourished together, winning countless awards and receiving national and international attention.

It's easy to understand the acclaim when you read the many fine stories collected here. And this is only a sampling of the excellent work submitted, because the editors were limited to ten stories each. As you'll see, some of the writers are among the best known in Canada and others are at the beginning of their careers.

It's always exciting to have the chance to look at the spectrum of work being done in a given time and place. I want to thank all the writers who submitted work to *Due West*. And I want to thank Aritha van Herk and Wayne Tefs, my co-editors, for taking on their tasks in the spirit of adventure and friendly cooperation that made the creation of *Due West* so much fun.

Geoffrey Ursell, for Coteau Books

It's twenty years ago, and you're sitting in a pub on Pembina Highway in Fort Garry and a clutch of dreamers is dreaming words, words in ink and cut pages and covers. You're dreaming the book, the tangible, tactile object. You haven't heard yet of perfect binding, of dingbats, of saddle stitching, Corel, Ventura, fulfillment, or financial statements. You have no notion that you're looking down the dangerous end of a telescope at more than two hundred published books, at Governor General's Awards, at GG nominations, First Novel Prize nominations, Lamperts, Leacocks, Lowthers, McNallys, the delighted faces of dozens of first-time authors. You certainly are not contemplating twenty years of labour, of screening twenty thousand manuscripts, of Editorial Board meetings, conferences with writers, proof-reading, copy-editing, launches, grant applications, Literary Press Group, the ACP, conference calls – if you had, you probably would not have hazarded the dream. The work alone would have thrown you off. No, you are in love with words, with story, with song, and you are doing nothing more than dreaming the book – a simple thing, a good thing, a thing that carries and sustains what you are and what the place you live in may become.

Wayne Tefs, for Turnstone Press

Strangely, and not by design, many of these stories declare themselves as being in some way preoccupied with bodies: bodies of land, bodies of water, bodies politic, and human bodies, flawed but indelibly fascinating to every reader for their boundaries and edges, their joys and griefs, their organizational strategies and negotiations. Whether the body is in hiding or on display or intent on transforming itself, whether the body is Godiva's legendary body eager to escape its famous nudity, or Joe La Mar's body broken in the service of the first Calgary Stampede, these stories evoke more than a material organism. They articulate the body in distress, the body ecstatic, the body invisible, the body revised, altered, disfigured, magical, mutilated, passionate, and disgraced. But in all these fictions, the body's true inheritance is its imagination, capable of making land out of the sea, capable of floating or vanishing, capable of transcending both corporate and corporeal. These stories disrupt the everyday world's insistent materiality; they enact a gesture of reconciliation between the physical and all that is spiritual, emotional, intangible. Such constellations of embodiment trace the vivid language that transforms solid flesh and bone into the realms of fiction.

Aritha van Herk, for NeWest Press

Eleanore, Remembering

SANDRA BIRDSELL

My grandfather was known for his ears. They were huge. He told me they came from the ocean.

"My birth was imminent," he said. He stressed the word, *imminent*. It was a new one. He'd learned it from "Increase Your Word Power," in *The Readers' Digest*.

"And wouldn't you know it, this angel inspector? He was assigned to me," he explained. "He was supposed to keep his eye on my development from a seed to a baby, but he feel asleep at the wheel. And there I was, about to slide through the trap door into the world, when Inspector #38 woke up. Lo and behold, it was not good tidings of great joy. He noticed that I was short two ears."

He tapped a jumbo ear that lay flat against his head, its ivory folds spiralling inwards, a giant scallop shell. "This is what he managed to come up with on such short notice. He claps these things onto me and away I go, out the trap door and into the wild bruised yonder."

I never knew whether the slip of his tongue was intentional or not.

My grandfather's ears could hone in on the flight of a monarch among the purple spikes of blazing star edging his garden. They quivered with the roar of land slides when he drew his finger through the earth to make a trench for planting seeds.

"So, where did the angel get the shells, hey?"

"He had them in his pocket, I guess."

"Angels have pockets?"

"His robe. He had them in front, here." He slipped his hand into his shirt. He knelt among melon vines,

1

his tweed cap, as usual, low on his brow and his face shadowed and seeming to be all nose and chin.

That day the air was for swimming in, silky with moisture and heat. But still, he wore his dark twill, double-breasted jacket. He had been married in it, wore it to church twice a week, to weddings and funerals, when he collected his mail at the Post Office, and to work in his garden. When he died, the jacket went with him. His skin was always cool and dry, and smelled of yellowing newspapers. My grandfather was a man of out-dated stories that none the less, must be told. He was a leaf withering and straining to be released by the tree. A garden kind of man.

"So how did the angel just happen to have shells in his robe?"

He yanked on his long pale ear lobe, as though to jar the answer from it. "They were a souvenir," he said, at last. "From Santiago. Spain."

His head pivoted on its scrawny stem as he looked out at me with eyes that had the transparency of a dream. He put his finger against his lip for silence and turned an ear into the earth.

"What was he doing in Santiago?" I asked, but I knew the answer. I had read "The Miracles of Santiago," in *The Readers' Digest*, too. "The earth rings, did you know that?" he asked yesterday, out of the blue. "It makes a noise." I knew that he had also read the story about earthquakes in the most recent issue. Volumes of *Readers' Digests*, his English language primer, filled a book shelf in my grandparents' bedroom.

"Inspector #38 went to Santiago to visit the remains of apostle James. Now, be still," he said. He pressed his ear against the brocaded skin of a musk melon. He listened for heart beats of musicians, an orchestra inside the melon, an orchestra of seeds.

2

"Playing a serenade. In B flat," I said, because it seemed to me that likely a lot of sleeping went on inside melons. It was the only way the vines and leaves could bear the crowding.

He shook his head. "Don't forget about the trumpets." He meant there were orange blossoms inside the seeds too, lifted, toasting the future births of other melons.

Seeds are the Alpha and Omega, he once told me. The beginning and the end of every garden. He had pointed out the strategy of garden warfare, how weeds most resembling carrots would spring up beside carrots, wild cabbage among the pure in heart. I had always heard in the telling a message for me to beware.

My city cousins were coming out for a visit later on in the day. That was why we had been harvesting the garden. My uncles and aunts would come with their monthly offerings, envelopes crackling with dollar bills slipped into his palm during the parting handshake. And he in turn would present his. Bushel baskets of potatoes rested against the side of the house, still wet; washed clean. He would fill gunny sacks with carrots, beets, and turnips. With melons? I wanted to know.

He smiled and said he hadn't forgotten his promise. It was time now. I could go with him and choose my watermelon. As he pushed the wheelbarrow through the garden I followed, setting my feet into his boot prints, my eyes moving up to the small of his back and a feather of dust on his dark jacket. The jacket had been a gift from a Count Nicholai Petrovich Urusov, chief of the Red Cross in Russia whom he had served as Secretary for the Department of Nurses in Odessa as a young man. When he said the word, *Odessa*, he lifted his head and gazed out over the garden, at the tops of plum and apple trees standing across the back of it. It was as though, for

3

moments, he was standing on the Monumental Staircase in that city, and looking across the Black Sea.

My grandmother was at the kitchen window that morning, vigorously cleaning an already spotless window pane. While my grandfather was the keeper of the garden, my grandmother was the keeper of the house and of the ghost in its pantry. She had seen the ghost of a young girl, a girl with yellow hair, several times in the pantry. A girl who had smiled at her while she reached for the flour tin on the middle shelf. My mother had explained that what my grandmother had seen the first time had been brought on by a flu, a high fever had induced hallucination. What she continued seeing after that was the creation of her imagination; a longing to see Neta, a daughter she had left behind in the old country. An extraordinary child, Neta, an angel in human disguise with saintly and perfect features.

I had heard the story of Neta several times. When the entire family had fallen ill with typhus, Neta had nursed them. She had played Schubert and Russian folk songs on the piano to soothe their fevered brains. Hammered the seams of their clothing to kill lice, washed their bodies clean of excrement, sang and prayed, brought them back to life and then died. *Please excuse me for not being perfect,* my mother would say to the hall mirror when she stepped in the door from visiting my grandmother. *But I have no desire to be six feet under.* When I told her that I preferred to stay with my grandparents for summer vacation instead of taking the train to the lake for summer camp, she said to herself, *Oh look at that one, will you? She wants to be a Neta.*

But I wasn't thinking of the ghost in the pantry as I followed my grandfather that morning, going to the back of the garden and the watermelon patch. I was thinking about my city cousins arriving. Of David, being able to choose his watermelon.

I selected, of course, the largest watermelon in the patch.

One day during my summer vacation, my grandfather had put a new twist to the story of how he'd come into such large ears. We had been sitting in the front yard on a bench, watching children pass by the lane on the road. Even though I had only travelled from Main Street and the suite of rooms where I lived with my mother overtop a Hairdressing Salon, to the end of Colert street where my grandparents' lived, it was as though I had entered another country. I preferred the stillness and intrigue of my grandparents' sadness to the tight clutter of my mother's rooms that always held the faint odour of face powder mingled with ammonia from hair permanent solutions. "Once upon a time," my grandfather had said. "Once upon a time, long ago and far away. I was on a ship. This ship was called SS Burton, and we were steaming to Canada. I was standing on the deck, watching the land disappear. Suddenly, he said, my ears started to shake. They had heard the ocean, you see. And before I knew what was happening, my ears pulled me across the deck to the railing and were about to jump over it and into the deep, when a man stopped me. Just in time. He was a Goliath of a man. He sat on me night and day. Stopped my ears from going home and taking me along with them. That's why we came here, to Manitoba," he said. "Because it was far away from oceans." His watery eyes had turned to the horizon as he spoke; to a far shore.

My grandmother had come upon us without our knowing. "Papa!" she scolded him. "Don't you make fun," she said and shook a finger at him. "Don't do that. You'll see what comes of it." She plowed across the front yard through a tangle of overgrown flower beds to the water pump. Its handle squealed and water splashed into her pail in a furious gush.

"Now, see what happens when you make fun?" she said, later. Her hands dipped rags into a basin of water. She pressed wet clothes against his brow as he lay still and silent, face white and rigid with the pain of a migraine. "You see?" my grandmother said as she parted his hair gently, showing me a ridge of proud flesh where a bullet had nicked his skull. *They tried to kill him,* my grandmother said, but would not say more. It was enough information for me to feed on while he stayed in bed the remainder of the day, half-dead.

I watched my grandfather flick a knuckle against the side of the watermelon I had chosen. "How do you know the angel was an Inspector #38?"

He turned his back to me, flipped out the tab on his shirt collar, showed me the #38 on its label. Then he rapped against the melon, on all sides of it, listening intently.

"I'm not sure if it's ripe. Maybe so. Maybe not."

Then he did something I had never seen before. He took a jackknife from his pocket and opened its blade. I was both frightened and awed that he meant to cut into a melon still attached to its vine. He made three small incisions the shape of a triangle that became a plug. He pulled it out and peered into the wound. "It's not," he said. "Take a look."

I set my eye against the hole. I thought I could see pale seeds floating among a stringy forest.

"Did you know that seeds have memories?" he said, as though it had only occurred to him. "They can remember every garden they came from. Even that first garden, Eden," he said with awe.

Seeds have memories, I thought, as I floated in a trough filled with tepid brown water. I wondered about my father. It was said that he was a baseball player who had come to town on a tournament. Or, that I was the daughter of a speed boat racer from Michigan who had attended a boat regatta. An Irish boxer, a light-weight champion with a singing voice like Mario Lanza. But more than likely because I was pale-skinned, blonde and blue eyed, my father might have been the son of a Ukrainian baker in a town close to the American border. The previous year I had taken the train, gone to Gimli for Summer Bible Camp, and when I unpacked my suitcase, the camp counselor had eyed my *True Romance* comic books, the bottles of nail polish, my painted toenails, and remained silent. I was a fatherless child, illegitimate, after all, acute forbearance was the order of the day; painfully apparent tolerance. I was special, my grandfather told me, I was wanted, and after that, I didn't lose an iota of sleep over who my father might be.

I floated in a corridor of shade cast by the house's extended roof, a wood colonnade, where my grandmother sat on hot afternoons with her basket of mending. My grandfather had set the trough under a drain pipe to catch rain and given us, his grandchildren, a pool to splash in. The trough had once watered farm animals, a left-over from his brief farming days, east of the Red River. Several volumes of a Royal Britannica encyclopaedia stood on a china cupboard. Evidence of an even briefer career as a door to door salesman in the city of Winnipeg. A row of gladioli, bent with the weight of crimson blossoms, arched across the bleached wood of his potting shed, off-spring of a handful of corms carried in a pocket on the voyage from Ukraine to Canada. In the china cupboard stood a cream jug his grandparents had brought with them from

Poland to their new home in southern Ukraine. My grandfather carried in his eyes the colours of all the seas his family had known. It seemed to me that the bringing and carrying, to and from, had stopped. That something had ended, here, in his garden.

My cousins arrived late in the afternoon. I heard a car enter the lane and went into the front yard to watch. Moments later, another car turned in from the road. Branches scraped against metal as the vehicles travelled the narrow path that opened suddenly to the front yard where I waited. A path that opened to a vine arbour, the water pump almost hidden among spikes of delphinium, phlox, oriental poppies gone wild in random spurts of colour. My grandfather waited in the garden while my grandmother came to the front door untying the strings of her apron. He had swept the yard with a willow broom and so the earth around the house, the paths in the garden and to the ice house and privy beyond it, looked darker, fresh and decorated with wavy lines. They had been anxious all morning that their feet, or mine, shouldn't be the first to disturb the symmetry of it.

Immediately the garden filled with the sounds of greetings as women reached for one another, exclamations, as my mother appeared at the end of the lane, a slender frame in a white and navy polka-dotted dress, carrying her hair-dressing tool kit. Before the end of the day the ground would be spattered with a confetti of hair trimmings.

When they had finished greeting one another, they moved to the side of the house and into the shade of its extended roof where spindle chairs sat in a row, boards covered the water trough, becoming a make-shift table with an embroidered tea cloth. My grandfather followed, but stood apart from them as they gathered in the shade. His hands dangled at his sides like spotted potatoes. Someone opened a car's hood and the men leaned over its engine, their oblique and truncated discussions beginning; and my grandfather returned to the garden.

David had grown taller I noticed, as he and I walked to the front yard and entered the diffused light of the vine arbour. His father had taken a longer route, he said. They had driven miles out of the way across secondary roads in order to cross the Red River on a ferry at Saint Adolphe, because David had requested it. David had rheumatic fever and was not allowed normal child's play; his parents compensated any way they could. He couldn't wait, he said, for the trip home and the danger of the car inching down a slope onto the ferry. He wanted to see the river again, its surface dappled with light; the dragon in its depths. He couldn't wait, he said, to read his newest story to me. David planned on being a writer, and already he'd filled half a notebook with stories. He'd learned a new rule for writing, he said, when he'd finished reading. That rule was, he said, his voice sturdy and confident, to never begin a sentence with the words, *and* or *but*.

And once upon a time, I thought, as I led David to the back of the garden to the watermelon patch. But once upon a time. I liked how it sounded. It suggested the extraordinary might happen. Like stepping into the pantry and finding a ghost.

Because I didn't have any new rules of writing or words to dazzle him, I showed him my watermelon. "It's not ready yet. Know how I know?" I pulled its plug free and told him to look inside.

"I don't see anything." He sounded as though he suspected a trick. The kind of trick that had once been played on me at a birthday party. I had been urged to look through binoculars, promised that I would see a tropical island in its lenses, but what I got were eyes rimmed with charcoal.

Inside the melon seeds there are orchestras, a symphony in the round. There are melons, inside melons, inside melons. The women began calling for us. It was time for lunch, they called. It was time for asking the blessing on the food, for singing and eating. Hurry, they pleaded, and as David began to run, they cried out in unison, "Stop! Stop! David, stop running." He slowed to a jog and I sprinted past him easily, and sang in passing, "Beat you."

He arrived moments later, scowling and obstinate looking, swarmed immediately by an angry mother and aunts who fussed and scolded. After what we've been through, and now, to have this. To have a child born in this new country, afflicted with a bad heart. Remember the hunger, the disease, they said; remember Neta. Yes, remember Neta, my mother said through the row of hair pins held in her teeth. Poor Neta, the angel in disguise. My grandmother cleared her throat noisily and the women fell silent. It seemed to me that it wasn't a silence they fell into with ease.

David pushed the women away and stomped off into the house to sulk. Let him, my grandmother advised. Sooner or later his stomach would overrule his stubbornness. I wrapped a bun and cheese in a cloth and went looking for him. I liked the fringe of his almost white eye lashes, was awed by his confidence. But when I looked for him, he wasn't in the house.

"David," the women called for him, their voices high with a faked cheeriness, but I heard their panic as I looked inside the ice house, in the tall grass beyond the fruit trees where we sometimes hid. "David," they pleaded when he wasn't found in the arbour, or anywhere in the front yard or back yard. Then my grandfather, his face taut with fear, left the yard without speaking. He walked down a hill that led to the river, his stride long and arms swinging, walking faster than I had ever seen him walk. Moments later he emerged from among the trees and stepped onto the road with David in hand. What next? the women's eyes asked, as they sighed with relief. They hurried to prepare a plate of food for the truant David; my mother slipping two sugar cubes beneath the plate's rim.

"Spiders talk to each other," my grandfather said. It was late in the evening and the company had left. My grandmother was in the house at the kitchen table, a lamp set down onto it and shedding its light across the pages of her open Bible. We sat in the semi-darkness, our backs against the house, looking across the garden. Fruit trees sprawled against the purple sky, their crooked limbs glinting with light as spider silk billowed in an intermittent and cool breeze. Spiders talked about what they were afraid of. I, too, had read "The Wizardry of Webs" in *The Readers' Digest*. They talked about hunger and desire.

"They talk to one another through their threads," he said.

Baby spiders fly away from their mothers on strings of silk, over fields. Over mountains. Over oceans? I wondered.

"It's good," my grandfather said moments later, "that David stayed away from the edge of the river."

Withering corn stalks rustled, the sound of it like hands clapping, applause echoing in a hall, far away.

"There was ice in the garden," he said, more to himself than to me. "And the children were sliding across it. Back and forth, back and forth, in their little felt slippers."

11

Moths battered against the kitchen windowpane, trying to get at the light.

"There had been so much rain. And the creek flooded onto the yard and froze. And so the children were having a fine time sliding on it. Little Neta, too. One would try and outdo the other." He gazed at the fruit trees, as though he might find the children among them, dipping and gliding.

"But then, a man came. He was leading a young man to the back of our yard. Towards the barn. The children knew something bad was going to happen. They'd already seen so much. They began to run home, all at once. The man was far enough away and so I didn't fear any harm. I turned from the window because I didn't want to witness another killing. And so I didn't know that little Neta had fallen on the ice and couldn't get up. I didn't realize that Neta had stayed behind."

The kitchen window shivered with my grandmother's knuckles rapping against it. "Papa!" she called, loudly, angrily. "It's too late for stories."

He sighed. His hands became large white fans unfolding against his thighs. "And now, it's time for tomorrow," he said, and with a groan, rose from the bench and walked stiffly, into the garden and into the purple shadows.

The following morning I set a shopping bag filled with my belongings among the watermelons. I wanted to inspect my melon before returning home. He was tired, growing too old for children and summer vacations, my grandmother had said. Please tell your mother. My heart skipped at the sight of the melon. Red ants crawled about the hole in its side. Ants crawled in and out of the watermelon, swarmed over the plug lying on the ground. In my eagerness to beat David to lunch, I had forgotten to put it back in. I looked frantically for a twig or a stick. I scraped the insects off the plug and gouged them out of the melon. I pressed the missing piece into place and left. The orchestras, I thought, the musicians inside the seeds would spill out, one by one, too soon, unformed like my grandfather without his ears. Because of me, the melons inside the melons, the memory of past gardens might be lost.

Years later, when my grandparents' house is gone, plowed under to make way for a gypsum plant, it becomes important to reconstruct it from fading images in black and white photographs, from the imagination, from what my mother can tell me. What I recall first is the bench I sat on at mealtimes. It was painted a muted blue and became my bed at night. A settle; I discovered the name for the sleeping bench in a book about Mennonites.

I also remember clocks ticking, and an enfolding stillness; hearing a gaunt lament in a clock chiming the hour. As my grandparents moved through their austere rooms, an air of tragedy entered and left with them. It had followed them from that other country. They had brought to Canada a single trunk, five children and a quiet, understated melancholy, as elegant and as rare as a Cecropia moth.

I remember the smell to the pantry, too, and its shelves lined with tins and jars of spices, drawers labelled in German Gothic script, and, that there hadn't been a single time I passed by it without expecting to see something other than a window hung with chintz curtains. Other than my grandmother at work, and the doughy swell of her pot belly beneath her apron. I had expected to see the girl, Neta, blue eyes and yellow hair as fine as cobwebs, lifting a tin of flour from the middle shelf.

What really happened to Neta? I wondered throughout the years of raising my own children; and when they had all gone away, I set out to try and uncover the mystery of the child my grandparents had left behind.

As I walked in the early morning, mist rose from furrowed ground. I tramped among herds of cows, their flanks gleaming, looked up at a Dutch windmill and imagined I was Neta. The wind off the Baltic was like sand blasting my limbs and made my body ache for days. The houses my grandfather's people had left behind in Poland were still there, crouched behind dikes and canals, braced for a wall of water the north wind shoved into the Vistula every spring, flooding its delta, a priest, a self-made historian explained. Red brick walls tumbling down were what remained of my grandparents' house in Ukraine. Broken fruit trees, bits of wire, a tangled garden strewn with garbage and pools of glass, thousands of tiny bottles. Nail polish bottles, an interpreter said, probably from a failed venture. And somewhere below the pools of glass lay Neta. What sounded like wind in poplar trees filled the air. It came from power lines strung across the valley. Above the village where they lived, a colony of summer houses spread up and across the gentle hills. *Dachas.* Tiny wood dwellings with not an inch of space more than necessary, their gardens three times their size. Identical dwellings to the one my grandfather chose to build in southern Manitoba. His was a temporary summer dwelling. A brief respite from the extraneous world.

When I returned from my travels I went to visit the site of my grandfather's last garden. I found it by following steam bursting from a chimney at the gypsum plant where the house had been. As I mounted a crest in the road, the skeletal steel framework above the plant's kilns, the steam rising from its chimney vanished. I saw his ectomorphic frame and felt his cool, dry skin. I put my hand in his and imagined our cells fusing.

What remained of his garden, a row of fruit trees, shone pearly white, as though coated in hoar frost, but it was powdered stone, I knew. White dust carried by the everyday currents of the wind. Look, I wanted to say to him. I am on to you. I wanted to show him the photographs of the *dachas*. To tell him that I now know he had never planned on staying.

But for all my snooping, prying and reading, for all the miles I had gone, I hadn't really learned anything more of him than what I had already learned as a child. Like the gypsum stone heated in the kilns, the secrets and mysteries of his antediluvian past have calcified, turned to powder carried by the wind.

Later I dreamt of him.

He was kneeling in the garden and his tweed cap dipped towards the earth as I came near. My hands were small like a child's as I set photographs around him on the ground, one by one. Look, see, there's your back yard. The creek is dried up now. That's where you saw Neta, sliding. His eyes met mine and brimmed with longing, an immutable sadness.

I heard myself say, "I want to know."

His finger jabbed at the earth as he drew a terse, vertical line, "Beginning," he said. He drew another vertical line, a wide space between it and the first one, and said, "The end." Then he drew a horizontal line between the two points, his finger stopping midway. He drew an ellipse the shape of a melon seed, enclosing all the lines. He reached for a pebble and jostled it in his palm before throwing it into the sky. As it arched up, he pointed to it and said, "You." The stone stopped moving, became a buff pebble frozen in the sky. He turned to me and said, "Just be. You just be."

15

When I woke up I realized that my grandfather had come to me in a dream. A strange dream. As my feet met the floor, the solidness of it had already dissolved and I was left with its residue, the essence of it lingering in the room as I put on a housecoat. I thought I remembered a glowing circle moving into a black frame. It looked like a tube of neon light and had wings attached to it on either side. Wings that looked to be porcelain. Large, like my grandfather's ears. I thought I remembered glowing hands moving into the black frame about to reach for the wings. The hands were going to take hold of the wings but were stopped by a voice warning. The voice said to me clearly, it was the clearest thing of the entire dream, "Don't break the wings off the desire to be."

I repeated the words as I went into the kitchen. They changed from don't break the wings off the desire to be, to, don't break the wings off the desire to be born. I was certain the first was what I'd actually heard. I took my dream journal from the top of the refrigerator and wrote them down. Later, I cross-stitched them onto a cushion that lies on my bed, so when I turn the blankets down at night, I touch it and remember.

David Goes to The Reserve

SHEILA STEVENSON

I invited one of my white friends at university from my Native Studies class back to the reserve. He offered to pay half the gas. It was one of the coldest days in January. The heater even on full defrost couldn't keep up, and I drove looking through a small clear area on the windshield, snow drifting from the sides of the road. The semis we met threw snow at us and at times you couldn't see a thing. That night we followed the taillights of the car in front. David was tired, didn't have much to say as we drove. He kept biting the inside of his mouth. We were both anxious to get in the house when we finally saw the turnoff. David really wanted to meet my Kohkum.

Kohkum had been waiting the evening through, and there was a light in the window and she had some food on the table before too long. Both stoves, in the basement and upstairs, were going. The TV turned up loud made it too hard to talk. Kohkum probably couldn't hear half what David said anyway. He was doing that weird thing of not looking at my Kohkum when he was speaking, that thing they teach you in university about talking to Indians. Cultural differences.

I hadn't been home for a long time. It's so far. No wonder my guest slept so late the next morning. At first I wanted David to get up and then I wanted him to sleep as late as he could. He managed to sleep through my Kohkum feeding the wood stove with scoops of coal, and I remembered how tired he'd been when we finally pulled in last night. I was still seeing highway, while he was just starting to butter up my Kohkum, making me jealous.

"If she brings a boy out there, he'll sleep in the

basement." I was visiting my Mom when she lectured Kohkum on the phone, her eyes on me. I could also "Stack some of that wood, do some good," even though Kohkom could ask just about anyone. My Mom has this myth that back home no one helps anybody.

I could tell that Kohkom was not too thrilled with David, his carrying on the night before with endless questions as he talked to the table, or the salt and pepper shakers. Kohkum was probably worrying – meeting David – that I must not be doing too good in school, but really it was for friends like him that I wanted to do the best I could, given my lack of serious ambitions.

Times like this when I come home, Kohkum eyes my clothes, my backpack, and she always makes it a wash day. She'd "dry the clothes for a bit in the dryer," she told me that night, hustling up some bannock and jam. "No – it's no trouble. Do you have any clothes needs washed? I have room in the washing machine," she asked David too, because that's the way she is.

That morning waiting for David, I went out to get some wood with the cardboard box. The coal smell in the air is oily and maybe an old person would feel it in their chest, taste it in the food, but Kohkum's gone to old ways even more since Mooshum died, and coal is cheaper and lasts longer. The coal is a part of Kohkum's old person smell. I can't get used to it on my Kohkum. I can't get used to her watching Oprah Winfrey either. Kohkum had just asked me if maybe David had been using drugs. I told her that David hadn't been using drugs, not since he'd been with me. Kohkum is always able to look anyone in the eye and know the truth.

The yard was ice with a pitted complexion, frozen and spotted with the soot. The wind was rattling the clothesline and the taste from the coal fire was on the lump at the back of my throat, on that somehow unexpected bit of homecoming feeling. To the right the Chevy truck stood marooned under a load of dried wood like some disintegrating buffalo in an ancient wallow. A magpie leaping was arching to the wind and doing jumping jacks, and there, my old car looking like it never left the reserve.

From inside my grandmother rapped on the window. She motioned – a skinny dog was just out of range, in case I threw a chunk of wood, or had scraps to feed him. I didn't know if he was a stray or not. He was kind of watching me and he would follow. I hoped Kohkum would think to put the coffee pot to the back of the stove to keep it warm for David, but then I knew she would.

I filled the box with wood, thinking we might as well use wood for the time being, while we're on "the reservation," that American word David used. Just that word makes me think of the reserve as somewhere exotic, like maybe Wounded Knee. Maybe it makes a place where my Kohkum is a wise elder, maybe where I walk in the valley deciphering meanings in the wormwood, churning up fresh paths on snowmobiles with my new university friends.

In Saskatoon, David was pretty excited when I had asked him if he'd come back home with me for the weekend. That felt good. The ice in the yard broke like glass in each frozen footprint. I stomped some and saved some for David to do. Suddenly again, I was fiercely glad he was here instead of gone skiing, or maybe at another skidoo party at his parents' cottage that I'd not been invited to. And he wanted to meet my Kohkum, that too made me feel good.

David finally woke up to the sounds he's not used to. I'd shut the door behind me loud and firm to keep the warm in. Kohkum lifted the lid from the stove, added wood, and the sparks flew upward. The door on the stove was squeaky. The wind was still whipping up a little snow. David must have heard the sound of the wind in the chimney change to country music when Kohkum turned on the radio, making him quit his "stinking in bed." Sometimes Kohkum's phrases make us sound like hillbillies. Kohkum asked me how school was going, and I made it sound okay, then again, not too okay, then she started the washing machine, the old tubs ready to catch the water to use again.

David finally came up in his baggy jeans and his poor boy sweater. He got the eggs fried hard and toast greasy warm under a bowl, and he was complimenting everything. He must have thought that he was really roughing it. I remember thinking that. Normally David is a vegetarian, vegan. He has that luminous transparent skin like those dolls with those baby shoes and tiny bottles.

After David finished, he wanted to go for a hike. If we were going out hiking, Kohkum had it that David could borrow the coat used for bringing in the wood and save his ski jacket.

"I hope we see some game," he said. I'd already told him that the reserve didn't have any game, no deer really, no moose – because if anything moved out here, there would be ten hunters go and shoot it up. David still had it in his head that Indians live on big game reserves or something.

The TV was on – Kohkum always watches talk shows from Los Angeles in the morning and does her work around and between that time she turns on the TV. Those old cook stoves heat up the house pretty fast, and so I was ready to go out again. There's always an extra coat, and a snowmobile suit from when my cousin was staying here before. I put on the snowmobile suit, having a silent fit of conscience about David wearing Mooshum's green coat, something my Kohkum keeps using and using, keeps hanging behind the door. Reserve style.

I stayed by the door as David got dressed in Mooshum's coat. It was like putting a mattress cover on a fence post. David is cute, he's got grunge style. He covered his throat with a flourish, and stretched a toque widely to cover his ears. I was half wanting and half afraid he'd ask for that coat as he put on work mitts and then the old corduroy cap; that feeling I get.

I had half forgotten the beebee rifle behind the door. It was one of the last of the toys not given away or hauled off by some kid. I slung it over one shoulder. I slipped the little orange tin of beebees into my pocket and I mimicked what I thought was David's exaggerated surprise. I said, "It's for targets, silly." He didn't know it was just a toy. He kept looking away, just watching his footing on the wooden step, I guess I hoped.

The wind had gone down as David and I emerged into the cold white and blue world. The sky was bright. The snow under the eaves was dented with the tiny avalanches of the day before, melted with holes and marked where a bird's flight disturbed it. It was preserved like a plaster mask and as delicate and hard as china. Dirt, curls of bark, and edges of crushed puddles marked the driveway.

"It's good you're up," I said as we walked. "This morning I already walked past the railroad tracks. That's far." Again, I could see the pile of exposed grain, a flight of winter birds, the chickadees, my cousin's horses huddled together in the coulee, and that dog with ice clinging to its muzzle. David, in the patched coat, kind of fit in like a happy tramp.

"Poor creatures," he said. I remembered he'd used that word first referring to us, that day I met him the first time

21

away from campus. He had been rummaging for vintage clothes at the secondhand store, and he remembered me from class. I didn't know him, except I'd seen him before; an artist maybe, I thought to myself. Afterwards we ran downtown in the snow, catching flakes on our tongues, laughing at ourselves on the mirror window of an office building – my hair wild and tangled and his face to me the face of a Dickens' boy in his Sally-Ann clothes. How should I act, what should I say, I often thought. I still can't explain "the grunge look" to Kohkum.

David walked on top of the snowbanks, jumping from peak to peak singing "Along the mountain track, Val-der-ree, Val-der-rah," his breath making frost on his eyelashes and on the edge of his scarf. When he turned his head, it was as if his voice came from far away.

There was a New Year's party hat on the road and I kicked at it, but its tassel was stuck fast in the frozen snow, reminding me of something. I remembered that other time, that New Year's night I was babysitting, running at two in the morning in minus twenty degrees, and I surprised some deer. I remembered I was telling Kohkum about surprising these deer that night, and how they rose round the edge of the clearing. All she could see was how dangerous it had been. I know that. It would have been irrational, except I know when to stop. I try and tell her that.

At night in winter the cold and dark makes the distance between landmarks shrink and expand, the scorching cold dilates and explodes inside your lungs. When that happens, it's like a warning. Burns you like a first kiss. But you forget sometimes.

It was the magic of how the first deer rose up and the rest exploded out in front of me, ice fog between their legs that swirled around me as I ran after them. I told

David that, so he wouldn't know I might have preferred to go to a party in the city. I don't know what he thinks we do on New Year's out here.

Kohkum had said, You shouldn't be out running in the cold. Even with a scarf, people freeze their face, their lungs that way, and you get tired and you freeze to death. Her voice rose and fell in the old time way. I should have stayed over at my cousins, and why did they let me walk home anyways. I should be more careful. Kohkum had kept her arms folded. You should listen. It's no joke, and you don't feel it coming on when you're freezing. Or you could get run over. You never know.

I was thinking about these "you never knows." It's like when you are driving and you see a car pulled over on the shoulder and you see a car coming towards you. Kohkum says you always pass both other cars at the same part of the road, and you've got to hope to hell that no one makes a mistake. You never know. After a while, I started to notice this phenomenon of passing parked cars when Kohkum wasn't with me, and so then that's when I tried to notice the times when it didn't happen. "You never know," my Mom and Kohkum say. But it's funny – it's like you get programmed and for the rest of your life you're resisting someone else's notion of Fate. That's what makes you act illogically.

My Mom and Kohkum, they're the same, no matter how differently they see the world, or talk about us kids. Kohkum will always think my Mom was wrong to start up with my Dad, maybe wrong to leave me there with her. Mom will be stubborn and they won't talk about it together, but I see it when Mom and her disagree about me, or about something my aunties or my cousins are up to.

But my Kohkum believes in a power and presence of what must be a God, and that God is in each of us, full of light. She made me believe that people have souls and we're only contained in our bodies and sometimes very lightly, like babies are sometimes, or the very old or dying are. Kohkum said that when she looked up in the sky, she was afraid of what was up there and I always think of that. I think of her telling me not to whistle at the Northern Lights. I'd do that when I was a kid. Just because. Just because that was superstition. They teach you about superstition in grade three.

I leapt from footstep to footstep, breaking through where David had been a second before. He didn't wait up. He looked like an old man from the back – Relic, from the Beachcombers.

But it was the old pattern, the way when I was a kid, Kohkum's talk as we left. "Kohkum, we're going walking, hiking! And we won't run, and I won't get lost." I had to laugh, Kohkum is always worrying. Just because that's the way she is, worrying about everyone. I remember wondering, the twin sundogs overhead, if she could ever see the Zen-like purity in a day like this one. A black crow's rush of wings startled me and the sound moved thickly in the frozen air. When I opened my eyes, David was below me, had jumped down to the road, just the two of us, our colours bold and vivid. Kohkum was too old to appreciate the crystal beauty, to be young, that must have been what I'd decided. I vowed, then, to remember and keep that day forever. I saw that scruffy reserve dog following us.

The snowbanks were piled up about five feet high to be a windbreak. The shock goes up your legs when you land. David was ahead again, disappearing behind the other side of the snowbank. It's funny how playful he is and it's one of the things that attracted me to him. I told him that, and he sort of dodged an imaginary punch, looking at me sideways. He was a clown that day, wearing Mooshum's coat and hat. Elmer Fudd. I've admitted to myself since then that I had a crush on David.

This car I recognised comes around the corner, I see it's the priest's car, him, so I have to say something to David. "It's the priest, now be good…" As the priest passed by looking at us curiously, I said, "I think his head turns all the way around."

I had gone to church almost every week with my Kohkum when my Mom left me on the reserve after Dad and she broke up. And I didn't like the priest. At the funerals, telling the people they sin, recycling sermons in the dilapidated church every Sunday. The sermon I remember was in the fall, after Mooshum died. How can we judge the servants by what each did with the money given him while the Master was away? In this Bible story, the Master is gone for years, and he returns to see how the money he has divided unequally among his servants had been invested. I know that I'm on the side of the one He called no good, lazy, the one with the least amount of money to invest in the first place, the one who was afraid to lose the Master's money and so went and buried it. The one the Master beats around the head when the poor bastard digs it up for him and tries to explain and loses everything anyway. That useless bastard of a priest left my old grandpa to die in hospital and he didn't bother to visit. We felt no need to explain that we only asked him to come for Kohkum's sake. Kohkum wanted him to visit. Often now I keep my opinion to myself, but I can't help the way I feel when I remember Mooshum's funeral. Kohkum still goes to Mass on Sundays, just like how she keeps that old coat. David must have looked like Mooshum too, to that old priest. It's funny the way now my memories spark around Mooshum that day.

We came up to the big coulee. The bush was like a venetian blind against the sun, stirring an illusion of depth and of distance, the filigree of a confessional. Single file we walked, like dropping to the bottom of a cool well. We followed the track of a snowmobile into wider white coulees, invisible from the view above. Everything was quiet, the berries of rosehips red like blood in the snow, the waxwings small grey flurries disappearing into the sun. The path itself was set above the snow and we sank up to our knees unexpectedly. And David, single-mindedly, obsessively followed the linked design in the snow in front, off in his own world.

I had never really known my grandfather. But he wanted me to go to school and get the education the whites get, get me off the reserve. He made me stay in town with my Auntie's kids, although I was back almost every weekend on the reserve, always just a few miles away. But then I felt he was just running my life, that he really didn't love me, I guess. It is a lifetime ago now, I convinced myself of that. I was having a good time I thought then. Came the day I didn't want to go back to my Mom's either. After I managed to finish high school, Mooshum hurt his back real bad. And after that he just faded away. He became an old man in the kitchen. He was there getting sicker, and after a while Kohkum and I did everything, and maybe just Kohkum after that. He didn't talk much except when he had an opinion. Except about the old days and about people I didn't know, and then never saying much to me anyway.

In those days with David, the schoolbooks just lay in the corner, and I would feel guilty. I was doing okay, but I could have been doing better. Now I think of Mooshum always there before, giving me money that he could have used for himself, helping me buy my first car and fix it up. And I think about that night of my high school grad. He was still wearing that label they sew on the sleeves of new suits. I think of that. I could have taken it off with my little pearl-handled nail file. I remember that.

David and I climbed the side of the coulee towards the snow that was less deep. When we reached the top we stopped to get our breath. Our clothes stopped rustling. It was quiet. By two hours after midday, the temperature was the highest it would be. I looked at David and his cheeks were like apples, his blue eyes clear like the sky shining behind them.

"This is great!" he repeated and I suddenly felt the same way. The blessing of that day. I wanted to say something.

He was yelling and whooping and then, far below I saw two humans appear at the edge of the clearing. They were hunting. They both had rifles. I nudged David, motioning him to be quiet. He shut up right away. He was holding the pellet rifle. The air seemed frozen and the trees below like smoke.

"Hey – who are you?" one yelled after a minute of sizing us up. We were sizing them up ourselves so I didn't answer.

"Who are you?" the bigger one yelled again, his voice cracking a little. Then I recognised them. I saw them lots before at the arena in town. They go to the hockey games, the Spencer boys, Rodney and Tom. They're just kids. I decided to see what they were going to do next.

I yelled back, "Who are you?"

I turned to David to share the joke, surprised to see the way he was holding the gun, his hand under the barrel. He looked ready to swing that gun up. He looked scared in his body, and us outlined against the sky. Maybe like a man to those boys. I must have gone grey. David said "Shsh." The boys below consulted each other.

"Jesus, David, its okay," I hissed at him and he looked at me without certainty. I pushed David to get him going, back from the edge, to break the spell and his robot expression.

"No – who are _you_?" Rodney yelled. That really gets my goat. It's like my Kohkum says, you never know.

"I _live_ here!" I threw back at the boys. I was annoyed at David. I didn't want to talk to him. I just walked, fuming, thinking. David was saying, "Wait, this thing isn't loaded. Hey, this is a beebee gun."

When my Mooshum passed away, this old man, the elder who gave his tribute at the wake, said Mooshum wanted me to go on and get my education. The undertaker had Mooshum wearing that grey suit in the casket for the funeral and that label that was on the sleeve was – gone. I found myself looking at that place on his sleeve where it had been and I burned with shame. I remember I was still skipping a lot of my classes then too. There was lots of food at the wake, and the band hall was packed with everyone from the community, Mooshum's friends and our relatives. I listened to the stories and the tributes, but all I could think of was how I never really knew him. I was just a dumb ignorant and ungrateful kid, and I couldn't stay around. I went home with my mom. I remember that I knew what I was.

After that winter break with David, I began to find something in university for my own reasons. I adopted the persona of little Oka Annie looking for Daddy War Buck. After a while I was able to start feeling right about Mooshum. And the reserve. I was the only one who knew what happened.

I have not been much for staying with Kohkum, spending my time in the city, "with friends, maybe." Monel, my mom, is always thinking she is covering for me, but it's tough going out to the reserve to hear Kohkum or my aunties. Sometimes it's us miserable kids, or then band office politics, or complaining about my mom or one of us kids who never grew up. Sometimes I can't stand it. I hate knowing I'm being used as an example – what to be, what not to be.

I am a year closer to getting a degree in the program they have for us and finally I am starting to learn how to pick electives. I find the professors and the white students will still look to me to give "the" Native perspective in discussions in class. Me.

David was the first of my university friends, White, Indian, or Non-Indian, that I thought I could just be myself with. "Just be yourself," is the advice you hear from people who enjoy beating their gums. They tell that to people maybe they think are shy, that don't know how to act.

I don't know if David noticed I was mad at him.

Kohkum had a hot soup and bannock waiting for our lunch that day. I'm thinking now of that day when Kohkum asked me about David. David went and called his brother-in-law to pick him up in town after lunch. I drove. We waited at the Service Centre until this car pulled up. A guy waved, and David was gone like a shot.

Kohkum never made any judgement that I know of when I told her what I thought had happened. She got a hold of my jeans and mended the fashionable rips before I went back to school and I guess she let me think about it, to make up my own mind. Now when I see the mending it makes me feel Love.

I guess David is okay. He's not to blame. We're still friends, or still just friends, or whatever you call it. He sure liked meeting my Kohkum, he said the last time I saw him. I think he must have been embarrassed to have been so afraid, that must be it.

Godiva Rides Again
PAMELA BANTING

Godiva was getting out of local politics. Out of politics altogether. She had said her sayonaras to all of that for once and for all.

It hadn't been the ride *per se,* she realized as she reflected on her reasons for leaving the sceptre'd isle. She hadn't minded the original ride. After she had gotten over her initial shock and misgivings and made up her mind to "just DO it," she was fine. But after the mayor and council voted unanimously to make it an annual event and to piggyback her ride onto the May Agricultural Fair and Exhibition, and as she began to go through the motions year after year, it wasn't long before she started to dread getting up on a horse. She even started making excuses to avoid the hunt. She stopped going down to the stables to pat and comb and talk to the horses.

Besides, although the ride had been her husband's idea in the first place, he was not any keener than she was on its becoming an annual event with commercial spin-offs – souvenir plates, mugs, key chains, baby rattles and pictorial fans made in Taiwan. Likenesses of his wife in every household in the country.

Face it, their marriage was suffering. More than once Leofric had yelled at her from across the room, "You like all this attention. You like it. Don't you? Go ahead, admit it!" He claimed Godiva was becoming a pin-up girl – just another Madonna. He stomped up and down the length of their dining hall cursing and spluttering and rhyming off the latest contribution by the poets in the Godiva Fan Club:

Ride a cock horse to Banbury Cross
to see a fine lady upon a white horse
With rings on her fingers
and bells on her toes
She shall have music wherever she goes.

Godiva swore that if she had to listen to that silly poem one more time she was going to ask Leofric to have the person reciting it or printing it up on the brochures for the Coventry Bed & Breakfast Association held in the stocks for three days. Such insipid rhyming verse. That was the trouble with England – every bloody hooligan and his dog thought they were goddamn Shakespeare. Bells on her toes indeed! The rings were accurate enough, but she had had to hock them to raise money for her getaway.

To be fair, her husband had been right in some respects. Before all the commercialism had come along to spoil it, Godiva had always taken pleasure in horseback riding, and her now-famous ride in opposition to Leofric's goods and services tax had been an extraordinary experience in its own right. Straddling the palomino naked. The horse without saddle, bridle or hackamore, her long strong fingers twined into his mane, her own long golden mane flowing free and spilling onto the horse's haunches. His muscular rhythmic gait under her, the breeze between her bare toes. The ride was a horse-crazy young woman's dream come true.

But like any peak experience, she had been changed by it. Ever since that fateful day, Godiva had had to struggle hard to quell an insistent yearning to travel. She wanted to see the world, experience other cultures, learn a new language. She wanted to live in a culture where the men were manly and wore something other than woolen Marks and Spencer trousers and sensible English shoes. Somewhere where a good horsewoman was appreciated rather than exploited.

After many sleepless nights, Godiva determined to make a new start. She wrote away for travel brochures from around the world and pondered alternate careers, what kind of life she truly wished to lead, and immigration requirements.

She considered Spain. Godiva had always been drawn to Spanish culture. Flamenco. The men in those skin-tight pants, little bolero jackets and fabulous black boots. The fierce women veiling and unveiling their beauty while at the same time getting an accurate bead on that strutting man down the length of their forearm and across the bend in their elbow. The bullfight, of course, with its snorting and pawing, the turnings in the dust, the collective excitement of the crowd. The Spanish love of the horse. *La guitarra*. And the Spanish language, which felt so incredibly good in your mouth. Spanish was like food. Godiva could have eaten and drunk Spanish.

But she knew that the English invariably became caricatures when they crossed the border into Spain, and since her famous ride Godiva had had quite enough of stereotypes, what with all that business about the white goddess-black goddess, virgin-crone, summer-winter, love-death, peeping Toms and blind seers. Albeit with great reluctance, she recycled the Spanish brochures and looked at her other options.

When one got right down to it, there were precious few places in the world hospitable to the English and their culture. Having tromped all over the world for several centuries now, the English had largely worn out the Commonwealth welcome mat. It had gone so far that nowadays the good citizens of colonial countries cringed with an almost English distaste and grimaced in the direction of their radios when they heard the rising and falling intonations and the arch syllables of a British accent reading the six o'clock news.

Godiva toyed for while with the idea of teaching English in Japan, but she had heard at a party once that the Japanese preferred to hire ESL teachers with a western Canadian accent. The Middle East had an aura of mystery and drama that appealed to her sensibilities, but she was not at all certain that in an Arab country where by law women were compelled to wear the chador she would be able to live down her famous political activism. She even looked into the feasibility of crossing the channel and becoming a Dutch milkmaid with long double braids down her back. Godiva liked working with horses, and she thought she might thrive managing a modest herd of dewy-eyed Holsteins as well.

Finally, after much research and deliberation, she was able to make an informed decision, and what she chose was the fresh green breast of the New World. She would emigrate to Canada, where on Christmas morning many Canadians still momentarily yanked their right arms out of the turkey cavity and, like freshly scrubbed surgeons with both arms aloft, ran to their television sets in order to catch a glimpse of the Queen delivering her annual Christmas message.

Her decision finalized, Godiva began to pack. At long last, she was getting out of Coventry, getting out of this one-horse town. She packed a few clothes, her journal, her blow drier and curling iron, a bedroll and guitar, and saddled the palomino.

Yes, saddled. She had no intention of riding bareback all the way from Coventry to London, and it would be unthinkable to arrive at the frontier without her saddle. To her embarrassment, it *was* an English-style saddle, and Godiva was resolved to replace it with a handsome leather-tooled western-style saddle as soon as she could manage. But her old one would have to do for the first while.

Godiva took one last look around at the castle and its environs. She scanned her eyes over the green sward round about. Then she drew a deep breath. Placed her left foot in the stirrup and pulled up into the saddle. With a flick of the reins, she and the palomino trotted off through town. Clippety clop on the old cobblestones.

Adios, she called to the neat hedgerows. *Adieu*, she whispered to the twittering English birds. *Auf wiedersehen*, hosts of golden daffodils. *Hasta la vista*, picturesque countryside. *Ciao*, she scribbled on the note she left for Leofric at his end of the long dining table.

As she approached the outskirts of town, she urged the horse into a canter and then a full gallop.

Eat my dust, she cried.

At long last, Godiva was lighting out for the territories. Now that her journey was actually under way, she felt her whole being yearning toward Canada – the great plains, the giant inland lakes of Manitoba, and the boreal forests of the north – and she could not get there fast enough. She had been utterly seduced as she paged through *Beautiful British Columbia* magazine, as she gazed at the photographs in the booklets sent, as per her request, in plain brown wrappers to her castle address by Alberta Tourism and Recreation, as she pored over the descriptive passages in the pamphlets put out by the Eastend, Saskatchewan, Chamber of Commerce. The gently undulating foothills, the flat plain stretching like an ache for hundreds of miles in the four directions. The jewelled emerald lakes, and peaks and valleys of the Rocky Mountains. Maybe in some former lifetime I roamed those territories, she mused, my hair blue-black in the shining sun. Or maybe I was a pronghorn antelope grazing the coulees, or a hawk measuring the arch of a chinook.

Godiva roused herself from her reveries and returned to the practicalities at hand. She dismounted, handed the palomino's reins and a handful of coins to the small, wide-eyed urchin girl blinking up at her, and traipsed into the ticket office to book a one-way fare on the Equity, a passenger liner sailing out of London in two days time.

On mild sunny days during the voyage, Godiva relaxed on deck, reading, soaking up the sunshine and, with her arms wrapped dreamily around her knees, rocking herself ever so slightly back and forth like a small child impatient to reach her destination. From time to time, she thought she could hear the palomino whinny and paw at the wooden floor of his stall in the animal decks below. A slow smile played across Godiva's lips. Both horse and rider were anxious to get on with their adventures in the New World.

To distract herself from her almost overwhelming eagerness during the long Atlantic excursion, Godiva wrote in her journal, passionately recording her nightly dreams and her hopes and aspirations for her new life. Such a land it was where she was headed. A land where history had not yet clotted meaning around every stone and tree, every patch of grass, every stained glass window and local cemetery. A place where history could still be made! Where history could still be invented, made up, fabricated, acted upon, bragged over, spoken into the record, testified to, disallowed, written down, punished, rewarded, fictionalized, and changed forever.

A land of wild horses! Mustangs! Horses which weren't all shod with heavy, clanking iron shoes and doomed to pull rickety old hay wagons from dawn till dusk, or sunup, she corrected herself, to sundown their whole life long. Not just broken-down old nags and drays. Nor hunters and jumpers carrying foppish, drunken lords and corsetted, laced and be-velvetted ladies after one poor, bedraggled Reynard the Fox.

No, we were talking wild ponies. Bucking broncos. Buffalo horses. Quarter horses skillfully working huge herds of shorthorn cattle. Saddle horses. Cutting horses. Mounts and caballos. Godiva's horsey imagination had come untethered at last.

She was going to be, or rather become, a cowgirl. She was itching and twitching to saddle up and ride on out. Godiva didn't hanker to be no equestrienne. Instead, she just wanted to try her luck with some of them bucking broncos.

Yes, Godiva had resolved to make her new home a home on the range, where the skies were not cloudy all day. Where your clothes dried overnight, and you had clean socks and underwear for morning. How Godiva hated the damp English climate! She had been forever tugging her long wool cardigan closer and closer across her breasts, shivering all the while. England's was a damp cold, and Canadian immigration pamphlets described the climate of Alberta, where she was headed, as a dry cold.

When she wasn't daydreaming and planning and making notes in her journal, Godiva pored over the catalogues she had ordered in advance: from Sadler's Saddlery in a little northern ranching and farming community called Birch River and from Diablo Boots in Calgary. She could hardly wait to try out a western saddle with covered stirrups and elaborate hand-tooling. She wanted to get a pair of chaps too. And a suede jacket with fringe along the sleeves and across the back. She read in the glossy news-magazine with a Scottish name that was lying on the nightstand in her cabin on the Equity that the Barenaked Ladies were extremely popular in Canada, but Godiva was happy to be leaving *her* life as a barenaked lady behind.

In fact, the first thing she had done right at the start of all this was to drop the Lady. She had gotten her documents together and filled out all the requisite forms and applied for an official name change, and then she had waited and waited for months. Now at long last, she weren't no Lady! She was just plain jane Godiva.

As the Equity sailed into Canadian waters and Godiva started to spot Spanish, Portuguese and Japanese trawlers hauling in cod, she could not help noticing that her speech was changing. She had begun to drop the g's from the ends of her words. From now on, she was not going to talk as if she had a clothes-pin stuck on the end of her pert, upturned English nose. She would deliberately cotton on to the Canadian vernacular. After all, she reasoned, she had abandoned the Land of the Poet Laureates. She was chucking the literati for the lariati.

As the sailors and the rest of the crew prepared to dock the Equity at Montréal, however, Godiva felt herself growing nervous. She accepted the little white immigration card from the steward, but when she sat down on a nearby bench to fill it out, her hair lifting in the breeze, she noticed that her hands were shaking. She hesitated, staring off into the distance and anxiously chewing the end of the little yellow pencil he had also given her. Her palms were clammy, and she could feel the blood rushing to her temples and her ears.

What if the Canadian Immigration border officials ran a random check on the CSIS computer? What if her husband had declared her a missing person? What if there were "Wanted" posters with her oft-reproduced image in bilingual text on the hydro poles of Montréal? Godiva remembered with palpable relief that only signs in French were permitted in Québec. But what if her famous visage had been printed by the authorities on the backs of milk cartons in her chosen country? Even worse, what if Leofric had reported the theft of the palomino? What if Godiva's name came up on the computer together with the words "Horse Thief – Reward Offered"?

The minutes passed. Godiva could hardly breathe. She gripped the pencil tightly and held it suspended over the line asking "What is your occupation?" After several long minutes had passed, she took a deep breath, pressed down firmly on the lead and boldly filled in the blank with the words LADIES' BARREL RACER. The next line asked for her final destination in Canada. She wrote CALGARY STAMPEDE. You only go around once, she thought.

Then she had to fill out the forms for Agriculture Canada concerning the importation of quadrupeds. Just as Godiva had dropped her ladyship, she thought it appropriate and practical, given the threat of being arrested for horse thieving, to rename the palomino. Godiva wanted something with the ring of the range about it. Merlin, the horse's English name, would be laughed off the rodeo circuit from Swan River to Morris to Ponoka.

The name Poseidon popped into her mind. The name connoted the kind of ideal masculine strength and vigour she saw in her horse. But Poseidon sounded like a black stallion, a studhorse, and her proud-stepping but good-natured horse was a beautiful tawny gold with an ivory mane. Godiva let her thoughts linger lovingly on the horse and down over the strong muscular lines of his haunches and withers. His contented snuffle as she walked up to him in the stable to exercise him on the heath. His beautiful mane the exact same shade as her own long hair.

As she mused on these pleasing images and memories, the name suddenly came to her. She would call this one-woman horse simply Palomino, her pal, pal of mine. They would be like Roy Rogers and Trigger, the Lone Ranger and Silver. Her reliable mount, her constant companion, her faithful cayuse. Godiva and Palomino. She completed the forms, signed them with a flourish and handed them back to the steward.

Before disembarking onto Canadian soil, Godiva had just one last mission. She hurried down the passageway to the on-board duty-free shop and with her last twenty-five English pounds picked up a bottle of Canadian rye whisky, which she would stash in her saddle bags as soon as she could invest in a pair.

After clearing customs, she proceeded directly to the Via Rail office and purchased two tickets for Winnipeg, Manitoba, the Gateway to the West, one for her and one for Palomino.

And Besides God Made Poison Ivy

ARMIN WIEBE

For six months your grandfather Kjrayel Kehler sat stone-faced with my father in the sitting room every Sunday afternoon answering a whole catechism of questions about his mother's arthritis and how much milk the schemmel cow gave that Kjrayel had bought from Harder's auction. And my father always asked Kjrayel a question about what Preacher Funk had said in Sunday morning church.

Kjrayel Kehler always had an answer for that question, too, and when the dinner dishes were all washed my father would let your grandfather come outside with me to sit on the lawn swing beside the lilac bushes. And I would laugh so much sometimes I got the hiccups because being with Kjrayel Kehler was like trying to stand up on a moving swing, and after he was gone I would still stay there on the lawn swing bench afraid that my legs wouldn't hold me up. I would stay there until my father rattled the upside down pails on the post. Then I would hurry to put on my milking dress.

A heavy rain held up the thrashing gang at the neighbours for a day and your grandfather said to me at breakfast that we would go to Yanzeed to pick blueberries. I don't think he was that interested in blueberries really, but he wanted an excuse to drive the Model T he had bought in Winnipeg even before the harvest. So sure he was that he would have a bumper crop. Your grandfather was so eager to drive the car that he didn't even go to the beckhouse after breakfast, which was almost like having the sun stand still in the sky, because in those days I could set the morning clock by his visit to the two-holer.

I hardly had tied loose my apron and put on my straw

40

hat before he was honking the Model T horn. He had a dozen syrup pails piled in the back seat and two ten-gallon cream cans standing on the floor and I schmuistahed to myself that my Kjrayel must be thinking he would get a bumper crop of blueberries, too. Not that I had anything against having lots of blueberries to put some colour on the table during the long winter, and I liked riding along with my man in the Model T after a rain when the road was too wet for dust.

And I liked watching how your grandfather gripped the wheel with both hands, the end of his tongue sticking out from his lips like baloney between pieces of bread. How he looked straight ahead through the window glass – until he saw something to laugh about. Like how that cow in the ditch looked like Milyoon Moates or how the new telephone poles looked like a row of upside down women's legs with high-heels on. I saw, too, how he was shrugging himself around a little oftener than seemed to be comfortable, even on those Model T seats.

Sure enough, as soon as we had picked blueberries for maybe five minutes your grandfather febeizeled himself into the bush and I didn't see him again until I came back from emptying my syrup pails into the cream can in the car.

For hours we picked, a bumper crop of berries, both cream cans and all the pails full, and before we went home we sat on the shade side of the car and ate *jreeve schnetje* and drank cool coffee from a jar and even popped a few blueberries into each other's mouths. If this Indian family hadn't stopped their horse and wagon right beside our Model T who knows what Kjrayel Kehler would have started there in the shade so far away from Gutenthal. The Indians soon picked their way into the bush and only the horse was left there to see, but an eye is an eye, even when it is looking out from the side of a horse's head.

Later, I was happy for sure that it was so schendlich hot that night we each had to stay on our own side of the bed. I mean, in those days your grandfather took it seriously what the wedding preacher had said about being joined together and with no children yet in the house a woman could let herself go, too, but this night it was good it was too hot.

The sparrows already tsittered outside the window when I heard a mourning dove. I listened to hear if your grandfather Kjrayel Kehler was going to coo back to it the way he liked to do. But instead he jumped out of bed and ripped his combination underwear off so fast the buttons flew all over the room. Before I could even say, "What's loose?" I saw that his middle was covered with gnauts, the poison ivy itch, front and back, between the legs, all over everything, and he danced there as broadlegged as he could without falling down.

I shouldn't have laughed at your grandfather like that, but sometimes a woman forgets to remember her place, and besides if it had happened to me, his dear wife, your grandfather Kjrayel Kehler would have laughed at me and blabbered the story to all who would listen, even unto the day when I will be lying in my coffin waiting to be buried in my best dress.

How could I help it? Could God himself have kept a straight face looking at your grandfather dancing naked from one foot to the other in the morning light?

But at the same time I had to cry, too, because such itchy gnauts between the legs had to be a bigger plague than anything God sent down to Job in the Old Testament. And I was happy for sure that it had been too hot in the night for any joining together into one flesh.

When I had stopped shuddering enough to talk, I asked, "What did you wipe yourself with yesterday in the bush?"

For once Kirayel Kehler couldn't say anything. He just looked at me and a tear sippled down his cheek.

I tried to wash him with warm water and lye soap but the red blisters were so sore and so itchy he screamed when I touched him, even with a soapy bare hand. I filled the wash tub and when he sat down in the soapy water he felt a little better and I gave him his porridge to eat. With his hands busy at least he didn't try to scratch himself. But every few minutes the itch got so gruelich strong he shrugged himself and schulpsed water all over the floor.

Your grandfather was still sitting in the tub when I came in from the milking.

"Suschkje," he said to me. "The thrashers are coming today. What will I do?"

"You can't wear pants with such gnauts, it would rub the skin too much."

"And I can't go naked to thrash barley."

"I'll just have to tell them that you are sick and they will have to thrash without you."

"No. I'm not sick. I just have gnauts. I just need some kind of clothes to wear that don't rub me between the legs There must be something."

"Well, I don't know," I said as I poured fresh milk through the strainer into the separator bowl. "Even wide pants would rub together and a person can't walk around broadlegged all day." I speeded up the separator crank until the bell on the handle stopped ringing so I could open the spout. The morning air blew in through the wire window and I felt it come up my legs under my skirt. That's when I laughed at your grandfather again.

I didn't think Kjrayel Kehler would really do it, and I could see that it wasn't easy for him. At first he wanted a manly dress, like one of my dark winter skirts, but the wool made him kjriesch out with hurting. And he didn't want flowers, he said, as he stroked each dress and skirt to see how smooth it was. But every dress that was light and cool had flowers and your grandfather just couldn't bring himself to wear flowers on the thrashing field. He kept coming back to my black winter skirt.

I could see what he was thinking. With that skirt he could wear his own shirt, and from far off the dark skirt wouldn't show so easy and with no flowers he wouldn't feel so much like a woman. If only the wool wasn't so scratchy.

I looked at your grandfather's freckled bow legs and his blistered hams. I looked at the long paper dry-cleaning bag at the end of the row of hanging dresses. I thought of how I would feel if it hadn't been too hot for loving in the night. Still, it was a hard thing for me to do.

The silk underskirt from my wedding dress fit him quite well, looser than it fit me, because a man doesn't have to have room to give birth to children. With his workshirt covering up the soft lace of the bodice and the black skirt covering up the rest Kjrayel Kehler stepped out the door to face the thrashers.

I don't know how much ribbing your grandfather got as they pitched the sheaves into the thrashing machine, but at meal times not a word was said about Kjrayel Kehler sitting at the head of the table with the air from the wire window blowing up his skirt. Maybe it was because Kjrayel Kehler kept telling one funny story after another so they forgot to laugh at his dress. Still, the few times I had a chance to look out to the thrashing field I saw that more people than necessary were stopping to watch.

Each night while Kjrayel sat in the soapy water I washed the barley dust out of the silk and hung it on the line to dry for morning. I cried on the second night when the spots of gun grease wouldn't wash out even though I rubbed till my hands were sore.

On Saturday at noon Preacher Funk drove into the yard just as the men were washing up for dinner and I heard the preacher say something about how he had heard that the Catholic pope was helping with the thrasher gang. I didn't hear what Kjrayel Kehler said back to him, but Preacher Funk didn't stay long after that and I thought I could see in your grandfather's eye that look he gets when he is planning something for a surprise.

That night Kjrayel was reading the Bible while he soaked himself in the tub. Yodel Heinrichs had brought him a box of baking soda to put in the water and your grandfather agreed that it took some of the itch away. I had laid out my second best underskirt on the table and was going to cut out a pattern for some pyjamas that he could wear under his Sunday pants for going to church.

"Suschkje," he said to me. "Don't forget to wash that underskirt for church tomorrow."

I had my cloth scissors ready to cut. "You mean you will wear a dress to church?"

"Well sure," he said. "In the Bible the men are always going around with dresses on. People who go to church should know such a thing."

I was so bedutzed by all this that I didn't know if I was going to shame myself the next day because my man had a dress on or if I should be happy with a man who thought church was so important that nothing could keep him away. Maybe I could hide myself on the women's side of the church.

So I washed that silk wedding underskirt with the gun grease spots on it and hung it up to dry. It had been a tiresome week what with feeding the thrashers and canning blueberries and making catsup from the tomatoes that were ripening all at once. I had no room to think about what dress Kjrayel would wear to church in the morning.

It would have been good to have a camera to take off a picture of your grandfather that Sunday, but we didn't have such a thing yet, and for sure in those days nobody would have brought a camera to church unless there was a wedding on. So I can't show you what your grandfather looked like.

At his funeral I wouldn't let them open the coffin and people figured it was because of the way the cancer had eaten away at him when it took so long to die. The people can think what they want.

We should have hidden the Model T in the barn that Sunday afternoon, closed our windows and pulled shut the curtains so it looked like nobody was home. But we didn't. Instead we sat at the dinner table longer than we should have and let the air from the wire window blow up our skirts. I still didn't know if I should laugh or cry or shame myself.

And then the first buggy full of visitors clattered into the yard.

When your grandfather Kjrayel Kehler died they took him from me before he was even gone. Funeral Home Fehr wouldn't even let me see Kjrayel till he had him all fixed ready for the viewing. Like your grandfather was some kind of Stalin and Lenin in Moscow or something like that. Well, one thing I learned living forty-three years with Kjrayel Kehler is that just because somebody in a Sunday suit says no, doesn't mean that it can't be done. And who anyways heard of a locked funeral home in Flatland?

We never talked about that Sunday, though I always felt that it meant something, something more than a kjrayel-hauns joke, though for sure a kjrayel-hauns joke it was. I am just a simple woman but I lived with your grandfather for over forty-three years and in such a man there is always something else going on besides the ploughing and the thrashing and the sitting on the church bench on Sunday morning. By the time we got up from that dinner table half a dozen buggies and three Model A's had parked themselves in our yard and we were like Adam and Eve with no place to hide.

Kjrayel Kehler gave me a kiss on the cheek and he fuscheled in my ear, "Don't even think about giving all these people faspa. If they don't smell the coffee they will soon get tired and go away." Then he walked outside in my white wedding dress and sat down on the lawn swing and shuckled all afternoon without saying a word. The next Wednesday evening when I walked into the sewing circle I overheard Schallemboych's Tien saying that your grandfather had looked like he was praying with his eyes open.

I have to admit that I was envying myself over your grandfather. I mean a woman only gets to wear such a dress one day in her life and then it just hangs there, though I once heard of a woman who made curtains out of hers. I was still crying on the bed when Kjrayel Kehler came in after the visitors had gone away. I wouldn't let him touch me in the night for a whole month after that, long after the gnauts had disappeared.

I don't know if it would have been his wish, but there are more things in this world than the eyes can see or what can be read about in a newspaper. I had sat up with your grandfather in the hospital for four nights in a row and the doctor told me to get some sleep. So your mother stayed with Kjrayel Kehler and I went home to bed.

When the phone woke me up in the middle of the night I felt like I had been ripped out of a dream I couldn't remember. And then after I was dressed and waiting for your father to take me to the hospital I suddenly felt like something was pushing me and making me do what I did.

It wasn't until late the night before the funeral that I was able to sneak into the funeral home to be with your grandfather alone. I had never undressed Kjrayel Kehler in those forty-three years we lived together, at least not with the lights on, and then a coffin doesn't have that much room in it, so it was scary and funny at the same time and I kept thinking that Kjrayel was going to sit up and tell me to stop tickling him. And it's not easy to dress a person who isn't helping, especially when Funeral Home Fehr could have walked in any minute. But I thought I saw your grandfather's lips smile just a little when the silk underskirt touched his skin.

The gun grease spots showed through the wedding dress but it was too late to rub them with bluing. And besides God made poison ivy and He planted it in the same places He put the blueberry bushes and I know I shouldn't say such a thing, but I have sometimes wondered if maybe God didn't make poison ivy with its three leaves and white berries just before He made Adam out of a lump of mud and set him loose running naked through the Garden of Eden. At least, if your grandfather Kjrayel Kehler had been God, that's how he would have done it.

A Book of Great Worth

DAVE MARGOSHES

My father was there when the Hindenburg went down, killing 36 people.

He was a reporter on one of the Yiddish papers of the day in New York, and, though labour was his specialty and he rarely covered regular news, had been assigned, because of a staffing problem, to cover the dirigible's arrival in New Jersey, after its trans-Atlantic flight from Germany. It was only his fourth day back at work after having been off for more than a week for an appendectomy and he was still sore, and after the long train ride to Lakehurst he was feeling quite a bit of discomfort. Gritting his teeth, he interviewed officials and some of the people in the large crowd that had come to watch, then found a chair where he could ease himself while he waited.

Ropes had been set up to keep the crowd at some distance, but that was more for the safety and convenience of the passengers than the sightseers, so he was no more than 100 metres from where burning debris began to fall immediately after the explosion. Like everyone else there, my father was stunned by what happened. Heat blasted into his face as if he had opened the door to an oven and peered in to check the roast. His eyes flooded with tears, an automatic response of the body, he supposed, to protect them from the heat. Standing up to get a better view of the arrival in the moments just before the explosion, he was just a few steps from the radio man, chattering into his microphone, "Here it comes ladies and gentlemen, and what a sight it is, a thrilling one, a marvelous sight," then continuing to broadcast after the eruption of fire, which seemed, my father used to say when he told the story, to literally split the sky with dazzling colour; and, except in patches where bursts of explosion obliterated his voice, my father could hear him clearly:

"It burst into flames, get out of the way, get out of the way, get this Johnny, get this Johnny, it's fire and it's flashing, flashing, it's flashing terribly ... this is terrible, this is one of the worst catastrophes in the world ... oh, the humanity and all the friends just screaming around here ... I don't believe, I can't even talk to people whose friends are on there, it, it's ah, I, I can't talk, ladies and gentlemen, honest it's a mass of smoking wreckage and everybody can hardly breathe and talk and screaming, lady, I, I'm sorry."

Everyone was running and, after a moment in which he was frozen in place, transfixed, my father was too. His notebook and pen were in his hands, and his mouth, he remembers, was open, and he ran, thinking not of his story or even of helping people – those in the dirigible or directly below it seemed beyond help, he said – but of his own safety, something which, when he would tell this story to us children, years later, he conveyed without any discernible sense of shame but rather a small pride for his prudence. But when he had reached higher ground and stopped to catch his breath and, scribbling in his pad in that illegible shorthand of his that used to fascinate me so much, begun to record the sights and sounds billowing in front of him like a film running haywire through a projector, only then did he feel the pain and wetness in his side and, holding open his suit jacket, see the spreading blossom of blood soaking his shirt.

His first thought was that he had been injured by a flying piece of debris, like the shrapnel or flak in the war he had heard so much about, but then he realized it was nothing that romantic or dangerous, that the stitches closing his incision had merely given way under stress and that, like a corroded bathroom fixture, he had begun to leak.

At that time, my father and mother were living in a small third-floor apartment in Coney Island with my two sisters; my birth was still four years away, but my mother was pregnant with a child which, had it lived, would have been my brother or, perhaps, rendered my conception unnecessary. In addition to the four of them, there was a fifth person crammed into the small set of rooms: a living room with the apartment's one partial view of the ocean, jammed with an overstuffed sofa, upon which the guest slept, and two frayed easy chairs, rough bookshelves, a coffee table, lamps, and my mother's piano, at which she instructed several wooden-fingered neighbourhood children; a kitchen so small that two people could barely stand at the sink to wash and dry the dishes; one small bedroom which was my parents'; and an even tinier room, not much bigger than a large closet but described as a den, in which my sisters slept, the eldest in a small bed, the younger on a folding cot permanently unfolded. This guest was a young woman my father had met a few weeks earlier and invited home with him. She had come from Montreal in search of a man she described as her brother, a poet my father knew slightly. She had, on a slip of grimy, much-folded paper, the name and address of Fushgo's bookshop, through which the brother had told her he could always be reached. There, standing in one of the narrow aisles sandwiched in among the groaning walls of second hand books my father loved to browse through, he'd met her.

"Morgenstern, I'm glad you stepped in," Fushgo said, beckoning him over. "A damsel in distress. Just the ticket, you are." He indicated the tiny woman standing beside the cash drawer so drably dressed and standing in so unimposing a posture my father had at first failed to notice her. "This is Anna," Fushgo said, winking in the sly way he affected when he was trying to interest my father in a book beyond his means. "She is that rarest of women. She cannot speak."

My father was presented with a woman of indeterminate youthful age – she could have been sixteen, so smooth and clear was her skin, or thirty, so severe was the expression of her cloud-grey eyes – whose dirty yellow hair coiled like a tangle of unruly wool down the back of her tattered shawl, which at one time has been maroon. Everything about her was in disarray – the buttons of her white blouse askew, the hem of a slip showing beneath that of her pleated grey wool skirt, even the laces of her high shoes undone – but her clothing and hair, even the nails on the fingers of the small white hand she extended to my father, were clean; and she smelled of the sea, not the rank, oily waters of the East River that often shouldered its way on the back of fog along the Lower East Side, where he worked, or the flat, hotdoggy smell of the beach at Coney Island, but the bracing salt spray of the pounding surf at Far Rockaway, where he and my mother would sometimes go walking with the girls on Sunday afternoons. "Show, show," Fushgo grunted, prodding her with a sharp, tobacco-stained finger.

The woman offered my father a small sheet of paper obviously torn from a pad, and freshly so judging by the clean ragged edge, and already scribbled on with a sharp pointed pencil. He took it from her, noticing that her delicately veined hand trembled. On the paper, in a handwriting that was both clean and immature, was written in Yiddish: "My name is Anna Fishbine, from Montreal, in Canada. I am seeking my brother, Abraham Diamond, the poet, who receives his mail at this shop. Can you assist me?"

My father had several small weaknesses – schnapps and cigarettes among them – but only one great one, and that was his love of books, not merely reading them, a love which in itself could have been satisfied by the public library, but of possessing them, feeling their weight on his knee and the rough texture of their bindings on his fingers as he read, seeing the satisfying substance of them on the shelves he had constructed in the living room, the heavy dusty aroma wafting off their old, roughly cut pages as they lay open on the kitchen table. New books, with their crisp, clean jackets and unsoiled pages failed to impress him the way a book with a life and a history behind it did, so he was an addict to Fushgo's constantly replenishing stock and devoted to the man himself, his irritating mannerisms, come from a lifetime of communing with dead authors at the expense of living readers, notwith-standing. But my father, who had from time to time seen the poet at the Café Royale and had exchanged words with him on one or two occasions, had never encountered Diamond at the shop.

"Diamond gets his mail here?" my father asked, raising his eyes to Fushgo, who, despite his stoop, was a tall man.

"Only invisible letters," Fushgo said, raising his brows, "delivered by invisible mailmen."

The two men exchanged glances redolent of the comfort with which they felt in each other's presence. Both were shy men but they had a mutual love, they'd known each other for over a dozen years and, over that time, my father had contributed to Fushgo's upkeep with the same regularity and consistency of a Christian tithing to his church. Fushgo shrugged his rounded shoulders, raggedly incised by the frayed stripes of his suspenders, and made a comical face with his eyes and blue-lipped mouth that suggested despair over the antics of women.

"How long since you heard from your brother?" my father asked.

At the woman's feet there was a brown cardboard suitcase. In her hands she clutched a blue leather purse from which she produced a pad and pencil, laying the purse awkwardly on the suitcase. She scribbled, looked up, scribbled again, then tore the page loose and handed it to my father.

"Six months without a word." Here was where she had hesitated. Then: "Our parents are frantic with worry."

My father nodded his head as he read. "Your brother often goes to the Café Royale. Do you know it?"

The woman shook her head, a look of mild fright briefly passing over her eyes.

"I'm on my way there now for a bite," my father said. "I'll escort you. Maybe you'll be lucky and he'll be there. Or someone will know where he might be found."

The woman seemed so grateful that my father was infused with a feeling of well-being that propelled them both out of Fushgo's shop onto East Broadway with the gentle force of a summer breeze. My father carried Anna's suitcase, which seemed so light as to be almost empty, while she clutched her purse to her chest. Because of her silence – he didn't know at this point whether she was an actual mute or merely too frightened to speak – there was no need to chat, but my father grew expansive and rattled on, describing the scenery through which they passed and, occasionally forgetting, asking her questions she could not – or would not – answer without stopping to write on her pad. "That's all right," my father said. "Forget it." Or: "That was only a rhetorical question. There's no need to reply."

She paused several times, hindering their progress, to gaze into a shop window or down the length of a street they were crossing, and one of the rhetorical questions my father asked concerned the nature of Montreal, for the woman gave the appearance of having stepped directly from the boat or the countryside.

At the Café Royale, there was no sign of Diamond nor any of the men my father thought he might have seen with the poet. Nevertheless, after he had placed the order – a corned beef sandwich with coleslaw and a pickle and coffee for him, strong tea for Anna – he inquired of the waiter, who asked several others. Most didn't know Diamond, but one who did said he hadn't seen him for several days. Perhaps this evening. Mendel and Solarterefsky, two playwrights my father knew, were at their usual table in a rear corner and he inquired of them as well. Both knew Diamond, and Mendel said he thought he'd seen him in the company of Ishavis Lazen, the actor, who was sure to be at the café that evening, after his performance. My father had a meeting to cover so he introduced Anna to the two men, spared her the effort of the notes by explaining her situation, entrusted her to their attention and left her there, promising to look in later. "Hopefully, you'll have found him, you'll be gone and happily ensconced in his apartment," he told her. "I'm sure all will be well."

My father went to his meeting, where he listened, took notes, and afterwards talked to people in attendance. He went back to his office and sat at a heavy oak desk where he wrote an account of the meeting on a standard Royal machine with Yiddish characters. He and another man who was working late had a drink from a bottle of Canadian whiskey my father kept in the lower drawer of his desk. He gave his story to Lubin, the assistant city editor, and he put on his raincoat before stepping out into the light drizzle that was falling in the darkness of East Broadway. He walked past Fushgo's shop, dark as an alley, and the Automat, closed but its lights still shining, and toward the café, from which, as he approached, he could see light and hear noise spilling. Anna was sitting at the table where he had left her, an island of mute and painful isolation in the midst of the tables crowded with loud men. Mendel and Solarterefsky were gone, there was no sign of Lazen, though the theatres had let out more than an hour earlier, and, of course, there was no sign of Diamond.

My father sat down and ordered a coffee. "I'm delighted to see you again, my dear," he said, "but sorry to find you alone. Was there no news?"

Anna wrote this note: "No. Mr. Mendel was most kind. He and the other gentleman introduced me to several men who know Abraham but no one has seen him for several weeks. There is a possibility he has a job with a touring company. Someone promised to inquire."

My father frowned and looked around the café, raising his hand to several men he knew. "Have you eaten?"

Anna nodded vigorously, but he was struck again by the emaciated quality to her small, smooth face he found so appealing, the cheekbones high, the skin tight and without lines except for the sheerest hint beside her nose where, though he had yet to see her display the ability, surely, she must occasionally smile.

"Are you sure? The cheesecake here is very good. I wouldn't mind one myself, but I couldn't manage the whole thing. Would you help me?"

She agreed and, when it came, ate all but the few forkfuls my father took to put her at ease.

She looked down at the plate, as if ashamed at the weakness her hunger had revealed.

"You have a room?" my father asked. "Someplace where you're staying? Perhaps I should take you there."

Anna looked up, then down again. On her pad she wrote: "I had hoped I would find Abraham."

"So you have no place?"

She shook her head and they sat in silence while my father smoked a cigarette and finished his coffee. "I want you to understand," he said presently, "that I'm a married man, with two wonderful children and a third on the way. So please don't construe my intentions as anything but the most honourable."

Anna wrote: "Surely your wife will object."

My father smiled. "Bertie would never turn someone away from her door."

Again he carried the suitcase, extending the elbow of his other arm to her on the dark street and, after a moment's hesitation, she took it. On the long subway ride home he wondered if what he'd said was true, but my mother, of course, was asleep, and if she did object, he knew, it wouldn't be until afterwards.

Not once, as the subway car lurched through its velvety tunnels or as he made up the bed for her on the sofa in the tiny living room, did he question his motives, not once did he long to heal her wounded tongue with his own.

My mother did have a generous heart, and patience which, after three weeks, was beginning to grow thin. She was four months pregnant and suffering greatly, her body wracked by cramps at all times and swept by waves of dizziness and nausea when she moved with anything but the most deliberate slowness. False calms would arise during which it appeared the worst was over, then the pain and sickness would come crashing back without warning. Inside her, the baby seemed to be warring with the notion of its own life. There was no question but that Anna could be useful. My oldest sister was six and already in school, but the younger one was only three and needed care and attention, and diversion during my mother's worst times. My father, who always worked into the evenings and often later, saw to the children in the mornings, getting the eldest off to school, while my mother stayed in bed preparing herself for the day ahead, but in the afternoons, after he'd gone, the little one often grated on her nerves, the older one was soon home demanding to be heard, and there was a meal to prepare, then bathing. As the pregnancy deepened and the nature of the ailment became more clear, a plan had taken shape to have my mother's younger sister join the household to help her; Anna's presence made that unnecessary. She immediately took charge; at the same time, her presence grated on my mother, aggravating her already stripped nerves. By day, Anna helped in the apartment, relieving my father of some of his morning duties, but, more importantly, being there in the afternoon, playing with the younger one, keeping her quiet and amused, while my mother lay propped up against pillows on her bed reading detective novels and feeling the muscles in her legs slowly turn to jelly. Sometimes, rising to go to the bathroom, my mother would open the bedroom door and find Anna and my sister sitting side by side on the piano bench, the little girl enthralled as Anna's fingers silently raced over the keys my mother hadn't touched in weeks, just above them, producing a music only the two of them could hear.

In the evenings, she took the subway to Manhattan and the Café Royale where, like an urchin awaiting her drunken father, she sat at a table by herself and passed notes to people asking: "Have you seen Abraham Diamond?" My father often dropped in on her there and, if his work kept him late, would stop at the café on his way home to give her company on the long subway ride, which still frightened her. My mother, without accusing him of anything, clearly resented the attention he paid to the girl.

"Three weeks and still no sign of that *brother*," she said on a Saturday. Anna had taken the girls for a stroll on the boardwalk, and she and my father were alone at the breakfast table.

My father shrugged. "It appears he's gone with a company on a road trip. No one seems to know for sure where they are or when they'll be back. What do you mean, brother?'"

"Oh, Harry, it's as clear as the nose on your face that the man is her husband. Or her lover. God knows if there really are worried parents in Montreal. The woman has been abandoned."

"You really think so?"

My mother rolled her eyes upward, as if to seek support from the angel of the ceiling. "Men are so blind."

"All the more reason to give her sympathy and support," my father said after a moment.

"You think so?" my mother said sharply.

At times like these my father would often retreat to his books, forming his own private library wherever he was sitting, the world shut out by an invisible, sound-proof barrier as he pored over the pages of his latest acquisition. Although he had gone no further in school than the fifth grade before he'd been required to begin to support his family, and English was his second language, he was partial to Shakespeare and — inexplicably — the

American Civil War, but his deepest passion was for the classics, and his most treasured possession was a richly illustrated edition of Caesar's Wars in Latin that he had taught himself to read. He had paid Fushgo ten dollars for the Caesar, more than four times the portion of his weekly allowance that he allotted to himself for books and, with the interest Fushgo charged, it had taken more than a month for him to pay it off. In later years, he would acquire huge volumes of Dante, rich with Blake engravings, and, though he wasn't religious, a variety of Bibles, in several languages, their oiled leather bindings giving off a smoky aroma of history, damnation, and salvation. At this particular time, he was engrossed in a book that appeared to have been hand-written, in the manner of monks, in a language he had not been able to identify. The handwriting was skillful and consistent through the several hundred pages, the unintelligible words clearly scripted in a faded blue ink, the capitals at the beginning of each new paragraph shadowed in a red the shade of dried blood. There was no date, no publisher's name or city, no illustrations that might serve as clues to the book's origin, and the title and author were just as indecipherable as the text itself. The leather of the binding was so thick – more like a slab of oxblood hide used for making shoes than the soft black grainy cloth publishers used – and the spine so warped that the book could not be fully closed, and when it lay on a table it seemed like a head whose jaws have sprung open, eager to share the untapped wisdom within it. "For you, Morgenstern," Fushgo had said when he produced the book for my father. "Read this, and you'll learn much the same wisdom you acquire conversing with your Anna." And he laughed, Fushgo, spraying the dark air of his shop with tobacco-scented breath.

For hours at a time my father would sit poring over the book, comparing the strange script with works from his collection in Latin, Greek, Russian, Hebrew, not that he thought this language could be any of those, but hoping for some clue, some similarity of characters that would provide a hook, an opening through which he might shoulder to some dim understanding of the message the old pages indifferently held. One night when he had come home early, he was sitting at the kitchen table engrossed in the magic letters, my mother asleep in their room, when Anna came home from the café, her small shoulders rising in their inevitable shrug to my father's raised eyes. She came and sat beside him and he poured them both drinks. She sipped hers, then wrote this note: "I fear I may never find Abraham."

"Surely not," my father said. Then, after a long silence: "But you should give some thought to what you'll do, just in case. Have you written to your parents?"

Anna hesitated, then wrote: "Neither can read."

"And the neighbours? A friend or landsman who could read a letter to them?"

Anna shook her head. "There is only me," she wrote. "I must return to them soon."

My father nodded. "You know you're welcome to stay here as long as you want. Bertie is irritable, I know, but it's the baby, not you." He put his hand on hers, marvelling at its smallness, the way her entire hand, even the slender fingers, disappeared beneath the cup of his palm.

Anna smiled and wrote: "You're very kind."

She gestured toward the book and my father slid it to her. "This is a book of great worth," he said.

She bent over it, puzzled, then raised her head, her cheeks and mouth and eyes molded into a quizzical smile of such sweetness it pierced my father like an arrow fashioned of the finest, purest gold.

"Eskimo?" she wrote.

As my father's one indulgence was his books, my mother's was her piano. It was an upright Baldwin of indeterminate age, the ivory of its keys yellowed like Fushgo's ancient teeth. It had been purchased at a second hand shop on the Bowery with $100 it took her three years to save and had been lifted by rope and tackle along the outside wall of the building and brought into the apartment through a window. My mother had studied the piano as a child, and music for two years of college. She'd long since given up any ambitions of the concert stage, but her greatest delight was to sit at the piano in the evening – the music students of the afternoon just an unpleasant taste in her mouth, the children in bed and my father not yet home from work or, perhaps, enveloped in one of the overstuffed chairs reading, one ear cocked – and play the concerti and sonatas of Mozart, which were her passion, or Chopin, which my father preferred. Since the third month of the pregnancy, the lessons had been cancelled and my mother, her head light, stomach lurching, legs and fingers aching, had sat not once at the piano, and the apartment resonated in the evening with a silence that seemed more like a presence than an absence.

Into this silence, where one would have thought she would be comfortable, Anna intruded, passing this note to my mother one evening: "When you are out and I won't disturb you, may I play the piano?"

"Of course," my mother said with irritation. She rarely left the apartment, but when she did she could care less what happened in her absence. "You play?"

Anna nodded, smiling shyly.

"Let me hear."

"Won't your head hurt?" Anna wrote.

"My head's fine today. I'd play myself, but my fingers have rubber bands around them."

Anna sat at the bench and raised the cover, exposing the Baldwin's soiled smile. She raised her chin, facing the window which looked out, past the roof of the hat factory across the street, at the ocean, stretching with calm indifference toward the horizon and the old world beyond it. After a moment, she began to play. Chopin. The 5th concerto. My father, who had been in the bathroom shaving, came to the door with a broad smile on his lathered face, saying, "That's wonderful, Bertie," then filled the doorway in confusion, looking from my mother, who stood by the window, to Anna at the piano and back again.

"I'm sorry, my head is hurting," my mother said after a while.

My father's appendicitis attack came completely without warning. At dinnertime, he had a sandwich, salad, coffee, and piece of cheese danish at the Automat, then went for a short walk to allow the food to settle, then stopped at Fushgo's for a chat and a drink from the bottle the bookseller kept behind his counter. He began to feel ill immediately after downing the shot, and Fushgo had to help him back to the newspaper office where he sat at his desk taking deep gasps, his face drained of all colour, until the ambulance arrived. My mother was telephoned from the hospital and she came at once, leaving the children with Anna, who had been just about to leave for her nightly visit to the Café Royale. The appendix was removed that night, and when my father awoke from the ether the next morning, my mother was sitting on a straight chair beside his bed, his hand in hers. She'd been there all night and her face was etched with pain and exhaustion.

"Who's the patient?" my father said. "I should get up,

you should get into this bed, the way you look. Or better yet, we should both be in it. The way you look." He squeezed her hand.

"It's too narrow," my mother said, smiling.

"Too narrow?" my father said. "According to who?"

She told him what the doctors had said. He asked for a cigarette and she told him they were forbidden. He told her about the drink he'd had with Fushgo. "It's the first time liquor's ever hurt me," he said. They laughed and gazed at each other fondly.

"Anna's with the children?" he asked after a while.

"Yes."

"Thank God we have her. Especially now."

My mother didn't say anything right away. Then: "She'll be a great help while you're here, yes. But when you're home I'd like to have Sarah come."

My father was silent.

"It's been over a month. We can't be responsible for the woman forever. She's taking advantage of your kindness."

My father nodded slowly. "After I'm home," he said.

He was in the hospital for four days and was under strict orders to rest and not go back to work for a week after he went home. The attack had come on a Friday and he was released on the following Tuesday. By the doctor's orders, he shouldn't have gone back to work until the following Wednesday, but the city editor phoned and he went on the Monday. He felt fine, just a little tired, the incision, already beginning to scar over with bright pink flesh shiny as fingernails, just a little tender. On Thursday afternoon, feeling completely fit, he went by train to Lakehurst.

It was well after midnight when he came home, my mother asleep, the living room dark. He'd served his editor as well as he could, though he'd retreated from the scene soon after he began to bleed and was unable to attract the attention of any of the medical people who rushed to the airfield. In the town itself, he found a small hospital and, while he was waiting, telephoned in his story. After several hours, a nurse whose hair had slipped out of its careful bun into shreds of haphazard grey cleaned his wound of the coagulated blood crusting it and bound him securely in bandages wrapped around his lower chest and belly. No doctor was available, though, so no stitches were taken, and it was this delay – the opening required seven stitches the following day, when he reported to the hospital where he'd originally been treated – that caused the odd shape and thickness of the scar he carried the rest of his life.

My father went to the kitchen and poured himself a whiskey, and drank it quickly and poured another. The ceiling light spilled through the doorway into the living room and he could see there was no one sleeping on the sofa. He went into the bedroom and sat down heavily on the bed and took off his shoes. My mother, who had been sleeping lightly, rolled over and opened her eyes, reaching out her hand to touch his arm.

"Harry? What time is it?"

"Almost one. Go back to sleep." He bent over her and kissed her head.

"How was it?"

"You didn't hear?"

"No, I didn't play the radio."

"I'll tell you in the morning."

"Okay." She rolled over.

"Anna's not back from the café?" my father asked.

"She's gone."

"I thought not till next week."

"We had an argument," my mother said. "I asked her to go."

"I see," my father said. He tried to imagine what such an argument would have been like, the flurry of notes being scribbled, torn from the pad, crumpled, thrown to the floor.

"I'll tell you in the morning. Sarah's coming tomorrow evening."

He took off his shirt and went out of the room, closing the door quietly behind him. He stepped into the small room where my sisters slept and gazed down at them, muffled in darkness, but glowing haloes around their heads formed by the streetlight from the window drawn to their hair. He bent over each head and kissed it. In the kitchen, he slowly drank the whiskey he'd poured. A dull red stain the size and shape of a strawberry had gathered on the bandage just below and to the left of where, he believed, his heart lay. His body was exhausted but his mind raced, filled with the dazzle of flame, its surprisingly loud roar, the plaintive voice of the radio man, "get out of the way, get out of the way, get this Johnny, get this Johnny." He walked across the living room to the shelf and found the book written in the mysterious language and took it back to the kitchen. He sat at the table, the open book in front of him, and looked first at its inscrutable script, then up at the icebox, standing silent and white against the wall. From the living room, he thought he heard the tinkling of piano keys, the first tentative notes of a Chopin concerto, but it was only the sound of an automobile passing on the street below, rising through the warm night air and the open window. His side ached, just beneath the strawberry stain by his heart, and he didn't know if it was the incision, or something else.

Nuri Does Not Exist
SADRU JETHA

My father answers to the call of Gulu but his real name
starts with the letter K. My uncle answers to the call of
Hassan but his real name starts with the letter F. And my
aunt Amina's real name starts with the letter Z.

"Why, Grandma?" I ask.

"Evil spirits, *beta*," she says, hands up removing her
horse tail bun.

I get up on our hard bed and go behind her.

"It is to confound evil spirits who might wish to harm
my children."

My hands close on hers. She slides them out from
under mine. Left hand on the bun, right pulling out
hairpins, first one, then another, then two more.

"But how, Grandma?" I give her the puff bun and
four hairpins.

She shakes her hennaed hair, tucks bun and pins under
the pillow.

"Shush, *beta*, we don't talk about evil spirits at night."

"Tomorrow then," I say as I move into her side. She
presses me close. Sandalwood scent.

"You will wake me, Grandma?"

A last squeeze. "To sleep, *beta*."

I sit cross-legged facing her. She closes eyes.
"Bissssmillllaah ... In the name of Allah ...," she begins her
whisper. Then silence, only lips moving, hands folded in
lap.

I look out the window. Moonless stars, thousands.
Nkhuuuu ... clearing of throat in the distance. Kaku's night-
watchman. Does he really keep awake all night?

"Ali, Ali, Ali," she breathes out, opening her eyes. It is

over. She blows gently, first across my right shoulder and then my left.

"There, *beta*, both the angels on your shoulders protect you now."

I lie down, face turned toward her.

"Sleep in peace, *beta*."

She continues sitting cross-legged, closing her eyes again, right cheek bulging with the last *paan* of the day, murmuring, then silent, then blowing to the right and to the left of her shoulders. "Ya Allah," she sighs and lies down next to me. I get closer to her, curl my right leg across her bony thighs, arm pressing spongy belly, smell her sandalwood smell.

When I stretch my arm she is not there. She did not wake me. I jump out of bed, look around. Everyone fast asleep. Down two flights of wooden stairs, three steps at a time. She is on her low stool.

"Why did you not wake me, Grandma?"

She does not look up but reaches for her brass plate, with betel leaves wrapped in wet cloth and three little tin boxes, one for chopped betel nuts, one for bitter white lime paste, and one for tasteless brown paste, fragrant. Chewing tobacco in the little handkerchief, knotted, in the middle of the plate. I sit on the floor, arms round drawn-up knees, watching, while she prepares her early morning *paan*.

"Could not sleep, *beta*. Got up early. Very early," straightening a leaf on the shiny plate. Rubs on it, with right forefinger, first the white paste, then the brown.

"But how Grandma?"

Adds betel nuts. Folds the leaf three times. Thumb and forefinger lift the tiny bundle. It disappears into her red mouth. I wait for her eyes to close as she takes her first slow bite into the *paan*, pressing out its sharp juices. She sucks in a deep breath, eyes on me.

"How what, *beta*?" she asks, mouth full.

"How are the evil spirits confounded?" passing her the spittoon under the stool. Cleaned to a shine every night by Mama Aya.

She holds it some distance from her, squeezes her lips into o…puuutch…twang. Her first thwack into the spittoon. Places it a few feet away to catch her squirts, short and sharp, for the rest of the day. A straight shooter. Comes with long years of experience, Mama Aya says.

Though I am in standard two, she lifts me into her lap. I lie facing up. My right hand on her jaw, feeling the quick movement of toothless gums mashing into the *paan*. She shifts the bulge to the right of her mouth. It will rest there till lunch time, getting smaller, invisible. Her mouth no longer moves so I drop my hand.

Mama Aya sits on the soft grass under the cool dark of the mango. Silken *bui bui* hides all but her bare feet, hands and face. She is still as air, eyes distant, blade of grass between teeth. I follow the long line of ants starting from a small hole under the flame tree. They are black. Not *majimoto*, the fat red ones which draw blood. Each carries a tiny load. Going…where? I look up. The sun not so hot, not so high as at noon. Her eyes are fixed on me, unseeing. I crawl into the salt breeze to where she is and stand across her stretched legs. My hands on her cheeks, face nearing hers. Our noses meet.

"Maamaa," I breathe into her mouth.

"*Mwanangu*, my child," she stirs, pressing me hard into her breast. Heavy musk heartbeats. I remove part of the *bui bui* covering her head. It falls on her shoulders. My fingers move along the parting of plaited woolly hair, fuzzy.

"What does *labek* mean, Mama?"

She turns me round. Lifts me like Grandma and lowers me into her lap. By the coconut palms is a man, Mama Aya black, tall and thin, binding his ankles with a cord. His hair curls, not as woolly as Mama Aya's, not straight as mine.

"Mamaaa. *Labek*. Tell me what *labek* means?"

A leap onto the grey trunk of the coconut palm. Feet up together. Arms gripping the slender trunk. A looping caterpillar.

"It is like this *mwanangu*," her hand dry, stroking my forehead. I place my hand on hers. She stops.

Now at the top of the tree, removing the heavy knife from loin cloth. Oonh. Whack. Thud of a coconut. Oonh, whack. Oonh, whack. Thud. Thud.

"Yes, *mwanangu*," she starts, removing her hand from my head.

Replaces the heavy knife. Slides down the swaying trunk. Collects the coconuts into a woven basket. Swings it onto his head.

"It is when the master calls his slave…"

"By his real name?"

"…and the slave replies *labek*, I come, I obey."

"Did Grandma…"

He looks at us, smiles and waves his right hand. Mama Aya waves back "*Heri*, good fortune, Bilajina."

I say, "*Kwa Heri*, goodbye, Bilajina."

Bilajina, Without Name. They found him under the upside down *mbuyu* tree, where the spirits meet at midnight, at noon as well. Not far from where Mama Aya lives. They waited for his mother to come and claim him. She never came. Some say nobody in the whole of Zanzibar knows his real name. Mama Aya does not agree. "Allah knows," she says.

"Did Grandma...," I begin again but her arms close in, hard, hurting.

"It is like this, *beta,*" Grandma begins, stroking my hair with her right hand. Her left hand fits into mine. "If an evil spirit wishes to harm you, he has to know your real name. If he doesn't know it, he can't find you."

Her mouth moves again, once. She looks down at me, eyes deep bright. She does not smile.

"And so we call you Nuri. If the evil spirit harms Nuri, well, Nuri is not your real name. The one called Nuri does not exist. And so the real you is unharmed."

She looks at me again. She is clever. Did not Grandfather say that he would be lost without her? When I grow up I will give not one but several names to my children, none of them real. That should take care of even the cleverest of spirits. I could call one of them Bilajina. Or give them no names at all.

"What does my real name mean?"

Her hand is brown, chick-pea like mine.

"Servant of Allah. But you mustn't tell it to anyone. An evil spirit passing by may hear it."

"Not even during day time?"

"No, not even then."

I turn her hand. Blue veins soft twisting snakes.

"Why did you name me Nuri?"

She closes her eyes. When she opens them on me, they are shiny sharp. She lifts me roughly, presses me hard against her. Her heartbeats strong as Mama Aya's. She pulls me back. And then ...too late. Her mouth crushes against mine, muffling her reply, "Because you are the light of my eyes. He, he, he, he."

I wipe the wet from my mouth, frowning, then get back into her lap, curled up hard against her stomach, feeling the laughter inside. Her hand begins stroking my hair again.

I rush up the wooden stairs and enter Grandma's room. Everyone is there. She is propped against two pillows in her hard bed, tired, except for two glints that are her eyes.

"I have been waiting for you, *beta*," she complains weakly, *paan* in mouth.

I enter her raised arms. Sandalwood scent. Her lips, limp, press against mine. I do not wipe the wet from my mouth. Right hand strokes my hair. Her lips move, then narrow, then blow towards me.

"She's getting weaker," Mama Aya whispers.

"Help me in, *beta*."

I do.

"Cover me, *beta*."

I do.

"Remember the things I told you, *beta*."

Right arm reaches out. I take her hand in mine. Her eyes, still on me, begin to close. She smiles, then heaves up, eyes rolling upwards. *"Labek,"* she cries. Her hand is limp.

"From Him we come, to Him we return," Mama Aya murmurs.

> IMPORTANT. *All persons entering the Colony and Protectorate of Kenya. Disembarking passengers are required to report to the Immigration Officer under Immigration Regulations, section x, subsection y, subsubsection z. They are required to complete the form prescribed by the Minister under the aforementioned Regulations and present it to*

> *the Immigration Officer. PENALTY. False*
> *statements will result in prosecution leading*
> *to a fine or imprisonment or both.*

The same slip of a form, Grandma.

> *Name.* "Nuri..."
> *Address.* "Khatpat Bazaar, Zanzibar."
> *Purpose of visit to Kenya.* "In transit. On
> my way home to Zanzibar."
> *Nationality.* "British Protected Person."
> *Race. Race?* "Human."

I join the queue, form in hand, waiting for interrogation. Fear in my belly, the same fear you felt but never talked about. This white spirit is red-haired, but then you said they all looked alike to you, Grandma. A pukka sahib, in gleaming white shirt, khaki shorts, knee-length socks, polished brown shoes. I face him. "Smart Alec," he mumbles, reddening. Crosses out "Human," scribbles something in its place and motions me on to the gangway for "Disembarking Passengers; Customs to the Right."

Customs. A brown sahib, all of him in whites, shirt, shorts, knee-length socks, leather shoes.

"Anything to declare?"

"No."

"London return Indian and nothing to declare?"

"I am here only for a few hours. On my way to Zanzibar."

"M.B.B.S.?"

"Beg your pardon?"

"M.B.B.S. - M for *miya*, husband. B for *bibi*, wife. And B.S. for *bacche saath*, with children," he laughs, turns his head and spits out a mouthful of *paan* juice. "Joke, you see. Good, yes?"

I nod, smiling.

His eyes narrow on my camera.

"Let's see," he demands.

I comply.

"Ah, a box Kodak," he sounds disappointed as he returns it. "Leica is much better."

He looks at me again, hesitates, then waves me on. I feel his eyes on me, hear *paan* juice splash against the wall behind me.

"Nuri, weh Nuri. Nuriii, Nooorrriii." Mama Aya, come to see me.

"*Labek*, Mama," as I hurry down two flights of stairs, three steps at a time. She is on the stool, Grandma's stool, draped in soft *bui bui*, her face leathery lean.

"*Mwanangu*," she cries, opening arms to take me into folds of *bui bui* musk. She pulls me back and squeezes my cheek with her thumb and forefinger.

"But you have gone so thin, child. No meat on you. And so pale, like a white man." She begins stroking my hair.

"They looked after me well, Mama."

"How about your meals?"

"My landlady cooked my meals."

She fidgets, then asks in a low voice, "A white woman?"

"Yes, Mama, a white woman."

"Eh?" She narrows her eyes, leans forward a little and asks in a murmur, "White man's truth?"

"Truth, Mama. God's Truth only," I say, swishing right hand under my chin. "Over there, white men work in coal mines, drive buses, and work as porters, Mama."

"Hah," as she claps her hands. "Now I have heard everything."

"And there were black students, blacker than you. And brown students and students from as far away as China. And we were all the same in the white man's eyes."

She withdraws from her face, her eyes unseeing on the line of ants on the wall opposite. There is much I want to ask, but I must wait and watch as I did long ago under the mango tree.

"Your Grandmother…" she returns to herself, looking at me. "She told you to remember the things she taught you."

"How could I forget, Mama?"

"About the good and the evil…"

"As with the spirits, Mama."

"And about the real and the false…"

"As with names, Mama."

She nods a few times and then withdraws from herself again, still, silent.

Born British Protected Person. Race Indian, 2nd class. Not White lst Class lst Division. Not Arab, lst class 2nd Division. Not African, 3rd class. Only blacks are African. They are natives.

Zanzibar becomes independent. Arab government passes a law. I cease being a British Protected Person. I am Zanzibari now.

Revolution. How many killed?

One, Hasnu the tailor.

Two, Bakari the teacher.

Three, Mzee Mohammed….

Ten? More like a hundred. A thousand. Ten thousand. Mass graves.

Zanzibar and Tanganyika are now one. They pass another law. I cease being Zanzibari. I am Tanzanian now, still 2nd class. Race Indian, capitalist, exploiter, blood sucker. Not African. Only blacks are African. Not native. Natives have been abolished.

I emigrate. Fill in forms. Become British Citizen. Part of the black swamping hordes come to sponge on the state. Race IndianPakiColouredBlack.

I emigrate again. To Calgary, Alberta. More forms. I am Canadian now. Of sorts. They call me Nick. Two false names. Doubly protected. Other Nicks here, Noormohamed, Nuruddin, Nashir, all Nicks.

Dastoor has become Dick.

And Sadruddin is Sam.

But Nuri persists, in the birth certificate, in passports, in school and distant university records, and throughout every changed nationality. Grandmother knew. Nuri can come to no harm. He does not exist.

THE DANGERS OF B AND E

Kathie Kolybaba

when someone touches me
I go crazy
really
I can't handle it
on the skin
For days it'll bug me, yeah, I'm scratching it
makes me crazy, I'd
freak if
you did it, if
but okay, gotta go

I'm alone in the house. She's alone in the house. Everything is white, still. The snow. The walls of all the rooms of this house. The scattered paper. The sheets on the bed. The credit card. The woman waiting, watermelon in her hands, rich.

She's alone in the house.

Lachinski's outside, it's his turn: I pull on my gloves, pull the door shut tight behind me. It's bloody cold. I'm wearing a huge old mouton coat, wrap it tighter about me, crunch up in the car. We're quiet for some time, listening to nothing much. It's ice clear on the road; the road isn't as straight as I thought.

At eight, the sky is still grey. We walk in slowly, trudging under the weight of winter gear, on ice. The guard at Control watches us watching him, waiting for him to let us through. His hatred for us gives him this pleasure – five slow minutes with slate eyes watching us watching him, waiting. And then release: the door rings, Lachinski swings it open, and we're through. Click. Past the kitchen and the tower guard and toward the school: two more gates, some minutes, tired jokes, and we're in.

Fontaine's finally shown up. Come back to quit, hang out. He looks edgy. I haul him into my office, make a big fuss so the other guys can laugh, so it's okay for him to come with me. I literally pull him in, as if he has no option.

His hands are frantic, beating the metal of the closed door, rapping, crashing against all the solid space between us in this small, windowless room.

"What's going on?"

"Nothin'."

"Fontaine, I'm serious, what's going on?"

"I just felt like quitting. I hate school. It's so fucking boring."

"Two weeks ago you were scrambling to get your work finished. You were doing good work. What happened?"

The tears come before the words, this big guy weeping, arching his neck back, crunching his face.

I sit down.

He moves harder against the door.

Moves his body in, head down, rigid in curled pose.

"They wanna send me away. To Saskatoon. The Psych Centre."

"Why?"

"They think I'm nuts. A whole gang of them. They've got piles of reports."

"So that feels bad – that they think you're nuts?"

"It feels fuckin' awful."

"Yeah. I guess I'd feel like shit inside if people had

78

lots of files on me, if they thought I was really crazy."

"Yeah. I feel like shit."

He's so quiet. His head in his hands, shoulders in, weeping. My body is folded; my head is down, too.

"The thing is, I know I can't handle it sometimes, I want to scream at those fucking bastards, I just pace and pace sometimes, I can't stand it."

"And with all these guys with the files – do you talk? Or do you banter?"

"Yeah. Well okay. I can't stand it, they ask everything; why the fuck should I tell them anything?"

"So you banter. And drive them crazy."

He smiles, the Fontaine smile, for one split second.

"Fontaine, I don't think you're nuts. I know it's not much, I'm just a teacher, but I think you're okay. I like you."

He's utterly silent, his frenetic energy stopped, his left hand suspended, fingers still, half clenched in air.

My hands separate, open over wood. The palms of my calloused hands touch nothing else.

"I'm up for parole in four months. But if they send me in there, I'll never get out. No one ever gets out of there."

Such terrible need and he cries again and I can't touch him, can't.

In the car with Lachinski, the talk is slow. No laughter today, a quietness, the words thought out, delicate, poised. Discussing the day, we drive home through the ice and the sad lonely fields, Fontaine on our minds.

A long still day: the sun in suspension, the sky perfectly clear. I enter the house, cautiously. The door's ajar, the stereo's gone, the phone's off the hook. Everything held.

Upstairs, all the drawers are open. Everything's unlocked, messed up. The sun lies still in the sky.

Had a rough time with him at the beginning. I know why they think he's nuts – the guy just about drove me crazy actually. Wanting attention always, and so bright, he would hang around and banter as if his life depended on it. I'd never seen anything like it: "So what ya doing out here anyway, teaching us this stuff? You think we care about this stuff, reading and all that shit, you think this matters to us?"

"Well, I…"

"You think we can even read or something? And what are you doing here, when you could be teaching some nice white kids in the city?"

"The city, I…"

"What's that you're wearing, what is that, and what's that on your hand there, are you married?"

"Fontaine…"

"You mean some guy lets you come out here everyday to these cons all these cons all these men? What kind of guy is he, is he crazy?"

"Well…"

"Or maybe he just don't love you maybe he's got some woman at home right now in your house. You got a house? Yeah, hanging out in your bedroom checking out your clothes, using your perfume, what do you think … sleeping with your man? Does it matter to you or do you care, hanging out here with these cons checking out all this shit?"

"Fontaine…"

"Or maybe you got kids, you got kids? What's the matter I say something wrong you got some problem there no kids something screwed up? Why do you look like that?"

"Fontaine go and sit down…"

"Well I didn't mean *hey* did I hit a nerve or something some raw spot hey I didn't mean to suggest…"

"Fontaine…"

"Well shit you looked nervous there a little edgy I'd say as if something bothered you. Hey you shouldn't let things get to you like that, I mean, *hey,* don't get so worried so upset."

"Fontaine, sit down, it's time for you…"

"Really it's not good to get so upset. Did I upset you? *Hey* what are we reading today what's on the agenda poetry or some story? I kind of liked that story the other day you know with the old man yeah not a bad story."

"Fontaine, take the book, take your body, sit down…"

"*Hey* why so nasty you look mad *hey* don't be mad I was just asking. *Hey* aren't you the teacher isn't it your job to tell me what book? *Hey* you look upset you shouldn't let things bother you so much, really, you look bothered."

"Fontaine, take the book, take off."

"*Hey,* I thought teachers were supposed to talk to their students. You're my teacher, right, so why can't you talk to me? What's the matter? You shouldn't be so sensitive. *Hey,* is it just because I'm some dumb Indian? Is that what you think? Is that why you're like this? That's it, isn't it? And I thought you were different."

One day he kept at it, until finally I told him to FUCK OFF. To really *fuck off.* It was in my voice, not mere exasperation, but sheer finality, violence. He stopped immediately; he sat down and got to work. We got along beautifully since then. I remember it well, the sheer sickness I felt just after I said it, until I realized it was okay, I could tell my students to fuck off if I wanted, in this school.

She enters the house, cautiously.

I told Lachinski about the Psych Centre but not the tears.
I kept that to myself, the tears and my aching. The words
were basics, sheer as ice; but he knew, was suffering too.

By the window. Only snow. Snow and bare branches of
trees. The house is warm, but my body, still chilled, aches.
Behind the kneecaps, under elbows.
    Everything is still, meticulous: everything necessary is
written down, locked up. Safe. I wait by the window.

Lachinski and I, drinking one long night into the dawn
find our bodies close. One hot summer night, watermelon,
brandy, sweet longing. His quiet hands and the slow dance
of the moon on the plants, my clothes white and all words
a nuance. Our movement together as natural as waking to
sunlight: our small touching poised on the moment of
fresh possibilities sheer in the night.

Journal Entry #8:
    *Exercise can be defined in many terms. For example, I used
to be a burglar and in my line of work, I had to scale high-rise
apartment buildings in the city for practice to get used to the
heights and help me get a better understanding of what and how
much work was involved. I also had to be in good physical
shape to endure climbing 10 or 20 stories high. But on the average
it was no more than 10 stories. When you look at it though, it is
very high. As much as I can say about exercise, it's a good way to
keep your body in tone and will help you to endure a bit longer
than the average human being if you're in this line of work.*

What does he see when he enters? What does he look at?
Does he go straight for dresser drawers, for closets, for the
stereo, for the computer? Does he turn on the TV, turn up
the heat, does he look out the window? Does he look at

the print on the wall, notice the blues of the rivers? Is he fastidious, efficient, gathering merchandise, rifling cloth and paper for money, credit cards, or does he immerse himself, look around, check other stuff out?

I imagine someone breaking in this house, someone looking. I have it straight from the beginning, but I don't know what happens next. I've never known what happens next; but it's Tuesday, it's the opening the basement window trick, quick, and he's in. There's only one: one man, but I don't know what he looks like, how big he is, how he moves. I know only that he looks: sees my leftover morning coffee cold in the machine, the food all crunched up, shoved in, in the fridge. I know he goes upstairs and sees the scattered make-up on the bathroom shelf, feels the towels half-damp from my bath. I know he enters the bedroom and sees the pillows crushed cradling still the ghost of my dreams. This is all I know: I fear terribly that he will enter my study, find my journal, begin a journey: I envision him opening this left-hand drawer, opening envelopes of photographs, letters, moments. I see him looking, not knowing what he will see.

I did not expect the tenderness, that long languid night, in my white house. Only banter and our camaraderie of laughter and rare respect. A strange loyalty, yes. But that cradling my small body, his open palms caressing my throat, tracing the veins on my wrist, my life, all this is a secret surprise.

Fontaine comes in bantering, swaggering, dancing: "I got parole, I got it! In three months: I can't believe it!"

"What'd you do?"

"*Hey*, I talked to them a bit. Just enough. I was fairly straight – *hey*, you'd be proud of me!"

"Yeah?"

"Yeah."

"Does it make sense? To level a little?"

"Yeah. A little. But I did tell those guys that I didn't like all those questions, I did tell them that."

The door is open; he's expansive, large, taking up the whole frame. I'm still sprawled in my chair, my legs on the desk, drinking coffee, looking up at him in the light of the early spring morning.

The risk is not to enter, the risk is to live there. Live there, secretive one.

"Once I was checking out a house across the river, a huge place on a little curvy street. Got in quickly and still I felt funny, had a strange feeling, so I was moving fast. Had the stereo, some cameras at the side door, some credit cards and cash in my jacket pocket, was just checking out the lady's dresser drawers. Looking for money, jewellery – you should see what some people have – and at the back of this weird kind of cabinet I found a bunch of stuff. I pulled out the whole fucking drawer and looked really carefully – this broad had everything there – a strop razor, six containers of sleeping pills, a semi-automatic, a long thin wire, a bottle of rat poison, even a note. Prearranged. I couldn't believe it. It was all laid out perfectly, at the very back. I felt really sick just looking at it, like I was right in there, feeling around with her guts. I packed it all back in, as best as I could, piled the other stuff back on top, and left."

Crazy, hey?

Secrets. Secrets of the men I keep. The terrible risk of entering this white house I wander about in, safe.

The radio is background; the sky is background. The ice slips under and past. We move through the white-out, watching the brief moments of yellow on the highway; our bodies arched forward, hoping we're on the right side of the highway. The city emerges, finally, as if untouched by the storm. Lachinski, Friday, February: our silence as natural as the constant cold. This song, "walking on sunlight," filters in through the dark white sleep of snow, of the fields, barren and enclosed; this ridiculous and almost hearty song makes us crash through the silence and into the city with hysterical, lost laughter. The suffocated fields sleep still, behind us.

"But sometimes, even now, I find myself wondering about her – wondering if she really did it, or if she changed her mind, or if she's still waiting for the perfect occasion. I find myself wondering what she looks like, what radio shows she listens to, what she likes to eat for breakfast, you know?"

He comes to my school, my new school, in the city, utterly Fontaine, wearing a bright red shirt. He's out. Laughing. I want to hug him, so I laugh with him, it's pleasure, this. I'm wearing a red dress; like a real teacher, he says, amazing.

For a brief moment I imagine loving him, my thief, my journal writer, my reader of people's lives: stripping off that cotton shirt, moving up and against that strong body. Clean hair, laughter in my throat. I imagine myself giving in to this strange and crazy desire, kisses on eyelids, the scent of him.

He's there by the window. Laughing. His body fluid now, an openness not there before. We're past words: he touches me, delicate stroking fingers on my exposed wrist. And is gone.

Little Boy Games

ALLISON MURI

The story lies, I think, in my association of the gun and the game. I remember orange feet, the bright green head, the cold eyes that had hardened over and puckered a little as the fluid receded. The day was hot, the end of a dusty summer, with wind stinging the alkali dirt and chaff into our eyes; or maybe it was later, cool blowing fall getting ready to step into winter, whipping the long strands of my hair and bits of straw into my eyes, billowing his open denim jacket out from his body. Perhaps the gun and the game were separate days, separate visits.

Then again, maybe not; but who's to say now what this particular little history was, what it wasn't? I don't know if he remembers, or if he would tell, even if he did remember. But those events have become linked together by a memory adept at symbolism, fashioned into this single story because I can make more sense of them this way, the game and the gun. Here on this page, those afternoons are the same warmish windy fall day.

At least, I assume it was fall because, out in the knee-high yellow grass of the square corral behind our house, alongside the twin tracks of dust that led out to the pasture where my dad checked his cows every day, was the dead duck. Though maybe not the same vibrantly coloured one I see in my mind; perhaps it was actually a female on this particular day, drab brown in shades of sandy-dirt and dry-grass. And yet ... is that my cousin's hand reaching down to stroke the brilliance? There was vivid colour, but let's make it drab. Let's make it female.

My dad had shot it. Or possibly, it was my uncle who'd bagged it, my uncle who had come up from Regina with his retriever, and my aunt, and my cousins. (Whether the men actually said "bagging game" I don't know for sure; it could be merely that I've come across the term and fallen in love with it elsewhere, in a Saki ghost story, perhaps, read when I was young and now associated with that time as closely as a piece cut to lock into a puzzle.)

We didn't eat duck. Neither did my cousins' family: the taste was too wild, the meat too greasy. And so this duck was dead there in the grass behind our house. It's likely they were using it to train the dogs, my dad's Irish Setter or my uncle's English one, to retrieve other inedible fowl they would shoot in future seasons.

But that's not where this story starts, really, since although I was aware of the duck's existence – we'd all searched for it the previous afternoon – no, make it two days before when we'd learned of its presence – we had mostly forgotten about it.

So on this particular fall day, my cousin – the younger one who was my age – he and I were stalking the barnyard. He had a gun carefully cradled in his arm, a real gun, and I wasn't to touch it. I think it was most likely a pellet gun, though he may have told me it was a .22. He might have told me it was a semi-automatic and I'd have believed him.

He was a hunter, even at that young age – and how old were we? Six or seven? Even then, he was a sportsman who got up before dawn to go fishing; who went with the men when they had room in the truck on early morning scouting expeditions; who shot at rabbits and gophers and magpies with a slingshot and heavy round pellets.

I remember my dad telling me how he used to trap crows when he was a boy. The Fish & Game League used to pay a few cents for every leg or egg of scavenger birds like crows and magpies, which were commonly believed to be robbing songbirds' nests. He couldn't remember how much for sure, since he never got paid as his older brothers had. By the time he was big enough to join in the hunt, it was just for fun. They would climb up trees to the huge nests of twigs and collect the eggs, or throw the hatchlings to the ground and then cut off their legs. I don't know why they still troubled to cut off the legs. Maybe they needed to prove to themselves their prowess, maybe they lined up the bony legs and sunken, softened eggs on a window sill in the barn. Maybe they needed to remind themselves every so often of the deaths, of their own power to cause death. More likely, they thought these tokens would be worth something again some day. (Like the coyote pelts that got chewed up by mice, just a few years ago, while he was waiting to see if the price would go up.)

They used to set gopher traps on the tops of posts along the fence line. When you caught a crow and went to kill it, he said, it would flop off the post and hang upside down flapping against the barbed wire and cawing. Then hundreds or dozens of crows would appear, first as black dots high above in the blue; then closer as dark menacing shapes swooping and screaming the whole time until you killed it. They're smart birds, crows. I think they knew.

The boys in my class at school hunted gophers, poured gallon pails of water down the holes to flush them out or drown them, sometimes poured gas down and tossed in a lit match, or they trapped them or snared them. (Or poisoned them, but that wasn't the usual method for young boys – partly, I suppose, because it was dangerous, but also, I suspect, because the action occurred underground, out of sight, long after the boys themselves would have gone.) If they wanted the tail, for which they were sometimes paid, they grasped it between thumb and forefinger, held the animal aloft, and snapped the tail off with a quick, hard jerk. The body would be left wherever it landed for the dogs or the crows to eat. Sometimes at school I would hear them bragging of these exploits; and once or twice, shrill giggles when one told of how he had snapped off the tail while the gopher was still alive.

Or they simply shot them, those curious animals who can't resist popping up out of their holes to see what's going on – the boys hunched alongside their fathers on a calm day, a fine way to spend a quiet Sunday afternoon.

Hunting was what my cousin and I were doing on the particular fall afternoon of this story. He would have pointed his gun at everything we saw, he would have adopted the stance, the stillness, the wide-apart legs, finger poised on the trigger, hand steadying the barrel, blue eye squinting down its length at gophers, at birds, at fence posts, maybe even surreptitiously at the cats. He didn't fire, of course. He wasn't allowed to shoot, and it wasn't long before he had tired of the pretence.

"I know a game," he said then. We'd played it before. On our last visit to Regina he'd met me at their back door, escorted me downstairs, in the basement showed me the elaborate fort he'd constructed on the couch out of blankets and cushions. Once we were both lying down inside the low darkened confines of his fabricated room, he wiggled out of his pants and convinced me to do the same. It was, I believe, an unremarkable event – and it went unremarked – though the memory remains clearly vivid to me over twenty years later. I was probably well used to the game by then. My first recollection of my youngest uncle, for instance, was when I was perhaps four years old, when he would have been thirteen or so. A little old to be playing doctor, surely, but I don't recall begrudging him that furtive inspection, or even being mildly surprised at it. And consequently my cousin's behaviour some years later wasn't unexpected, just something boys did.

Later we ate pistachio nuts out of a crackling plastic bag my cousin bought from the convenience store on the corner. Our fingers and our tongues were stained red with the dye; it was the very first time I'd tasted them. He told me about a girl in his class at school, one he didn't like, how he'd grabbed her by the ankle and twirled her over his head, how she was wearing a skirt and no panties, how her cunt looked. He used that word; it was a word I'd never heard before. He made a V with the index and middle fingers of his right hand to show how it looked.

"Why don't you like her?" I asked. He showed me how he threw a stone right into her cunt, the index finger of his left hand wedging firmly in the V.

"How could you twirl her over your head and pick up a rock at the same time?"

"That was when another boy was twirling her," he said. "I forgot to tell you all the boys in my class were there. We took turns."

I didn't believe him, really. How could he have enclosed her ankle with a grip so strong and loose without dropping her? How could he have lifted someone above his head with one of those skinny arms? I doubt that I questioned whether he was capable of such cruelty, though I cannot be certain.

I know I didn't like the pistachios, their blandness, the occasional sickly shade of unripe green inside, the stains they left on my fingers like a ledger of what I'd touched.

"I don't like that game," I said much later, on that fall

day at my parents' farm. It would be different this time, he told me. Let me show you first, then you can decide. I can't remember the threat he used, or even – to be honest – if he used one, but very soon he led me to the overturned outhouse that had been hauled into the pasture by the barn. The original door was now the floor, so we squeezed in through the crack where the roof had separated from the wall.

At this point, the story falters. I do not remember that gun. Where did he put it? He certainly would never have left it alone, outside, leaning abandoned against the outhouse to signal our presence there. He brought it in with him. Surely I remember it leaning, dark and slender, against the burred splinters of dusty white-painted wood inside? That would explain why we didn't crawl through our usual entrance, the round holes cut into the wooden seat that now made the south wall of our tiny hideout. We squeezed in through the narrower opening so that he could hold the gun upright, safe, like his dad had taught him. If my uncle had caught my cousin mishandling that gun, he would have strapped him on his bare bum with a leather belt. And he would have taken the gun away.

I must have worried about it, that it might fall over and go off when he set it down. He would have leaned it up against the wall when he showed me the game. That gun's presence must have made what we were doing seem even more precarious. If it was there. And surely it was. I can see it there, right there beside me. I could reach over and touch the smooth, cold barrel as I stood there with my legs slightly apart, my head almost touching the ceiling.

My cousin lay on his back with his head pillowed in the sling made by pants and panties pulled down to my ankles. The examination was brief, almost chaste, neither pleasant nor unpleasant.

"Now you have to do it to me."

"I don't want to." I didn't want to look at his thing, I didn't want to touch it, I didn't want my head between his legs, I certainly didn't want my head touching his underwear.

Finally, exasperated, he told me if I wouldn't play this game, he would pick another one.

We squeezed outside again and he led me, without speaking, past the house and the caragana hedge, beyond the garden to the corral.

He led me to the dead duck.

"You have to touch it." He stroked it. And then his fingers reached down again without the least hesitation and poked it. Right in the eye. I had never touched a dead animal.

"No."

"If you don't, you have to play the other game. You choose which."

"Well, I don't want to play either." I started for the house.

"If you don't, I won't be your cousin anymore." This threat had worked once, but I'd asked about that: I knew he had to be my cousin forever.

"Well, maybe I'll still be your cousin, but I'll never play with you ever again." I stopped short. Never? I turned my shoulders toward him.

"Yes, you will."

"Never. Not ever again." I had thought we were friends, buddies. We were pals. I can remember the smart of tears starting but I would have willed them away, would never have let him see me cry, would never have shown him that I was susceptible to that most hideous weakness of girls. I turned around and walked back to where he stood. How could he say that with such finality, with such arbitrary purpose? I know – I'm sure – I believed him, at least partly because lying was the worst sin I could think of. Maybe I believed others feared the consequences of such a sin as well. I did not understand how our own solitary truths can distort or shadow both experience and voice.

I kneeled down in the spiky grass, reached out and gently, gingerly, touched the dead body. I think I felt the stiff feathers of the wing, the hard smooth shaft of the elongated primary flight feather; I was surprised to discover I didn't mind so much. I stood up again to go back to the house.

"That's not all," he called after me, the anger and threat in his words whipped with the wind through my hair and against my ears. "That's not enough. There's more. You have to do this." He grabbed one of the legs and dragged the duck up the dirt path of the tire track. *How could he touch it like that? What could be fun about this game?* I wouldn't have doubted his sincerity: the enthusiasms of boys were foreign to me, inexplicable and strange.

"How far?"

He pointed down the track. "A long ways." Touching a feather was one thing; actually grabbing a dead leg and moving a dead body was another. There was no way I was going to touch that scaly, curled-up, *dead* claw.

"Either this game or the other one. Or I'll never play with you again. And I won't be your cousin, either."

I suppose I sighed. I suppose I said, "All right then."

Did we walk purposefully, striding back across the yard? Did I lag behind and hang back? Resolute or reluctant? I was an obedient child and had given my promise, so in this story I will say I was solidly determined to get the thing done – although I do seem to recall an uncomfortable shame as we passed in view of the windows of the house, where my mother and aunt would have been keeping an eye out from the kitchen table. And the gun, that gun has disappeared from the story again, though it must have been there with us, held up and across his body like a soldier's as we made our way back.

Once inside the outhouse again, the examination was conducted quickly, silently. One or two gentle nudges to those clammy, enpurpled, loosely filled pouches. (The more I think about it, the more I remember a surprising shade of dark pinkish-red. But – oh, *enpurpled, enpurpled*, such a lovely word.) Nothing on God's earth would have convinced me to touch the place where he peed.

"I'm done," I said. "You're okay." He nodded, satisfied. And out we went into the wind again. It must have been windy, as it is always windy on that treeless plain where my home was.

Later, when we are walking back to the house for supper, he aims at a row of sparrows perched along the power line above our heads.

"I'm going to kill one. Think I can get it? I can, you know."

"Don't shoot them! Please – don't."

"I will. I'm shooting at them right now."

"No, you're not. I didn't hear your gun. You didn't shoot at them." I can't resist adding, "Did you?"

"Yes. This gun has a silencer. I shot a bunch of them, and they're going to die."

"Why aren't they falling then?"

"It takes a while to work, when you use a silencer."

"Why?"

He pulls at my sleeve. "Let's go. C'mon. I'm hungry."

"Why did you shoot them?"

"I'll feed them to the dogs later, they like them."

"Wait. I need to see if any die."

"Naw, it'll take too long. I'll come back and get them later after they fall. Let's go now." He grabs my arm and we head toward the house.

As we pass under the wire, the chain of earth-brown sparrows lifts in flight. I remember looking over my shoulder at the doomed, dead birds arcing away from us, back toward the barn.

I remember the sadness, that full aching in my chest that accompanies loss, the ache before tears. That sadness, that I do remember.

Bottom
BONNIE BISHOP

It's pain which drives me out into public places. Like my
friend Lydia who allows herself to cry only at the theatre
or opera. She knows at some point she will have to pull
herself together among all those other people. Alone, with
nothing to distract her, she may cry into forever. Here, in
the shopping mall of brass, mirrors, and escalators, I lose
my equilibrium but, if I should fall into my pain, someone
at least will notice. It's just my period, that time of month.
Joke: Why do women get periods? Because they deserve
them. This is a bad month, with the cramps and flow.
I've stuffed super absorbent into me and wear maxis big
as pillows. I imagine I have a slightly bowed walk. What
do other women do? Stay home, probably.

I'm buying lingerie to wear for my lover. Mostly, these
days, I don't know where I'm going. To be forty, alone,
with nothing more than a clerk typist's job for security,
these days I don't know if I'm up or down. The escalators
give me acute vertigo. Joke: One man to another – she has
acute angina. Other man – oh good, that'll make up for
her small tits. The only thing I'm certain of is Thursday
from four p.m. to seven p.m. I will be with Michael. That's
something, isn't it? It's a start.

Woodward's welcomes me with its hum of shoppers,
cash registers, solid walls and floors. I feel more secure
but the pain won't stop. In among the see-through
negligées and underpants I move; and one other, a burly
man with dark beard and brown overcoat. I see his thick
fingers touch a cream satin pair of panties. I can tell his
hands are rough because of the way they pull on the satin,
catching the thin, soft material, the way my lover's hands

sometimes catch on me. Joke: What's forty thousand men at the bottom of Lake Ontario? A start. If my lover were at the bottom I'd dive clean through and pull him back up. The man with the beard looks up and sees me watching him. I don't know how long I stand like that but when I open my eyes he is beside me asking me if I'm okay. I say yes and he moves away. I can't remember what I'm doing here. Oh yes the pain. The lingerie. My lover. My list of things to do. Why did God invent men? Because cucumbers don't take out the garbage.

Here's a sexy little two-piece, red, lace item that'll make Michael's eyes pop out. His hands won't be able to resist. Men are like that. Territorial. Have to get their scent all over you and your things. No wonder women are constantly buying stuff. Keeps their men interested. Why did God invent women? Because sheep don't do dishes.

I'm moving along the line-up with the other shoppers toward the cashier and her multi-coloured machine. Everything is orderly and functioning well expect for my pain and the child crying in her stroller beside the rack of marked-down housecoats. The mother of the child offers her something bright and plastic. The child ponders it for a moment then begins to wail again. I feel the blood in me rush out. This might be like my friend Anna, whose breasts fill and leak every time she hears her five month old baby girl cry. If it wasn't for the cramps I would go over to that child and pick her up and hold her fast against my heart. I would. I can't understand a mother who won't pick up her crying child.

I'm paying cash for the bikini set. The designer sheets and duvet I bought for my bed and to impress Michael put me over my credit card limit last month. "Excuse me lady," I feel the grip of a hand on my arm and I turn to face the burly man, who has the satin underpants in his other hand. He can barely look me in the eye. "Lady, I don't think you're well." I follow his eyes down to the pool of blood between my feet and see the trail which this man has so carefully avoided stepping in. My stomach seizes tight with pain and I lean into the counter to stop it. Forget the blood, I think I'm going to throw up.

> *Here's me in my favourite dream: swimming. It's the only place I can. I buoy along using strokes I have no knowledge of — the back stroke, the side stroke. I use my feet and hands like delicate flippers. The water and I must be lovers, it sinks into my pores and holds me up unfailingly. And I am inside its skin, inside its heart, wrapped inside its very being. No two others could ever be that close. I swim toward a white light who happens to be a nurse.*

I see the intravenous running out of my wrist so I ask her what happened. She tells me how a day and a half ago I had a miscarriage in Woodward's. She asks me if there is anyone I want to call. I say no. She asks me if I live alone. I say yes. She tells me I was lucky I wasn't home alone. I might have bled to death or died of fever because the miscarriage was complicated by a staph infection caused by the super absorbent tampon. She tells me the doctor will be glad to see that I'm awake. I ask her the time and then she leaves.

For as long as I can remember I have desired a child. The older I get the more resentful I have become watching mothers with their children. Like my friend Jane who goes grocery shopping with ten bucks in her wallet to try and feed her young son and herself for a week. She tells me of her anger toward all the shoppers with their grocery carts piled high with expensive meats like sirloin tip steaks and lamb, and exotic fruits such as pomegranates, limes, and artichokes. All Jane and I want are the necessities that will make us feel secure and nourished. What have I lost? The anchor that would have secured me? The nourishment to help me survive?

In one more hour Michael will be knocking at my door. And I won't be there to wrap my arms around him like a life jacket, or he to me like a buoy. But this is all superfluous. Michael is superfluous. At this moment he has no idea of what has happened. If he does find out he will gracefully, perhaps gratefully, exit the scene and consider himself lucky that the cliff of the abyss didn't crumble before he backed away. Sometimes I think of all my lovers and what might have been if we had come this far together. Sam, the carpenter, and I would have been building our second home by now and I would be an alcoholic. With Jason, one of us would be up on murder charges. If my life reads like a bad novel and all my men have been minor characters, then how will it end? And what page am I on now? Joke: How many men does it take to wallpaper a room? Thirteen, if you slice them really thin. I sit up in my hospital bed and swing the tray around toward me. I lift the lid and fold out the mirror. I am surprised to find that I don't look any different. Something should show on my face, shouldn't it? Loss or grief? Why do my hands feel so empty?

The tray has a cubbyhole which has a plastic bag stuffed into it. I open the bag. For Christsakes. It's the little red bikini set. For Christsakes. I now have this great impression of being rushed out of Woodward's on a stretcher with vomit spittle running down my chin, clutching this underwear. Or is it the bigger question? Who made sure I didn't leave the store without the string bikini set? Was it the bearded man who notified me of my impending death? Or the sales-clerk whose shoes I vomited over? Whoever, I am grateful to them for their faith in my absolute recovery.

The doctor arrives, and like the nurse, tells me I'm lucky I was out shopping. I tell him all over the world women are dying from tampons and contraceptives, why should I be any different? I ask him a riddle: What's the difference between men and boys? He tells me I'm not taking this very seriously. I tell him men are taller. He understands that I'm in no mood to deal with the situation so he turns to leave. "Hey," I say, "Hey would you like to see my new bikini underpants?" He turns and says, "Is that some kind of joke? You women, you all try and act so tough these days." He frowns at me stern and yet not without sympathy. This man has pulled god-knows-what from between my legs. Blood, soft bone, and the haunt of my dead baby's cry. And here I am grieving him with my crude jokes.

Myself? Myself, I feel like I'm belly-dragging along the bottom of Lake Ontario, dark and dank, with all the pressure of the cold, cold water upon me. I know where I am now.

STEEP DEEP KEEP
SHELDON OBERMAN

So I'm just fuming in this tourist boat with Laura crying down below. I flick ashes into the grey sea chop and snap out, "I don't need this."

Maybe I shouted. I don't know, but everyone near me shuts down like I'm some psycho terrorist; all of these package-tour tourists packaged into yellow vinyl rain gear. Some toothy guy next to me shifts a space away. All the while, he's watching me sideways-weird, like I'm going to jump overboard. As if that was going to spoil his trip. Or maybe it would make it a five star success.

I didn't care what any of them thought. If they thought. If they ever had a goddam thought that wasn't about credit ratings or travel points, like they only drank white wine and pissed Perrier. Anyway, I wasn't going to jump.

But who's to know? When Laura and I were thumbing up through Quebec, we read about this guy at Niagara Falls. He was perched on the rocks alongside his fianceé. They were just looking down, checking out the drop. He said, "It sure looks steep." And then he's gone. She didn't even see him fall.

So Laura and I had this joke. Whenever one of us got sentimental, maybe about some place we both liked or about staying together, the other one would say, "It sure looks steep!" We had lots of jokes like that. They kept us sharp, kept everything clean and clear.

We hit it off real good all summer. It didn't matter that she was a college kid and I got by any way I could. When the rides didn't come we'd put on shows for each other, right there on the side of the road, singing and goofing around. We'd just shine.

But here I'm mad and worn out. Wet and cold. I couldn't care less if those Kens and Barbies set their cameras on high speed action. Let them. They wouldn't be getting a jump shot out of me. I am just wishing to hell we were anywhere else, that's all. Because everything's gone sour.

The loudspeaker is droning about some Arctic current flowing into the St. Lawrence. That's what draws the whales; this ice cube flow chock full of plankton.

It's making sense, because all the night before we'd felt that chill coming through our sleeping bags. We couldn't even keep each other warm. Laura was wrestling around with dreams, and I was frozen wide awake and thinking how close September was. We gave it up by sunrise and stamped around the town. The streets were all like dry ice and the coffee shop still shut tight. So Laura curled inside a store entrance and stared at the window full of school supplies, both of us knowing what was on her mind.

Then it was thirty bucks for the boat ride. We'd been living on ten a day since we'd left Banff so I said forget it. But Laura had to go. So I paid, too, but let them know it was a rip off. And we get on board just in time for rain.

"Oh, great!" I say, "thirty bucks to get soaking wet."

She says, "Why hitch all the way to Tadoussac if we're not going to see the whales?"

I say, "I don't know. I don't know why we're doing anything."

She starts to cry. She says, "I'm going below."

I say, "Go."

So I'm wrapped tight around my cigarette, blowing smoke into the grey. There's no horizon. Just this empty seasky and the railing is rising, falling, rising, falling with me hunched over it like I'm trying to keep it down.

The tour guide is cracking static with her bullhorn but I'm not listening. I'm just playing some angry scene with Laura in my head. Still, all the stuff about the whales is slipping in.

It turns out that whales aren't fish at all. They're really smart animals like us. At least, if you figure that we're so smart. Somehow millions of years ago, they decided to go back to sea. So they lost their legs and grew fins and for millions more years they swam around and ate and talked whatever whales talk about. They learned these moaning sounds like radar that go for hundreds of miles. And they found certain places where they can bounce their voices right across the ocean. So I figure it's not so bad being a whale.

But no way. The belugas are stuck here in the St. Lawrence and it's so polluted that they're dying out. I'm thinking about how whales die, how they must roll around underwater and start drifting off or maybe how they decide the sea's no good anymore and they want back on land and they'll end up dying on some beach. I'm thinking about what kind of strange sad stuff they must be moaning out all across the ocean.

My mind is going *steep deep keep*. These are sounds in my head; *steep deep keep* over and over like a song with no tune. I'm humming down into me, *steep deep keep* and into the ship's belly where Laura's rocking and crying and into the water as if the sounds can bounce all the way to Niagara Falls where that poor jerk got lost.

And just as if I called it, something swells out of the water. This thing plunges out of the water only so huge that it seems slow. Like the sea is shaping out a curving rubbery wall, rolling on and on while I'm going "What? What?" until it crashes.

All the yellow vinyl people shout, "Hey, look! A whale.

Get it! Get it!" They're pushing around me with their cameras while the bullhorn is roaring about what everyone is supposed to see.

It's flowing out of the water, this dark fleshy part of the ocean – it's not water, not rock – it's impossible. Like a massive organ coming right out of your body. Something crazy, groaning out such a colossal sadness and spraying salty water.

I think I'm splashed because my face is wet. It's like that big by-Jesus tail has gone and slapped me because my chest is heaving, gasping and then I'm pushing past all the yellow vinyl tourists to the steps, to Laura, just wanting Laura so I can cry on her lap, "Don't go," crying to her because it hurts so much to go.

Puerto Escondido
WARREN CARIOU

The air was the temperature of skin.

They walked in the *zocalo*, Gregory in cutoffs and short sleeves, Alicia in a woven Guatemalan shift she'd found at a roadside market.

With one hand on her hip, he steered her through the crowds of Mexicans and past the occasional clutch of sunburned tourists – forgetting, for the moment, that she hated being steered.

The waves were sounding on the distant beach.

They had come here for the sun, but had switched allegiances after the first day.

Everything in daylight seemed overexposed, like photographs of snow.

They found the true beauty of the place in the warm chiaroscuro of lanternlight, the tantalizing sense of half-glimpsed things.

After sunset, vendors lined the sidewalks of the *zocalo*, offering silver and lapis lazuli and aquamarine jewelry, batiked cotton dresses, and lustrous black pottery.

The dark-muzzled mongrels that lurked in the daytime streets disappeared at nightfall, perhaps to stalk the *campesinos'* chickens.

It was the next best thing to nakedness, this air.

They turned in at the *Hotel Cortez* and walked through a stuccoed corridor to a beachfront terrace.

The rush and drag of waves on the muddy sand was louder here, though the water was not visible.

Out on the beach, before the boles of the palm trees, was a row of bamboo torches with pale writhing flames. Alicia tucked her hair behind each ear.

She had nearly killed Gregory, and herself, two days ago.

But this was nothing like the surfing beach, where it had happened.

Here, the little cove which ran the length of the *zocalo* offered shelter from the deep-sea swells.

They walked past the bar and took a table close to the beach.

She thought she heard voices down there, children playing, laughing like cartoon characters.

The bartender brought red wine in earthenware goblets.

Perhaps these were the same kids they had seen fishing for mackerel from the gunwales of anchored boats, swinging tiny silver hooks above their heads and tossing them out.

The mackerel had moved like swarms of bees, breaking the surface in unison.

One boy had fished by himself from the buttress of volcanic rock that divided the cove from the surfing beach.

Twenty-foot breakers had curled into the rock face and exploded in geysers of spray, and as the water had cascaded down, the boy had scampered out onto a jagged promontory and hurled his hook.

One slip on that treacherous surface and he would have been lost.

Alicia was crying again.

"Don't," Gregory said, reaching for her hand.

He had always thought this would be a dangerous place.

He'd read the guidebooks and knew what to expect: malaria, diarrhoea, sunburn, earthquakes.

Alicia had laughed at him, but now she brushed her teeth with bottled water.

The undertow was a danger he hadn't considered.

No matter how far the waves flung themselves onto

the shore, the ocean always gathered them back in.

He hadn't seen her cry until recently, and didn't know how to react.

The tears were barely visible, trailing down over her cheekbones and underneath her jaw.

"Sorry," she said, trying to laugh.

"You shouldn't be sorry for anything."

She turned to face the beach and inhaled sharply through her nose, then fumbled in her purse for cigarettes.

When Gregory saw that she had no matches he walked to the bar and asked for some.

In mixed English and Spanish, the bartender tried to tell him about a two-hundred-pound sailfish that an *Americano* had caught that afternoon.

"*Non quiendo*," Gregory said, though he had in fact understood.

Along with the matches, the bartender handed him the business card of a friend who would take *turistas* out fishing for only five thousand pesos an hour.

"*Gracias*," Gregory said.

When he handed the matches to Alicia, she avoided his gaze.

They were alone on the terrace, which was not surprising since locals never came to these places and tourist season was already finished.

The summer rains would be here soon.

She dried her eyes on a tiny pink napkin, then rolled it into a wad and dropped it in her purse.

According to her mother, her grandfather had died of cigarettes.

Cigarettes are not a disease, Alicia had told her.

The sounds on the beach came again, boys playing tag among the palm trees.

She wanted to have a child, but she hadn't told Gregory

because she didn't want to scare him off.

They had only been seeing each other for three months.

She put the cigarettes back in her purse without taking one.

"I like how the people here smoke," she said, "as though they didn't know it was bad for them."

"They have no concept of safety," he said.

She wondered if he thought the same thing about her.

She had talked him into coming here in the first place, had discounted every one of his excuses.

She almost always got what she wanted.

That was what she'd told him the first time they went out, and he had laughed, thinking it was a come-on.

He was not at all like her ex-husband, who would have sat there on the beach drinking tequila while she drowned.

She would have almost preferred that.

Gregory took his sunglasses from his shirt pocket and cleaned them on the edge of the tablecloth.

In the lenses he saw reflections of himself.

The Mexicana DC-10 they had taken from San Francisco to Mexico City had shuddered during takeoff, and the engines had wailed like huge saws.

The cars here had no seat belts, no emissions controls.

Every female dog in the place was either pregnant or nursing, the rows of shrivelled black teats swaying under their concave bellies as they loped from one piece of shade to the next.

Alicia touched her tongue against the glazed edge of the goblet.

She was thirty-two.

Gregory was only twenty-seven, and though they both said age didn't matter, she wondered if maybe it did.

Everyone said they made a beautiful couple.

She had almost killed him.

She remembered his hand gripping her wrist, the riptide sweeping them out toward a breaker which was lifting itself above them.

He could have swum back to shore on his own, but refused to let go of her.

That was why she'd screamed for help.

She had never imagined herself needing a rescuer, but the screams had come easily, even with salt water in her throat.

Afterward, she hadn't properly thanked the surfer who saved her, had instead collapsed on her beach blanket, coughing violently and shivering.

Gregory would have kept holding onto her.

Two beautiful young women had walked by, wearing dental floss bikinis and carrying expensive cameras.

She couldn't remember what the surfer looked like.

Gregory had thanked him for her, but that wasn't the same.

When she had climbed on the surfboard, she had spread her knees across the back of it and paddled weakly with her feet.

The surfer had pushed the board from behind, and could have looked right up between her legs.

The beach was quiet now, except for the waves.

The children here always went home at the same time, without being called.

When Alicia was a child and spent summers at Manitou Lake, she used to hide in the bushes near the public beach every warm evening, stealing a few more minutes of the night while her mother called out her name again and again.

Gregory leaned forward on the table and looked into her empty goblet.

"Another?" he said.

"Please."

He waved to the bartender, who was leaning against the cash register, eyeing Alicia, like they all did.

"Dos otros, por favor," Gregory said.

Of course, he had eyed her himself when he first saw her.

It was at the welcoming reception for the new Minister of Justice, whom Gregory had supported in the election.

She was standing with her husband in the foyer of the Minister's office, talking to a policy analyst.

She had a slender neck and large grey dissipated eyes, though she spoke with quick authority like all the other lawyers.

The husband stood sullenly beside her, staring into his glass of rye and water.

Gregory thought: this is the kind of man who could be violent.

After the separation, Alicia never once mentioned his name, as if she was afraid of invoking him.

She looked at Gregory now, over the rim of her goblet.

"What are you thinking?" she said.

"I don't know. That we're still here."

"A miracle, is it? We've survived four days."

He took a short breath and exhaled through his teeth, a washing sound.

"Time is going slower than I thought."

She had a crack in her lower lip from sunburn or salt water, and the wine had seeped in, so it looked like she was bleeding.

He would rather taste his own blood than salt water.

He had gone into the ocean before her, diving beneath the cresting breakers and drifting out with the backflow.

The water was as warm as the air.

It was surprisingly shallow for a long way out.

They had watched the surfers slide down those glistening walls all morning.

Some of the Mexican children were playing in the surf, running just ahead of the upwashing waves.

When he turned back toward shore he felt the undertow dragging him further away.

It quickened to the strength of gravity.

Then the next breaker extinguished it, tumbling him shoreward.

He recovered in time to body-surf on the next wave, windmilling his arms to stay on top of the water as long as possible.

The salt made his tongue swell up like a blowfish.

He rode several more waves, until his foot brushed against the bottom and he stood up in waist-deep water.

Alicia was lounging in the surf only a few yards away.

"Go back," he said. "Go in!"

She smiled and splashed frothy water in his direction as the riptide pulled her further out.

"This isn't funny," he said.

He was already swimming out to her when she felt another surge of undertow.

It swept her out thirty feet before a huge wave broke over her head and rolled her under.

She couldn't find the surface.

She inhaled anyway, found air mixed with foam that caught in her windpipe like gravel.

When she opened her eyes she saw Gregory standing on a sand bar in front of her, the water only chest deep.

She stretched out her hand and he grabbed it as the undertow started again.

He pulled against it, but the sand sifted out from under his feet and in a second he was floating with her, rushing out toward the next wave.

"Swim!" he said, but already he felt her sinking.

The sand had dissolved like a pillar of salt.

They were lost in the surge and heave of the ocean, casting pieces of itself on the shore and gathering them back in.

She knew he wouldn't let go.

The ocean always gathered them back in.

Gregory sipped the last drop of his wine and felt it evaporate from his tongue.

There was a hint of rust in the aftertaste.

Alicia looked past him and saw the bartender leaning on the stump of a straw broom, watching her.

"He must think I'm a goddess or something," she said.

"Finish your drink, and we'll go," Gregory answered.

She stared back at the bartender and lifted her wine toward him in an extravagant toast.

"If only he knew," she said.

She drank quickly, then placed her goblet back on the table.

They stood up and Gregory led the way to the south end of the terrace and down a concrete staircase to the beach.

The wind was picking up, bending the palm trees like reeds.

They took off their sandals and walked toward the water.

When they reached the wet sand at the water's edge, they turned down the coast toward the string of orange patio lanterns that marked their hotel's poolside bar.

Shaggy whitecaps bore down on them out of the darkness, and the spray flew with the wind.

Gregory wondered what would have happened if the surfer hadn't been there.

He put his arm around Alicia's waist and she leaned against him.

He should have known he couldn't save her by himself.

At some point he would have had to decide: either let go and watch her drown, or keep holding on and join her.

When they reached the rock where the boy had been fishing, they turned toward the road.

The surfing beach was unlit, and bandits were said to wait there for tourists. It was safer to walk near the lights of the private cottages.

The only things Alicia remembered about the surfer were his suntanned arms, his California accent, and the word "Pipefitter," which was scrawled across the front of his surfboard in hot pink lettering.

They passed a tiny rust-pitted sign which they hadn't noticed until the day after the incident: *Playa Peligrosa*.

Dangerous beach.

The waves were a few hundred yards away, but they seemed to travel through the sand like tiny earthquakes.

At the edge of the hotel grounds, bougainvilleas and birds of paradise shuddered in the wind.

A group of young couples sat near the pool, sipping colourful drinks and talking lazily.

Perhaps the surfer was among them.

Alicia found the key in her purse and walked ahead of Gregory to unlock the door.

It was cooler in the room than previous nights.

She flipped off her sandals and padded across the concrete floor to the bathroom.

Gregory chained the door behind himself, then he lay down on the bed.

He would have let go of her.

Whether he'd wanted to or not, he would have let go. The fan above him wobbled, as if one of the blades was about to fly off.

Alicia came out of the bathroom carrying her shift, which she draped over a chair.

The tan lines on her shoulders and along her neckline gave the impression that she was still clothed.

She lay down beside Gregory and kissed his temple.

The sand sifted out from under his feet and he was swept out with her.

She switched off the bedside lamp.

She unfastened the buttons of his shirt, then opened it and kissed his chest, circling his nipples with her tongue.

Pipefitter.

She pulled his shorts and underwear down to his knees, and he kicked them off.

The fan whirled like a child's fishing line.

She moved onto him and they made love slowly, eyes closed, listening to the muted concussions of the waves.

The ocean always gathered them back in.

The Last Work of a Hired Hand
CLIFF LOBE

The first time I saw Uncle Abel without his left arm, at the funeral, I couldn't keep my eyes off the stump. I remember thinking that he looked unbalanced, with his shirt-sleeve pinned up, like a peasant mannequin someone forgot to assemble. I was hypnotized by what he was missing.

My fascination was nothing abnormal. We are stitched together by rhizomes of nerves much older than memory, we share the salt of one ocean. Which is why I can stare with impunity into mangled wrecks on the highway, or hospital rooms where unfamiliar corpses lie under sheets, waiting for the mercy of death. Those exhausted, barley-wheezing contraptions could as easily be me – my body wasted by carnivorous diseases too dangerous to name.

So don't tell me it's impolite to stare.

I felt that man's disaster as if it were my own, and in a way it was. Uncle Abel was something of a father to me, when no one else wanted that job. I'll say he gave me a leg up in the world, if you'll pardon the expression. Abel did his best, and for that I have learned to be grateful. Of course, I can say that now: time has cauterized my memory and I too am one step from my grave. At the time it was different. A fascination made possible by the ignorance of youth drew me to Quiring Acres.

But I have to clear something up.

I don't know what happened, we Quirings are usually substantial. I need only look at pictures of myself to be reminded of classical Greece – not that I'd chase little boys. But through some biochemical wrench, my father was betrayed by his genes, lungs strangled by asthma.

I suppose every family must have one – a piglet who gets the hind tit, not to mention one who gets all the land. It's Biblical. I didn't ask to be the accident-son of a Professor Emeritus and his Teaching Assistant. I prefer the chthonic rhythms of private property myself. I can't count the corduroyed knees I was bounced on: pedants from Britain with PhDs in whining, booze-breath Americans with fake Oxford accents, turtlenecked graduate students with chronic brown noses, people who quibbled over iotas.

I revered my uncle Abel and his agricultural kingdom, was embarrassed by my family's lack. Abel was as big as a granary, and with his stump wound-up in sterile gauze he possessed a heroic aspect. I thought of him as a partially-mummified Pharaoh, a Brigadier General, half-dead from nerve-gas, in a trench teeming with starved Nazi rats. Most times he would be clutching a picture of yours truly to his eviscerated breast.

That's the imagination I had.

But it was nothing as dramatic as that. Abel had simply made a mistake – he was a run-of-the-mill farm casualty. While greasing his New Holland baler, Abel caught his sleeve in the power take-off. "It's nobody's fault but my own," he admitted. "Any city boy'd know better."

I didn't doubt that for a second.

It was the last of seven bad years, or the first, depending on who you were. For his part, like anyone who plants things, Abel believed in a future – ignoring loans that had been called, a decade of soft markets, notices from Eastern bankers. I wasn't fooled by fatalism in disguise. I remember the eulogy well: *There is a time for everything … a time to plant a time to uproot … a time to be silent a time to … be born a time to….*

I seemed to miss the part about comfort. But Abel

listened intently, he was as religious as any land-owner could be. I imagine he wondered if he would be one-armed in heaven. Eternity's a long time to be handicapped. I kept thinking about the arm and the baler and the way my father died on the same day. I played the accident back and forth in my mind during the sermon: a slow-motion stew of blood and flying fingers. I thought about dying myself, and in my folly imagined it would be an important event. Definitive. Operatic. Needless to say, I now know better. I hear the whimper of death in my ear, feel the confines of a coffin.

I still do my best thinking in churches.

Abel couldn't do much while we shovelled in the grave. He had never learned how to weep. Waving his good arm out over the hole, he was candid. He explained the advantages of life with one hand: "It'll take half the time to wash up for lunch," he said, "or to prune my finger-nails for Sunday. And I'm half-cured of nose-picking, a habit I confess that I practice. You all know I loved my brother."

Abel's bravado fooled no one, least of all me. Like most human beings, he was trying to convince himself that the vagaries of chance are benign, that death isn't The Holy Terror. Like the rest of the crowd, I simply stared into the hole, smelled the cold clay that would one day embrace us, and dared myself to jump in. Who, unable to sleep in the vise grip of midnight, hasn't heard the thudthump of the first shovel of dirt?

The following week *The Chronicle of Thirteen-Mile Corner* reported: "**Local Farmer Loses Arm, Stalls Tractor.**" If you don't believe me I still have the clipping — it's as yellow as my lizard skin. For the first time in that paper's history, the phrase "one tough bastard" was printed. It was no typographical error, no bug-eyed editor's lapse.

There was no other way to put it. My uncle had beaten a machine; this was a victory for the whole human race.

The PTO shaft drives the baler, connects it to the tractor, as I am sure you did not know. It spins at a thousand revolutions per minute. It caught my uncle's sleeve and reeled him in like a noodle, rolled up his arm in less than a second. The tractor stalled when the shaft reached his armpit. You can check most of this information in a library.

Abel blinked and found himself disabled, unarmed, attached to his baler, a patina of blood streaming down his white hairy belly and bandy legs, congealing in pools in his boots. After what seemed like hours of cosmic wrestling (in fact about seven minutes), it was clear to Abel that he would die there if he didn't do something. Dark waves of unconsciousness loomed behind him, welled up his spine and the back of his neck, festooned his peripheral vision. He would have to sever the remaining tendons of his arm with a tin-snip, and cut through what was left of his humerus with a hacksaw. His free hand could just reach the toolbox bolted onto the back of the tractor. Abel reasoned: "Who wouldn't bisect himself just to live half a life?"

Then he made the first clip: a scream, a high-voltage shudder, convulsed his body. When he made the last pass with the hacksaw – cutting bone was like cutting wet lumber – Abel felt unbearably light. Time seemed to dilate. Each moment felt like the very last, elastic, second which precedes the end of the world. Life, it became clear, in that industrial mishap, was too absurd to measure in good or bad, right or left. In the end, it was a matter of litres.

Once freed, Abel wrapped baler twine around his stump, cinched the tourniquet tight, and stumbled toward his truck. Unforgettable smells seared his mind: blood vapour, jute, dust-dry alfalfa, dollops of warm bearing grease on his skin, diesel fuel laced with the tang of his urine.

Abel was blood-caked and naked when he staggered into the hospital and collapsed. Abel was in shock. He was bled dry. His body was running on empty. Except for his boots, Abel's clothing had disappeared: coveralls, blue jeans, Stanfield's underwear. Even the silver buckle he won in the Herbert Gymkhana was missing: spun off and whipped into the southern sky. In one great yank that spinning shaft had undressed him, he was a spool of human thread. It left a bloody mess: shredded tissue, muscle strings, mulched bone-meal, which hung from his shoulder like farmer sausage spilled out of its casing. Abel would recall, weeks later, as he narrated the accident to me: "I thought that bloody shaft was going to yank me inside out through my own armpit. Billy B. Damned if I can't still feel it pulling." Then he'd wiggle his imaginary fingers and remind me that what was left of his arm had been ignominiously buried in the town dump.

It was nothing less than a miracle that he lived, that his agricultural brain was spared permanent damage. "How horrible," the town whispered behind his back, fascinated by the idea of a man they knew amputating himself. "It would take some kind of man to hacksaw his limb! I couldn't do it! How disgusting!" They said things like that to each other for years, I heard them, while they clutched their meagre biceps and thought foolish thoughts about pagans and cannibals.

How could such fools know that life is an exquisitely painful necessity?

The arm made Uncle Abel famous despite his insistence that the whole thing was a stupid mistake. He was turned into a local hero, a mutilated man to be revered. Who wrestles farm equipment and wins? Who can say they stalled a Case Agri King tractor with their armpit, and lived to start it next season? Abel was an organic marvel in an evanescent world. He was an anti-machine.

Abel's mishap proved to be my good fortune. After the funeral, I signed on as Abel's new hired hand. Don't look at me, I wasn't thankful. In no way did I relish the thought that I'd profit from Abel's loss. In fact, I refused to make that comparison, just as I refused to carry any primogenital territorial grudge. Forget the past, this was business. Besides, I was probably adopted. Let the dead rest.

That's more than you need to know about me.

I had my first career. Like most lumpen proletariat, I sold my body for Room and Board, for Minimum Wage. Work at least until freeze up. I would stand in for Abel's left hand. He would be able to count on me to tie off burlap sacks when we bagged oats, or to lace his boots up in the morning. I would hold wrenches when we repaired machinery, butter his bread when we ate lunch in the fields.

I should tell you that Abel had no children of his own, no sons to pick up the slack: his loins were defective. It was a source of perpetual shame to him, that degenerative truth. There is a powerful gene in us Quirings to extend our munificent line at any cost, to plant our seed. I have more than once felt it myself. At the time, I could see its weight pressed into Abel's sun-pedigreed face. "'They tell me it's a problem with my plumbing," he reasoned, "a malfunctioning hydraulic pump, a sticking master-cylinder." Abel confessed to me later that summer, as we castrated pigs after lunch, that he'd been to a specialist in The States. "They said conception wasn't out of the question," he reported, "but it would have to be artificial. They said don't count my chickens."

It's no exaggeration to say that it caused me great pain to hear my uncle speak with such pathos of his nether condition. He slunk like a beaten farm mutt. It murdered his spirit to think that his lineage would disappear into the ground with him, his body one more asylum for worms. "This is Quiring land," he said, "it's always been that. I want more than my name on this place."

I thought of my father in his premature grave, his bowels and dreams obstructed by cancer.

The accident didn't help Abel with his dynastic plans. He took the wound personally. At first he brooded and moped, hating his body which, for the first time, had proved unreliable. His face ached because he refused to smile. The stump lit up like a red exit bulb when someone mentioned the baler. He would look no creature in the eye. Soon he began to kick at the cats that lived in his milk house, to terrorize his chickens when he fed them. In a word, he ignored his vocation. Weeds took over his fields. The cows in his barn starved while they wallowed hock-deep in the ammoniac broth that spilled out of the neglected gutter.

I did my best to keep up. I now recognize the behaviour of a condemned man who has just read his death sentence. Instead of work, Abel preferred to spend his days sketching what were supposed to be farm machines of the future, contraptions with fool-proof shields. My uncle pined over these drawings like a new bride ordering china. Or he would pore over the catalogue Dr. Unger had sent him: *Artificial American Limbs*. He scribbled notes. One day at lunch he told me he was thinking of a prosthesis. He began to make long distance calls during which he gripped salesmen with a litany of questions: "Does this model come in stainless-steel?" "Could I weld a crescent-wrench to the end?" Each time, my uncle hung up, dejected. Then he'd resume his anatomical sketches – new plans for what he thought a farmer's artificial arm should look like.

"There's room for improvement," he confided in me one evening, pulling me aside, waving a blueprint. "Was the Lord an ergonomic engineer? Not in the most modern sense. A farmer's a mechanic, a veterinarian, an inventor. He's an artist, a banker, a seer. My new arm will do everything...better."

I don't think Aunt Kate cared much either way about the absent arm, or the paucity of her husband's seed. Nor was she troubled by the strange things that began to happen once Abel got back from the hospital. She was content to approve of his mechanical schemes to replace the limb and to kiss that deluded genius on the top of his unsuntanned forehead at breakfast. She simply nodded when Abel insisted that the arm be chrome-plated, agreed when he changed his mind and insisted that it be cast out of anodized aluminum, with titanium bushings, and assembled by Boeing Aerospace. She was the kind of woman you can't imagine being concerned about anything as unelevated as anatomy.

She was a remarkable beauty, Aunt Kate. She possessed the arrogant posture of a ballerina and the humility of a mendicant saint. And she never failed to look clean and composed, whether gutting chickens or digging beets. She was a lot like a movie star that way, a stunning angel of loveliness: barns or vaporous coops atmospherically framed her rare beauty. I happen to know that she sun-tanned in a two-piece bikini, in summer, topless when she thought that nobody was looking. Most of her friends wouldn't even wear pants.

I could talk about Aunt Kate forever.

It occurred to me, years later, that that was why Uncle Abel and I got along: our devotion to Aunt Kate's wordless beauty. Yet, with only one arm, Abel had become introspective, a fraction, a novice at despising himself.

Clearly, Aunt Kate was too perfect for my dysfunctional uncle to embrace. There was no doubt she deserved something better, something tangible enough to fill out her dreams: children as numerous as sand grains on a beach, the glow of a gestating belly. Not a one-armed man trapped in a low-grade depression, compromised by a faltering pipe.

But Aunt Kate was oblivious to my observations. She shared none of her husband's maniacal need to propagate, to implant an agricultural dynasty that would extend into the mists of the future, at Thirteen-Mile Corner. She would have been happy to adopt. And she hardly noticed his missing appendage. She treated the injury as if it were a half-page torn out of *Company's Coming*. She loved that man for what he was. I imagine she would have loved him even if his body were covered by hairy warts and draining sores. What else could a man ask for?

By any standards, Abel was blessed. With a wife like Aunt Kate, that sod-buster had more than enough. Every night she testified her undying devotion: "I love you, Abel, you Quarter-Horse Stud." She would coo this in a cloying, newly-wed voice, not even trying to whisper. "Now fire up your Cockshutt and get that tractor to bed!"

It was all I could do to stomach such language.

Of course, Abel's heart and mind were elsewhere. But when Dr. Unger showed up to remove the stitches from Abel's stump, he pointed out that it could have been worse. "By rights, you should be dead," the doctor lectured, and my uncle reluctantly agreed. He *was* lucky. He still had two legs and, statistically, more than half his life. I remember the doctor's words now, as if I were just hearing them: "You're lucky, Abelard Quiring," he said. "I deliver a baby into this cesspit we call a world every day, I do a half-dozen autopsies each week! In my spare time, I like to read Nietzsche."

A Conversational Philosophy elective in his fourth year of medical school had been Dr. Unger's favorite class – supposed to improve his bedside manner. By now it was an avocation. He swabbed Abel's stump with peroxide and began tweezing out stitches: "I can't count what I've had to amputate," he said, "eyes, ears, noses, several dozen toes, and three or four feet. I've cut off more legs than Picasso. Even a tongue – due to cancer." The doctor punctuated each sentence by plucking out a silk stitch. "In total, I've clipped twenty-four vas deferens."

The doctor finished the stitches, and rinsed off his tweezers. "Life is an anthology of disease, a fugue of protracted suffering. Please hand me that anaesthetic." He splashed some onto the stump, droplets darkened the linoleum at his feet. "A body is no more than the sum of its parts, many of which are unnecessary. I see each of you as a walking pathology. Keep this wrapped up for a month."

Abel manipulated the buttons on his work-shirt.

Weeks later, the stump had healed over nicely, although it remained rather tender. Abel was gradually remembering how to laugh, and when he did, the stump bobbed like an insane, hairless tail. The prosthesis finally arrived from *Der Roboter Fabrik* in Stuttgart – delayed by a strike at Lufthansa.

Things began to get better. My uncle was almost himself. I was his field-hand, his personal secretary, his new nineteen year-old son. Abel could do little without me. I was authorized to forge my uncle's signature all over town: I ordered hundreds of gallons of diesel fuel, calculated herbicide and pesticide needs. When necessary, I discretely peeled oranges, or flipped the lids off his Pilsners. I even tried to teach him to write, but progress was painfully slow. The untrained nerves and the thick calloused fingers of his reluctant right hand were sluggish. His calligraphy, I must say, was the scrawl of an idiot, the spasmodic penmanship of an octogenarian seized by horrible shudders of senility.

I could write better with my left foot, but then again I am a fast learner. In a matter of weeks I was the farmer my father had never been. Of course, Abel gave up on the writing lessons. He bought a Collegiate Smith Corona from Sears. He began punching out simple sentences with one finger, when he had to. Before long, I noticed that he was trying his remaining hand at poetry. Simple pastoral limericks that he stored in a UGG binder.

By this time, I had mastered the rhythms of life at Thirteen-Mile Corner. I could milk cows, bale hay, grade eggs, build fences, butcher any number of animals. I could cut cattle and vaccinate steers, or cultivate long straight rows that turned fields into pungent corduroy tapestries.

But within a month I began to suspect that the accident had altered more than my uncle's physiognomy. He complained of being cold and damp in the middle of August, he flinched when nothing had touched him. And he still reached for everything with his invisible left hand, a habit which excited the muscles attached to the stump, making it contort in its sleeve like a sack of drowned cats.

It had a mesmerizing quality, the stump. I hated to think of it touching my aunt. I imagined her sheer revulsion. So I planned an excursion in my head in which we would leave that farm together – an elaborate, romantic rescue. One night I overhead my uncle: "I can still feel it, Kate. It shouldn't be in the dump."

Remember, I am old enough not to be given to exaggeration and I am hardly a liar. I am telling you exactly what happened. I heard Aunt Kate giggle and say, "I'll make some Spam sandwiches, Ab. We'll dig the thing up tonight and give it a decent burial!"

I should have left that crazy man's place then and there. I wanted to forget that simpleton farmer and his hideous stump, his binder of one-finger poems. I wanted to convince his celestial wife this was no place for a woman who belonged in the *Sports Illustrated* Bathing Suit Issue.

That stump became my daily bane. By degrees, it drove me crazy. I ducked and swerved around it when we passed in the hallway. I shrank from his touch when he sneaked up behind me with my pay cheque (which I had written up the night before) tucked up under the nub. I did my best to fake gratitude and avoid contact. He expected me to shake on every month's wages.

He heaped coals on my burning head, that man. But even if he was insane, I couldn't lift a finger to hurt him. I had our patronymic to respect. And I could hardly run off with his wife – this was no Old Testament era. Which left me to despise the grotesque remnant of arm, and my uncle's invalid weakness. Bound by our common genealogy.

Bound, that is, until the body-less arm appeared. That was too much for my nerves.

The first time I witnessed the malcontent arm it was cleaning itself at the pump. It proceeded to shake the paw of Abel's dog, Thunder, who, like any senile German Shepherd, glad for attention, slobberdrooled and wagged his mangy tail. The dog acted as if a disembodied arm appeared on the farm every day, and I am convinced that I could have been murdered in my sleep and that furry bag of arthritis they called a watch dog would have quietly waited for someone to toss him my thigh bone.

I kept the news to myself. Who would believe me? Maybe it was I who was touched by the hand of unreason. Maybe it was my brain that was addled.

I need not have doubted myself. The arm was in no way discrete. I realize now that it was overjoyed to be back, that hideous member. It knocked on the window, threw open the door, made a dramatic entrance. It draped itself across my aunt's sculpted shoulders, announced its utility by serving us supper. I thought I was going to be sick.

It did not take long before Uncle Abel and Aunt Kate were treating the arm like a first-born child, a long-lost prodigal son. Kate dressed it up in a sleeve she cut off of one of Uncle Abel's Arrow dress shirts. In a word, they were delighted. They behaved like children at their first circus. They acted as if they didn't know that miracles are nothing more than a willingness to be deceived.

I believe the arm craved attention. Soon it was twisting lids onto sealer jars for my aunt while she made preserves, or helping her shell peas. It pinched her when they passed in the hall, jived in the kitchen when she wasn't too busy.

Out in the yard, we prepared to harvest by rebuilding the combine. Of course the arm had to help. It handed Abel the correct sized wrenches — standard or metric — before he could ask for them. It spun fine-threaded nuts onto rusted studs in the most awkward, unreachable locations. When machinery broke down, the arm welded straight and uniform beads. The arm was so skilled at milking that soon Abel and I did little more than trip over each other trying to stay out of its way. It wasn't long and the cows would bellow complaints when my uncle or I tried to touch their milk-swollen teats with our three calloused hands. We were shipping record amounts of milk.

I must say that I could have learned to appreciate that appendage. I have always liked to sleep in.

Certainly, the farm did not suffer: the place was never in better repair. The arm knew what to do even before we did. All Abel had to do was think of a task and the arm saw to it. If he thought about an itch, the arm would be there to scratch it. Happily, it completed the most menial chores. Soon Abel began to refer to it as "we". Aunt Kate whistled "Mother's Little Helper" while she ironed. On Sundays, before breakfast, the arm wound the imitation grandfather clock, cranked up the organ, and played solemn bass-lines to their favourite hymns.

Before long, the arm was balancing the books, cutting and raking the grass, and sculpting the shrubs along the driveway so that the front yard looked like a Renaissance park. In its spare time the arm painted the barn. Then it weeded the garden and tagged the steers. The arm learned how to artificially inseminate the Holsteins when they came into heat, and each of the cows conceived twins. That obsequious limb even did the dishes. "This arm," said Abel, "is the genuine article. It's a labour-saving device. And it's cheap. Everybody should have at least one of these."

Cheap all right, I could see through that. The arm was doing me in. I was trapped in a rural postcard. In a matter of days, I would be out of work. Laid off. Replaced. A victim of surplus production. It wasn't hard to see why. The arm didn't worry about wages. It didn't even bother to eat. I ate as if there was no tomorrow, as if my stomach was an expanding black pit. And it was no secret I was expecting a raise. My uncle and aunt noticed. They exchanged knowing looks. They taped the inflated grocery bill to the fridge. They didn't invite me when they took the arm out on picnics, and to add insult, they let that upstart appendage steer the new Ford pickup Abel bought with the disability cheque.

But their schemes were wasted on me. I remained undaunted. While they picked at their French pastry desserts, at plates full of dainties whipped up by the proficient appendage, I dug into second helpings, or thirds. All this while heaping praise upon the cook, between mouthfuls of meatloaf and ketchup, home-made bread sopped in gravy. Praise, I might add, that was nothing less than poetic. I did it every night. I didn't gain a pound. In fact I became slighter. My bowels were as regular as the three-engine freighters that hauled our wheat to the Lakehead. When Dr. Unger came for Abel's next check-up, he looked into my eyes, sent me to my room immediately, and told me to undress. He entered and sized me up: told me to breathe deeply while he listened to my chest. He poked and he tweaked. Depressed my abdomen. Then he inspected my manhood. I coughed on demand. I was then told to assume the fetal position. He explained and I complied. I felt intrusive fingers inch down my posterior. "It's probably a parasite," he said, "Giardia, most likely. Or a tapeworm. But smart money's on Beaver Fever. Do you drink out of sloughs?" He shook his head, I was sure he said something or other about Diogenes and a puddle. Then he produced a thermometer from his bag, flicked it twice, and took aim at my hitherto unexplored sphincter. To be blunt, he probed the defenceless raisin. He said he'd need a sample of my stool to do tests.

Oh, the indignities of the infirm! The thought of worms in my guts made me unwell, I was mortified by the picture of me, to be polite, voiding myself in a shoe box. Heed a turd mandate? Be exploited, as I always have been, by the laws of supply and demand? Never! What did that horse-doctor know? He rummaged in orifices for a living.

I had to keep eating. I had to keep up with my rival. I wasn't about to be bettered.

The arm knew that I didn't like it. It could sense my

acrimony, the same way a dog can smell fear. The more I contemplated my hatred, the more it laboured to gain their favour. How could I compete? It scratched Kate's scalp while we watched TV. It cut her hair in the latest *Cosmopolitan* fashion. It performed reflexology on Abel's troubled feet and once a week cut his fifteen nails, trimmed his ulcerous bunions.

What did it ever do for me?

At night I planned a spectacular revenge. I would set up a minefield of gopher traps for that precocious limb. I would lure it into the mixmill. Or I would chop it up and feed it to the pigs the day before they were to be butchered. I mail-ordered molybdenum hand-cuffs. Did it think that I was expendable? An unemployed, hungry statistic?

That sinister limb didn't know everything.

I was consumed with the orchestration of my magnificent plot. I would show that arm who was boss. I dreamed skewed dreams of terror and hatred. Each night the arm would be on top of me, clawing at my oblong good looks, tearing at my considerable anatomy. I woke standing in bed, drenched in an acrid sweat and the bile of revenge. I listened to the sounds in that harmonious house, its nocturnal creaks and whispers, its somnolent sighs of bliss. Each decibel was information to be sorted and stored. I kept track of everything that relentless arm did.

It wasn't difficult. The arm had the run of the place. Downstairs each night, my uncle would watch television, with the arm curled across his shoulder like the vainest Siamese tomcat. It helped him clap when Paul Henderson shovelled his famous goal past Comrade Tretiak, held his beer when we rose for *O Canada*. There was nothing to do that the arm would not see to, no need to be up with the sun. The arm had things in hand. It flicked through the channels – a remote control. It carved out his nostrils when it thought nobody was watching.

Upstairs, things were hardly better. Imagine my disgust when I saw the arm head to my aunt's bedroom. I have to confess, houses built before the advent of forced air heating are amphitheatres. The passages and vents designed to facilitate convection form labyrinths of duct work and ornate cast-iron gratings: it's a matter of knowing where to look, and one or two small modifications. I could hardly believe my eyes. That perverse arm was attending to every one of my aunt's corporal whims: performing Swedish massages using ancient techniques, rubbing her temples with an elixir of dew, drawing baths filled with Body Shop potions or organic sea salts. The arm ignored not an inch of her willowy body as it administered its agenda of digital indulgence.

I retreated to the solitude of my bedroom. Beaten. Unamused. A man half himself.

Imagine my shame. Imagine my terror. That night, in the middle of my recurring tropical dream – I'm shipwrecked on the South Saskatchewan River with Marianne and Ginger – I awoke to find the pyjamas I had been wearing folded at the foot of my bed. The room was infused with the pale neon of moon, my radio reset to the CBC, softly piping in jazz. The house was preserved in a deep midnight silence. Then I found that officious limb poised above me no doubt ready to crush my wind pipe with one karate chop, to rip off my member, itself half hoisted from terror. I could do nothing but close my eyes and emit several loud, primal cries. I am not boasting when I say that I woke up the house.

There I was, trapped. Caught between the quicksilver mirrors of desire and regret. It is a moment I would like to forget.

But it's not that easy. I have the kind of mind that has trained itself to retain information. I can summon up the most insignificant facts, embarrassing details of my life, frames of a film advanced in slow motion. The older I get the clearer the pictures are focussed. I might mix up a few dates, confuse a name or a face. But it's all in there: a private kaleidoscope of disgrace, a catacomb of humiliating niches and rooms that I must endure in silence.

No, it's not easy. I have to live with myself. I suffer lunar cycles when the two hemispheres of my brain feel like repellent magnets, days when my cranium is too small to contain everything I have done. There are no words for that kind of pressure. I once tried to bore a hole in my head to relieve it, with a Black and Decker one-half inch speed drill.

There is nothing to do but wait.

The past fills my head, my temporal lobes, with its spools of inferior data. The past is a whisker on a stinking corpse, a fingernail that won't quit growing. It's the only thing in this world that's not temporary.

My condition is hardly surprising. I am an old man. I am said by many to be wise. I should be. I have seen enough to wear out two sets of eyeballs. On the days when my head is most congested, when my shame is acute, I relive that summer. I remember immaculate Kate, her lunatic husband and his disconnected limb. My father's academic death.

It is a child's luxury to forget.

Needless to say, I left that farm without explanation, without collecting the wages I was owed. I know when people are out to get me. The blank cheques I had stuffed in my duffle, like the tools and the ersatz silverware, were worthless. The cheques came back marked STOP PAYMENT. I expected imminent retaliation, so I sneaked off like a criminal, with the virus of self-doubt in my raven's eyes. I thumbed a ride on a cabover Kenworth hauling hogs to Intercontinental Packers. I dissolved into the anonymity of a long city winter. It was a season of unendurable hunger. I eventually sent a forwarding address.

A certified cheque arrived, drawn up in a flourishing, eighteenth-century script. The deposit cleared and I ate well for most of a month. In a gesture of goodwill, they had factored in a raise – retroactive to the first of July. That was my last contact. No doubt they are long dead, and Abel's land has passed into the hands of an estate lawyer, or some other parasite. I have tried hard to forget Quiring Acres and its thwarted history. I have tried to erase the benighted echoes of that barren house from the recycled pages of my mind. But it is useless. My head is a quarantined village.

I used to tell people what had happened out there, that summer, over tepid beer, over institutional desks. I couldn't say enough about that place. I saw through their uneasy laughter.

I have no choice but to carry the arm, preserved in my head, a fistful of self-disgust. Its five fingers inch through my brain like roots of quack-grass. They push out against the perimeter of my skull, feeling the ancient bone for cracks. For aneurysms to pinch. Every day it tightens its migraine grip.

It has been all I can do to keep myself together these years, drifting from one Provincial Hospital to another: Riverview, too mossy and gothic for my tastes; North

Battleford, hidden by trees; of course historic, tyndall-stoned Selkirk, where the food is not actually half bad. And finally Ponoka. It's all in my file, if you can't take my word. I've enjoyed the best architecture in the west, the most practical Shrines to the Mad.

I've said enough. I am bored by what's left of my life, it's too mundane to bother to mention. And don't proffer your bourgeois pity. We're all children consigned to oblivion. Of my pending death, I am neither afraid nor surprised: my lungs gurgle with phlegm, I eat nothing, but still fill this bedpan. The young Stripers blush at my prolific excretion, steal peeks at my comely backside. (Please excuse me if that fart's an eye-stinger.) Each day, they try to pry this pen out of my hands.

Well I'm not dead yet. Much as you wish I was. I don't care if you disbelieve what I've said. In the end, it comes to nothing. Spare me the cards from Seven/Eleven. What good are words when you're dead? I slide over the country, these stubbled fields I see out my window, like blades of November wind. Who knows where I will be buried. The grit of the past is there, in my memory, a desert of shifting sand ribs. I'm the last Quiring alive, one more perpetual tenant.

No More Denver Sandwiches
MEEKA WALSH

It's cold. Dead cold. The middle of winter. They're sitting in Robin's Donuts looking at the Saturday paper. Holidays are discounted. The economy's lousy. Fly to Mazatlan, air and hotel, for less than it costs you to stay at home. Or Hawaii, Cuba, Jamaica, Palm Springs.

"Hey, you've been to Palm Springs," he says to her. "How about let's go there. It's cheap. What's it like?"

"It was another life," she says. "I'm not going back. Not only can't. Won't. Finished, final, over."

"Yah, but what's it like?" he persists. "Every year it's advertised. Bob Hope is there if he's still alive. Dinah Shore and the Dinah Shore Open. All the tennis greats and Elizabeth Taylor and Betty Ford and the drug people. There must be something there."

So she tells him.

I was young, married. A good idea at the time; finally not such a great idea. His parents went to Palm Springs every winter. All their friends did. Dozens of couples, married for years, well-off. The men would pack cardigan sweaters in light colours and their clubs in leather bags. The ladies had florals, pastel knits and bathing suits with skirts.

My ex-husband was sick with colds off and on all winter. His parents were concerned. They sent us tickets. Come down, we have an extra room. They always took a condo near friends. Why not, I figured. I hadn't travelled much. Palm Springs was where the movie stars went. They told me – sure I'd see some. My father-in-law claimed he'd seen that guy who had a TV series, who owned a baseball

135

team. The one with the pale eyes. Why not? I liked the idea of getting on a plane in winter and getting off in summer.

It was night when we landed and really late. The plane had been held up in Minneapolis and by the time we arrived it was maybe 10:00, maybe later. They opened the door of the plane and I remember walking through the opening onto the top step of those stairs they wheel up and the air just smacked me in the face. Dark and hot and wet. Soft with flowers and diesel and the smell of earth, rubber on warm asphalt and the flat sound of cars honking in the heavy air.

People moved around in short-sleeved shirts. The dark men unloading the plane had bare arms. To me, coming from winter, they looked naked. I couldn't breathe and I remember being so excited by all of it that I felt like running and running to say how great it was. Palm trees. I'd never seen palm trees. They were so exotic I couldn't believe they'd grow around an airport. And flowers, fat flowers everywhere. People were wearing sandals. My nylons were hot. My hair was back-combed and sprayed stiff and I could smell the lacquer softening in the humidity.

We had to rent a car and drive through Los Angeles to get to Palm Springs. We had no idea how far. The guy at the car rental said just follow this road to the turn-off and then left onto the highway, we'd see signs. I was hungry. I wanted a burger and fries. I wanted a chocolate milkshake. I wanted to take off my nylons and knit suit. I wanted to trot beside the car in the fluorescent green grass. I wanted to check those palm trees to see if they were real.

Why can't we stop for a burger first before we leave LA, I wanted to know, but he said his parents would be worried, we were already late. We'd find something once we got on the highway.

Of course, neither of us had ever driven on an American freeway. If you have, you know there's no getting off, there's no where to eat, there's just four lanes of cars each way and that's it.

Then he said we could eat once we got there, at a Denny's or a Sambo's. Can you imagine a restaurant called Sambo's today? I think, if you can believe it, they served pancakes in the Aunt Jemimah tradition. But I knew what would happen. We'd go straight to his parents' place because you couldn't worry Mom and Dad and once we got there she'd offer to make us a Denver sandwich. It's gruesome. Scrambled eggs with little pieces of pink salami chopped in and green onion which never got fried, only warm. Warm green onion, wet eggs, pink meat bits. No one young eats that. Or she'd say cereal. A bowl of cereal. No one young eats cereal at night either.

That food did a lot of damage and in fact I figure it killed his dad. Colon cancer. Forty-seven years they were married and he never had roughage in his diet. Nothing fresh or whole. All those years she never let him near uncooked food. He loved fresh corn in the summer. She'd ration it, counting the cobs like he was on an allowance. Maybe she should have let him have all the corn he wanted. I bet she wonders.

Sure enough, "I'll make you eggs. How about a Denver sandwich," and he says "Okay, Mom." The trip was like that.

We ate and unpacked and I changed and went outside to the patio. All the shrubs had lights under them and they floated in the dark like little clouds of vegetation. The pool was lit around the edges and the water was turquoise like in the movies. There were crickets or frogs and a TV was on in someone's condo. What at first I figured was a round kiddie's pool turned out to be a Jacuzzi. The sky was very dark and up in the mountains I could see the lights of houses which I knew belonged to movie stars. I figured this would be okay and I knew what I wanted.

I wanted to go to the restaurant where Frank Sinatra ate. I wanted to have drinks with fruit on plastic swords, a shrimp cocktail, Caesar salad, Chateaubriand, rare, a stuffed baked potato and something flaming for dessert. I wanted to sit in a leather banquette in the corner against the wall, facing out so I could see everyone and they could see me. I would wear my black dress with the low back and my shoulders would be tanned. I would have a pearl bracelet on one wrist. I would wear my hair up in a French twist and a few tendrils would escape at my cheek and neck and they would curl a little from the heat. Sipping cocktails, whoever I was with would lean near my ear and whisper that the man who'd just come in and taken a chair at the table near ours was a known Mafia figure.

"Right here, here in this restaurant right now?" and I wouldn't believe whoever it was telling me that, because even though he might have been wearing too much hair tonic he looked quite nice and handsome in a rough kind of way.

I knew, eating my shrimp cocktail, that this was a man who could order what he wanted in a restaurant and get it. I could tell, when I got up and excused myself and walked right past him to the ladies room that he didn't have to raise his voice to be heard. I was certain, when I saw him ordering from the wine list, that when he was cruel it hurt him deeply and I couldn't finish my steak after he looked directly at me, smiled, and lifted his glass.

I wanted, at the end of my dinner, to get up and walk past his table again. I wanted him to stand up and be close enough so I could smell his hair tonic. I wanted him to take my wrist, the one without the bracelet, very firmly but not to hurt me, and insist I sit down with him at his table, stay with him, be with him dark and dangerous, go with him where it was dangerous, quickly and never be frightened, to a place with horses and fast cars and elegant casinos and maybe yachts, to turn night into day if we wanted, to be so quick and beautiful that New York composers would write songs about us and to never eat Denver sandwiches again.

Everyday the men golfed. The ladies played cards which I didn't know how to do and didn't want to learn. I read in the sun by the pool, only me and some kids, somebody's grandchildren and their nanny, and after I'd had enough sun and done I don't know how many laps in the turquoise pool I'd change and walk the few streets over to Palm Canyon Drive, the street with all the shops, and I'd prowl the stores looking for movie stars. I didn't see any, not one. I did see a lot of blonde people, young and old, even one old woman pulling her own oxygen tank, poor soul, and everyone was really dressed. A lot of big flower prints which I knew I couldn't wear back home and never figured I'd be in Palm Springs again so while I tried on lots of clothes in those stores looking for movie stars, I didn't find anything much to buy.

A couple of times, at night, we went out to restaurants and I kept on the look-out for stars and my Mafia man. There I was, a kid really anxious for everything. Life in gulps. I wanted the edgy stuff, the gentle stuff. I wanted to spin and never catch my breath, spin until I fell.

Most nights we ate in with his parents. After dinner their friends would come over for coffee, instant decaf and Sara Lee baking. I would sit between two people on the sofa, someone on either side of me, nice enough people, no, actually they weren't nice now that I'm telling it – small, dull, smug people is really what they were, the friends of my ex-husband's parents. I'd sit there with my wonderful tanned body. I'd sit there with my dark hair and my big eyes. I'd turn my head from one to the other to answer their questions. I'd look across the room at the wives and husbands of the friends of my in-laws, and language I'd heard but never uttered would bubble to my lips. I knew if I sat longer I'd shout, "Have you ever fucked someone you're not married to?" and I'd get up and clear dishes. I'd run water and look out at the hot green shrubs and the turquoise water and then I'd excuse myself and go to sleep.

I kept hoping I'd see someone famous. I hadn't given up on that. I wanted to know how tall were they. Did they have perfect skin or did they wear thick make-up? If I saw them in person I knew I could tell. I was curious about their mates. Did stars attract beautiful mates or could someone handsome be married to someone they just loved who might be plain? Did they drive their own cars when they were on vacation and did they pay cash? Did they in fact have to buy their clothes or did people give them gifts just to have them wear their things?

So late afternoons I'd be on Palm Canyon Drive and like I wanted to know everything and be everywhere, I wanted to be glamorous too. Why not?

I was trying on a pant suit and this was one I could see myself wearing at home. It was a dark green linen. The jacket was sleeveless which I liked for my tanned shoulders and it buttoned down the front. The neckline was wide and cut a little low but if I had to I could pull it closed with a pin. I thought, with all the blondes young and old showing everything they had, day or night, I could wear a jacket with the neck cut in such a way that the tops of my very young breasts showed too. Why not? I was quite pleased and was close to buying the outfit, thinking I'd maybe come back for it when the saleslady said to me that it looked just as nice on me as it had on what's her name, the movie star from France who was involved with the skier.

She packed it for me and that night I insisted we eat out, alone. It turned out my in-laws were eating out too and had gone early. If you eat early there, there's a discount. All these wealthy people vacationing in an expensive resort lining up to eat almost before dark to save five bucks. My ex-husband was in the living room, watching TV.

Here I come. I could see myself from where he sat. Young. Made crazy by the smell of orange blossoms in the air every night. Brown shoulders. Dark hair, big dark eyes. Excited. Wearing something new. Me and a French movie star in the same outfit. The air outside smells good. So do I. I walk into the living room slowly. I'm in high-heeled sandals to go with the outfit and I don't want to trip on the shag carpeting. He's going to be wild for this. The whole time we've been here he's been looking at everyone's cleavage. I'm offering the tops of my young breasts. Just a little showing. I walk in slowly, my heart pounding.

He looks at me. I smile. "Do yourself up," he says. "You look like a tramp."

I stayed with him for a couple more years.

Hollywood Legs
SHELLEY A. LEEDAHL

In 1979, when I was twenty-two and coming to grips with the fact that I would never be an interior designer, my mother was forty-four and finding herself. I blamed Mrs. Gudmundson in Home Economics for putting the seed in my head, and I blamed my father for everything else. I'd rebounded from the city and was facing the deathly prospect of working in one of Dad's stores. I favoured the lumber yard, because I liked men who were handy, but the choice wasn't mine to make.

"You could work in groceries," Dad said. He talked and chewed simultaneously, then washed his words down with milk.

"Swallow your food, then drink. God, that is so disgusting." We bullied each other, nightly, over beef and turkey TV dinners. Neither of us had learned to cook, Home Economics or not, and Camille, my seventeen-year-old sister, spent more time at her boyfriend's than at home.

My older sister Sherry had married Everett Lundquist, an electrician from Marvin. "Sparks are really gonna fly now," Dad joked, insinuating that Sherry's erratic temper would ignite some blazing fires. At the wedding reception, Everett blundered through the typical thank you to my parents, "for raising such a great daughter." Dad and Mom agreed he was a decent enough guy, if not a bit of a Clydesdale. Across the dance floor, his family sized us up, too. We were Norwegian, at least, so Sherry couldn't be too far from wrong. Aunts and uncles on his side tossed blessings like confetti: lots of blonde, blue-eyed children. Sherry learned to make *lefsa* and a sugary pastry called rosettes. Within two months of the day she was deliriously pregnant. She called frequently. "What do you think of Lief for a name, if it's a boy of course?" I could hear crochet needles clicking. "Or Svend."

"You'd name your kid Svend?"

"So you don't like it then."

"I just think you're getting a little carried way with this Norwegian thing, Sher. It's not like we're even third generation. What's the big deal?"

"It's important to Everett."

There was nothing more to say. Sherry was hypersensitive where Everett was concerned. She resented Camille and I because we weren't wildly ecstatic about our new brother-in-law. He had lovely long eyelashes, but frankly, I had to work up to touching him in the receiving line.

Dad washed down another forkful of tinny peas. "Well, do you want the job or not?"

"I hate that store. I hated working there in high school and I'll hate it more now."

He chased a sliver of roast beef around the foil. "At least it's a job." His voice was a mosquito at midnight. Buzzing and pissing me off.

"Did you know," I said, "that when I started I couldn't figure out the produce scale, so I used to make prices up?"

"I don't want to know this."

"Three-fifty for a bunch of bananas. A buck for a head of lettuce. I never knew how far off I really was, but no one ever complained."

"Do you think you can figure it out now?" He pushed his chair away from the table. He looked tired, and, since Mom had left for university, battered.

Mom's apartment in Saskatoon was five blocks from the university, with low lighting and lots of plants. I thought it was funky. She was taking first-year arts classes and drove home every third weekend. All this school business had, as far as anyone knew, erupted within one volcanic year. Prior to that, she had taught piano for twenty years. She was a good teacher, with several students. A friend who'd taken lessons from her said my mother had been an inspiration. I never guessed. I don't know how much she made, but she said she gave it all to us kids anyway, and I was sorry to hear that.

She was home on one of her weekends. Thankfully, she still cooked, but where before she'd scramble to clear the table as soon as we'd finished eating, she now mooned over tea while food particles barnacled onto plates. The vacuuming, general room-to-room straightening, and laundering of Dad's dress shirts fell upon me. Even when she was home.

There were other changes, too. She'd never given her appearance much thought, often wearing Dad's dowdy cardigans or brown socks, so when she came home in a new jumpsuit with a brilliant scarf draped artistically around her neck, her lips glossed pink and blue eyes like skylights opened wide with mascara, I began to suspect. I came across her in her bedroom packing for another three weeks away. There were several colourful piles of clothes on the bed's white comforter. She folded each article before setting it in the suitcase. Her back was toward me, and I watched for a few moments in the doorway. Then something black shimmered in her hand. "What's that?" I asked, plopping onto her bed. The suitcase hopped and she half-turned toward me.

"Panties." She held them up. Bikinis with a tiny black bow sewn onto the waistband, front and centre. "Like them?"

"Nice." I flipped through a *Time* magazine, several months old. Very nice. "So ... how's school going?"

"I study a lot. At my age everything takes twice as long to sink in."

"You're not that old."

She seemed not to have heard me, because when I looked up from the magazine she'd already left, her feet dancing down the hall.

The weeks back home caterpillared into months. I felt like the life was being sucked right out of me, like I was being pulled into a black hole. I knew there was a place for me somewhere in the world, I just didn't know where to start looking, which rock to turn over. My work at the grocery store was sheer drudgery. The boss's kid had to work twice as hard as anyone else. I hated the blue fortrel uniform, the customers who didn't know enough to separate their produce from their detergent on the spinning counter. My first go around, in high school, I developed an obsession with one of the packers that made going to work bearable, but I didn't have even one stolen kiss to show for it and he'd since moved away. I felt a quiet storm stirring between the meat manager and me, but he was married with a new baby and I didn't have the energy to make the effort. It never got beyond wistful looks except once. We collided in the stock room and he put his hands on my ribs, just below my breasts, and held on. His touch fuelled my dreams for weeks.

I'd only fallen hard once before, and when distance put that relationship to the test, it failed. While I was selling beds in Saskatoon, he was sharing one with Carol Friesen back home. When I confronted him, he did not deny it. "Bastard!" I grabbed handfuls of his hair and smashed his head against the wall. "Bastard ... you fucking bastard!" Over and over I smashed, and he let me. Shortly after, he moved to Alberta. The whole thing had left me totally dry, like the skull of an animal bleached by the sun.

I tried wearing the metropolitan persona for several months, but it never quite fit. I was lost in the street lights and sirens, and my heart was not in selling beds, although it was as close as I ever got to a career in interior decorating. Money was another problem. Perhaps later, I thought, but not right now. I circled back home like a child who runs away, then slinks in the back door when she realizes no one's missed her.

At home I made an attempt to see old friends, but all those swears we'd made as teenagers, I swear to be best friends forever, etc., hadn't held. Besides, many of my school friends were already mothers and I got my share of those conversations with Sherry. She lived in some kind of ga-ga land that I could only tolerate at intervals. Camille and Tom were still hot and heavy. I couldn't believe what she got away with.

"You never let Sherry and I stay out all night," I said to Dad across the table. We were having cereal. "It's not fair." The music on his transistor radio was far too lively with Dolly Parton's warbling.

Dad chewed toast and slurped Bran Flakes. He was reading the newspaper and had slopped strawberry jam on one corner. "What?" He kept reading.

"Camille. She gets away with everything."

He looked at me over the paper. "She doesn't attack me every chance she gets." It was an old argument that had run out of steam. Camille had graduated from high school with honours and now also worked in one of Dad's stores: the pharmacy, where I'd done a short stint when I was fifteen. She claimed to like her job.

One Sunday afternoon after another Saturday of late-night

movies and over-salted popcorn, I cornered Mom in the bathroom. She was preparing for another departure. She was curling her hair.

"I was thinking about moving back to the city," I said.

"Mmmm."

"If I do, could I stay with you for a while?"

She clipped two red hoops onto her ears. "I thought you hated the city."

"Bad timing, I guess. It could be different this time. I could get a better job." She unplugged her curling iron and coiled the cord.

"So ... could I stay with you?"

"I hope you don't mind," she said, "but I'd really rather be alone."

"Just a few weeks? Until I find a job and get my own place?" I closed the toilet lid and sat.

Mom sighed. "You can't keep bouncing back and forth between your father and me. You're twenty-two."

"Twenty-three. Last month."

"Right. Anyway, you know what I'm saying, it's time you found your own way. Do something with your life. You're making money, why don't you save and take a trip?"

"I don't want to go anywhere." This wasn't true. The idea of a long vacation to exotic locales excited me, it was having no one I liked well enough to come along that was depressing. She seemed to read my mind.

"You and Camille could have a great time together."

"I'm not going on any trip, with anyone."

"Okay Miss Woe-Is-Me."

"Oh, please."

"Someday you're going to look back on your life and you'll see this grey area of wasted time." She gathered her make-up and earrings and scooped them into her cosmetic bag. "You'll think about it when you have a million things to do and no time and would do anything to have this precious time back." She opened and closed a few drawers. "Have you seen my toothpaste?"

"On your dresser. Is that what happened to you?"

"What?"

"You know, you started running out of time."

"I just know how precious time is. I don't want to waste a minute of it."

"So you move to the city and take arts and sciences. And you're fulfilled."

"You don't understand."

"Hey, I'm proud of you. Remember, I was the kid who was behind you all the way."

"You don't sound 'behind me all the way.'"

"I'm just down." She stepped toward me, squeezed my shoulders and kissed my forehead, something she hadn't done since I was a child.

"Your ship, my dear, will come in," she said. "Trust me."

"You drove her to it, Dad." He had just returned from a Chamber of Commerce meeting and found me, as usual, watching television in what was formerly the piano room. Mom's grand piano had been moved into the living room where it sat like a ship on dry land. No one touched it.

"I never drove her to anything. She wanted to go to school. What could I do or say to change that?" He cracked open a beer. The theme song from Hawaii 5-0 blared.

"There's another beer in the fridge, if you want one."

"No thanks. But about Mom, if you hadn't been so … stereotypical, she wouldn't have felt compelled to leave."

It was the first time I'd put it that way. It had always been a going away before, not a leaving.

"Your mother's never been satisfied with anything. She always wants more but doesn't know what." I didn't believe this. On the contrary, I'd always felt my mother was the picture of contentment, teaching all day, spending her down time in quiet ways.

"This family is so screwed up I can't stand it." I reached over and turned the television volume down.

"Turn that back up."

I left it. "Take last Christmas."

"What about it?"

"Ever since I can remember, Mom's prepared a huge meal. You eat, then hit the couch. You're snoring before we've even got the table cleared."

"What's that got to do with your mother going to university?"

"Everything. Don't you see?" I threw my hands in the air. Too much television; I was more melodramatic than usual. Dad had kicked off his Hush Puppies and was now fully reclined in the Lazy-boy. "Women aren't falling for that cult-of-domesticity shit anymore."

"I can't figure you out," he said. "Who are you mad at?"

He had no idea. I had no way to tell him. "I'm going to bed," I said, leaving him there in the television light. I turned up the thermostat as I passed it in the hall. The furnace protested, but in a few minutes the comforting sense and sound of hot air pulsing through my register hummed me to sleep.

In 1980 my sister Camille went to Montana for an abortion and Sherry's pride and joy turned one. Mom missed the abortion but made Nels's birthday, although we all thought she'd have rather been elsewhere. It was too cold and wet to sit in the backyard, but the late

September air was sticky in the house and we felt trapped by it. Our words got stuck. It was Mom's idea to take the festivities outdoors where nature helped obscure the long silences.

Everyone was home for the party. Camille and Tom slouched in lawn chairs, a respectable distance from the picnic table and the rest of us. They were living together now. Common law, Mom said. Shacked up, according to Dad. Tom smoked incessantly and only moved when he finished one beer and got up to get another from the house. Beside him, Camille chewed on a strand of long hair and read a paperback. She dropped it twice. Everett, Sherry, and Mom tossed a ball to Nels. The birthday boy was magnificent in a pastel green sweater and matching bonnet. I took pictures. Dad was taking an incredibly long time to bring out the cake.

"Camille, go check on your father," Mom said. Camille put her book face down on the lawn chair and her sliver-thin shape disappeared into the house. She'd lost weight since the abortion, and hadn't had much to spare before it.

Nels lost interest in the ball toss. "Come to Auntie," I said, coaxing him to sidestep around the picnic table. "Tell auntie what a kitty says?" He sucked on his pudgy fingers and ignored me. "Meow," I tried, "meow."

"I don't know why he won't answer," Sherry said. "He talks a mile a minute at home."

"They're always like that," Mom said. "You guys were like that."

"You can't tell me you remember." I felt I was talking to the ghost of my mother.

"Sure I do." She smoothed Nels's wild blonde hair. "Who's Grandma's boy?"

Footsteps rustled in the fallen leaves behind us.

"Mom." Camille put one white hand on Mom's shoulder. "Something's wrong with Dad."

Mom bolted for the house; Camille stood there, trembling, her hair falling forward into her face.

"My God," I said, standing. "What's wrong?"

"His face – I think he's having a stroke." She started to cry, and then Tom was there, holding her and stroking slow circles on her back the way a mother soothes a child. Sherry and I found our parents in front of the bathroom mirror. The right side of Dad's face drooped like melted wax. He touched the sagging skin with hesitant fingers.

Sherry stepped closer. "Dad?"

"It's okay," Mom said, steering us out of the room. "Everything's going to be fine."

In January, 1981, a long list of resolutions snaked through my head. Writing them down or saying them out loud would have been too much of a responsibility. I desired universal change for my non-life, beginning with my job and my residence, but I procrastinated. I couldn't bear to think about the revolution that needed to occur. If I let things continue, perhaps change would come of its own volition.

During the peace of another motherless Sunday afternoon, I was sifting through treasures in a basement trunk. Mom's wedding dress lay crumpled in the bottom drawer. I tried it on over my clothes and checked myself out in the basement bathroom mirror, noting that it was no longer white but a sickly shade of yellow. It fit. I went through piles of loose photographs, then stumbled onto several boxes of slides. The first was a collection of slides taken at my parents' wedding. I'd never seen them before. The cake cutting, gift opening, get-away in the tin-canned car; my parents were radiant. I marvelled at the changes that had taken place since then. The physical changes, like Mom's grey-blonde hair and Dad's softer shape were, I knew, natural processes of the passage of time, but what, I wondered, what trick of nature could separate two people, once so evidently in love?

"What in God's name are you doing down here?"

I looked up. "What in God's name are *you* doing down here? Geez, Dad, are you lost?"

"I'm out of shirts. I'm doing laundry." I watched my father take his dress shirts from the basket on the floor and drop them, one by one, into the washing machine. There was a gracefulness to his movements that I wouldn't have thought possible from him. He dipped a cup into the detergent and held it high above the washer, letting it pour like a waterfall. Then he turned the knob and the machine rumbled on, the jets coming to life.

"Dad, come here."

He shuffled in his slippers to where I was sitting on the floor. "What's that? Old slides?"

"Yes. From your wedding. Did anyone ever tell you that you looked like Elvis when you were young?" He chuckled. I passed him a slide and he held it up to the light.

"Well it's one for the money, two for the show…" He did the Elvis swivel. Half of his face, the half unaffected by Bell's Palsy, seemed to light up and I thought I saw a moment of the man Mom had married.

"Pull up a hunk of cement," I said, slapping the floor. He sat, cross-legged, on the cold floor beside me, and one by one we viewed the slides against the bare bulb.

Hours or minutes passed. I opened the last box. Someone, presumably Mom, had penned "1957" on the white border of each slide. I drew one out and held it up. "Oh, my God."

"What? Let's see."

It was a slide of Mom in a chair with a young Sherry sitting side-saddle across her. Mom was wearing a short skirt and heels. Her legs, unbelievably long, tanned and shapely, were swung glamorously to the left and crossed at the ankle. Hollywood legs.

"Let's see," Dad said again. I passed the slide and he framed it against the light. For a long time there was nothing, not even a breath to disturb the air. Then he puckered his lips as if to whistle, but nothing came out except a faint, wheezing sound. He held on to that thing forever.

A Year Before Emery Legrandeur Rode Red Wings to a Standstill and Avenged the Death of Joe La Mar

FRED STENSON

> *The promoters of the Calgary Frontier Days*
> *Celebration have not even the merit of*
> *originality to commend them but are just plain*
> *every day citizens of Rangeland. Having in*
> *mind that what has happened in the South —*
> *we speak now of the oldtime cowman's being*
> *forced to the wall — Guy Weadick conceived*
> *the idea of organizing a monster celebration*
> *patterned after those in vogue in the great*
> *Cattle States in the South.*
>
> *Calgary, 1912*

All up and down Whisky Row the hitching posts were full. The wind and dust were for the moment down and the August night was still and pungent with the smell of horse. Weadick's boot heels clapped the boardwalk and his head was lively with argument about the program introduction he had written that day. It was good to come across humble — you had to — but should he have said "patterned after" when he meant "better than?" If his Stampede wasn't going to be the best ever, then why do it? Why go to so much trouble?

Earlier, in the hotel room, he had read the whole thing to his wife, Flores. She had been sitting on the bed sliding her hands along one of her trick ropes. The rope had got wet in a leaking baggage car and she was working it supple again. When he finished reading, she said, "Feed that to a cow, she'll bloat up and die."

Weadick stopped in front of the King George Hotel and considered the effect Flores' remark might have on the bar patrons inside. He imagined a burst of laughter and hands slapping the mahogany, a beefy rancher shouldering through the crowd and yelling at the bartender, "Hey, Baldy, get Weadick here a drink. That was a damn funny story." Or would they take it serious? Agree with the assumption that his Stampede could never live up to its promotion.

As Weadick stood and mulled, a buggy drew up beside him. A woman leaned out of the canopy's shadow into the cone of electric lamplight.

She said, "Hey, Guy?" And then, "How come you never visit anymore?"

The woman drew down her fan, her pink-piped bosom yellow-tinged in the glow.

"Dolly, you should take off some of that jewellery. You could blind a man."

"I might have to pawn some soon. You and your cowboys been negligent."

Weadick set his boot on the buggy step. "Not negligent, Dolly. Truth is we got a Stampede to put on. You Nose Hill sporting ladies are some of our toughest competition."

"You told me another time we were the city's top attraction."

"Both things are so, Dolly. And if you send your buggy drivers to line up outside my Stampede like they do down at the railyards on paydays, it could be a sweet arrangement."

As Dolly drove on, Guy thought of a line in his program that could have been written just for her.

Not alone the kings and emperors of Rangeland but citizens of all classes have

*united to make the Stampede a worthy tribute
to those grand old men whom we delight to
honour.*

To a cowboy crowd in the Yale Hotel, Guy said, "I got a
bronc coming up here, gentlemen, that's never been
rode."

"Hell, Guy, I got one of them in my field at home."

"That's interesting, Elmer. Question is, has it piled
anybody but you? Horse I'm talking about has bucked
off over a hundred of the top bronc busters on this
continent. That's over a hundred straight."

"What's it go by, Weadick?"

"Cyclone, and that's just what he is: a flesh, blood
and muscle cyclone. When Clem Gardiner sits down on
Cyclone…"

And, just before he left, in case anybody thought
Cyclone was the only good horse he had in his show,
Guy told them about the umpteen other snaky horses
Joe La Mar had brought back to Calgary from all over
the province. Why, right now, Joe and the boys were
down at the pavilion testing those broncs to make sure
there wasn't a dud among them.

*Enlisting the aid, which was readily given,
of several of the most prominent cattlemen of
Alberta, organization was effected, and
preparations made to present this
entertainment on such a scale of magnificence
as would be a fitting finale to the glorious
history of the justly celebrated range.*

In the Alexandra, to get the topic off real estate, Guy
talked about Indians.

"Make you fellas nervous if all the Indians in the country come and pitch their tipis on the outskirts of town?"

"Only thing would bother me is the smell."

"Frankly, boys, fond as I am of Calgary, I don't think you can criticize anybody on account of smell. When the horseshit gets half this high in an Indian camp, they move on,"

"Get to the point, Guy. Why are all these Indians coming?"

"For my Stampede. Given that the Indian was here before any of us and that I want my Stampede to be absolutely authentic, I've sent letters to all the chiefs and invited them and their Indians free of charge."

"You made a wrong move there, Weadick."

"You reckon?"

"People got no use for Indians. They won't pay to mingle with them."

"I say you're dead wrong, friend. People's memories ain't so short they won't see that a frontier days reunion without Indians would be a farce. How often in these bars do I hear the boys bragging that a white man can out-ride a red man. Well, at my show, they can put an entry fee where their mouth is. At my Stampede no one will be barred on account of his colour or his creed."

"The Indians are going to compete in the same events as white men?"

"That's right. What's more, I wrote a letter to Pancho Villa and he writes back that his best Mexican vaqueros are on their way. I just wish my old friend Bill Picket was still bulldogging. I was in Calgary in 1904 alongside Bill, and plenty of Calgarians showed up that day to see a black man sink his teeth in a bull's lip and drop him to the ground."

Our Motto: A Square Deal for Everyone.

In the brand new Palliser Hotel, the angle that worked best was celebrities.

"Weadick, come clean, is Teddy Roosevelt coming to this show of yours or not?"

"I've come as clean as I can. Mr. Roosevelt won't confirm but he won't say there's no chance of his being here either."

"Sounds like he ain't coming."

"I'll tell you who ain't coming is your Prime Minister Borden who didn't give it a second thought. Difference is Mr. Roosevelt wants to come, just doesn't know if he can."

"Who is coming then?"

"The Duke of Connaught, Canada's Governor General, his wife and their beautiful daughter, the Princess Patricia, have confirmed their attendance for both Labour Day and the cowboy breakfast to follow next morning."

"Com'mon, Guy, they was coming anyway. Ain't you got anybody coming special?"

"How about my old friend, Charles Marion Russell, cowboy artist, and his wife Nancy?"

"That the best you can do? An old horse wrangler with some paints?"

"Pardon me, friend, but your ignorance is showing. Charlie Russell was indeed a horse wrangler in the Judith Basin, and he, like myself, is proud of those days of hard work on the range. But Mr. Russell is also one of the up and comingest artists in North America. Last winter, while my wife and I were touring the capitals of Europe, Charlie had his show in New York City's famous Folsom Galleries. If you boys were smart you'd go to Charlie's exhibition here and buy one of his western pictures. Be a better investment than all that bog-hole real estate you keep buying on spec."

> *Calgary Eye Opener*
> *May 12, 1912*
> *Get it out of your noodles that this is like the*
> *boring exhibitions of bucking we've been*
> *subjected to in recent years. Guy Weadick's*
> *Calgary Stampede shows early signs of being*
> *at least half worthy of its advance billing,*
> *some of which will be appearing in this*
> *publication as paid advertisements.*

When Guy said his line about real estate speculation he heard a laugh he recognized from the other side of the crowd at the bar. He excused himself and followed the sound to where a squat man in a bulging waistcoat sat alone with his chin on his chest. He was staring down a bottle of whisky. Edwards, the newspaperman.

"That you, Bob? I barely recognize you in this watering hole. You come up in the world or what?"

"Good evening, Mr. Weadick. Pull up a stump and I'll serve you a glass of this frontier liquor. It costs more in this boozorium but goes down just as rough."

Guy sat opposite, held his glass while Edwards poured it full with a slightly shaking hand.

"Your health, Bob."

"Let's drink to something with more of a future. Your Stampede."

"All right. The Stampede. Say, by the way, I haven't thanked you for the good write up you did last week."

"Anyone who buys a regular half page ad deserves my unstinting praise."

"You can say that, Bob, but I swear you're excited about my show."

"Quite so, Mr. Weadick. I can't wait for the *monster* parade, particularly. It takes your brand of showmanship to convince whisky traders of yesteryear to sit on a float a few yards downwind of several Mounted Policemen."

Weadick looked to the sides and back over his shoulder. When he was sure no one was listening, he said, "To be honest, Bob, I'm having a little trouble with those whisky traders. They talked big at first but some got cold feet about stepping back across the Medicine Line. I swear some of them think I'm in cahoots with the law."

Edwards chuckled, sipped from his glass.

"Yessir, Mr. Weadick, I can't wait to see that bullwhacker from High River knocking the lids off gentleman onlookers with a sixteen foot whip. And the real estate float promises to be a once-in-a-lifetime attraction."

"Come again. I don't know of no real estate float."

"The big glass tank filled to the brim with water? The two sharks swimming inside staring hungrily at the crowd?"

"You ain't planning to make fun of my show, are you, Bob?"

"On the other hand, if I treat it with total respect, the public will think money has passed hands – which of course it has."

Guy knocked his hat to the back of his head and laughed. "You're not what I'd call easy company, Bob Edwards, but by damn, you're good company."

> *Calgary Eye Opener*
> *September 7, 1912*
> *As for the "Monster Parade" that we heard about so eternally beforehand, without the Indians, it wouldn't have been much of a show. As far as we were concerned, there wasn't enough music.*

A cocky boy of barely eighteen had come to listen to the conversation between Weadick and Edwards. Liquored, he stood too close and couldn't, in the end, keep quiet.

"He ain't such good company, Guy," the boy said into the lull. "I'd say he's half crazy."

Guy tipped onto the back legs of his chair.

"You watch yourself, friend. That talk's outa line."

"I read his rag, that *Eye Opener*, and he sounded like he was supporting temperance."

Bob took a drink and said with the mildest of smiles, "You find something strange about that, son?"

"Hell, you're the biggest drunk in this town."

"That's quite a compliment. This town has many excellent drunks."

The boy fidgeted with the over-sized buckle on his belt. He'd drawn a crowd and their laughter was turning on him.

"You going to explain your temperance or not, *Eye Opener* man?"

"Bob, you don't have to say a thing to this pup."

"I don't mind, Mr. Weadick." Edwards looked up with his sad hound eyes. "But I do wish you would stand back, son, so I don't have to crane my neck. The answer to what you see as a conundrum is simply that I have been there and I know."

"Been where?"

"The Banff sanatorium, among other places, which has a very impressive collection of snakes and other curious reptilian phenomena."

"What's he talking about, anyway?"

"If you don't understand, boy, you'd better retire."

"It's that damn girly lisp of his makes it hard to follow. He's damn sissy if you ask me."

"You just said one thing too many, friend."

It was clear the boy did not want to fight Weadick. It wasn't altogether certain that Guy wanted to fight the boy. Before anything could happen, Otto Kline split the crowd and knocked the kid aside. He said, "Guy, I been looking all over. It's Joe. I just took him to the hospital."

Happiness has a way of coming and going without warning.

Inside the horseshow pavilion at Victoria Park, Guy Weadick, Otto Kline and Johnny Mullens looked at the patch of dirt where Joe La Mar had fallen. Guy had spent the last three hours in a hospital room at the Holy Cross with Joe's wife and Flores. Joe's back was broken and there was nothing to do but watch him die. Now Johnny told the story of Joe's ride on a big sorrel gelding called Red Wings.

"Joe rode him a few jumps and looked like he had him. But then this Red Wings hit a wet spot and slipped down on his knees. Joe kicked out of the stirrups in case it was going to roll on him but, right then, the horse jumped back up and into another buck. That threw Joe forwards. He'd'a been thrown clear but his spur caught up in the mane. He just hung there, snapping."

Johnny ran out of words and Otto spoke.

"We couldn't get close enough to pick him off, Guy. That old sorrel was scared loco…"

"That's okay, Otto. I see what happened."

Were we to die tomorrow, the only comment would be: "When are they going to plant the old…?" And then: "I wonder where I can rustle a buggy."

Guy rented a buggy and drove up and down the street biting the dust licked up by a rising west wind. A bottle of bootleg whisky lay in his lap. It was the middle of the night and the townsfolk and bulls were asleep. Guy was passing the Grand Union Hotel when the side door flew open and Bob Edwards fell out. He pitched against the brick wall opposite and, leaning there, took a piss. Guy stopped the horse and waited.

"Bob, you look as if you could use a ride."

"Aw, it's you, Mr Weadick. I'd accept but I can't climb that high."

Guy got down and helped the man up. They continued in silence.

Edwards spoke first. "I'm sorry about Joe La Mar. He was a friend of mine as well."

"Guess we'll have the funeral day after tomorrow. Saturday night at the Stampede, I'll get the cowboys and cowgirls to do an exhibition performance, proceeds to his widow."

Edwards pulled cigars from an inside pocket and offered one. Guy kept the rig rolling. He cupped his hand to catch a light, to seal out the now stronger wind.

"Bob, what say we take this bottle across the river to Dolly's?"

"What, so I can mount a woman and prove myself a man?"

"That's your business. I just want a place to drink where I ain't alone and choking on dust."

They rolled on down the sidestreet. Guy whipped the groggy horse up to a trot between the dark shapes of houses. Then the hollow sound of the Langevin Bridge. Because the wind was sweet-smelling there and free of dust, Guy stopped the rig.

"This put a damper on your show, Mr. Weadick?"

"No, Bob, that's not how I'm built."

"As I wrote somewhere or another, nobody's so religious that he considers dying a pleasure. Presumably that goes for the death of others as well."

"You see, Bob, something like my Stampede is already a kind of funeral. We're burying the Old West with honours. And we'll bury Joe La Mar right alongside."

The wind sang through the rips in the canopy. The invisible river moved beneath them.

"I'll tell you, though, I wish that when my Stampede was done, that the winning bronc rider would come and ask for Red Wings to be driven into the arena and snubbed down."

"It's a horse, Weadick, not Lucifer incarnate."

"Don't get me wrong, Bob. I'd do that horse no harm. I just wish the top rider would ask to ride Red Wings in a no time-limited exhibition. That big sorrel bucking end to end of the arena, cowboy waving his stetson, until the horse stands still, sucking air. That would be the best ever monument to Joe La Mar."

"What if your top bronco rider is an Indian or a Mexican and doesn't give a damn about Joe La Mar?"

"I wouldn't mind. Let the best man win regardless of race, colour or creed. I was just saying what would be ideal."

"Ideal," Edwards repeated. A few seconds later, he added, "You're a born maker of myths, Mr. Weadick."

Guy turned and looked intently at Edwards. "And what are you?"

"Oh...a born slayer of myths, I guess."

"I'd rather make 'em than break 'em, myself."

"And given that there's more satisfaction in an act of creation than one of destruction, I expect you will always be the happier man."

"Then why the hell...?"

Edwards flipped the stub of his cigar up in the air. It sailed and, sparks trailing, lit in the water downstream. Guy watched and waited.

"Drink's a bad vice, I admit," Edwards said finally, "but the worst vice of all has to be advice."

Guy took his cigar out of his mouth to laugh but no sound came. He carefully shaped off the ash on the corner of the seat and replaced the grooved stub between his teeth. Then he snapped the reins over the horse's back and the buggy kicked forward. He drove toward a cluster of lights at the base of the hill where the jangle of a piano rose faintly above the wind.

> *While this is to be a season of joy, a period of rich reminiscences, an occasion of hearty greetings, and renewal of old friendships, there will be just a tinge of sadness as we gaze upon the* Sunset of a Dying Race.

Uncle Timothy
DAVID BERGEN

Just after the birth of Theo, my brother Timothy phoned. Bea talked with him while I listened in. I knew immediately who it was because the tenor of Bea's voice went lower and softer, as if Bea and I had been walking along a country road together and Bea had seen a rare flower in the ditch and stopped and said, "Oh, look." After Bea hung up she said that Theo's name had been mentioned only once – Timothy asked if he was healthy. Bea added that Timothy had been calling from Vancouver; he was just passing through on his way back to Irian Jaya, and couldn't come visit. I thought then that I had lost my brother, that I might never see him again, and I did not mind that thought.

And then on Theo's first birthday, Timothy sent a card. The front showed a sketching of an Asmat *bis* pole, like one of those carvings that Michael Rockefeller had bought with steel and dark tobacco and shipped back to a museum in New York just before he was supposedly eaten by the local people. The drawing was in black and white and for me held some unstated portent. Inside the card, close to the bottom, Timothy had scrawled, *Happy Birthday, Theo, from your Uncle Timothy*.

When Bea showed me the card, I stood in the centre of the kitchen and saw myself years from then standing in the same spot, being handed, by my now-grown boy Theo, the thirtieth in a series of birthday greetings. "Another card from Uncle Timothy," he would say, and I would take the offered quarto and find on it a sketching of a skull or a gourded penis. And on the inside Timothy would continue to cryptically describe his life, offering nothing of substance save the evidence that he was still alive and a missionary and remembered once a year the birthday of Theo.

I wondered if Rockefeller's skull still hung from the rafters of some Asmat hut or if it lay, bleached and smooth, against the cranium of some other unfortunate victim of a revenge killing: a long ago feasting of brains and tongue. I have read that even the bravest of Asmat warriors, in order to thwart psychic attack, sleep on the skulls of their fathers. What do they do if there are two brothers? Fight for the skull of the father? Is the mother's skull worth nothing?

It was evening. I bathed Theo and got him into his blanket sleeper. "It's raining," I told him. "Tomorrow we'll put on your slicker and boots and go puddling." I kissed his cheeks. Left. Right. I pounced with my face on his stomach. He scowled. Kneed me in the jaw. Grabbed fists full of hair. I stood, Theo still on my head like a burr, his legs kicking at the ceiling.

Bea came upstairs and stood behind me and held Theo's cheeks. "Come sweetie," she said. She stretched and plucked him from my head. Her breasts touched my back. Her hips my bum. "He's all excited now," she said.

I straightened the sheets on the crib, lined up the board books and teddy bears. Bea settled into the rocker, lifted her shirt, slipped a breast from her bra and gave it to Theo. Theo closed his eyes and worked for the letdown. When it came his mouth moved more slowly, with a steady rhythm. Bea stroked her baby's ears. I turned off the light and left the room.

I went downstairs and found Bea's mother, Alice, eating rice pudding and reading at the kitchen table. Alice had lived with us since the birth of Theo. I helped myself to a bowl of pudding and sat across from her. Alice, when she reads big cumbersome books, takes a pair of scissors and cuts them into quarters or fifths. Right now she was well into the second quarter of a fifteen hundred page novel on India. The effect on me was disturbing, to come upon her and see in her hands a tattered book that had neither beginning nor end. "You've got rice on your chin," I said.

She brushed it away. "I'm getting old and sloppy," she said. She kept on reading, turning the pages too quickly I thought, as if she were looking for a particular phrase or word and wouldn't rest till she found it.

"Timothy sent a card," I said, and slid it across the table. She took it and held it at an angle, her glasses sliding to the tip of her nose. She fingered them back. "Well," she said. She looked at me and I had the urge to tell her all about Bea and me and Timothy. The urge passed.

Bea came down, served herself some rice pudding, and sat.

"I'm happy," Bea said.

"Me too," I said.

Bea had begun attending this church called "The Meeting Place." I asked her once, *What's the point?* and she shrugged and seemed a little sheepish, as if this were just one more method of betrayal. I went with her one Sunday. She took me to this old warehouse downtown. The interior was clean and brightly lit. There were chairs instead of pews. We sat near the back and I bobbed Theo on my knee. Bea was wearing a brown dress with small black flowers printed on it. The hem went just below the knee and it had buttons up the front. I thought that Bea looked particularly beautiful that day. Her hair blended with the dress and during the service her black-booted foot swung to the rock and roll piped in through huge speakers and I could see the outline of her calf through her black tights.

Several college students presented a drama about Job and then someone sang a Van Morrison song. Theo got restless so I took him outside and we sat on the curb beside a red BMW. The sun was hot on our heads. Theo chewed on crackers and a banana. Later, after the service, Bea came out and stood by the doors and talked for a long time to a man with a blond pony tail. I watched her hands touch his and scatter upwards and then one hand rested on the man's shoulder and escaped again. Theo caught sight of Bea and wanted her but I distracted him by walking over to our car which was sandwiched between two highly waxed foreign models. We climbed into our sedan. The heat inside made me groggy.

"Who was that?" I asked Bea when she joined us.

"My cousin Vern," she said. "He's just back from Chile. He was breaking horses down there."

"Whatever happened to old fashioned hymns?" I asked.

Bea didn't answer. We stopped for an ice-cream and walked down by the river and watched the boats. Theo was in his stroller and kept screaming for licks, his little legs beating the air. Bea picked him up and offered him her breast. He fell asleep so we put him over in the shade; his leg jumped once or twice and I thought that he was probably dreaming. Bea wanted to rest awhile so we did that. We sat on a bench and held hands.

The next day Bea fell and hurt her ankle. She was walking outside to pick something from the garden and on the last step she twisted her ankle and crumpled. I had been following her and from my perspective it seemed the fall was almost deliberate. Bea's ankle turned on the last step and she toppled forward and her knee struck the pavement. It gave off a dull sound, like a block of wood being hit by a hammer. Bea began to moan, a heap at my feet. How helpless and useless she was. A child, at least, I could pick up and comfort. I looked out across the lawn. My son's red trike stood in the middle of the yard. The gate on the new cedar fence was swinging in the wind. I leaned forward. Patted Bea's shoulder. Touched her hair.

"Get up," I said.

Bea had broken her ankle in two places. Surgery was required; a steel pin was inserted. "Our family has weak bones," Bea confessed to me that night. I was sitting beside the hospital bed, holding her hand. Theo was with his grandmother. "My father broke his wrist skiing in Switzerland," Bea said. "And my mother fell while ice skating and fractured her hip."

I balled my hand and knocked the plaster. I'd bought some flowers; roses and carnations. Lots of green things besides. I mentioned to the girl in the florist shop that they were for my wife and she looked up and said, hopefully, "Oh, a baby?" "No," I said, "A broken ankle." I laughed then, and the girl pulled back and tipped her head in surprise and I could see the vein along one side of her neck. I thought of that vein now as I smelled the flowers and palmed the still damp cast. Later, before I left, I bent to kiss Bea and found there overly sweet breath, made so by demerol perhaps, or morphine.

Sometimes when I'm holding Theo and talking to someone I want to say, "This is my brother's baby. You see, he came to our place for a visit and he fucked my wife Bea and got her pregnant. So, that makes me the uncle. Funny, eh?" But I haven't actually said those words yet. I just think them. And that's okay. We do what we have to do. I know my Barth. Grace exists because it is so. People are sinners.

My wife Bea, she is a sinner. The thought is lovely

really. So much more meaningful than the nonsense that assumes everyone is good. When Bea lies on me I imagine bones inside her as thick as the limbs of trees. I smell her and come away with a hint of earth, a composted scent, or rain and dirt, or the sharpness of a freshly dug potato. She likes to straddle my chest and if I feel like it I hold her thighs while her hair falls across my throat and into my mouth. When she knots her hair up behind her neck I think of the dolls my brother and I got from an aunt one Christmas long ago; dolls with mops for hair, thick red strings of wool that became knotted and gnarled and were eventually cut. I wake sometimes during the night and think that now is a good time and I imagine cutting Bea's hair above her ears. Sap her strength. All that gloating joy and self-satisfaction. Instead, I hold her and think of this story Timothy told me, long ago, about a Dani ritual. They have a large dance and the women dress up to make themselves pretty so that they can be stolen by another man, and the men dress up too and go with the same intent; to steal another man's wife.

I asked Bea once, in a mood of generous curiosity, what it was like to hold a body like Timothy's. "Must be very light," I said.

"Don't be silly, Thomas." Bea's face pinked up and I thought, really, that in the end she was a prude.

"I mean," I said, "It must be different than me. He's a feather, I'm a sack of stones."

"True," Bea said. Then she paused and said, "A sack of stones is kind of nice."

One afternoon I found Alice reading in the den. There was a soap opera playing on TV. A beautiful man and a beautiful woman were arguing. Then they were kissing. The picture faded.

"How can you read?" I asked.

Alice removed her glasses and held a finger a third of the way through her cleavered tome. "They're very similar. This is like one big soap opera," she said, referring to her book.

"But surely better," I said.

"Not necessarily," she said. "Are you hungry? There's some fruit and a boiled egg on the counter."

I stood and fetched the egg and poured a glass of apple juice. I returned to my spot beside Alice and peeled the egg. The bluing of the yoke filtered through one side. Alice said, "Eggs always remind me of Ralph's head."

Our legs were touching. Alice's breathing was feathery and she crossed her hands at her stomach. Her feet lined up nobly on the floor: bare feet, second toe longest on each foot. I recalled Alice and Ralph on the beach one day long ago, before Ralph died. Alice was thinner then, though her tummy was round and the backs of her thighs were loose. Ralph kept putting his hand on her bum. I liked that. I thought then I wanted to do that to Bea when she and I were fifty.

The soap was over. I must have dozed, for a few moments anyway, because I imagined Alice's hand on my crotch and when I opened my eyes, she was nestling a cup of tea in her lap.

"Are you going to eat your egg?" she asked.

I looked down and found it lodged under my thigh. It was slightly misshapen now and a thread from Alice's shift clung to its filmy exterior. I pulled the thread away and ate. Theo cried out later and I went up to his room and held him and rocked. I remembered that first early morning in the hospital, holding him as Bea slept, observing the rubbery features of the newborn, the puckish mouth, the eyes pressed tight in sleep, the squeezed angry brow, the bronze tufts of hair, reddish down on his arms, the beating of blood in the straight vein on his forehead. Yet, for all that marvellous willing of creation, I was frightened by his existence, as if he didn't really belong or perhaps shouldn't belong, and the impulse arrived to put my palm over the little bugger's mouth and hold it there and then to lay the body down and run.

Perhaps it was the card sent by Timothy that spurred Alice's comment one evening. We were sitting down to a supper of biscuits and soup when Alice, in the distracted manner she has, held her spoon in the air and said, "It surprises me sometimes to think of your brother as a missionary."

"You think I'm incapable of belief?" I said.

"No, not at all. I remember Miss Pankratz. She was a missionary in Nigeria. She came home on furlough and spoke in our church. She told the people that she was not going to suffer and would not live without some of life's finer things. She said she expected at least enough money to buy new panties. Well, her saying that diminished her in my view. It was as if she had talked about sex and shouldn't have. She came over for Sunday lunch. Shook my hand at the dinner table. Her own hand was very light, like holding a baby mouse. This surprised and frightened me."

Bea, who was mashing banana for Theo, waited for Alice to finish and said, "It has little to do with belief, Thomas."

"Of course," I said, "Witness Timothy."

Bea burbled at Theo. She said, "I don't understand why we expect missionaries to be sexless."

"I think," said Alice, "that as a child I saw missionaries as angelic creatures. And so for one of them to speak so easily of panties seemed a travesty. It was like, *wear them for goodness sake, but don't talk about them.*"

"Did she actually say *panties?*" I asked. The word was full of sex, I thought; the two syllables evoking a shortness of breath, a popping gasp that stretched and descended into that tease of the final 's'.

"Oh, Thomas," Bea said.

I smiled at her. She emitted a heat this evening. She was wearing a T-shirt that had three kittens on the front, their heads going one, two, three, number one and three sporting the whiskers for Bea's breasts. The T-shirt was large and so hid much of Bea, but when she leaned back and held her hair in a temporary grip, I could see the outline of her and I thought how tonight I'd like to lay her down and touch everything.

Alice was still considering. "I don't know," she said. "I imagine she used the word underwear. Panties does sound too intimate, doesn't it?"

Bea was swiping at Theo's mouth with a warm cloth. Sometimes, her efficiency with Theo irked me. As if sensing my thoughts, Bea hobbled up behind me and pressed the kittens against my neck. She squeezed my chest. Her hair had that familiar dry, hay-like scent that came from being combed too often. Horsy.

Alice asked, "Do you ever think Timothy might visit? Just walk in and say, 'Hi, I'm home!'?"

"He's on the other side of the world, Mom," Bea said.

"I think that," I said. "In fact, I dreamed it the other night." Remembering, I thought how disproportionate dreams can be and so I did not describe the images. In the dream Timothy came and scooped up Theo, threw him high into the air, and Theo fell to the ground and smashed his head open on a rock.

I could feel Bea's breath on my neck. Her weight was suddenly cloying and so I stood and moved away from her and I gathered up the dishes, rinsed them, and stacked them in the dishwasher.

"You didn't tell me you had a dream," Bea said that night. We were lying in the dark, on our backs. The air conditioner had just cut in and I could feel the cool air on my arm which hung over the edge of the bed. For an answer I laid my hand on Bea's pyjamas, down by the belly. My knee knocked against her cast.

"Peg leg," I said.

She ignored me and said, "Remember that dream I had once, about Timothy being eaten? That was awful."

"Not so awful," I said. I undid a few buttons and slipped my hand inside, onto the loose flesh of her belly.

"That tickles," Bea said. I pressed harder, felt the sponge of her, my fingers sunk down around her belly button now. "It *was* awful," she said, "Because it was so real."

My fingers pulled at the elastic and slipped under. "Panties," I whispered. Bea laughed. Or maybe it was a groan. Then she was quiet, breathing quicker, lifting her healthy leg and letting it drop. Lift, drop. "I read the other day about this Rockefeller," I said. "Thirty-five years ago he disappeared in Irian Jaya."

"Yeah?" Bea tried to kiss me. She opened her mouth wide.

After she pulled away, I said, "His father had all kinds of planes out there: coast guard, Navy, local missionaries. Nobody knows to this day what happened to him. Some say he was eaten by the Asmat people."

Bea turned and heaved against me. I found her centre and said, "Others say it was sharks. Or crocodiles. Sometimes," I breathed in Bea's ear. "Sometimes I imagine Timothy dying out there, just dropping out of the sky and disappearing. Forever."

As Bea finished, her stomach tightened and she grabbed my free wrist and twisted it up towards her mouth. The light of the summer night coming through the window shone off my fingers and her knuckles, creating the illusion of two hands fighting for the possession of a single object.

Act of Love
SHARON BUTALA

This is perhaps not a story to tell, she thinks. Then, no, this is perhaps the *only* story to tell. It's the story of how she was raped, once when she was maybe thirty-one or two, and how all the bad things that ran wordlessly through her culture about herself and about women as a species flooded over her, and she blamed herself and was ashamed and never told anybody till she felt securely beyond her youth.

Not that it helped. By then she had gone too far for rage, too far for thoughts of beatings, castration, murder, or a life lived without men. What she thinks, increasingly, glumly, since that first telling of it, is that there was nothing she could have done about it then, and there's still nothing she can do about it. In fact, she's just grateful he didn't break any bones, subduing her easily with his weight and implacability, so that she acquiesced as the only way to avoid being hurt. Nor did he force her to any act of extreme perversion that would have haunted her dreams for the rest of her life. Even her children weren't in the house, but were away visiting their grandparents. Yes, she thinks, I was very lucky.

Not that she doesn't see the irony of her conclusion. As far as she knows, she was the only one he followed home that night, she was the only one he raped. But for years she didn't even call it rape. She didn't call it anything, she didn't even think about it. One night she was sitting talking about a mutual friend with a man she'd just met that day, when she heard herself say, calmly, conversationally, that was the night I was raped.

Since then she's been thinking about it a lot, has been going over all the details one by one, as far as she can remember, since it happened twenty-five years before. Stop that, she tells herself. If you doubt each detail as you remember it, you'll soon doubt that you were raped at all. And she remembers the ugly muscles of his upper arms and the way he pushed her, relentlessly, inexorably, till he was inside the house, then in the bedroom, then lying on the bed on top of her.

She doesn't understand why she didn't feel like the woman she'd seen in a television movie who'd been raped and who went a little crazy afterward, took a dozen baths and was afraid to go out at all, and then set up a trap for the man, inviting him over, planning to say, "Come in," when he knocked on her door, and then to blast him with a shotgun. And there were other stories too, in magazines and on radio and television, about women reacting to rape. She'd found them all excessive and self-aggrandizing, reactions of women who couldn't have been too stable to begin with, who clearly harboured some very bad notions about themselves as sexual beings. For years that was what she'd thought.

But the older she gets, clutching her secret to herself, the less sure she is that those women were wrong, and that her reaction – to keep silent, not to think about it, to count herself lucky among those who'd been raped – is perhaps the less rational approach after all, and that maybe *she* is the one who values herself too little, who suffers from an absence of self-esteem, and a badly developed sexuality. They'd been outraged at their violation; she hadn't even been surprised; she'd resisted till she saw resistance was useless, then she'd gone limp till he was done. All those years, whenever it popped into her mind, she'd quickly thought of how she was lucky compared to being a concubine or forced to commit suttee or being a tribal slave. Even now, when she's learned to value herself quite a lot, she's still not outraged and isn't sure why not.

And she tells herself, if you never told anybody, you can hardly be the only raped woman who reacted that way. Remember dating when you were a college student? Most dates wound up in wrestling matches. You expected them, there was an unspoken accord: he would try, you would say no, at a certain point you'd either give in or he would realize you meant it and stop. Sometimes he went further than the accord allowed, and if he did, you didn't go out with him again. It was a dangerous game, but the only one. Now she thinks that maybe she'd been lucky there too and that her girlfriends were being raped and not telling anyone.

Besides, the only reason she didn't give in was that her mother had told her she shouldn't; so had the nuns and priests who'd educated her, and her girlfriends, even the boys who were her friends, counselling her sagely and whispering about girls they all knew who were easy. If you didn't resist, it was absolutely clear, the life you were being groomed for would be over, and that was a price too high for anybody to pay.

Then, abruptly, when she was in her late twenties and newly divorced, all that ended. Suddenly, making love was socially acceptable, a positive good; everybody was doing it; it was expected. She thinks that probably almost nobody was doing it as much as they implied they were, she for one wasn't, but the point was that you could if you wanted to and nobody would call you a slut or a whore or easy. Nobody would say anything at all.

I never even noticed him, she thinks. A dozen of them together in a club at one big table, her girlfriends, somebody's husband, a few male friends who were always around, and him, the rapist, a stranger, a houseguest of one of the men. They hadn't even sat close together. When she thought about that night, she remembered he'd sat on the opposite side of the table at the far end, and when she thought harder about it, she remembered he'd asked her to dance, that he hadn't been a good dancer; that they'd danced once, then sat down. She hadn't even talked to him, and she hadn't liked him because he was so silent and his silence had a heavy impenetrableness to it that made her wonder why he'd asked her to dance.

The reason she didn't at first remember dancing with him was that sitting at a table behind them was a man she'd had an affair with and in a forlorn way was still in love with. He was sitting with a woman; by the way he was acting she could tell he was in love. When she'd noticed him and smiled and waved, he'd deliberately looked away without even nodding. She'd been so wounded by this unexpected, deliberate, and undeserved slight that all enjoyment was leached from the evening and after a while, it was barely midnight, she'd gotten up, and said goodnight, and left.

But then, she thinks, I do remember that the man I'd danced with stood up when he noticed I was leaving, that as I was walking away he was hastily trying to make change to settle his share of the bill. And I hurried out of the club, and I kept telling myself he wasn't leaving because of me. And yet, as I passed the shadowed street behind the club, I thought seriously of stepping into it and hiding against a building till he'd gone by. I didn't, my training to stay on well-lit streets was too strong, and besides, I kept thinking I was imagining things, that he wasn't going to follow me, or if he was, it was only because my house and the house he was staying in were near each other.

Even now, after all these years, after all the times she's remembered the details of that night, she can still see the comforting shadows of that narrow side street. She remembers clearly how she hesitated, how close she came to taking those few quick steps that would have saved her, and how she didn't, telling herself not to be silly, not to be melodramatic.

I never told anyone, she thinks, because if I did how could I maintain my dignity, my good name, my social standing as a decent woman? I was a divorcée, I was in a nightclub unescorted, I'd had affairs, I'd slept with men I'd just met. I'd violated all the codes I was raised with, had become all the things a dozen years before I'd fought with my dates not to become. This is why for twenty-five years I couldn't tell this story. Because it was all my fault; I had been asking for it.

Is that why I refused to think about it? she asks herself. Because I couldn't face that awful truth? That everyone would think I should have expected it, given my lifestyle? That because of it nobody would care? She knows that was part of it: her pride kept her silent, and her stubborn belief in her own strength to endure even the worst that fate might have in store for her.

For all those years she hasn't allowed herself to think about it – except inadvertently, stopping herself as soon as she noticed she was – now, her dark secret out in the open at last, she's driven obsessively to remember it clearly, in every detail. Despite the new climate of opinion, she still suspects it really was her fault, as she'd thought for all these years, something she'd earned, and has no right to be troubled or angry about. She needs to know the truth about it, either to accept the blame or to at last feel the outrage she's told she has a right to.

No, it's more than that, she thinks. She's reached a time when she needs to study her rape from every possible angle in order to discover its true meaning; she's driven to gathering together all the details of her life, every single one. She's weaving them into a precise tapestry – her finished life – something, when she reaches old age, she'll be able to glance at with awe and in contentment, everything sorted and in its place, all passions wiped away, everything clearly what it is and nothing more.

She knows that what happened to her was trivial compared to the rapes other women have endured. She wasn't even really frightened, not at any time during the whole thing. He scared me, the way when I got my key out he stood close to me, and when I tried to slip inside first and shut the door on him, he put his leg in the gap, shoved, and was inside. Then I was scared, she thinks, but not terrified, just scared, because I knew he would try to force me to have sex. I didn't think beyond that, because he was a close friend of a man I trusted, and I couldn't believe anybody that man cared about would be capable of anything really bad like maybe – murder. As he pushed his way in, I believe I clung to that thought.

She remembers he put his arms around her and kissed her in the darkness of her living room – I don't remember anything about that part, she tells herself – and said, "Where's the bedroom?" He thought it was upstairs and was pushing her toward it and she said, "No, not upstairs," thinking if he couldn't find the bedroom she'd be safe, but the moon was so bright and they were at the bottom of the stairs and it was through the open door beside them, they could see the moonlight shining on the satin spread.

She can't remember about the clothes part. She would have been wearing jeans, but she doesn't know how they came off. She remembers his belt buckle hurting her and him raising up to undo it while he kept one forearm across her chest. She fought with him, pushed against him, tried to hold her legs together, to bring her knees up, to shove him away, but it was hopeless. In the one effort when she used all her strength to throw him off, he responded by using his strength to hold her down. She knew when she felt his whole masculine power, if she didn't stop fighting him he not only could hurt her, he would. It seemed the only sensible thing to do was to give in.

Somehow the sex didn't matter much, not at the time, anyway. It was horrible and disgusting, but it was his action, not hers, so she wasn't disgusting, he was. That was what she was thinking as it happened, that it wasn't much, it wasn't anything. After, she pretended she was asleep. He pushed her a bit or something, she doesn't clearly remember what, and then he just left. Got up, pulled on his pants, walked out.

She remembers how the second she heard the door shut she leaped out of bed and locked it. She doesn't know if she saw this through the window or if she imagined it, but she sees him hesitate and look over his shoulder when he hears the bolt snap shut. Like it just occurred to him she might be mad at him or afraid of him, like up to that moment it never occurred to him that she had any feelings at all. Or maybe she was going to call the police. She remembers she thought of them for only one brief instant, shuddering at what they might say to her. No, she never seriously considered the police, but she thinks at that moment it might have crossed his mind, and for an instant he was afraid.

Then I just walked around the house in the dark, she remembers, didn't even put on any lights. Just walked around from room to room and looked out the windows at the moonlight. And I felt so bad. I felt like life was too awful to want to live. That I wasn't loved by anyone, that I wasn't – I was going to say, fit to live, she thinks, but that sounds like all those women on tv and radio and in magazines who are so excessive. Anyway, it wasn't quite like that.

I was fighting this terrible sense of loss and the ugliness of life. Like this was something I would never recover from because I had been so defiled, and all the things I'd believed in, all the things I'd tried to be, one silent, well-muscled stranger could destroy in a minute. Could make me feel I was a fool, and alien to the loving, clean world I was raised in because I was so bad, so guilty, so big a liar about myself.

Yet, as well as she can remember, she didn't think of suicide. Instead, she'd been plunged down into an echoing underworld whose very air was made of something more resonant and more meaningful than mere pain, and the place was so far down and so dark she couldn't pull herself out of it, couldn't even think of escaping, couldn't think at all. Now she sees it was the place that at bottom holds death, and she'd been aware of it then, but beyond action of any kind.

Eventually she must have simply gone to sleep. The next day she got up and went to work and looked after her children when they returned from visiting their grandparents, and kept on going to work and doing all the things she was supposed to do – doing them badly sometimes, fitfully, failing as often as she succeeded, being an ordinary, normal human being, she supposes – and didn't even try to kill herself.

She regards it also as ironic that the night she heard herself say out loud she'd been raped, the mutual friend she and her new acquaintance had been talking about was the man who'd sat behind her in the club that night, the man she'd been in love with, who'd refused even to say hello. She remembers how his deliberate turning away from her had hurt as much as if he'd slapped her. Even now she can't think why he'd done that, and she's surprised to find it stands out in her memory as one of the worst hurts she's had to endure.

Nor did she once think *why me* as she'd heard victims of misfortune do: it was where she was headed, it was a fate she could foresee – not that she had, she doesn't mean that – but it hadn't surprised her, it hadn't seemed unfair, because it fit within the context of her life at that time.

This is why she feels no outrage, only this bottomless, unending sorrow whenever she thinks of it. That he had no right was never in question but – if only she could hold onto that glimmer she sometimes catches of some greater wisdom that might tell her what she really wonders: why so small a thing, that didn't even leave a bruise, made her feel so bad.

Now she remembers something else that hovered on the edge of her memory all these years. The day afterward, coming home from work to discover she'd forgotten her keys, she'd had to break a pane of glass in the French doors in the dining room to get in. A few nights later a male friend walked her home from the movie she'd been to with her friends. She must have invited him in, because she remembers when he saw the broken glass lying where she'd left it on the dining room floor, he'd picked up every shard and put it all in the garbage. She remembers the strange way he did it, glancing at her once, not listening to her feeble protest that she'd do it herself in the morning, but bending so quietly and carefully, with an air of the most complete gentleness, a sort of tenderness toward her for which she could find no explanation.

Neither of them spoke as he worked, but it was as if they both knew this was something she was unable to do herself, something she needed help with. Even now she doesn't know why she couldn't do it, and she remembers how as she watched him work she had been filled with gratitude, she nearly wept for his kindness. Yet try as she might, she can't remember his face or his name, only his gentleness, and the sound of his broom brushing over the hardwood floor, sweeping up the last particles of broken glass.

The Organized Woman Story
BIRK SPROXTON

Carol is an organized woman. You will understand what
I mean by an organized woman when I tell you about
her love life, or what I know of her love life, for she has
never been in love with me. Not like that, anyway. I
have the wrong name.

By organized, I don't mean that she can always find
her car keys, though it is true, or that she can remember
to phone her third cousin Sally on the third Sunday of
every third month, though she does that, too. She phones
me on the same day, the third Sunday of every third
month, and she tells me that Sally has taken to lassooing
the children at supper time, or whatever it is that Sally
is up to, and she tells me the latest news about Michael.
Michael and I correspond every few days on electronic
mail, but no matter. She calls me regularly. On the third
Sunday.

I first realized she was an organized woman when
she fell in love with my friend. He is her second husband
named Michael. The second Michael, my friend, is a
different man from the first, but they have the same
first name. Then I realized that she always falls in love
with men named Michael. Not every Michael, of course,
for she can be a very fussy woman, but every man she
falls in love with turns out to be named Michael.

You may think that because her brother is named
Michael and her father is named Michael that she is
simply picking variants of her father, each man a copy
of her father with his quiet laugh and confident walk,
the way you fall in love with, say, a special kind of
doughnut and each time you hanker for a doughnut

you go to the same shop, the warm yeasty smells as you open the door always remind you of what you want, and you order the same kind of doughnut you did the last time you were struck by the doughnut urge. Something like that.

Now you may argue husbands are not like doughnuts, but I must tell you I once said that to her, I said, men are not like doughnuts, you don't have to choose the same kind every time, and she pointed out, in a rather peckish way I thought, that I certainly had not divorced myself from my last round of doughnuts, that in fact I seem to embrace and nurture and hold on to doughnuts and let them root and ripen and grow into huge balloon tires around my waist. I, she said – meaning me, your story teller – seem to have clutched those chocolate doughnuts to my very loins for life. She has this way of zeroing in on your weak spots. So I dropped the subject.

But she was not looking for variants of her father.

I know this because she was once courted by Wayne, a pharmacist in my neighbourhood. In fact, she was infatuated with Wayne, quite wrapped up in him, you might say, after she chucked out her first husband named Michael, even to the point of trying to persuade her brother to go by the name Wayne.

"After all," she said to her brother, "Wayne is your second name, and this Wayne is very nice. I'd like you to be Wayne, too." She did not approach her father, of course, whose second name is also Wayne, because she knew that he would give in to anything his darling-poo wanted and so it would not be a proper test. Therefore she approached her brother first. But her brother remained adamant. Michael was the name he preferred. Wayne wouldn't do, even if it was his second name and one she was currently infatuated with. So she dropped him. The pharmacist, I mean. If she could not get all her men to go by the name Wayne, if she was stuck with Michael, then Michael it would be. She'd have to find another Michael.

Wayne the pharmacist had to go. She thanked him very much for giving her the cardboard boxes she had used to pack up her first husband's things, and for allowing her a small discount on the several tons of packing paper she had used to wrap every single item that Michael owned, each sock in its own wrapper, before she chucked him out.

That was the Saturday she broke tradition. She phoned me, even though it was Saturday, to say that Michael had departed, his possessions all neatly wrapped in tissue paper and tucked in solid cardboard cartons the nice pharmacist had given her. I thought I would say something to cheer her up, though she gave no sign of being upset, so I said, No, Michael hadn't gone, in fact he was sitting in my living room.

She said, "Oh, you silly man, what's he doing at your place?" And I, thinking she deserved a diversion though I knew she would find my place a deplorable mess, said, "Well, why don't you come over and find out?"

So she came over and that's how she met Michael, my friend, and that's why Michael and I now use electronic mail to talk. She phoned me the next day, Sunday, the third Sunday of the month, to say that Sally was building a huge jungle gym for the kids to climb on, she was bolting planks onto the third storey Sally was, and then she, Carol, apologized for hauling Michael off like that last night, and wasn't he a nice man?

I said, of course you think he's a nice man because his name is Michael.

It was the wrong thing to say. I won't tell you exactly

what she replied because it might make her look bad, but it had something to do with my feeling sorry for myself about all the poems I can't get anybody to buy, or read, and why didn't I get off my blossoming derrière and lift the telephone receiver and give Sally a call, she of the lasso and the jungle gym and the herd of howling kids.

So I did. I lifted the phone and did that very thing. That very day. The third Sunday of the month. Right after I fortified myself with a little nibble of chocolate doughnut and a somewhat larger nip on a heel of Johnny Walker Red Label and a thorough re-read of the more kindly rejection letters I have in my files.

"Sally," I said, in my most charming poet-voice, "Sally, I'm coming over."

"But," she said, "I don't even know you."

"So what," said I, "I don't know you either. That makes us even. Besides that, you have a lasso."

She said, "What will we do when you get here?"

I said, "I will read you my poems."

She said, with only a small hesitation, "What kind of poems?"

"Apple poems," I said, "Peach and orange and banana poems. Pomegranate and eggplant and rhubarb poems. I have apricots, I have blueberries, I have kiwi and squash, I have scarlet runners and carrots and beets, I have peas and pumpkins and pears and kohlrabi. I have delicate grapes and crunchy celery, I have potato poems, flowering reds and bristling whites, I have turnips and cabbage and broccoli and brussels sprouts…"

She interrupted me. It's a small failing of hers, not to be a telephone person; long telephone calls don't agree with her.

Then she said, in a quiet voice, she said, "I want a salad, I want you to read me a salad."

A minute ago the phone rang. You can hear it plainly from up here on the third floor of the jungle gym, despite the cries of the children and despite the tiny wet bottom planted on my knee. That will be Carol calling. She will be talking now to Sally. It is the third Sunday of the month. Carol will be asking us to drop over after supper for a visit. Bring the kids, she will say. And Wayne, bring him too, tell him I have some chocolate doughnuts.

She's an organized woman, Carol is. They won't talk long. We will drive over, and sit and visit, and Michael will ask about my latest crop of poems. Have I thought of maybe doing some weeding, he will ask in his gentle way. Then I will say, no, no weeding, I'm a fertilizer man, let them grow.

And Carol will agree with me, "Fertilizer, I'll say," and then give the little laugh that makes Michael's eyes shine.

And Sally, well, Sally will say in her sing-song voice how she likes the fruits and vegetables we grow together and how the kids grow like bad weeds and maybe we should gather them up now if we can disentangle them from the jungle of Michael's computer cords and get on our way, for we have to stop at the pharmacy to buy some radish seeds.

And then Sally will turn to me and say, "Wayne, it's time to lasso those kids and tuck them in the back seat."

And I will lasso those kids and tuck them and strap them tight with belts and hugs and kisses, and Sally will drive us home to make poems and salads together until the next time the phone rings on the third Sunday of the month. Then I will dust the fertilizer from my latest poems. The kids will howl as only kids can do. Sally will twirl her lasso as she picks up the receiver. It will be Carol. She's an organized woman.

The Bad One
JAKE MACDONALD

One afternoon in late summer, a hot day with the sun beating down on the humpy streets of Keewuttunnee, Sonny Copenace went uptown to do a little shopping and ran into the Bad One.

It happened outside the bait shop. Sonny had just purchased three dozen chubby chubs, paid for them, taken the plastic bucket and stepped out the door when a flying shadow came out of nowhere and blasted him down onto the sidewalk.

In the cartoons they always show a guy knocked out cold with stars whirling around his head. That's exactly what it was like. Sitting on the sidewalk with his legs splayed in front of him, Sonny saw tiny blue points of light dancing in front of his eyes. His pants were wet and minnows flipped around on the sidewalk.

A little kid stared at him.

"What happened?" Sonny said.

The boy gestured with his hand, pointing to a hunched-over guy who was walking off down the street. "He did it," said the boy. "The Bad One."

Sonny climbed to his feet. He knew the guy who had punched him, recognized the broad shoulders and weaving walk. It was Roy Paypompey. He was a sniffer and a murderer. Sonny knew Roy, had even saved his life once, pulling him out of the river when he was drunk. Maybe this was Roy's way of saying thanks.

Sonny started picking up his minnows. They were flipping around, covered with dust. The store clerk came out. "What happened?"

"Roy hit me."

"That prick. I told him to stay away from here."

"He's supposed to be in jail."

"He got out," said the clerk. "New trial, and then he got acquitted. The sonofabitch."

Sonny salvaged his minnows and went down to the wharf. On his forehead he could feel a welt the size of a fist. His two American guests asked him what had happened.

"Guy hit me."

"Why?"

"I don't know." Sonny dabbed cold water on his forehead. *Roy kills a little kid, then instead of apologizing he goes around punching people.*

At the end of the day Sonny cleaned his fish, collected his tip, and walked up the long hilly road to his home. He and Diana lived in a blue aluminum-sided bungalow they rented from the government. Sonny made a coffee and got his smokes and went out on the back steps with Diana. She touched the swollen bruise on his head. "So he didn't say anything?"

"Not a word."

Diana lit one cigarette off another, a definite signal that she was mad. In the back yard the kids played on the Jag, which was parked on a piece of plywood waiting for the snow. Macy tugged at the hand grips and made varooming sounds while Darryl-Ann begged for a turn. "So now what," asked Diana, "we gotta keep our kids inside every minute of the day?"

"I don't know."

"You should have let the asshole drown."

Sonny used to be proud of the fact that he'd saved someone's life. He even got a medal from the government. They made him wear a necktie and jacket and go to a luncheon. But ever since, he had all this other stuff to deal with. Like Kim's death. He could still remember the day she disappeared. The police cars. Dozens of them. More police cars than he had ever seen. Helicopters clattering overhead. Big scary-looking police dogs. And long lines of men moving through the bush. People thought a bear had taken her. But then only two hundred yards from the police station the searchers found an orange garbage bag with her body in it.

So even though he wasn't in jail, you'd think that Roy would stay away from Keewuttunnee. Kim McIvor's relatives were great big guys, tough guys, Metis pulp-cutters, and Sonny knew that if the law didn't take care of Roy, the McIvors would do it themselves. But over the days following Kim's death nothing happened. Roy went into the grocery store, hung around, stood on the street corner trying to bum money. Early in the morning Sonny would see him sitting on the guard rail by the Forestry base, grinning and waving at the trucks going by. Sonny figured that Jim McIvor, the 250-pound arm-wrestling champion of Keewuttunnee, had to be out of town or something. But then one Saturday night Roy came to a town dance. And just around midnight, Jim McIvor walked in.

Roy was drunk. In a hard hat and a torn-up shirt, he weaved around in the centre of the dance floor, bobbing and staggering to the music. Everybody else sat at the plywood tables, refusing to take the dance floor as long as Roy was there. There was a thick feeling of tension in the hall. Sonny stood leaning against the wall, watching Jim McIvor. Sonny thought the big man would finish his beer, stand up, and just walk over and kill Roy Paypompey on the spot. But nothing happened. The dance finally ended and everyone went home. The next day Roy was sitting on the guard rail, waving at everybody and grinning just like always.

Somewhere at home – probably in the bottom drawer of his dresser with his pocket knives and old spools of fishing line and hand-warmers and other assorted items of junk – Sonny had a little blue cardboard box with a medal inside it. It was the Star of Courage. He got it for saving Roy's life. The day it happened, Sonny was installing a chimney. He was up on the roof of the Keewuttunnee Bay Inn with Sam Morrison and Joe Hudson.

Mid-afternoon, Roy Paypompey came through the narrows in a boat, obviously drunk out of his mind by the way the boat was hopping and caterwauling across the waves. Roy crossed a boat wake at the wrong angle, and the boat leaped into the air and Roy somersaulted into the water. The boat skittered across the wake and then inscribed a fast circle and came back at Roy and whacked into him as he was floundering in the water. Sonny didn't think about what he was supposed to do. He leaped off the roof and hit the grass running.

He ran into the water and swam out to the boat but Roy was gone. Sonny dived underwater a few times and looked around. About three feet beneath him he saw a checkered lumberjacket sleeve go floating by in the underwater sunbeams. He seized the jacket and felt Roy's arm. Surfacing, he pulled Roy to shore. Joe Hudson and Sam Morrison waded out into the river and took over, hauled Roy up onto the beach like a sturgeon. Somebody called the First Responders. A veterinarian who was fishing at the Inn came down to the shore and helped pump the water out of his lungs. The medi-vac helicopter from Kenora clattered down into the parking lot and whisked Roy off for several tens of thousand of dollars worth of emergency medical care. A few weeks later, Al Chaput of the OPP recommended Sonny for a Star of

Courage. But if Sonny had known how Roy was going to end up, he'd have gladly just let him sink.

So nothing happened at the dance that night.

Sonny was beginning to realize that there are two versions of life: there's the way you think things are, and then there's the truth. Everybody has a stereotype about life in jail, for example. The guards are supposed to be bad guys, bullies. But Sonny had been in jail a couple of times when he was young, wild, on the bottle, and the guards were all nice guys. They'd give you smokes or lend you five bucks. And the jail was quiet too. You always heard that sex molestors got beat up in jail. But Sonny had never seen that. There were a couple of rapists on their unit and they played cards and ate at the same table as everyone else and nobody batted an eye. It bugged you sometimes in a small community. No matter what happened everything just carried on, quiet and normal, quiet and normal.

A few weeks after the dance Sonny got a visit from Chief Romeo Star. It was a cold autumn Saturday. Sonny had been out all night hunting beavers with Johnny No-Cash. Johnny No-Cash had an Indian-sounding name but he was actually a white guy from New Brunswick. He had big cheekbones and he played the guitar and sang in a deep gravelly voice, just like Johnny Cash, but he never had any money like Johnny Cash so he wound up with his nickname. He was poor enough to come out beaver hunting with Sonny once in a while and they'd been out all night the night before. They'd sat on a beaver house in the freezing rain, trying to catch beavers in the flashlight glare and bean them in the ear with their .22s. There was a tiny spot the size of a dime just behind the ear. If you didn't hit them just right they'd dive down wounded, die, and you'd have to spend a long time trying to snag them with a hook lashed to the end of a long pole. Sonny was just about the last guy in Kewuttunnee who hunted beavers. The trapline had belonged to his father. But the fur market had collapsed, beavers were multiplying like rats, and Sonny (and maybe Johnny No-Cash) were the only guys willing to work for three or four hours for a skin that was worth fifteen dollars.

So anyway that Saturday morning Sonny was skinning beavers over at Johnny No-Cash's house when a truck pulled into the yard and Romeo Star climbed out. Romeo was looking well-rigged for winter, driving a new wine-coloured Lariat XLT purchased with funds he'd probably embezzled from the Bingo hall. Romeo's stomach jiggled as he waddled across the yard towards them with a brown paper bag in his hand. "Shut her down, boys. I'm buying."

Sonny jabbed his Buck skinner into a stump and sat down, searching through his pockets for a cigarette. Romeo opened up the brown paper bag and extracted three styrofoam cups.

"Thank you my good fellow," Johnny No-Cash said.

Romeo lit a cigarette and rested one cheek of his fat rump on the sawhorse. He launched into a bullshit story about the time he was a high-paid fur grader. Finally he got down to business. He said that people were "expressing their concerns" that Roy Paypompey was back in the community.

"Me too," said Sonny.

Johnny No-Cash shivered and buttoned the denim jacket over his skinny chest. He licked the edge of a rolled cigarette, lit it, picked a shred of tobacco off his lip and squinted at Romeo. "Just shoot him."

"We've spoken to him," Romeo said. "Trying to get him into counselling? But there's no way. He's too jagged up."

Sonny asked, "Why can't the cops run him out of town?"

"They don't give a care. It's their fault he's out anyway."

"How do you figure that?"

"It was that Sergeant's fault," Romeo said. "The one who got killed in the car accident?"

"McCandless," said Sonny.

"Yeah, that Sergeant McCandless guy. He was the one interviewed Paypompey. But he didn't tell him about his rights."

"The way I heard it," Johnny No-Cash said. "That's because Roy confessed while McCandless was washing the cop car in the driveway. Roy wasn't under arrest or anything. He wasn't even a suspect. He was just walking by the cop station. So he walked up to McCandless and confessed. And that turned out to be their main evidence. But the judge threw out the confession because McCandless hadn't warned him to get a lawyer before he talked."

Romeo sniffed. "Pretty dumb."

Johnny No-Cash asked, "Why would McCandless warn him when he was just fuggin standin' there washing the car? Hey, I hate cops as much as anybody, but don't be ridiculous."

Romeo shrugged. "Anyway, I been talking to a lot of people. And most of 'em think you should do something."

"Who, me?" said Sonny. "What's it got to do with me?"

"You're his friend."

Sonny snorted, "Like hell I am."

"You saved his life."

Sonny stood up angrily. "This boat goes by, I didn't even know who was in it! What do you want me to do?"

Romeo shrugged. "I don't know. Somebody's got to do something."

"Well one thing is guaranteed," Johnny No-Cash finally said. "He's gonna attack another kid. Even the judge said that. It's just a question of when."

Romeo and Johnny No-Cash sat there drinking their coffee, while Sonny sat off to one side on the sawhorse, feeling accused by their silence. He finally spoke. "Romeo, you always want me to do the dirty work. It pisses me off. Why don't you go and get one of those forty grand-a-year social workers?"

Romeo laughed, a dark chuckle. "They're afraid of him."

That night at dinner Sonny had a big argument with Diana. And then in bed she slept over on her own side of the mattress, curled up, trembling and angry. That Star of Courage, Sonny thought. Romeo and his buddies had been ribbing him about that. The big hero.

So Sonny kept to himself. He ignored Diana and he ignored Romeo. But deep down inside, he knew that they had a point. He had saved Roy's life. On Thursday afternoon when Diana was in Kenora buying groceries Sonny decided he'd go and see Roy and tell him to leave town. Just get the hell out. We don't want you here.

At the dock down by the river Sonny climbed into his boat and snugged the camo-patterned DU baseball hat down low on his eyes. He started the motor and drove across the slate-dark water. Where the railway bridge crossed the river he took the short cut, speeding carefully through the narrow passage between the concrete bridge piers. On the far shore he killed the motor, tilted it, and used the hooked beaver pole to pull the boat into shore. Tying the boat to a tree he walked up the path into the woods. A couple of snowflakes eddied down, the first of winter. Hiking along the path he passed some railway sheds, a derelict sawmill, and a field of wooden grave markers. At the top of the hill he came to a row of shacks, the shanty village where most of the sniffers lived.

He had a plan. He'd get Roy in the truck and take him far away. Maybe go to Winnipeg. They had places there, treatment and detox centres. Failing that, he'd just drop him on a street corner at Higgins and Main Street. Maybe he was too stupid to find his way back to Keewuttunnee.

Sonny stopped in front of a rain-blackened plywood shack with spray-painted graffiti on the walls. The door hung open. A big message was scrawled across it. COPS SUCK PIGS. Sonny climbed the rotten stairs and looked inside. It was dark inside, utterly bare. A yellow T-shirt was nailed across a window. In the centre of the floor was a large onion.

Sonny'd been here once, several years ago, searching for Kim McIvor. A nest of sniffers lived here then. One of them had been lying on the stairs, with a flies crawling out of his mouth.

Sonny tiptoed into the shack and peered into the bedroom. It was dark inside, and there was a torn mattress on the floor. A few scattered clothes. A torn-out page from a *Victoria's Secret* underwear catalogue on the wall. He turned around. His heart jumped.

Roy was standing in the doorway.

Backlit by the light of evening, Roy was a humpy silhouette. He carried a large sack over his shoulders. Sonny had a momentary nightmare image of a child's body inside.

"Copenace!" Roy laughed. "You scare me like that!" He dumped the bag. A dozen tin cans clattered onto the floor. Roy dropped to his knees and began sorting through the cans. "C'mon Copenace. Too much bullshit. Help me, eh?"

"Put that stuff down. I want to talk to you."

Roy ignored him. He unscrewed the top of a Coleman fuel can, sniffed the interior, shook it, and tossed it over his shoulder. Checking each can, he tossed the empty ones aside and hoarded the others in a pile. "What's goin' on, Copenace?"

"Come on outside," said Sonny. "I want to talk to you."

"Too much bullshit."

Sonny had a vague plan to get Roy out of the shack, get him moving. Like a drunk in a bar. If you just get him moving towards the exit, that's half the battle. "Let's go," he said. He patted Roy on the shoulder.

Roy stood up, but still resisted. "Wait wait!" He dribbled a paint can into the garbage bag, then held the bag up to his face. He inhaled deeply, shivered.

"Come on," Sonny said, wrestling Roy towards the door. Roy's shoulders and arms were bulky and hard. Sonny thought, *He's way stronger than me.* "Let's go for a walk!" Sonny insisted, pushing Roy towards the door.

Roy laughed. "That's bullshit."

He pushed Roy out the door. Outside, the ground was turning white. Snowflakes drifted down as Sonny led Roy down the stairs and towards the woods, holding his arm, leading him like a disobedient child. When they got to the boat, Sonny pushed him into the boat. "There we go."

"What the fuck is this bullshit?"

"Never mind." Sonny poled the boat away from shore and got the motor going. Roy slumped down in the bottom of the boat, rolling his head back and forth, mumbling some private song under his breath. Sonny cruised out onto the river, threading through the narrow place in the bridge where the current heaved and spooled between the mottled walls of concrete. Roy abruptly climbed up onto one knee and began unscrewing the fuel tank's gas cap. It was a narrow passage way between the walls and Sonny had to keep his hand on the steering tiller. "Hey don't touch that!"

Sonny pushed Roy and he shoved Sonny back. The boat slewed out of control and they swerved into the concrete wall with a bang. The boat reared up one side and the propeller came free of the water, cavitating and roaring. Within a split second, Sonny felt himself falling over the side into the river.

Sonny, half in and half out of the boat, grabbed the gunwhale and hung on. Frantically clawing for the tiller, he caught the red plastic safety lanyard and gave it a yank. The motor stopped. He threw his leg over the gunwhale and climbed back in. His pants and jacket were soaked. His heart pounded. *Man, this is bad,* he thought. *I can't believe this.* For a minute he crouched in the boat, wringing the water out of his jacket, trembling with shock. Roy was gone.

"Roy!" he barked, standing up. He took a life cushion out of the hatch and looked for someone to throw it to. "Roy!" he yelled.

Silence. The snowflakes coming down, hissing into the water.

Maybe he's drowned, Sonny thought. *Raped a seven year-old girl, and killed her with a cinder block. Now the sonofabitch is dead. What do I care?*

Sonny clipped on the safety lanyard and sat down to start the motor. But then he heard something. He listened hard, his heart thumping in the rustle of falling snow.

A shout.

Sonny started the motor and cruised towards the sound. The current was strong and he travelled fifty yards before he saw anything. Then Roy suddenly appeared – swimming slowly and purposefully towards the shore. Sonny accelerated gently, moving towards him.

Sonny thought, *nothing's easy. But there's no one watching and I know what I have to do.* Coldly, he shifted the motor into neutral. Roy's hand came out of the water and clamped onto the gunwhale. Sonny lifted the beaver pole and aimed the hooked end down at Roy's face. Sonny twisted the hook in Roy's jacket and pushed him under. He pushed the pole downward until six or eight feet of it was under water. The pole bucked and shivered in his hands but he held it firmly, kneeling, feeling the current turn the boat slowly as they drifted downstream.

Finally the pole stopped shuddering. Sonny could feel the weight still there, tangled in the hook. He jiggled the pole up and down until the hook came free. Then he threw the pole in the bottom of the boat and sat down.

He waited, listened.

But there was no other sound except the soft rustle of falling snow. Suddenly the realization of what he'd done rushed over him like a huge wave and his stomach heaved.

He leaned over the side and vomited.

Kneeling in the boat he drifted, stared down at his hands. After several minutes he splashed icy water on his face and stood up. It was utterly silent. Snowflakes scribbled down, clicking against the canvas of his baseball hat. Finally he yanked the starter cord and the motor roared to life.

He sat down, weighing some deep personal decision, and thought about Diana. What was he going to tell her?

It was dark now. Snowflakes as big as feathers twirled down and disappeared into the smooth black water. Across the river, through the gauzy snowfall, he could see the lights of town. Five minutes went by and Sonny didn't move. Then he came to a decision, shifted the motor into gear and drove the boat towards home.

Egyptian Sunday
VEN BEGAMUDRÉ

The first time Melissa Jameson brought her boyfriend out to the valley, her family thought she'd got his name backwards. Her sister, Amanda, figured Melissa was nervous they might raise objections, and that was why she introduced him as Prakash David. Melissa wasn't nervous and she didn't get it backwards. He was Hindu on his mother's side and Christian on his father's, and his last name really was David. Amanda, who was older than Melissa, didn't raise an objection. She raised an eyebrow. It stayed up till she noticed Melissa wanting to ask, "Something wrong?" Then the eyebrow came down. Amanda could have said, "Everything's fine. Heck, he's one nice-looking fella. Nice clothes, nice manners." But getting to know him was another story, since Melissa brought him out only on weekends. Besides, there were complications. Three, in fact – a grown-up one and two little ones.

First came Amanda's husband, Norm, who worked for the CPR. Since Prakash also worked with his hands, in a frame shop, the two young men should have had plenty in common. Not so. It might have helped if they could have gone fishing, but this was out. Prakash didn't fish. It might have helped if they could have gone hunting, but this was out, too. Prakash was a city boy, born and bred. Fish and fowl were things he picked up at Safeway. Worst of all, you could tell Prakash thought Norm was a bore. During their first Sunday dinner, Prakash asked Norm how he liked working for the railway. Norm told him, and told him – especially about the little-black-box which might spell the end of the caboose. Norm said, "As if microchips could replace a real man!"

Next came Amanda and Norm's two children – first Becky, then Lilah, short for Rebecca and Delilah. Good Bible names even if Delilah had given Samson that fateful haircut. At the second Sunday dinner, the little girls called Prakash "Uncle David" till he said David was his last name, so they took to calling him just Prakash. Even if he wasn't a real uncle yet, Amanda guessed it sounded funny to them to have one with a foreign name. Not like Norm's brother, whom the girls called Uncle Horst.

Edna, Mrs. Jameson, didn't raise an objection either. Not really. Her little girl had gone to the city for an education and found herself a bonus, that's all. Mind you, the boy was nearly five years older than Melissa and, as any mother knew, a decent boy of twenty-four would be succumbing to the nesting instinct. As Edna kept telling Amanda, Melissa should spread her wings and keep flying. Wasn't that what she meant to do between university and helping out at the Downtown Mission? Then there was her plan for social work in the Third World. Better yet, it seemed Melissa might not stop at a BA. She was already thinking about grad school – maybe even a PhD. "Imagine!" Edna told her friends in the coffee klatch. "Our Melissa a doctor, kind of." Guarded looks dropped on the card table and snagged on cribbage pegs – looks which warned, "Don't count your chickens before they hatch, Edna Jameson." She was, though. Heck, what was the point of even being a mother if you couldn't count your chickens?

Edna had always known Melissa would amount to something – even if she had been average in high school and hadn't socialized much. Not that the boys ignored her. She didn't have curly hair like Amanda's, but Melissa could wear hers long. And even then she had what the coffee klatch called a full figure. But Melissa always said,

"Maybe next time," if some guy asked her out. Good thing, Edna thought. She wanted her favourite girl to wait before adding two and two the way Edna had, too early on. Amanda – the one who couldn't wear her hair long, the one who still hadn't filled out – had been born seven months and two weeks after Edna's wedding. Such things didn't bear much notice, though. There was something about small town, Saskatchewan, something in the soil or the water, even the air, which caused a lot of babies to drop early. That's why Amanda had been especially careful.

Ray, Mr. Jameson, took his cue from Edna. He liked Prakash because he opened another window on Ray's world. Ray had been to Asia, thanks to Edna's church tours. They couldn't go on all of them, of course, so he'd missed the latest one – to India – and here was someone who wouldn't gloss over it the way *Maclean's* did. Didn't bother Ray that Prakash had come over when he was five, or that all he knew about India was what he'd picked up from his folks. Ray took to Prakash right off. Soon they bantered like pals. Mind you, there was always an edge to their banter, something Amanda never noticed between Ray and Norm. The edge came from Prakash not knowing as much about India as he would have liked. Times like this, Ray would try to lighten things up by asking, say, whether India might send an alpine ski team to the Lake Placid Winter Olympics. Then they talked as if they were tossing a football back and forth – a football wrapped in barbed wire.

"Still think it's a shame for his mother!" Ray said. "San-jay Gan-dhi crashing his plane, heir apparent and all."

"Sanjay's better off than all those people he had sterilized," Prakash said. "Would you settle for five bucks in exchange for the family jewels?"

Ray again: "Any jewels we hung onto during the Depression got mortgaged long ago."

Edna snorted in the kitchen. Then she glanced at Melissa, who was making gravy while Amanda mashed potatoes. You couldn't miss the flush on Melissa's face. "Men talk," Edna said.

Melissa, nodding, hoped her mother didn't know everything. Couldn't guess, for instance, she was debating whether to give up her virginity, and here she'd known Prakash only a month.

Amanda knew. She knew his type. They might not believe in sex without love, but once love came knocking they saw no point delaying what might follow.

Edna already suspected as much. After all, wasn't the course of love as predictable as a thunderstorm on a hot prairie evening? Mothers might not like it, but Mother Nature couldn't have it any other way. And so, when Melissa forgot to turn the heat down under the gravy and had to lift the pot off the stove, Edna dropped a hint: "Just don't hurt yourself."

"I think she's made gravy before," Amanda said.

Melissa bit her lip. It was her way of biting her tongue.

Edna, sighing, squinted at the roast through the glass in the oven door. There was so much she'd wanted to tell her girls when they'd been growing up – so much she still wanted to say – but such things usually came out in passing, when there wasn't time for a proper heart-to-heart. Like what to expect later, when you see how well a high school sweetheart you dropped has done. And you wonder how it might have been with him – the one who left town, the one who got away. Like how she knew what small town, Saskatchewan, could do to a girl – ruining her chances of a real life if she didn't get out, too. Even if she did come back from the city the way Amanda had, with her lab tech diploma. Amanda had been following her guidance counsellor's advice: "Remember, girls, it's important to have a career as a back-up in case your husband dies young."

Edna straightened and retied her apron strings. The apron was her Sunday best, linen with a map of Ireland in green and brown. She finally chanced, "Remember what Dad says in his workshop. Measure twice. Cut once."

Melissa and Amanda groaned an agonized, "Mo-om!" Melissa let the pained expression stay on her face to show she didn't read any of this as criticism. "Don't worry," she said.

"I'm not," Edna said. She brushed at Melissa's bangs, then smiled the way mothers did when they reminisced. Once, she'd cut both the girls' hair herself and still did Amanda's. Now Melissa got her hair cut in a real city salon. It was her only extravagance. She'd grown up so used to wearing hand-me-downs, she bought her clothes at the Sally Ann Thrift Shop. "Really," Edna said, "I'm not worrying," and laughed off the lie.

Amanda asked, "Am I allowed to worry, too?"

Getting back to the children – and in the end most such worlds revolve around them – Becky was in kindergarten, but Lilah still hadn't graduated from potty training. Prakash didn't seem to know much about children, because his own sister was older than him. He sat at dinner one Sunday looking blank while Amanda discussed how long Lilah was taking to learn. Edna tried to object to such talk since Lilah was right there, but Prakash interrupted. He asked, "How long can it take? To learn not to fall in. Isn't it just a matter of balance?"

"Huh?" This was Norm.

"Pardon?" This was Amanda.

Melissa started laughing first. Good thing, too, since

it let Prakash sit there grinning while he tried to figure out why everyone thought this was funny. Becky and Lilah laughed the loudest, but only because the grown ups were in high spirits. "Well," Prakash asked, his words broken up by laughter, "how long ... can it take?"

Melissa stopped laughing long enough to explain potty training had nothing to do with balance. "It's about keeping in what's best kept in," she said, "till it's time to let it out."

"And there's a time and place for everything," Edna blurted. Which set Norm laughing so hard he nearly spilled his Baby Duck. And Ray guffawing till he had to wipe his eyes. "This sure ain't it," he said. Which made Edna cover her face with her apron. And Becky and Lilah, who wanted to look like her just now, covered their faces with serviettes and went, "Uh-hah. Uh-hah."

Anyone watching closely would have noticed the one person who barely laughed was Amanda. Oh, she did once it became a general sort of laughing, but not a moment before. Because even while Melissa explained things to Prakash, it occurred to Amanda he might be pulling everyone's leg, especially hers. He wasn't. His people simply didn't talk about things like how to test if a roast is done, and they sure didn't talk about potty training. It was all so new to him, he said, he was fascinated – this after everyone had settled down. But on weekends to come, if he asked Amanda about anything domestic, she replied in a voice which suggested men shouldn't take an interest in such things.

To her credit, Amanda added to her list of Prakash's good qualities – nice looks and clothes and manners – a nice sense of humour. Or at least timing. And that's when she started thinking he had a problem. He brooded too much, but, still, if Amanda had been in Melissa's place and hadn't been engaged when she'd gone off to the city, she might have fallen for a guy like Prakash. Not a reserve Indian, of course – definitely not, given what happened to Norm's sister – but Amanda had to admit she might have fallen for a charmer. A charmer like the Doc.

Dr. Khaladkar was the only other professional Indian the Jamesons had known till now. With a name like Khaladkar, it was no wonder locals called him the Doc. He worked at the hospital and Amanda found she could talk to him about things she couldn't mention to Edna. Like the fact Amanda came from a family cursed with four girls in two generations. The next child with Jameson blood might well be a boy, but he wouldn't be Amanda and Norm's. Two children were a handful, and the Doc agreed when she mentioned this each time she took Becky or Lilah in with a cold. Amanda liked him. She liked him a lot. No surprise there, since he looked like Omar Sharif, if you caught him in the right light. Mainly, though, she liked the Doc because he was so unflappable. Years ago, when Norm had put his foot through a window at his own stag, the boys had taken him to emergency after phoning Amanda. The Doc's wife had left him, and he always seemed to be on call. The boys were more than a bit drunk, so the Doc asked her, after he strapped Norm on the table, "Should I expect anyone else from their party?"

A real charmer, all right, and that was the problem with Prakash. Why a problem, Amanda couldn't say. But sometimes, when Norm lay snoring beside her, she would find herself wondering how life might have been if she'd married someone like the Doc instead of settling for her Norm. How life could still be if she married someone like the Doc. Wouldn't that raise an eyebrow or two? People might notice her for a change instead of always asking about Melissa. Then Amanda would fall asleep and dream about riding a camel while someone sang "The Desert Song," and she would turn to find it was Omar Sharif and – oh, yes, yes, yes! – he would crush her lips with his, and his mouth would taste like figs, and she would flick the tip of her tongue, real slow, across that gap between his teeth.

Their first winter together, Melissa brought Prakash out every weekend. He liked the visits even if it meant sleeping in different rooms, because he fell in love with the place. Every house had a bird house near the gate, and each bird house was painted like the real house behind it. The Jamesons' house and their bird house were purple with green trim. Soon a folk art magazine accepted Prakash's first photo essay, "The Bird Houses of Lilac Grove," but even as the lilacs started to bloom, Melissa stopped bringing him out so often. Father Haygood's sermons were only partly to blame.

You couldn't accuse Father Haygood of intolerance – though there were times his outlook seemed as narrow as the valley – but all that winter he asked things like, "How come it's people like Mother Teresa who do the most good in India? Start mission schools and houses for the dying? Because the Brahmin priests are too busy kowtowing to the authorities." He was talking about what his flock had seen on the last church tour, the one the Jamesons had missed. Either he didn't see the new face in his church, or he didn't realize anyone might object to his sermonizing.

No one, not even Melissa, realized Prakash was taking it personally, till Easter long weekend. That was when he surprised everyone with, "Maybe some Brahmins grow fat, but this Haygood's got his needle stuck in a groove."

"It's nothing," Edna said. She brought the good pepper

211

mill to the table. "Three years ago we went to Thailand, and the rest of the year Mr. Haygood criticized the Buddhist monks. It's just his way of livening up the sermons."

Prakash asked, "By attacking people who can't defend themselves?" Then he dropped the subject, though not before Melissa gave him a strange look.

And not before Amanda gave him an even stranger look. She was thinking of a dog she and Norm once owned. It was an Irish setter Norm had taken from his ex-brother-in-law, Eddie Lavallée. Eddie had rescued it from Norm's brother, Horst, who'd used it for calf roping practice. Norm only took the dog from Eddie to stop Horst from going on – about Lavallées being good enough only to keep mongrels. If Amanda held its dish out, that dog came at her sideways, in case it had to make a run for it. Eddie would laugh at her and say, "Ya can't feed a dog that walks sideways." And even if the dog never did learn to trust her, she was sorry to see it go, lost one night in a blizzard. She didn't tell this story now, because she didn't think Melissa would appreciate it.

Father Haygood aside, the reason Prakash and Melissa no longer drove out so much was that their relationship was changing. That was what it was now, no simple city romance. Early on it had depended on those endless discoveries about the other person which fuel love like the first phase of a rocket. Now that the booster had burned itself out, things were a bit less novel and a lot less frantic. Prakash didn't like attending every church concert in the city, and he said so. Melissa didn't like making love in his makeshift darkroom, and she said so. Their romance slowed into that second phase where the rocket starts its climb to a stable orbit. They got on with their lives – Prakash with his job at Ye Olde Frame Shoppe, half-time so he could spend the other half with a borrowed enlarger; Melissa with her second year of classes and the Downtown Mission. Their new routine didn't include every weekend in the valley, though Prakash was more welcome than ever. Thanks to the Egyptian.

He wasn't really Egyptian, but that was what everyone called him since he reminded them of King Tut. He, or it, was a ceramic Polish coffin cover made by a real Saskatchewan artist – a coffin cover for a king in yellow, green, and blue. His face glowed with a healthy, oven-fired tan. Prakash won the Egyptian in an art gallery raffle, but he looked out of place in Melissa's house. They gave him to Edna and Ray for their anniversary. Ray was touched, though his way of showing it was to ask Prakash, "Imported just for us?" Ray chipped out part of the wall in the dining room, then plastered around the coffin cover. The first few evenings, Edna left the light on in the dining room – that Egyptian looked so spooky. Then she told Ray to build a cabinet with its own light. She said she would prefer Becky and Lilah smudged the glass, not the Egyptian. Even so, she left the dining room light on if Ray was out late.

Amanda didn't say what she thought besides, "Makes death look real colourful." She clearly gave it some thought, though. She and Norm had bought Edna and Ray a barnboard coffee table.

The Egyptian plastered into that wall cemented Prakash's place in Melissa's heart. She let him help her finish her basement and even let him frame in a darkroom. If the house was ever sold, the darkroom could be converted into a full bath. Good thing, too, since it wasn't really her house. Edna and Ray had bought it cheap – a handyman's special – as an incentive for their girls to get a taste of city life. It was also for the Jamesons to stay over when they drove in, which didn't happen much now, since they didn't want Melissa to think they were checking up on her. They knew, but pretended they didn't, that Prakash spent almost every night in the house.

Amanda suspected as much. You couldn't call her a prude. It was just that, like everyone else, she had her limits. She'd slept with Norm before taking her turn down the aisle, but at least she'd waited till they were engaged. Not only were Melissa and Prakash not engaged – they never once mentioned marriage. Since Amanda was Ray's favourite, he should have known something was up, but she kept things to herself till it was too late. Edna could tell. When the family got together now, Amanda watched Prakash so closely she reminded Edna of a marsh hawk. Except that sometimes there was a soft look in Amanda's eye you never saw in a marsh hawk's. Other times, the look went hard, but Edna couldn't know Amanda was remembering Norm's sister. The one who'd married Eddie Lavallée.

Finally Amanda decided to get things off her chest. She waited till she and Melissa were washing up while the rest of the family was out back trying their hand at croquet.

"Remember Gert?" Amanda said. She meant Gertrude, Norm's sister.

"Why?" Melissa asked. No one had mentioned Gert in years.

"Oh, nothing. Just wondering what she's up to." So much for getting things off your chest, Amanda thought.

Melissa rinsed and Amanda dried, while they watched Prakash help Lilah make her shots. It was so obvious, Amanda could scream – the connection between Prakash and Eddie. Eddie had been Indian, too. Not East Indian. But because he lived on a reserve, people in town saw only one side of him. They shrugged when Gert reminded them how, during rows between cottage owners and reserve people, you could trust Eddie to find a way of sorting things out so everybody won.

Gert moved to the reserve the day she married him. They had two boys and, at first, she would drive in for Sunday dinner with Norm and Horst and their folks. But after Eddie and Horst fell out over the dog, Eddie stopped coming, even after Horst moved to Alberta. One night, Gert was at bingo and Eddie stayed home. He wasn't much for drinking, but just to be sociable, he was helping a friend scrape the last drop of swish from a barrel. The older boy, all of four, had been playing outside since supper and got his hands frostbitten. It scared Eddie near to death. His friend decided to set things right before Gert came home. While Eddie went looking for a car to borrow, the friend boiled water and tried to pour it on the boy's hands. Gert moved her boys off the reserve the next day.

Amanda saw Eddie around for a while till he, too, drifted into Alberta. As for Gert, she and her boys were long gone, out on the west coast. The last card from her had been three years back, before Prakash's time. Amanda didn't think anyone would see the connection – the good as well as the bad – but she had no intention of taking the blame for what might happen to Melissa's children. And Amanda sure wasn't going to let Melissa get away with things Amanda could only dream about.

This business of getting away with things – it lay at the heart of the problem between the Jameson girls. And it kept simmering on the back burner. Not that anyone could put a finger on it, even if everyone had taken turns adding to the broth. A pinch of this, a dash of that. Edna especially, though if you asked her she would have frowned as if it didn't bear thinking about.

Like so many things, it had started innocently enough – years ago – when other children had been bragging on the school bus about the different languages their parents knew. Amanda said Edna spoke Ukrainian, even a bit of Polish. When Melissa asked Edna about this later, Edna shouted at Amanda, "I'm a Jameson now, not a Lapchuk!" Edna dragged Amanda into the laundry room and washed her mouth out with soap. Amanda didn't speak to Edna for days after that, till Edna got so upset she threw one of her best cups at the fridge. Amanda and Edna cried and hugged. Then Amanda told Edna she was proud her mother knew those other languages even if Edna wasn't, herself.

But Melissa – if she did something equally bad, she got away with it. She'd gotten away to the city. Now she was getting away with living part time in sin. Not for much longer, though, because Amanda was worrying about the impression it might have on her girls they found out. And they were curious. Becky said things like, "When's Melissa getting married?" If you asked Amanda, the girls were in danger of being exposed to a bit much. More than a bit too soon.

Take the time Prakash told everyone how he'd been hitching a ride on the Number One Highway and an old man had picked him up. The old man asked, "Are you East Indian?" Prakash said, "No, but I was born there." After a while the old man said, "Did you know a lot of East Indians are bisexual?" When Prakash said, "Really?" the old man said, "Are you bisexual? I'm bisexual." This certainly piqued Amanda's curiosity. She'd heard a lot of Egyptians were bisexual, too – or was that Greeks? – and it made them all the more appreciative of their women. For some reason, Prakash told the last part in a Jewish accent, as if the old man said, "You Jewish? I'm Jewish." Edna and Ray laughed. Norm managed a smile. Melissa elbowed Prakash and he went, "Ow!" Amanda wanted to laugh, but she wasn't about to, not with Becky and Lilah right there. Not understanding, maybe, but taking it in all the same. And when it came right down to it, if most such worlds revolved around children, even a fellow who didn't know much about them had better watch out. As Amanda could have told anyone who asked, hell hath no fury like a mother losing control.

One day in Melissa's second winter with Prakash, they phoned to say they were coming out for Sunday dinner, though it wasn't a long weekend. Since Norm would be ice-fishing with the boys, Melissa said she and Prakash would stop in town to pick up Amanda and the girls. So far, so good. Becky answered the door and yelled, "It's Pra-kash." Melissa was waiting in the car.

"I'll just be a sec," Amanda told him. He dawdled in the foyer looking lost, not knowing whether to take his boots off. "Leave them on," she said. "Norm does."

Prakash tiptoed in and stood at the door to the living room. He looked at the photo he'd given them last Christmas, a photo of the bird house in the Jamesons' yard. Then, while she bundled up the girls, he picked up mitts and scarves till she told him, "I can manage." She only said this because he was mixing things up. Becky would look awful with a pink scarf over her green snowsuit, and the red mitts clashed with Lilah's purple one. To change the subject, Amanda said, "Place gets smaller every day. Can't wait till Norm starts on the new one, skylights and all."

Off they went with Melissa at the wheel and Prakash scraping ice from all the breath frosting up the glass. The springs in back squeaked from Becky and Lilah bouncing, the way Amanda and Melissa once had on their way to Sunday school. But when Amanda asked Melissa how her classes were going, Melissa said, "They're going." She didn't even nod when Amanda commented on the trees. These days the trees on the hills looked like bristles on a sow's back, brown on white. They weren't really hills. They only looked like hills because the ground climbed up, back to the level of the prairie, from the narrow lake. Amanda asked, "You know how the local Indians say the valley traps spirits? Because it traps water, and spirits like being near water. What I think is – " She stopped and shrugged, to herself. Melissa didn't seem to be in any mood to talk about spirits.

When the car pulled up, Edna waved through the picture window. Amanda had to run after Lilah when she climbed up on a snowbank. Melissa and Prakash weren't out of the car yet. They were arguing about something, or at least disagreeing. Even after they got out and Melissa headed for the porch with Becky tagging along, Prakash stayed near the car and frowned at the bird house. Amanda knew what he was doing. He always frowned at the bird houses these days, but she couldn't decide if he was comparing his photos to the real thing, or the real thing to his photos.

They finally got inside and out of their parkas. Prakash flopped down on the sofa and put his sock feet on the barnboard coffee table. He flipped through an old issue of *Maclean's* while Ray set up the crokinole board.

Melissa was already in the kitchen when Amanda finished putting the girls' snowsuits away. Amanda thought Melissa would chat with Edna, then watch the game, but Melissa started mashing potatoes. "You go in, relax," she said. But Amanda stayed in the kitchen, and the longer she stayed, the tighter Melissa's brow knit. Amanda wasn't about to leave. Potatoes were her job. Since Edna had the gravy under control, Amanda tried to feel useful by setting the table. Soon Norm stomped in. The cold air reached the kitchen before he got the front door shut. Amanda called down to the girls and everyone took their seat for grace, Ray in his captain's chair in front of the Egyptian.

As usual for Sundays, Edna passed around Baby Duck. As usual, Amanda dropped a maraschino cherry into Sprite for the girls. And, as usual, Prakash didn't want any wine. Amanda knew he drank, though never in front of them. There he was walking sideways again. Melissa nodded for wine, but she barely touched the glass to her lips before setting it down. Prakash took the glass for himself.

Edna said, "Looks like we've finally converted you!"

Ray chuckled.

Prakash said, with an Irish accent this time, "A Papist I was born, a Papist I shall die!" The grown-ups laughed, because they knew he was High Anglican – almost RC, but no follower of the Bishop of Rome. He squinted at Edna as if he might have offended her by mocking her faith. She just laughed, especially when Becky sang, imitating the rhythm, "A hunting we will go, a hunting we will go!"

Amanda shushed her with, "Rebecca Louise!"

It started out as one of the best dinners ever. Prakash asked Norm about work and didn't look bored when he got on to the little-black-box spelling the end of the caboose. After they ran out of small talk, Ray turned up the stereo and everyone listened to the "Music for Unicef" tape. Lilah tried to sing along with John Denver, but Becky glared at her. Then Ray tried to bait Melissa into talking – by saying how much he appreciated all those singers donating their royalties to the Children of the World. It didn't work.

Finally Edna started clearing the table, but the way Melissa said, "No, wait," made Edna stop and sit there with the stack of dishes raised up. That's how Father Haygood held the goblet at communion, with his eyes closed and his lips moving as if he was practising verses tattooed behind his eyelids. Melissa took Prakash's hand in plain sight of everyone and said, "Mom, Dad, we have an announcement." They knew what was coming – it was so obvious – but she couldn't very well stop. "I'm ... we're going to have a baby."

You couldn't hear a thing then except David Frost saying on the tape, "From the General Assembly of the UN, good night." And applause.

Edna kept staring at Ray, so he cleared his throat and said, "That's great." He meant it. He really was thrilled.

All Amanda could think of was, "There she goes getting away with it again." Before Amanda could stop herself, she asked, "Melissa, how could you?" If only Amanda hadn't said this – if only she hadn't been looking at Prakash and thinking of the Doc – things might have turned out different. Then again, maybe not.

Prakash let go of Melissa's hand. He stared at Amanda as if trying to decide what shutter speed to use. "You've got two of your own," he said. "Don't you know how?"

She tried to say, "That's not what – "

"I know that," he said. "You mean how could we without getting engaged first."

"Don't worry, Amanda," Melissa said. She was tracing the flowers on the tablecloth. "I wouldn't dream of trying to outdo your wedding." Melissa had every right to be disappointed with Amanda, but it was still the wrong thing to say, and from that moment on the conversation became the kind where you say only the wrong thing. Worse, even people who weren't in the room played a part, all those ghosts squeezed around the Egyptian – Gert, Eddie, and Horst. And even the damn dog.

"At least we had a wedding," Norm said. He would have said more if Amanda hadn't frowned at him to warn that Becky and Lilah were all ears.

"Auntie Melissa," Becky cried, "if you don't get married, me and Lilah can't be flower girls!"

Melissa said, with heartfelt sympathy, "I never thought of that."

All this time, all of a minute or less, Amanda tried to think of a story to explain how she felt. She thought about Mary and Martha. How the person who does all the work – like Amanda, who'd come back instead of staying in the city – doesn't get the credit. But she didn't want to raise this now. Then she remembered Gert and Eddie Lavallée and started with, "Oh Melissa, can't you see what you'll do to your kids?"

When Amanda stopped to choose her next words carefully, Prakash jumped in with, "What you mean is, you don't want mixed blood in your family."

"That's not what she meant at all," Melissa told him. He didn't hear her lame, "And you know it."

"That's right," Amanda said. "Can't you see all the love in the world won't help your kid when he comes home crying? Because some bully called him a – "

"Brownie?" Prakash made it sound like a swear word. "Paki? How about Nitchie? That's what they call Indians around here, isn't it?"

Becky and Lilah were all eyes now. And open mouths.

"Some people might," Norm said. "We don't."

When Prakash snorted, Melissa dug her fingers into his arm. "Amanda's just trying to be practical," Melissa told him. "No, pragmatic."

He lowered his eyes and said, "Like the polka-dot woman?"

"The what?" Edna asked.

Melissa took Prakash's hand under the table. "Last week," she said, "we went looking for a place of our own —"

"What's wrong with the house?" Ray asked.

"A place of our own," she said. "Prakash called about an ad, and the woman said they had two vacancies. We got there an hour later, and this woman in a black top with white polka dots opened the door. Prakash said we'd come to look at the suites, and she said they were taken. It hadn't been more than an hour! He wouldn't believe her. She said she could show him the receipts for the damage deposits."

Ray asked Prakash, "You called her bluff?" Then Ray leaned forward. "Didn't you?"

"She slammed the door in his . . . in our faces," Melissa said.

Amanda had to admit, "I don't get it."

"She was lying through her polka dots," Prakash said. "She thought I was white when I phoned. Probably just pragmatic, worrying what the neighbours might think."

Ray reached for the Baby Duck and cleared his throat. "I don't know what all this is about," he said, "but I don't care for it. Melissa's going to have a baby and maybe it'll be a boy, and we've got a great excuse to celebrate."

If he hadn't said this, Amanda could have walked away without another word, but here was one more hurt she could chalk up on the list she kept to herself. Even if she was his favourite, she was tired of feeling guilty for not having given him a grandson.

"No," Amanda said, "let's talk." She looked at Edna, who kept her eyes on the Egyptian, safe behind the glass. Norm was distracting the girls by tearing their serviettes into snowflakes. "Don't you people get it?" Amanda cried.

"There'll always be someone reminding the kid he's not all Canadian."

Prakash asked, "Someone like you?"

"Come on, Melissa," Amanda said. "He's filled your head with crazy ideas. Just because you're thinking of spending your summers in India working on some ashram doesn't mean you can keep it up. What's going to happen to the poor kid if you shuttle him back and forth?"

Prakash slapped the table so hard, he winced. He took a deep breath and spat out the words like broken teeth. "Jesus H. Christ," he said. He stopped long enough to mumble, "Sorry," to Becky and Lilah. They'd clapped their hands over their mouths. Then he carried on with, "I keep telling her not to go! You don't hear me talking about the good-old old country. But I still love her for wanting to do it."

Melissa tried to say, "You never told me that," but he still wasn't listening to her.

"Your idea of vision," he told Amanda, "is planning the dream home Norm's going to build if you keep serving him hand and foot."

"Just a goddam second," Norm growled. He got up by pushing down on his fists. He was shorter than Prakash but Norm was no slouch. Then he blew it by saying, "At least I'm not such a tightass I store up my farts!"

"That's enough," Edna cried. "Both of you stop it right now!" She balled up the end of her apron, the one with the map of Ireland. "I never thought I'd hear such things in my house! Prakash, I like you a lot, but you've got no right to say anything you please."

He bit his lip, a habit he'd picked up from Melissa. He glared at Amanda as if she'd set him up – not himself, more like, by worrying the whole drive out.

Next Edna ordered Norm, "Sit down," and he did.

"As for you, young lady," she told Amanda, "I'm ashamed of myself for having raised such a … *durnie doynka*!" This meant "crazy daughter" in Ukrainian but it sounded a lot worse. Edna pressed the crumpled end of the apron to her face.

Amanda tried to say, "But, Mom – !"

Ray glared at Amanda and snapped, "Save it!"

Lilah was tugging at his arm for some Baby Duck, so now she thought he meant her. Quiet tears rolled down her cheeks. If it wasn't one thing, Amanda thought, it's another.

"No apologies, no goodbyes," Ray said. "All of you leave and don't come back. Not till you settle this. I don't care if you have to meet halfway waving white flags, but don't expect Mom or I to do it for you." He got up, parked himself in front of the TV, and switched it on. Too loud.

Amanda and Norm left first. Norm carried Lilah. Becky whined, "Des-sert!" Amanda shushed the girls in the ranch wagon while he scraped the windows. He hadn't plugged it in, because Melissa's car was in the way. He was in such a hurry to leave, they stalled at the end of Bird House Lane. He dropped Amanda and the girls in town and went back to his ice-fishing hut, the one place he really felt at home. As for Amanda, it took her all afternoon to calm the girls. She decided it would snow on Waikiki before she let them near Prakash again, family ties or no family ties.

If Amanda learned anything that day, it was that you couldn't teach people from another culture a thing. Not Dr. Khaladkar, who thought the best of people. Not even Eddie Lavallée, who'd laughed at her once and said, "Ya can't feed a dog that walks sideways." Then she knew she should have reminded everyone about Gert and Eddie – made them listen for a change – but of course she only decided this while rocking Lilah to sleep. Seemed like the way of the world. Either you never got the right words out, or you got up the nerve too late. Then Amanda fell asleep, too. She dreamt about riding a camel through a blizzard, and when she woke up, she knew the awful truth. Here she was pushing twenty-six and if she didn't do something drastic, Omar Sharif would ride right by. What could she do? It wasn't the kind of thing she could discuss with Edna, or with Father Haygood, and she certainly couldn't mention it to the Doc.

There wasn't much else. No throwing of cups at the fridge to cause a tearful clearing of the air. No blissful revelation like the one Saint Peter got when he tried to leave Rome. Life went on as life has a habit of doing.

Melissa had a girl she called Rani. This means queen in Hindi and it's easy to spell. After Melissa graduated, she joined Social Services. Next year she's starting on her Masters, in Admin. Prakash stays home and works in the darkroom when Rani's asleep. He's printing photos for his first solo show. It's on fringe prairie religious groups like the Moslems of Lac Labiche, Alberta. And, yes, he's an expert on potty training.

Edna and Ray talk about retiring to the Okanagan, but this would put them too far from the grandchildren. It may not be such a problem now, what with Amanda moving to the coast. If Edna and Ray can't be near all the grandchildren, better to be near two than just one.

Who would have thought Amanda and Norm would split up? No, who would have guessed it would take so long? To get the girls' minds off the separation and the move, she took them to Expo '86. One morning, waiting in line with them at the Egyptian Pavilion – made up like the tomb of Rameses the Second – she got talking to an electronics engineer. Tall fellow with a tan she could tell didn't stop at his collar. He'd done some work for the pavilion and was going through for the third time. Even wangled them a tour behind the scenes to show the microchips controlling the lights.

The week Amanda's divorce from Norm came through, she moved in with her new man. They might get married if they have children of their own. Then again, they might not. He's from one of those Sikh families, though he doesn't wear a turban and he keeps his hair cut short. Problem is, his family's not too keen on him marrying a divorcée. You'd think they'd be happy he found himself a Canadian girl, but they do have their standards.

There's plenty of time to sort things out. First things first. He's working on his mom, who says maybe – just maybe – she'll let him bring Amanda and the girls for tea.

Minor Alterations
BARBARA SCOTT

On the cold vinyl bench, cold she can feel through her jeans, cold transmitted along her spine to bare breasts bumping against the pale blue paper gown, Marnie sits. The stickiness that always lies between her breast and ribcage itches. She hopes he won't have to pick up her breasts and touch that sticky spot with its permanent film of sweat. She hopes this can be decided quickly. If it could be done in the office while she waited, she would do it immediately. It, this, the thing she can't name.

The chart on the other side of the closed door rustles. A rapid knock-knock, the handle turns. Marnie shivers.

His coat is pristine, black trouser legs jutting out at knee level, squeaky leather shoes. He closes the door precisely, smiles beneath greying eyebrows.

"I assume my receptionist explained the procedure to you, that this is just a preliminary visit to give you an idea of what to expect," he says through even white teeth.

"Yes," she says, though it was Harold who phoned for the appointment, made all the arrangements. She wonders if the doctor has had his teeth straightened. A plastic surgeon has to look good. To give the patient confidence. A smile glimmers within her but doesn't quite make it to her face. She can feel herself receding from her exterior, deeper and deeper within, away from the hands that will eventually have to explore her surface.

"Good." He is at the sink, washing those hands. Squeak of lather on skin. His hands are very pale. She hopes they will not be cold.

"All right then," he says in a smooth voice. "Let's

just have a look." And he peels back the gown, whisper of paper on skin, cool air a breath behind. Gooseflesh springs up around her nipples.

He probes each breast, fingers sinking into the heavy, blue-veined globes. "Mmm, no problem there," he says. "What size were you thinking about?" His hand rests just under the breast, as though weighing it.

Marnie forces herself not to pull away. His hand is warm, more repulsive to her now than the cold she dreaded. Her mind wheels. Size? Does he want inches? God in heaven, will he pull out a chart and convert to metric? Deep below her surface, a rumble.

"I assume you've thought about this a good deal."

But she hasn't really. It was Harold who suggested she look into getting a breast reduction. One night he traced with his finger the permanent bruises, caused by her bra straps, on her shoulders, and said it couldn't be healthy, that much weight, now, could it? And when Marnie said she was used to it, they didn't even hurt, and after all she'd been this size since she was thirteen, he very gently said that simply getting information didn't do any harm, did it? She let things slide. Hoped he'd forget if she did nothing. But after a couple weeks he handed her a piece of paper bearing the time and date of her appointment. The surgeon was booked solid and couldn't fit her in for a month, and for almost that whole month she managed not to think about it at all. Instead, she found herself thinking again and again about the Mykonos Restaurant and Lounge. Crash of dishes and swearing of cooks in the kitchen, steamy dishwasher going full blast, garlic and feta and tomato strong in the nose and sly sips of retsina strong on the tongue – all the details sunk low in her memory, labelled Life Before Harold. Before everything.

"Waitress, over here."

The lounge was packed and she was run off her high-heeled feet. When she first started the job she wore brown loafers that matched her pleated wool skirts. And blazers, or loose-fitting sweaters, feeling as though she were living at home again, with her mother checking her over for the first day of school, lips pursed and hands pulling down on her blouse with sharp tugs, "Really, Marnie, you must wear looser-fitting clothing. When you tuck in like that you look all bust."

After a couple of days Zaros took her aside in the coat check room and said, "Look kid, it's a restaurant, not an office, why not get yourself some sexier clothes and shoes and raise your liquor sales. That's where the money is. Liquor sales, and the tips, too," he added, tapping her ass lightly with a coat hanger. So she bought a black sweater with rhinestone buttons, and a purple skirt that was tight over the hips but flared out to just above knee level, and she thought she looked pretty good. Not slender, never that. But good in a fleshy sort of way. If you liked curves she was passable.

"Yes sir, can I help you with anything?"

He was with his wife, at least Marnie assumed the woman was his wife. He'd ordered for both of them, steak, baked potato, salad with house dressing. Maybe the steak wasn't cooked the way he liked it – medium rare, he'd said. She could see brown and red juices leaking into the baked potato, but wouldn't know if that meant it was medium rare or not. Marnie liked her meat cooked.

"Sir?"

"You know," he said with a smile, eyes not meeting hers, travelling somewhat lower, "I've been watching you for some time, and I have to say, you must have awfully big feet."

"Excuse me?"

"I said you must have awfully big feet."

Marnie glanced at his wife for some kind of clue, but the woman's eyes were fixed on her plate as she searched for a crouton beneath layers of lettuce. The man's eyes were riveted to her rhinestone buttons, more tactile than any touch, and Marnie had to make an effort not to move her hands to her breasts. She stared at him dumbly, not sure what to do. He was taking up her time, people at other tables were watching, and she probably had an order up in the kitchen. Why wouldn't he just get to the point? His wife was scraping up some creamy house dressing with her fork. The man's eyes were still at her chest as he said, with the same friendly smile, "I can't figure out how it is you don't fall right over."

Marnie inhales deeply.

"Yes, I've thought about it," she says.

"Good. Well, what I always do is show the patient where the scars will be and then send you home to think about it."

He pulls out a ball-point pen, pushes one breast up against Marnie's upper chest to make things a bit easier, then pulls the skin around her nipple taut between his thumb and forefinger. Her skin snags the nib as he draws a circle round the nipple. It tickles, and sends a shiver to her groin. She blushes and tries not to squirm. He pushes the breast up still farther and draws a line straight down from the nipple along the curve of the breast to the ribcage. But when he tries to draw a semi-circle along the lower curve of the breast, his pen slides over the sweat there, refuses to leave a mark. Marnie's cheeks burn as he flops the breast down, goes over to the sink and comes back with a tissue. He lifts the breast again, wipes away the faint trace of sweat, then goes back to his task. Marnie stares over the top of his head at the certificates on the wall. McGill. Harvard. Shiny black type on cool white paper. Gold seal and flourishing signature biting into the linen matte.

She never did say anything to the man in the restaurant. Just walked away. She thinks now, though she has remembered and restructured the scene so many times she can't be sure, that she may have cast the woman one long look of pity before turning her back. Funny. To turn it all on the woman like that.

She didn't even quit the restaurant. The man wasn't a regular and, as it turned out, he never came back, so there was no point in making a fuss, though she did invest in a bra that encased and controlled her breasts with underwires and thick straps, an ugly contraption with lace trim. A few weeks later she met Harold and never looked back. He was dining alone. She was drawn to him from the moment she took his drink order, the touch of grey at his temples and in his moustache, the neat press of his suit, paisley tie with single diamond pin. Before carrying his martini to the table she straightened her sweater, smoothed down her skirt, sucked in her tummy muscles and held them tight. Under those cool grey eyes she felt the rhinestone buttons a shade large, the purple a touch gaudy. He took an appreciative swallow of martini, rolling it round his tongue, then carefully unfolded his napkin while he waited for his food order. She made it her business to give him perfect service, alert to the exact level of wine in his glass, the moment his knife and fork lay parallel across his plate. And as he dropped his credit card lightly onto the bill tray he said, "Are you free for a drink after work?"

"I really shouldn't," Marnie wavered.

He smiled. "I'll pick you up at midnight."

She tumbled into bed with him that same night and he tended to her body with the same care and precision she had observed in his handling of napkin and cutlery. His cool fingers on her hot skin etched indelible patterns of desire, intricate and involved, until she pleaded for him to let them dissolve into release. They stayed in bed three days. "Don't leave," he said. "Phone in sick," and so she did, Harold nibbling at her ear, teasing her nipples with his fingertips, while she tried to convince Zaros she had the flu. Harold wouldn't even let her go out for groceries, and they ate their way through his refrigerator, bringing back to the bed bread and cheese, fruit and milk or wine, so as not to be too long absent from the mingling of their moist scents in the sheets and pillows. At one point when she got up to go to the bathroom after yet another tangled coupling he held her hand, pulling her back, and cried, "That's *my* body, bring it back here," and she laughed and laughed and loved him from that moment. When he finally gave in to her pleas and let her go she stood before her reflection in the mirror, tousled hair, eyes slightly bruised with lack of sleep, mouth swollen with kisses rough and sweet. For the first time she thought, "I am beautiful." And she ran her hands over the breasts he had kissed, the hips he had strained against, the pubic hair that had been entwined with his, cherishing this body that he had cherished until the cold defeated her and she scurried back to bed. Shivering, she slid beside him and tried to nuzzle in close, but he held her back so that he could look at her. With strong hands he scooped her hair up on either side of her face, cradling her skull. "You have such beautiful hair," he murmured, the strands tumbling between his knuckles. "Look at all these gold highlights. You really should cut it to show them off more, you know."

She lost her job because Zaros phoned her apartment to find out how she was doing and her roommate hadn't seen her for three days. But she didn't care. She packed up her things, leaving most of her clothes behind on Harold's suggestion. He would buy all she needed. And she was delighted. Make me new, Harold. Mould me, shape me. Make me yours. When I am yours I am lovely. Loved.

"Now these marks are where you'd have scars." The doctor says, flicking the nib of the ballpoint back into the barrel. "First we make an incision round here and remove the nipple, then make another down the mid-section of the breast and along the bottom, and kind of fold the skin over." His fingers trace the lines on her skin. "Do you sew? My wife does; says it reminds her of making a dart, just tucking in the excess material" – he pinches together a fold of her skin – "like so. Quite simple really." He releases her skin and it relaxes into its original contours.

"What about ...pain?"

"Well, that's a problematic question since people experience pain at different levels. Most of the women I've seen seem to feel the end results are worth the discomfort. Pain is a relative thing, really."

From the first Marnie loved Harold's drive for perfection, the way he pinched the skin at his taut belly and grimaced if he could capture more than a quarter of an inch, added an extra twenty situps to his nightly routine. She would lie in bed and watch him, delighting in the ripple of stomach and chest muscles. "Why not join me?" he asked, on occasion, and she chuckled, whipping back the sheets in invitation. "Why bother when I can get all the exercise I need lying down?" Shortly after that she started finding self-help books all over the house, in the bathroom and bedroom and kitchen, splayed open with the spine bent at chapters on diet and exercise and self-esteem. One night as she lay in bed waiting for Harold to finish his routine, she flipped through a book called *The Psychology of Winning*, the chapter on how to see yourself as you really are. Strip completely, and then put a paper bag over your head, with holes cut so you can see out, then examine yourself from every angle. The author's theory was that when you look in the mirror and see the friendly face you are used to, you are able to rationalize the flab, the flaws, the wrinkles. Cut off that face, the book said, blot it out, and you see the headless body of a stranger.

"Harold, listen to this!" She read him the passage as he worked through his side push-ups.

"Why knock something you haven't tried," he panted. "It might prove helpful."

"You've got to be kidding!" She hooted at the thought of Harold standing nude in front of the mirror with a paper bag over his head. "You haven't tried this, have you?"

"No," he grunted between push-ups, "but I think I have a pretty fair idea of how I look, what needs improving."

"Oh, I see," she giggled, "and I haven't, I suppose."

But Harold had turned to leg lifts and didn't answer.

Marnie went back to the book, which told her that men should maintain their optimum body weight at about one hundred and seventy pounds. And women theirs at about one hundred. Oh come on, she thought. It reminded her of some *National Geographic* special she'd seen on sea lions, with great galumphing jowly males pushing around sleek little lionesses half their size. She turned to share this joke with Harold but thought better of it. Underneath the bedclothes she pinched the skin at her waist.

The doctor walks to a cabinet in one corner of the room and pulls a piece of paper from a file. "This is the waiver you'll have to sign if you decide to go ahead with the procedure." He has not once called it surgery. "It tells you the things that could go wrong."

Marnie holds the paper between numb fingers. "Can you give me a rough idea…?"

"Well, for example, with all cases involving a general anaesthetic, there's some risk. That's laid out here." He points at the paper, then runs his finger down a few sentences. "Here you'll see that, even though we try our best, we can't always guarantee that both breasts will be exactly the same size. And of course, because we actually remove the nipple and then re-attach it, there can be, in rare cases, some problems with blood supply. Occasionally, very occasionally, the nipple doesn't get the proper blood supply, and in that case re-attachment fails to take place." He clears his throat. "What I mean is, the nipple could detach itself. Permanently." For the first time he looks directly into Marnie's eyes, and says, quite kindly really, "I'm sorry to be so blunt, but you do have to know all these things before you decide to go ahead."

Marnie and Harold were having coffee in the mall when the sign caught his eyes: Hair Removal, European Wax Expert.

"Why not check it out?" he said to Marnie.

"Oh, I don't know, Harold."

"You could probably get everything done at once," he said after a slow mouthful of coffee. "Sideburns, chin, even your upper lip. You have a little bit of a moustache, you know."

Marnie's hand went to her chin. Only last night Harold had complained again about the poky little hairs digging into his chest as she lay within the circle of his arm, and she had moved to her side of the bed, poking and pulling at a stiff bristle with her finger and thumbnail until Harold finally asked what on earth she was doing, she was shaking the bed. She tried to keep the hairs controlled with the tweezer, but every now and then she missed some.

Marnie's face flamed. "Maybe later, Harold," she said. "I'll phone them, find out the rates."

"No time like the present. Maybe they could even take you now." He put a few coins on the table. "Come on."

"Oh, I can see exactly what you mean," the receptionist said, holding Marnie's face in her hand and turning it this way and that. "Don't you worry about a thing." Her touch so candid, so accepting, a cool promise of smooth and glowing skin. "We can have you fixed up in no time."

"What exactly is involved in the procedure?" Marnie asked.

"It's quite simple, really." The receptionist smiled. "We spread melted wax over the area, let it cool slightly and then pull it off and voila, the hair comes with it."

"See, Marnie," Harold said, "simple."

And in no time Marnie was in the chair, with the petite blonde waxer showing Harold the routine. The electrically heated bowl of wax, a sickly yellow colour, the wooden pallet knife.

The hot wax on her lower jaw and chin brought tears to Marnie's eyes. She saw herself a blur in the mirror, ugly yellow splotches over her face one minute, a tearing wrench, and the yellow splotches became an angry red. "Darn," the waxer said. "Missed some, we'll have to try again. How are you doing? Okay?"

Of course I'm not okay, Marnie wanted to say. You

just yanked off half my skin with the first try and now you want to pour molten wax on what's left. But she could not say anything, not with Harold standing over her. He had asked if he could watch.

"Okay," she said.

"Sometimes we have to go over the area up to four times to get all the hairs," the waxer said, scooping up a blob of yellow.

Marnie's tears edged up over the rim of her eyes, leaked back into her hairline.

Harold peered at her forehead. "Do you ever do anything with the hairline itself?" he asked. "I've always thought Marnie would look lovely with a widow's peak."

The next day Marnie stared at her winsome heart-shaped face in the mirror, and spread the cooling lotion the waxer gave her over the sullen red patches on her upper lip, her cheeks, her chin and hairline. Tiny white dots sprang up over the red patches. She hadn't had pimples since she was thirteen. Her hand trembled so hard she dropped the lotion. Splatter all over the sink, the mirror.

"Well, I think that about covers everything," the doctor says. "You haven't said much, but perhaps you need to go home and think it all through. If you think of any other questions, just call and talk to my receptionist and she'll put you through to me on anything she can't answer." He hesitates, glances at her left hand. "You're not married?"

"No, not exactly. There is someone though. Someone serious."

He looks relieved. "Oh, well that's all right then. You go home and talk it over with him. For most women the scarring fades with time, and sometimes vitamin E helps. Still, he'll have to live with it too."

"Yes, I suppose he will."

After he leaves, Marnie dresses, then stands in front of the small mirror in profile. She presses her hands down on her breasts, flattening them, trying to imagine how she'll look. How her clothes will hang. Whether the contours of her belly will be more noticeable once the upper curves are gone.

When Marnie gets home there is a message on the phone machine from Harold. She phones his business number and he answers on the first ring.

"How'd it go?" he asks.

"Fine, Harold, just fine." A buzz on the line makes it difficult to hear what he's saying.

"Well, what did he say? Can he do it?"

"Oh yes, he said it would be perfectly straightforward, really." Marnie holds the phone slightly away from her ear, but the buzzing only gets louder.

"Did he say how soon he could fit you in?"

She twists the phone in her hand, winds the cord round her finger. Coil after coil of black rubber twining round her finger. The connection is appalling, the crackle threatening to become a roar. "Oh yes, that's all fine. I have to go now Harold."

"Wait a minute, Marnie," Harold calls, "I wanted to know…"

"Yes, well, I have to go now Harold. I'll talk to you when you get home." And she slams the phone down in mid-sentence and stands by the desk holding her head.

You've got a bit of a moustache you know…
You must have awfully big feet…

In the master bathroom she strips off sweater and bra. Stares at the blue lines round her nipples, under her breasts, these lumps of flesh that hang halfway to her waist, stuck onto her without her consent at age thirteen, not really her at all. Belonging to anyone who wanted to crack a joke, cop a feel. And now they stare at her, rimmed with blue lines, daring her to prove how much they don't belong to her.

With her pointer finger she traces each line, fingernail cool on hot skin, then runs her finger along her breastbone and neck to her chin. The faintest stubble of hairs returning. She grips one lone hair that escaped the waxing and yanks. Hard. Depilation, she mutters. The word rushes up howling from someplace hidden deep inside her and she clenches her teeth against it. Mammoplasty.

A nip here, a tuck there. A whittling away.

Wrenching the taps on full blast, she runs hot water into the sink, lathers up her hand and a washcloth and scrubs and scrubs at the lines. What about breast feeding, she hisses as she scrubs. How do you breastfeed a baby without a nipple?

When is a breast not a breast?

Panting, she stares at the breasts she has rubbed red and raw. Nothing. The lines haven't faded at all.

Half naked, Marnie walks uncaring past the open windows, soapy water dripping from her breasts onto her jeans, onto the hardwood floors. *How about the one where you draw two stick men with a blob between them: two men walking a breast. Get it?* She fishes in the writing desk in the kitchen till she finds a red felt pen with a wide nib.

When is a breast only a breast? When there's no woman attached.

Eyes fixed on her reflection in the kitchen window, she slowly and methodically draws over every blue line, pen digging into her skin, scoring over and over the lines on her flesh, until she looks as though she is dripping blood.

When is a breast not a breast?
When it's a blueprint.

Gripping the uncapped pen in her fist she sits at the kitchen table. The kitchen is cool, she is shivering and goosefleshed. But she shouldn't have to stand it for long. Harold will be home soon. And before he can even open his mouth she will say

Knock Knock Harold.

Just so she can hear him say, Who's there?

Fourth of October
LINDA HOLEMAN

On the fourth of October, the pain in Melanie's back explodes. It hurts when she stands, hurts more when she sits back on the edge of the bed. Walking with hobbled steps out to the living room, pushing hard on her back with the heels of her hands, she eases herself down onto the couch, and lies on her side, her knees drawn up.

"What are you doing there?" Seamus asks, coming in from the bathroom, rubbing at his hair with a towel. He turns on the TV to the weather channel. "Doesn't your shift start at seven?"

"Yeah. But there's something wrong with my back. I can't go in today."

Seamus comes over and stands behind the couch, staring at the TV. "Are you sure?"

Melanie closes her eyes. "Sure about what? About whether I've got a backache? Or that I can't go to work?"

"It's just that it's…" He stops. A big band version of "Don't Cry For Me Argentina" shrills from the television. "If you don't want to go to work today, stay home. You don't have to pretend there's something wrong with you, Melanie."

Melanie's eyelids fly open. She slowly turns her head so she can look up at him. "Pretend? What's that supposed to mean?"

Seamus's expression doesn't change, his face still directed at the TV. The figures of the temperature and humidity and last year's highs and lows reflect red and yellow on his glasses.

"I thought because of today…because…"

Melanie struggles to raise herself, grimacing, using her

hand along the back of the couch to tug her body into an upright position. A tiny intake of breath, almost a gasp, slips out from between her sealed lips.

"Say it, Seamus." At his name the volume grows. "Say it!" The loudness of her voice seems to increase the pain.

It had started the day before, just a poke, a nudge, each time she turned a patient or leaned across a bed, but by the time she got home from the hospital it was settling in, a tight, hot band across her lower back.

After supper, sitting on the deck cradling a mug of luke-warm coffee, she started to cross her legs, but the band tightened, stopped her with a sudden sharp stab just above the swell of her right buttock. She took a deep breath and put her feet flat on the deck and looked at the darkening of the leaves on the low, bushy mounds of chrysanthemums that edged the garden.

Melanie used to love the colours of fall; something about the velvety golds, the bronzes and dusty burgundies reminded her of well-aged wines.

"Melanie," Seamus called, up to his thighs in coneflowers. Melanie took a sip of her coffee, then leaned forward, carefully, and set the cup on the splintering cedar railing. She looked at Seamus across the small stretch of crisp browning grass, saw the slight stoop of his back as he carefully studied the blossoms, peering into the bristly black centre of each hoop of orange-gold as if waiting for the flower to tell him something, as if it might whisper "I'm ready" or "Go away, not yet."

"Want some of these for inside?" he asked, not looking up.

Melanie shrugged. "Sure."

Seamus had never shown any real interest in the long, narrow perennial garden. But this particular spring, as soon as the last crusty traces of snow were gone, he'd started to work.

Melanie had watched his activity from the deck. It seemed unnatural, the feverish mulching and weeding, the excitement about overnight growth, each sudden cluster of fresh, luminous green that broke through the soil in its predicted spot.

It had been her, not Seamus, who had loved the garden; she had laboured for five springs, adding and separating and cutting back.

"Come see the peonies, Mel," Seamus had called in May, his voice almost disappearing as he bent over. "They didn't even show yesterday."

Melanie imagined the shiny shoots of the peonies, the tiny nubs of shocking pink, thinking how in other years they had amazed her, the quickness of them stretching up and up, changing colour, so that in less than seven days the stubby domes were gone. In their place were slender green stalks, delicately waving in the breeze she made just walking by.

She remembered showing the starting sprouts to Jeremy, holding his hand, squatting beside him and pointing to the fat shafts of pink, like curious worms poking their sightless heads out of the soil to sniff the spring's warmth. Remembered his fingers, the round baby knuckles and almost transparent nails, reaching out, reaching for the peonies.

And she didn't want to see the peonies starting again, so she stayed on the deck.

Seamus had kept up his reports all through the summer. "Looks like this stuff has really spread. All the little mauve and white things. What did you say they were?"

"Artemis," Melanie said, her voice just loud enough to reach Seamus.

"Yeah. Didn't it just go to the edge of the border last

year? Now it's all the way back to here." He stood still, looking at her, his hands in the pockets of his heavy sweater even though the July sun made long bright pools of heat on the grass and garden.

Melanie looked back at him, but she couldn't see his eyes because of the sun's glare on the lenses of his glasses. She smiled politely.

"Oh, and look," he'd said, pointing at his right foot, "you should see how big the…" He stopped, suddenly, but kept his hand where it was, the long thin index finger still aiming at something on the ground in front of him.

Melanie knew what he was pointing at. She had chosen each spot and put in every plant herself, after all. And as she watched Seamus standing there, pointing, it was as if there were one of those cartoon balloons over his head, filled with the words "baby's breath." Melanie felt a sour rush of anger surge up her throat. Anger at Seamus, because she knew he knew what it was, but he couldn't speak the words, couldn't even say "baby's breath." But she kept quiet, didn't call out, "What is it? What is it, Seamus, tell me," forcing him. She let him move on, move away from the bush of tiny white blossoms.

But now, with her curled up in agony on the couch, he has the nerve to question her, question her pain, make her feel there's something wrong with her because her backache coincides with October fourth.

"I *know* what day it is, Seamus," she hisses. "I also know there's something really wrong with my back. Maybe the sciatic; it feels like it's going into my leg." One hand still clutches the back of the couch, the other runs over the top of her short hair, back and forth. "And how dare you say I'm pretending? What have I got to pretend about? What? You're the pretender; *you're* the one who's always pretending nothing's wrong. That nothing happened."

Seamus stares down at her, but the colours of the TV are still there, on his glasses.

"You just go on, every day, like everything's fine. But it's not." She licks her lips. "Our baby died, Seamus, he died, and it's horrible, but you won't even say Jeremy's name, or talk about him." The words push so hard that her jaw feels like it's dancing on an electrical circuit; she knows that her lips and tongue will be zapped, black and lifeless, if she doesn't get the words out fast enough. "You pretend nothing's changed. You want to pretend Jeremy never existed, for Christ's sake." She stares up at him, but it's as if he has no eyes, behind those kaleidoscope lenses. Suddenly she realizes how much it infuriates her, all of it. His glasses, his still body, his quiet acceptance. "It's not normal, Seamus." Each shouted word causes a new river of liquid fire down the back of her thigh and into her calf. "What's wrong with you? Why don't you do something, anything, to show me how you feel? WHAT'S. WRONG. WITH. YOU?"

She realizes her fist is up, over her head, like she's going to punch him somewhere, but he's not close enough, and she uses her clenched fingers to wipe the tears away from her cheeks. "And don't keep your face like that, like it can't move. I hate it." She doesn't really hate it, not his face, but she hates the gauze that wraps his features now. The millions of tiny threads that seem to hold everything together have changed his features into the preserved mask of a mummy.

Seamus turns away.

"Don't you go, dammit. Stay here and answer me. Fight with me." She's shrieking. "Tell me what *you're* going to do today. It's a special day, right? Sort of an anniversary, right, Seamus?" He's standing still, his back to her. "What are you going to do? How are you going to celebrate

Jeremy's death?" She's sobbing, the words coming out in great aching gulps, but she can't stop them. "I guess I'm celebrating by playing sick, is that what you're saying? So? What are *you* going to do?"

Seamus starts walking. He walks across the living room, to the bedroom, then out again, and Melanie hears the dull thud of the front door.

She loosens her grip on the back of the couch. Her fingers are cramped; she lowers herself and grabs a small vermilion cushion from under her head and presses it against her face, screaming into it. Much later, she lifts the cushion and looks at it, wondering if the stains will ever come out.

Eventually she phones the hospital to say she won't be in, swallows two small orange capsules from a bottle in the bathroom cabinet, and goes back to bed. She's not tired, but the pills let her drift into a kind of desperate twilight.

Around eleven she rouses herself enough to take two more pills, but no more of the dazed sleep will come. It's after one o'clock when she gingerly moves her legs, gets out of bed and pulls on her plaid flannel housecoat. Then she lets two more of the capsules slide down her throat. She knows she shouldn't; it hasn't been four hours since the last ones, but she needs the numb, far-away feeling they give her.

She shuffles out of the bedroom, stumbling a little as her thick socks catch on the edge of the hall carpet. She goes to the kitchen and runs water into the sink, scooping a handful into her cardboard mouth.

When she turns off the tap, she notices it keeps dripping. She knows it needs a new washer, knows there's a whole jar of washers downstairs in Seamus's room, his basement workshop.

The room is beside the furnace, a cubicle with a long countertop, the walls covered with that board with all the tiny holes in it. In this small warm room, brightly lit with a buzzing fluorescent tube, Seamus keeps an assortment of tools, dog-eared piles of magazines, an ancient office chair of wood smooth and rich as old honey, and mayonnaise jars and rusting coffee cans filled with nails and screws of all sizes, none of which are ever the right size.

Over the winter evenings, while Melanie sat in the living room holding a book in her lap, Seamus was in his workshop. Melanie never heard any sounds coming from it, never saw any evidence of work, like the bookshelves he'd once built for her, or the bird feeder he'd made when Jeremy was six months old. He'd put it up outside Jeremy's window, so from his crib the baby could watch the desperate flutter of the brave sparrows pushing and digging through the soft snow that kept falling on the tray of seeds that whole winter.

A few times she'd asked him about it, what he was doing, all those hours in the workshop.

"Just sorting through things," he'd say, "re-organizing," although when Melanie had gone in there, a few weeks ago, to get a screwdriver to fix the bathroom doorknob, it looked as messy and chaotic as always.

She runs her hands along the collection of river rocks lined up on the windowsill over the sink, feeling the fine silty layer of dust coating them. Then she glances up, out the window, to the backyard.

Seamus is sitting on the top step of the deck.

She walks, slowly and carefully, to the back door. She opens it, but has to stand still for a moment, her hand on the door jamb, and steady herself, blinking a few times in the cool bright light of the October afternoon. When she calls to Seamus, her voice sounds higher than usual to her own ears; it has a thin, hollow ring, like music played in an empty room.

"What're you doing home?" She leans against the door frame.

"Slow," Seamus finally says, in his usual voice, as if it had been a usual day. "Hardly any customers."

Melanie steps out onto the deck, looks down at the top of Seamus's head, at the thick, red-gold hair. Hair the colour of a maple, after the first frost. Then she sees the box in his lap. He's holding it with both hands. She recognizes it, a rectangular metal cookie tin decorated with a castle, and surrounded by billows of fog, or mist. Scottish shortbread; she got it as a gift once, long ago, from someone at work. She knows she's seen it, the tin, somewhere recently, somewhere that surprised her, where it didn't seem quite right.

Even though Seamus has spoken to her, there's something in the air, some stillness that Melanie can't understand. At first she thinks it's Seamus's anger, like a cloud, like the mist on the tin, swirling and hovering. She lowers herself beside him, one leg stretched out to take the strain off her back, and her knee brushes against his. When he leaves his leg touching hers, she realizes it's not anger, after all.

She doesn't look at him, but at the cookie tin. His thumbs rub slow small circles on the patterned top. She remembers where she saw it.

"Got one of your nail collections in there?" she asks. Stupid question, but she wants to start something, wants him to talk, wants to somehow puncture the dense atmosphere, make a hole in it with her words, so she'll be able to suck some air through, be able to breathe easier.

Seamus makes a small sound, not a yes or no, just a faint murmur, and she looks up from the tin. Studying his profile, the long straight line of his nose, she notices he hasn't got his glasses on. He only used to wear them for driving, but sometime over the winter, she's not sure when, he started wearing them all the time.

He still doesn't look at her, but his thumbs stop moving. One perfect oak leaf corkscrews gracefully in front of them, landing on the toe of Melanie's sock.

Seamus looks down at the leaf, then takes the lid off the tin, and opens the creased tissue paper.

Melanie sees shoes, the small white shoes with scuffed toes, each shoelace threaded through a little bell.

Seamus picks one shoe up, out of its nest of rustling yellow paper. The bell gives a muted chime, a tiny protest at being moved, as he puts it in his left palm. The shoe reaches from the base of his wrist to the middle of his heart line.

"Remember when we bought these?" he says. "He was just starting to walk."

Melanie can't look at him. She keeps her eyes fixed on the shoe, although it's gone all flat and blurry.

"You wanted to get him those little red ones, with straps, but Jeremy wanted these. He kept reaching for them, and shaking them so the bells rang. Remember?"

Melanie leans her head against his arm.

"And we always knew where he was, by the sound of the bells," Seamus says, putting the shoe back beside the other, covering them slowly, his hands resting on the tissue paper before he puts the lid on the tin. Then he sets it down on the step, beside him, and looks at her.

Melanie lifts her head off his arm. She can see herself in his pupils, but there's something wrong with his eyes, or maybe it's hers, from all the pills. She sees herself over and over, reflected back, like a room of mirrors. "I forgot how green your eyes are," she says, and wipes her nose with the sleeve of her housecoat.

He turns away, looks at the garden. "I was thinking of transplanting some of the peonies this afternoon. Didn't you say that fall is the best time for dividing peonies, for moving them?" He looks back at her, his eyes still that brilliant green.

Melanie nods. "I'll come with you," she says.

"Won't it hurt your back?"

"No," Melanie says. She brushes a piece of dry brown leaf off the front of Seamus's sweater, stands up and takes a step towards the garden. She feels Seamus move behind her, feels his breath on the back of her neck.

"No," she repeats, "It's better if I walk."

Turkle
DAVID CARPENTER

A long time ago there was a great storm, a blizzard that pummelled the prairie for one night and one day and another long night. Oldtimers from the district use it as a benchmark for other memories. One of the hardest hit was a farmer who owned more than a section of land along the North Saskatchewan River. On the morning of the great storm this man awakened before dark, walked out into the yard, and noticed that even on the path he took to the barn the snow was up to his knees. In the midst of doing his chores, he discovered that during the night his cow had wandered away through an open gate. He was fairly sure that, unless something had driven it off, the cow was not going to wander far. The cow's name was Turkle, but the farmer never used that name. This was just the family cow as far as he was concerned, and it didn't pay to get sentimental about animals.

On the morning of the storm, his wife and children got up as though nothing were different. The immense snowfall was exciting, perhaps almost a novelty for them. And so the children dressed for school.

It was a three mile walk. The farmer announced that he would take his almost new 1924 Model T out of the shed, put on the chains, and drive them all to school. This would give him a chance on the way back to check for the missing cow because *someone had left the gate open*. He knew every pebble on the road, he was proud of what his new car could do with chains on the wheels, and he was too stubborn to let a snowstorm divert anyone in his family from their daily routine.

Apparently his wife protested. She felt that the children

should be allowed to miss school, stay home, and do their lessons in the kitchen next to the wood stove. It was twenty-five degrees below zero that morning and dropping. But the farmer must have brushed aside her protests with his usual admonition, that *only babies are meant to stay home in bad weather, and the children aren't babies any more, so why baby them?*

He went outside and cranked up his new Model T, and in a minute they were gone. They were gone long before it was light.

For some reason, perhaps a small act of rebellion, the youngest daughter, the one who they say left the gate open, smuggled her cat from the barn into the car beneath the folds of her winter coat. The cat was a tabby named Albert. The names of the children were Clarence, who was ten; Eleanor, who was nine; and Berta, the girl with the cat, who was six.

The farm was less than one hour's drive north of Saskatoon, a section of grainland with a large coulee that flows into the river southwest of Hepburn. The road the farmer drove runs through this coulee, and so in a tough blizzard, it would be sheltered from a north or a west wind. Away down in the coulee, you could underestimate even the severest storm, which explains why the farmer thought he could negotiate the road in his car. But when you climb up out of the coulee and onto the flat land, these prevailing winds can catch you very suddenly with a wall of driving snow.

And that's what must have happened to the farmer, whose name was Elmer Foster, as he wheeled the Model T out of his coulee so many decades ago. Still more than a mile southeast of the schoolhouse, he drove into a massive whiteout, and before he could stop or turn back into the coulee, he was off the trail and spinning his tires in snow up beyond the running board. The farmer tried to extract his car from the snowbank, but when he spun his wheels, something seemed to blow its top (my grandmother's words), and the car's engine went dead. He tried to crank it up again, but to no avail.

The farmer waded all around the car. He was almost blinded by the driving snow which by now was propelled by a barncrushing wind that greeted the first rays of daylight with one long demented howl. As the story is told, the farmer was a fearless man, and less unnerved by the storm than angered by this turn of events.

As well, Elmer Foster was a tall man. Ducking his head back into the car, he must have had to hunch over to deliver his speech to his three children. He was by reputation a man of few words, so this speech must have seemed something of an occasion to the children. "Better stay put," he is reported to have said. "I don't care how much yiz want to go out there or how long yiz have to sit in the car, do not I repeat do not leave for so much as a minute in that storm. If it gets cold, huddle up, light this here candle, sing songs, nibble away at your lunches, and keep the blanket over top, but don't try to make it to that school or yiz won't last three gulldam minutes."

One of the children asked him where he was going.

"I'm going to get the horses."

With his coat flapping like the wings of a great stricken bird, he staggered back towards the coulee and disappeared into the driving wind.

The three children and the cat arranged themselves together in the back seat, and their voices were almost silenced by the terrible wind. They sat so that little Berta was in the middle between the bodies of the two older children. In return for this favour, Berta allowed them to hold her cat inside their coats, and all day long they passed Albert back and forth beneath the blanket.

As I write this down (in a warm house in the city), I'm sitting merely one room away from the same blanket. It is a faded and worn but still red Hudson's Bay blanket with black stripes. In one corner are four parallel black bars woven into the wool. These indicate the heaviest gauge, a fourstar, as they used to say. The four bars are there for native trappers who could count but not read. This family heirloom is probably about seventy-five years old.

But as I was saying, the children lit the small candle offered to them by their father and nibbled away at their lunches until the last crumb was gone.

The farmhouse was sheltered from the storm at the lower end of the coulee. The children's mother could hear the wind rising, she could see the snowfall increase, and for half an hour or so, she went about her chores half distraught and half denying the peril that had enveloped her children and husband. When at last she went outside to the henhouse, she had to catch her breath in the cold. Instead of feeding the chickens, she plunged a short way up the road to see if she could see her husband's car coming back. But there was no sign of the car, and the tracks the car had left had already filled in with snow and disappeared. Elsie Foster retreated to the house, filled the stove with firewood, and waited by the kitchen window. Even down in the protected coulee, she could now tell that this was one of the worst storms she had ever seen.

The window she waited by looks out onto the trail her husband took to drive the children. On all but the foulest days, the view from this window conjures a remarkable illusion. The viewer is closer to the river bank and to the cottonwoods and willows that line the river than to the vast prairie up above, and so from the Foster house, the table land that constitutes this prairie looks more like the top of a ridge of hills or a plateau – anything but a prairie. If you *had* to live away out there, my grandmother used to say, that was the place to be.

There was no telephone, so Elsie Foster waited. The wind got worse and worse, and the temperature sank below thirty. Several times during the day, in moments when the wind seemed to taper off, she left the warm house and tried to break trail up the road through the ravine that led to the schoolhouse. Each time, the driving snow forced her back inside. Sometimes she imagined her husband and her little ones safe inside the schoolhouse and merely unable to return home in the storm. But these short respites of desperate hope soon gave way to agonized mourning for each one of them. She never slept that night.

When she got up in the morning long before daybreak, the storm had passed, the wind had fallen, and the temperature had risen dramatically. When she left the house the temperature was still rising. In Alberta, this sudden warming after a cold spell is called a chinook, but in Saskatchewan, this phenomenon is so rare that back then it didn't even have a name.

The farmer's wife harnessed two horses to the cutter and grabbed a scoop shovel. She sat in the driver's seat beside a supply of blankets and a large round stone heated on the stove that she had wrapped in cloth. She urged the horses all the way up the coulee to the place where the car had gone into the deeper snow. It looked like a huge humped animal asleep in the ditch. She could not scrape the snow off the new Model T; she had to shovel it off in great scoops. It was some time before she managed to yank open the door on the driver's side.

The first thing she discovered was that her husband was gone. The second thing she saw, as a waft of candlewax and urine passed through her nostrils, was her three little ones still as death beneath the blanket, and then, nosing its way out from where they lay, the tabby named Albert. She cried out the names of her children, *Clarence! Eleanor! Berta!*

Slowly, one by one, they opened their eyes as though called back from the dead. Their candle had burned to a stub.

She carried the children from the Model T to the cutter and bundled them in with the cat and the hot bound stone. Then she led the horses back on foot and carried the children into her own bed. She massaged their limbs and fed them tea and soups and anything else they would take down, and though the two eldest turned feverish, she could see that her children had a good chance of making it back from their long sleep. One of them told her that their father had gone for the horses, so she realized he must have fallen somewhere between the Model T and the barn.

Berta, the small one, seemed strangely unaffected by the ordeal in the model T. Her mother spent more time tending to the needs of the two older children while little Berta slept between them in her parents' large bed. When Berta woke up, she said that she would come with her mother to find their father. But her mother made Berta stay home to care for Clarence and Eleanor if they should wake.

Elsie Foster knew she had to hurry. Once more she climbed into the cutter, though this time without the heated stone and the blankets, and urged the horses up out of the coulee and toward the schoolhouse. The snow was whipped and banked in bluewhite folds beneath a clearing sky, yielding not a sign of her husband. Perhaps he had gone in the other direction and found his way to the schoolhouse. If not ... and she prayed all the way to the sound of the wheezing horses and the hissing runners.

There was a jubilant crowd of survivors at the schoolhouse. Some of her neighbours had kept their children home; others had accompanied them to school and spent the entire day and night in the teacherage. When Elsie Foster broke into the schoolhouse, the happy mood gave way to one of great urgency. Elsie's neighbours set out at once to find her lost husband. All day long they kept arriving with food and fresh horses for the search. A team of horses managed to tow the Model T back to the Fosters' yard. The men waded back and forth over the trail poking and kicking at anything that might have fallen in the deep snow. But no one found a trace of Elmer Foster, the children's tall, strong, fearless father. Their indestructible father.

Elmer Foster, people said, would sooner have taken a horse or a car than walk a hundred feet. When he left the Model T, he half sailed, half stumbled down the trail back through the coulee, but even there, the wind was almost unbearable. It drove him along like a tumbleweed, sliced through his winter coat, and every time he drew breath, the air sank like a cold thin blade into his lungs. He managed to walk for half a mile, and then the trail turned west so that he had to face almost directly into the wind for a painful stretch. At this point on the trail, he must have seen very quickly that he wasn't going to make it. As the story goes, he ran into something huge and motionless somewhere near the trail. It was Turkle, the missing cow. She was still alive, in fact still standing and covered with a deep layer of snow, but the storm had been so intense the poor animal was played out, her breath coming in short feverish whistles. When he kicked the unfortunate creature, she scarcely even moved.

Foster always carried a big jackknife in his pants pocket. Perhaps the knife was in his hand before any clear messages had reached his half-frozen cranium. He had no sledge, of course, with which to stun the animal before he stuck it, so with the cow standing there in a state of frozen immobility, he probed the dewlap for the hole that cows have at the front of their brisket, and drove the long blade into the lower part of the cow's throat. As he had always done at the smokehouse, he twisted the blade, severing Turkle's jugular. The blood fountained out, the cow shuddered in the man's arms, and her old legs buckled.

Away from his ropes and pulleys outside the smokehouse door, Elmer Foster had never slaughtered a cow, so the work was clumsy and rushed. At first he could scarcely feel the knife in his hands, but when the warm blood covered them, the hands seemed to revive on their own. He opened up the cow, pulled out her intestines, and with them a sizeable calf fetus, and slowly wedged himself inside. Caught in a lesser storm, he might have chosen to fight his way down the coulee, but something must have told him that this was absolutely his only chance. He went into the foul steaming carcass feet first so that his head and nostrils would remain closest to the opening, and like the womb's former inhabitant, Elmer Foster closed his eyes to the awful storm. It howled over his head all that day and all the following night.

I have always wondered what Elmer Foster thought about in his moments of consciousness. Did he fret about his children in the car or his wife alone in the house? Did he hear his own words to his wife that same morning? *Only babies are meant to stay home in bad weather, and the children aren't babies, so why baby them?*

During the warmest part of the day, the search continued up and down the trail from the point where the car had foundered to the Fosters' yard. Clarence and Eleanor, the two oldest children, slept and woke throughout the day in a state of feverish recovery. Their mother left them in the care of her sister and joined in the search. As the afternoon wore on, a neighbour boy brought little Berta out on the trail so that she too could search for her father. She had been told that either they would find him and take him home, or that God would find him and take him to Heaven. This seemed a reasonable explanation, so the little girl, bundled up and drawn by her older companion on a toboggan, remained calm all through the waning afternoon. The boy left her and went to help the men search through some snowdrifts a short way off the trail.

Sitting on her sled, Berta thought she heard a noise. She made her way over to the sound and discovered after some vigorous digging that she was standing on a massive object beneath the snow. She began to dig down, singing and talking to herself. From time to time, the men would walk by, and perhaps note with some surprise that the girl was helping in her own way. As the light began to fade, she had uncovered the head of her beloved Turkle.

The name, I'm told, had come from Berta herself, a mispronunciation of turtle, and was applied to the big cow for her painstakingly slow movements around the farm. Apparently the name had stuck for everyone in the family except Elmer.

"Moo," Berta said to Turkle, and the cow seemed to moo back.

"What are you doing in the snow?" said the little girl.

Turkle grunted a faint reply.

"Are you deaded?" said the girl. This time there was

no reply. "Turkle, you are a bad cow. You should go home and get warm."

The cow seemed to agree. It even growled her name, or seemed to. Turkle had spoken many times to Berta, but never in a voice so strange and anguished. The girl stood up and began to back off.

When her mother came to take her home, she found Berta hitting the massive head of the cow with her mittened hand. She explained to her mother that Turkle was a bad cow, but that was because she was sick and cranky, and maybe they should take her home too.

"It's too late for Turkle," her mother said. "Turkle is dead, Berta."

"No, she's not," said the little girl. "Are you, Turkle?"

Without so much as the flicker of an eyelash, Turkle stared like a mother, sadly, and perhaps a little bit offended, up at the rising moon. *I know what I know*, she seemed to say.

"Come over here," said Elsie Foster. "Mummy wants to have a word with…" She never finished her sentence.

Much of this story, perhaps too much, was told to me by my grandmother. She signs her name Mrs. Judson Gerald Steward, but back then she was a girl named Eleanor Foster. She has a small flare for the dramatic, and I find I have pared her story back some. For example, she swears that the coyotes had already gotten to Turkle and her precious cargo, which is highly unlikely. She has little Berta standing triumphant upon the head of Turkle, signaling to the searchers in a gesture made all the more dramatic by the setting sun and the rising moon. If this were such a big moment for little Berta, why does she still avoid talking about the day they found her father? My grandmother simply shrugs. This is an older sister's gesture. In her rendition, brother Clarence is holding Albert the cat and openly weeps to a reporter as he tells the story his mother cannot bring herself to tell. This description doesn't quite square with my old taciturn Uncle Clarence, a solitary alcoholic whose memory of his father seems pretty shaky.

But the story survives in an even more pared down version in the *Saskatoon Star Phoenix*, and from there it was carried all across the nation. It is typical of my family that the only national fame they ever attained was entirely unsought.

But one dramatic detail of Eleanor's that I cannot bring myself to leave out is the moment in the smokehouse when all six feet of Elmer Foster's body were finally pried free of the great carapace of Turkle's body like a thawing T-bone, and o, she moans, o, the sight of his clotted head when he first smelled the air of the barn and he opened his mouth to wawl and cry in mother's arms.

Orizaba, North of Havana
NORM SACUTA

The rhythm of a slow ship in water makes any man seem possible, even the most violent – bristling short hair like a boy's, his shoulders too wide for his shirt, the faded thin-blue of a dagger tattoo just beneath his skin and the dark hair on his forearm. In the bottom of this ship, below water-line where he's brought you, where this circle of men call Spanish into each other's ears, you play poker by the roar of boilers and are expected to know the rules. You don't, but have brought enough money to lose, and they realize they might not have to cheat each other. Only you. Just you.

The turbines make a constant low thud, like something large patting the hull from the outside waiting for the rivets to pop. They never do, and the rhythm goes on, the men around you more and more choreographed. No one can talk to anyone else unless they lean forward, their dark eyes signalling conversation, the slow movement of two men towards each other as if about to kiss, then gently veering to the side of the other's head. It's the same movement men perform on the periphery of dance floors, discussing women, who to ask, the soft confidences they try to build before going out alone to choose someone on the other side of the hall. This is a movement only six inches from what you want, the low tilting of your head just in time to avoid disaster in front of the others, your lips against the dagger-man's ear. You ask him to look if the cards you hold are any good – his head lowers in front of your chest to check, then rises so his nose almost brushes your shoulder before his breath can be felt rushing a voice inside you.

"Pretty good, there, Yankee. Too good. I fold."

So do all the men who watch the dagger-man for signs, and you take the small pot of antes for your own. Every pot you win is small. You'll ask his advice several times, as many as you can get away with, and hope for difficult hands just so you can lean close to his ear, your head almost sidling against one of those shoulders that don't quite seem possible.

"I need a piss," you say, after tossing a hand and he, also folding, waves for you to follow him around the side of a boiler. Other men are stoking astern, out of your view, and this boiler is only kept flickering with infrequent shovels of coal in case speed is needed later. He opens the wide door, stands in front of the low fire and buttons open his fly. You stand beside him, begin to do the same, and watch the thin blue glow of heat in the bottom where you're expected to piss.

You stop then and turn towards him before he has the buttons completely free. This time your lips do not drift, and the mark you leave on him is almost invisible, even less glistening than the sweat that's on his brow. He looks at you only once – the vague, disinterested stare of a scientist – then lowers his eyes to continue with his buttons. You suddenly feel cold, and know something's changed. You want to relieve yourself but can't.

Almost as sudden as the kiss, you see one of those shoulders shift in front of you, the dagger-man's thigh forced against you from behind, collapsing both your knees backwards as you're crushed into a slanting pile of coal.

He moves so fast.

Your hands are pinned cross-like, biceps beneath his knees, the sharp edges of coal like diamonds in your back. He's seated on your chest and his hands are full of shadows.

When the rocks begin to fall you lose sight of his eyes in the hard blackness that fills your own, the coal ground and ground into your face until the scars run dark. Then he stops, though his knees keep you down, and in the moment you hear your own breathing above the boilers your eyes suddenly sting – a pain you've never felt before. You understand before actually knowing. He is pissing in your face, his cock shook a few inches from your eyes.

The pressure on your arms is gone when he finishes. You raise palms to your eyes but the coal only makes them sting more, so you drop your hands and listen to the ship. You have no ideas where he is. Then he lets you know.

He has something metal. A shovel perhaps. And with it he slams the side of the boiler, then the floor, then the boiler again back and forth, an irregular rhythm that is sure to bring the poker players. A single word he shouts out, over and over – a Mexican word you know. You keep your eyes closed and wait for them to come. Of course, they do.

The word is a rallying point. As your hands and feet are held, your pockets emptied, your ring and watch removed, they each stand over you, a positioned leg on either side of your chest, and piss. There is no other sound than it hitting you, a dull splatter against the shirt and pants they've let you keep only because they want them soaked.

They've left you on the coal and after a time you stand, almost blind, and wait until you see the dim light above you. You know that's where the spiralled ladder rises up one level, and walk towards it away from the circle where they still play for your money.

You've never been more careful than you are now.

Not for fear but humiliation. You're the cat you once saw in a neighbour's garden in Paris, walking without sound, low and crouched because an angry man called out after seeing something buried. When your hand sticks and unsticks on the railing, all the way up, you wonder if anyone hears it happen. The turbines have become white noise.

The passage lights are dimmed all over steerage, the curtains drawn at each cabin entrance so no one sees you pass. You've only seen them when looking down with Peggy from the second-class promenade anyway – their faces refusing to look up except when they're not watched. They want that power, at least. Most wouldn't recognize you now, black steaks on your face like dripping Chinese characters.

When you reach the open promenade you take the long route counter-clockwise on deck to avoid Peggy's cabin where there's sure to be a steward keeping watch. You'd been locked in your own cabin near midnight after pounding on her door for the fourth time, drunk but articulate, carrying a pail of melting ice to soothe the buttery red burns that circled her face. You weren't at the ship's bar when the incident happened, the box of matches suddenly aflame in one hand as she lit a cigarette, the other holding an overproof glass of rum. But not being there only made the image more real, the blue and purple flames shooting up and encircling her head until she looked like some bearded, haloed saint. She sat in the doctor's quarters and smiled when you told her this, said not to be ridiculous. You asked her how anyone knows when they're acting ridiculous, and left.

It's now after two a.m. The stars waver slightly in a soft wind from the south, and you can smell yourself for the first time as a small section of uncaked hair, just behind your right ear, moves in the air. Most of the cabin windows are dark – those that aren't send you heel-toe away from them, closer to the railing outside the wide cones of light. You feel unsafe so far into the night, the black coal pressed beneath you now inverted on the sky.

Finally, inside, you're afraid to sit anywhere, don't want the scent of ammonia left on the sheets, and stand silent for several minutes in the centre of your cabin. The basin will not be big enough. And you've brought only one other change of pants, some pyjamas, two shirts, underwear and another pair of socks. Everything else is in your trunk down in the hold.

No one sees you walk the promenade naked, stand at the railing and drop your stripped clothes into the sea.

You repeat this trip four times, only slightly less naked each occasion the bassinet is emptied over the ship's side. The first parts finished are your crotch and legs so you can pull on fresh underwear, the urine rubbed off with fragrant soap and two fresh bottles of tequila you planned to keep for New York. You stand in the bassinet and rinse with an unused chamber pot, hoping the short bursts of water from the taps in your room haven't disturbed the Babbs, the middle-aged couple from Boston next door. You decide they're listening and like their quiet compliance.

The last part you wash is your head, low to the floor, on your knees and pouring the tequila like champagne over your hair. You realize you've done the washing-up in the wrong order, from bottom to top, but decide you like the nearness of the floor as you finish. The coal scratches on your face finally become clear, and in the mirror you touch the tracks that look red like ringworm trails. When the last bassinet is dumped three stories to the sea, you stand barefoot in the dark and feel your arm hair rustling like silk. No one has ever been this clean.

It's four when you're finally in bed, the sheets folded white-out at the top, a thick band of cotton just beneath your arms. You had imagined the dagger-man coming here with you, his body coal-marked by shovelling, his movement in bed marking the sheets like pastels as he moved with you. You would have stood by the door after he'd left, the sheets pulled back, and re-lived his shape on the mattress.

Have you ever known how to tell, or is your whole history a fluke? The way men move in full knowledge the world is meant for them used to be a way of picking out the pretenders: you watched once in Cherbourg from another boat deck as two Frenchmen embraced on the pier. You decided they were brothers – the same dull eyes and dark features – and read their signals perfectly. The sound of their embrace was audible even where you were standing, and a steward waited impatiently for one of them to enter the ship. Their hands, flat palms, pressed tight on each other's backs and then they slowly patted the fabric of their overcoats two or three times, the slapping sound a clear message to everyone what their connection was.

Perhaps you were wrong even then – the men you've fucked since merely a run of luck, a fortunate turn of phrase, a caress at the right time and in the right place. Were you ever acting any way other than ridiculous?

The doctor sent you away twice while he dressed Peggy's burns. Each time you had a lot more to drink before returning, and when she was finally ready to walk to her cabin you wondered what a man should offer his stricken woman. You could only think in clichés – flowers that couldn't be found; a poem you knew you couldn't write – and finally settled on trying to carry her down the promenade.

Peggy thought you were falling over from the alcohol as you dipped to sweep her off her feet, the two of you stooping lower and lower into a crouched position. She had to ask what was being offered and when you told her, refused. You were angry, and fought with her all the way to the cabin, attempting twice more to knock the knees out from under her; but she wouldn't grab your shoulder and let herself be lifted, and you refused her offer to calm down and come inside to talk. She wouldn't answer her door after that.

When you first seduced her three months ago in Taxco, you were on the run from Indian boys you'd been seeking in the alleys of Mexico City; Christmas took them away from you – even those smooth, clean bodies needed redemption – and you fled to her rented villa. The house staff, Maria and Jesus, saw you approaching and knew from a photo album that Peggy's history and yours were mostly aligned and smiling. Maria fled into the bathroom and wrapped Peggy quickly in a housecoat, calling *hurry! the señor he comes!* When she was dragged down to the landing, you both laughed, realizing the assumptions they'd made. But nothing was corrected. You winked at her, and the game went on for two days, a fantasy performance for the servants, until you both woke on Christmas morning with limbs wrapped around each other.

"It's a poem I'll write for you," you said when she awoke, hoping your block was finally gone. She only smiled and knew you were lying. You spent the next three months trying to prove you weren't, but not a word was written before the *Orizaba* left Vera Cruz.

Last night, at ten after twelve, after using a fork to jimmy the lock on your cabin, you tripped again towards her door to pound your true desire against it. The dagger-man was leaning beside a steward in a small staff hallway within view of her cabin, his arms folded like a boxer posing, his hair short and thick, his shirt and pants clean as sheets. It was probably Peggy he'd been hoping to see, expecting his protection would convert into desire. But you were there, instead, and didn't understand. You didn't understand at all.

You sleep until eleven-thirty. As your eyes open, the room does not let you forget, a wide circle of damp wood by the bed where you washed yourself last night. The ship is slightly rocking, waves in a stiff breeze, and you sit on the bed's edge wondering if you can speak. No one is likely to demand it anyway, so you stand, put on your coat and go outside.

The ocean looks in transition, as if the ship were entering cooler water or the point where two currents meet, small crests moving out in random directions. In this kind of weather, the boat not rocking enough to make a difference but enough to end illusions, a new start seems possible. You turn and walk towards the stern, nodding to the Babbs, who've stepped out of their cabin.

"Mr. Crane!" Mrs. Babb calls, a slight concern in her voice. But you know what's upset her are the pyjama bottoms and slippers just below your coat.

You stand at Peggy's door and knock once, so lightly you might be a steward. She answers and smiles, the gauze wrapped around her head like an ivory frame.

"Hart," she says, "I'm feeling better today. Dress and we'll have breakfast."

What you say has no rhythm.

"I – I'm disgraced, my love. I won't be continuing."

She doesn't understand, but smiles, and repeats the earlier instruction before closing her door. You continue towards the stern.

The wake is only a few hundred yards long, then loses shape in the choppy sea, leaving no trace of direction. There is possibility in that lack – water without origin, a history the sea re-covers. The trail behind keeps up its constant erasure, the wake always fading in the slight turbulence as the ship moves forward. It occurs to you that you're headed for New York, a colder climate full of sharp friends already gossiping about your conversion, and the definite trail back to Mexico beings to regain shape, to return to a particular point on the ocean last night.

That wake is the only poetry you can possibly make, and when you take off your coat and leave it on deck, folding it carefully like a clean sheet of paper, you feel like you're finally writing again. You jump, both hands on the railing as if vaulting a neighbour's gate, and take three seconds to hit the sea.

All That Summer
MÉIRA COOK

No-one needed a miracle half as bad as Ally that summer. That summer was like living in a head of cabbage, every breath thick and clammy, the garter snakes oozing from the undergrowth, fat ripples of black and gold. That summer was the summer of the slow burning from the inside out. Ally drove north along the highway with Zack Hladun's son Billy in his father's '72 pickup looking for a place to park out of the glare of sun and scrutiny. Outside the light burned down to a stub, the windshield beat with the wings of scorched insects, inside the truck the air was bloodwarm, taste of bottled beer. Ally opened the front of her shirt and unhitched her bra, more for the relief of air than the distraction of Billy, although she achieved both.

Afterwards, after the slow itch of day burnt down to the wick, after the scuffle & cut and Billy's mouth flung cutfruit against her own, Ally was to remember this moment only as the time before the garden. Because it was then that she set off down the suggestion of a path that led in the beginning to the stone garden, the garden of beasts, and in the end to promises made & broken, girls lost & found and something like a homecoming at the saline peninsula of her heart although she would not have used that word herself, heart is not a word she would have used.

As for the garden, it was dusk. In the fugitive half-light she saw the wild bestiary, the garden that forever after would stand in the place of her virginity. So she was quiet at first, Ally who could never settle, wild Ally striding the high street in her black knee-length city coat, Ally whom the town called Ally-cat, tough Ally. Ally was quiet. It was Billy waking in the backseat of the pickup, feeling the sweat between his haunches, a lazy curl of wind on his forearm, who made the first sound. Yes, he said. Ally was startled because he answered the question she hadn't asked, although afterwards he was to deny having said anything, having any word in his mouth or thought in his head.

The truth is he had fallen into something at that moment, love or disease he would never know. The truth is, coming upon her suddenly like that, the flare of her thin body against rearing dinosaurs and dragons, a spectacle of monkey and bear - no this is not yet the truth. He stepped towards her and noticed suddenly the small dark mole at the juncture of neck and clavicle at the reticent hollow of her throat.

She moved towards the dragon, its sunken gothic face gazing east, she walked around the mermaid stranded in her stone pool, the three wise monkeys, the double-headed serpent, perhaps she touched the tip of one prehensile claw. Afterwards she encountered this moment precisely and with grave preoccupation, the derelict house on the outskirts of the garden, the apple orchard and the rows of oblique stone faces, but she never then or ever after thought of Billy who had turned like the weather, surly, and was mooning against the hood of the pickup while the clouds unravelled ragged and linen behind his head. So they had to leave and did not as a consequence discover the statue of the fallen woman, the wife of Armand, until the second time, by which time weeds had sprung in the crevice of her thighs and the wincing smile that was both jubilant and profligate had begun to crack against her lips.

If it had not existed it would have to have been invented for me, the stone garden. This was years ago, I am a woman after the chop, headless I sit crosslegged, telling tales. All this was before, you understand, before the lovers and the books, the gnawed distraction of children, the wounded nights, the sanity my life is bound to now, like a wheel. My name was Ally and I wore black.

I call myself Alix now, at least others do and seldom wear black except in the way of underwear and patent leather shoes. Ally wore black because it was the one colour not duplicated in nature, she was a thing apart, an outcast. No, that is not true she was not cast out, she cast herself out, out beyond the city gates and human understanding, she would stalk down the centre of the highstreet like a cat, talk to nobody, fuck with anybody. It was a point of honour, Ally, thin-boned bloody-minded Ally-the-cat. Let me begin again.

The garden was the beginning. It was in the image of the garden that she first coincided with herself. Although she saw it afterwards, often and in all kinds of weather, when she remembered, she remembered the garden that she first imagined that dusk in the cooling down steam of the first hot day of that hottest summer. I don't remember how many days before they went back to the garden, Ally and Billy Hladun who looked at her now and ever since that day with a kind of bruised emphasis, in truth he wanted to snap her thighs for a wishbone, there was no extinguishing himself in her anymore. I remember it was breathless, birdless, a mad gasp of a day, the prairie grass feral in the expectation of wind. Ally was itchy with sex, something hot and wedge-shaped at the bottom of her belly, a steam iron burning from the inside. As soon as the pickup rolled into the shade at the Grahamdale turnoff she twisted into his arms, her mouth a wound rubbing salt.

There is an image I have of these two, Ally and Billy Hladun as if I have watched them in the backseat of Zack

Hladun's pickup, a wild rout of arms and legs, her quick wrists, the triangles of his field-reddened flesh, the grain of bone beneath her skin. The truth is they were never naked with each other no time, just unzip unzip a cry a sigh, her jeans round her ankles, his open at the waist. In this memory she turns to look at me beneath the overhang of his shoulder and her fallen hair. Then she looks away. There is a border in my mind and I am moving toward it.

When they went back the second time they found the wife of Armand. Billy wouldn't leave Ally alone that time, didn't sleep but tracked her up the path toward the house. The house was quarried from stone with eaves hanging low and lentern, blocking out light so that the inside was quite dark save for flinching squares of sun fallen on torn linoleum. The rooms were low, alluvial with the sediment from old lives, bedsprings, worn out kettles, bottomless pots and the horsehair stuffing from chairs. The front door hung crooked on its latch, there were no windows in the peeling frames and the kitchen had a burnt-out grief-stricken look as if gutted by a fire more hungry than flame, bewildered now into a little heap of dust and ash. Ally walked thriftily through a wild disorder of rooms long abandoned, she had the feeling she was looking for something, a room a cupboard a book, something closed that could be opened. There was an apple orchard off the side but the trees were woody and would not bear, Billy said. The stone garden at the front of the house extended all the way around to the yard and was surrounded on all sides by the overgrown thatch of prairie grass that had once been cultivated land, Billy said. Ally was frantic with impatience, she longed to be alone, she wanted him to leave or fall asleep or die. He followed behind everywhere she walked so she went to sit on the dinosaur rock in shade thick with wings and turned on her Walkman. He wandered off then slapping flies and good riddance, looking hurt so that she would have struck him if he had come within an armswing. After a while he came back.

I've found something, he said.

> Welcome to my place I am the wife of Armand.
> We never quarrelled, he left me in the cold.

Some of the words were so worn against the syntax of stone, they could only make them out with their fingers. The wife of Armand lay supine, her stone thighs curved and sickle, a flourish of weeds sprouted between her legs. The smooth oval of her head was balanced on an arm pivoting from the elbow and her eyes were half closed, instinct.

Ally who was to learn stillness from the fallen woman did not, at first, move. Billy walked round and round bewildered into a rotation of parts, the wind from the west a hot flush of potato pickings, boiled cabbage and gasoline. They never then or ever after talked about her, the wife of Armand, in her presence, so it was only when they were back in the pickup and heading home into the sun caught in a snare of socket and sky, the seagulls hot off the lake and sour in their displeasure, it was only then that one of them spoke.

I think it was Ally, it may have been Billy. They decided not to tell. Already Ally knew all about secrets, her body was sewn with the crisscross of silence, scars like little stitches along the seam of her back, she had prepared all her life to accomplish this secret. The pickup breathed oil into the night, they passed cows standing solitary in fields, patient blue tongues held fast against slabs of salt. Billy also knew about secrets. His mother had had every secret of his childhood locked up in her head so that when she died he lost not only her, the woman he hardly knew except as a pair of grudging arms and the unrecollected murmur of a Chopin prelude at the bottom of an empty dusk, but himself, the child nobody could remember, the little boy only a mother could love and only in parts and only at times. As for his father, he is a farmer and a Lutheran, his hair a field of dead stubble. Like Lot he never looks back.

Ally's eyes are dipped and glazed, her eyelids at halfmast. Billy looks at her sideways as he stares along the long arrow of highway; she yawns an abandonment of jutting breasts, a loose muscle in the side of her jaw clicks amiably. Who is this stranger, this pale eastern creature beside him, he owes her no allegiance save in the ragged tear of pleasure given and received, the persistence of a secret. In his father's house, in the lowslung homestead swinging a latch between earth and sky, there is a book. This is the only book apart from the Bible, the catalogues, the ledger. It is used to prop one end of the sideboard, the silver framed picture of his mother before she was dead, before she was wife before she was even his mother. He has no idea how it got there, this book, and he cannot remember the last time he wondered about it, it is just there now, nights when he can't sleep for the pulse in his thighs, he reads the book. It is a collection of Celtic legends, mist and malarky, nothing could be further from this thick vegetable country. Watching Ally, he thinks now of the sealwomen who cannot be trusted. One night sure as the tide they will leave their children asleep in their beds slip into their pelts and return to the sea. Billy who has never seen the sea knows something of abandonment, already he imagines a look of wetness about her lashes, her ears flatten against her skull when the wind changes.

That summer they went often to the stone garden after the farm chores, after school, they would head north toward the turnoff and the incurable sunset. Because it was so far out of town and she had no vehicle, Ally tolerated Billy Hladun, his weight of bones grounding her to the hollow wingspan of pelvis. She had no pity, on him on herself, she moaned & clawed, blood and wince and thrust all synonyms for love. Afterwards she would stuff a kleenex into her opening would shrug into her T-shirt, her headphones, wander through the cool slant house, the stone topiary of beasts. Shunned and exhausted, his eyes cut to the bulb from staring down lines of flax and rapeseed, Billy would stretch out in the shade of the pickup, and studying the colour behind his closed lids, fall into a dream of magenta. As for Ally, her progress was at once more defined, more random, this was her first garden, a secular ordeal.

Billy is running. Billy Hladun is running through the fields. Running his disease and his cure, another translation of the same sluggish desire, a religion empty of belief, a politics empty of conviction. A synonym for love. Billy is running his lust to earth, it is the fox he will blood in the dark loam of his belly. As he runs his thighs stretch taut, his lungs unpleat, his muscles begin to remember the subtle excess of road and feet. He is running along the road that runs along the railway track that runs along the outskirts of town upon which the train runs twice weekly, three times in the fall. It is summer, the train has already passed through.

When I think back to the beginning I am undone by the hysteria of the wind, the sticky taste of sap at the back of the throat. All that summer the wind burnished the edge of days bronze and birdless, ransacked the trees. It never got any cooler. Nothing in my life will ever be as those days, those people, they were there when I was fifteen,

I will always remain fifteen with them. It was June and the winds flinched off the horizon hot and sour, breath of a fever before the illness has turned. One by one the people maddened in that lunatic wind, driven to acts not easily redeemed come fall.

It was hotter in the trailer than outside, no it was just as hot. The air outside the air inside, a thick skim of affliction on the surface of things. Ally was sick with the heat, all that season she would suffer in the rind of the summer, but tonight she was sick with it, her tongue swollen to the root. She fell asleep, dreamed she was sucking her own tail, woke with these words in her mouth, *somewhere in the world it is January.*

That summer Ally was fifteen and seeding like a dandelion on the wrong side of the tracks. Topheavy with the anticipation of breasts and a habit of measuring words like eyedrops, her knuckles clenched with the effort of conversation. Nothing articulate in her beyond the way she had of walking swaybacked down the centre of the road, a cold thrust of hip. By the time she was properly sixteen every dog in the neighbourhood had had his bone of her, but she was possessed of a high white purity that had little to do with the uses she put to her body. In the gothic cathedral of her soul she ran pale and highminded, the space between her legs nothing but the silence between words. Then she parked off the Grahamdale turnoff with Billy Hladun in his dad's '72 pickup and discovered the stone garden, the wife of Armand.

Billy runs in the night, it is the summer break but his father's fields of grain and alfalfa require tending, the men work in the fields until the last split seam of light. While he runs along the railway tracks he thinks of parallel lines, the sound they will make when they collide. He thinks that now the snows have melted it is hard to believe they were ever there, he remembers the dark coffeespill of Ally's eyes. What has survived his education, a mind lost for words, a body hungry for love. It is not a word he would use, love is not a word he would use.

He is obsessed with Ally, obsessed with the garden. The garden is the place for him of his lover's desire, the place from which love speaks, will always speak, when he is an old man he will come to a sunken garden and weep finally for the first betrayal. Love is the cold beak in his flesh, he does not know yet of Ally's treachery, her casual lovers, that she is known as the town bicycle. When he finds out he will want to die. He will not die, instead he will get drunk for the first time in his life at the Sharptail Shooter public bar and poolroom off Main, then he will drive down to the Grahamdale turnoff with seven companions similarly indisposed and wayward as skittles in the back of Zack Hladun's '72 pickup. After that nothing will assuage the garden in him. When Ally finds out she will leave him, the trailer, the town.

He will remember the moment he stepped towards her and saw for the first time the dark mole at the corner of her throat. All love centres upon an image remembered long after the final betrayal. Billy runs in the night toward home, a bright noun between transitive verbs, coming from and going to. Nearly there nearly there, Ally-ally.

Homefree.

I was mad for a time in my wounded youth, it was the hottest summer. The birds fell stunned from the sky, eyeless and struck to mica. Children stood in shrivelled fields, vacant as scarecrows, our voices thinned to dust. The river that, for as long as anyone could remember, had flooded its banks every spring to reclaim itself from the town, turned fossil, etching a record of its repression upon a memory of fishbones and scattered bedrock. It was so hot that year pregnant women leant up against their dryers and cried. Five stillbirths, eleven newborns whittled away in the season's frenzy. Homer the idiot pushed a nail into his palm at the funeral of Jalmer Guttman the embalmer, and sucked. After that bodies began to blow in the heat and the town had to use the curling rink for the viewings. Everyone went mad that summer, blame it on the heatwave.

In the camouflage of days that followed, Ally sickened with the thick phlegm of summer, the sky ticking in blue spasms above her head. If there were a man we would say about one in her condition that she was lovesick, if there was a home we would say she was homesick. There are no words for her sickness, let us say rather she was sick with longings, with the sad gasp at the end of the word laughter, with the presumption of the first person, that weary journey from the first apple tree. The bestiary was in her now, a hawk climbing the wild steeple of her understanding.

Billy is trying to outrun his life, he does not yet know that Ally is gone, he is so busy training his muscles to remember, his hands to forget. Running is the only way to remain in the present tense between memory that drags him back to the past and desire that flings him forward in the future. Billy does not know where the pain is coming from, it would be so easy to say I have sprained a tendon. Yet he does not sprain his leg, the cells go on without him, the small bones in his ankles hold fast, nothing he can do to disrupt the body's fine fascist replication, see boy run, see Billy. See Billy run.

When he gets over his pain at her defection Billy will begin to think he can save Ally. Learning that it is not in his power to save her, learning that he will need every stored memory in his body to save himself, will be his first trial in this fallen world. Perhaps he will finish high school, move to the city, become an x-ray technician. Perhaps he will marry a woman so plump that he cannot count the bones beneath her skin, live in a frame house on a crescent road, the kind of place where children make snow angels and jack o'lanterns, play in treehouses. He will grow up and marry, become a father, perhaps he will own a barbeque, in time a house by the lake. Once or twice a year he will take his children to visit their grandfather: this is where I grew up, he will say, we had very little but we were content. One day in old age he will come to a garden and weep. That is all, not a bad life, no sequel to this first disabling gush of pain. One thing is certain, he will never again make the mistake of believing he can save anyone. He will never again fall sick with love, he will take up golf and give up running.

Every madman loves a fire, so do children and anarchists and women in flight. Everyone else is afraid. Billy Hladun sees a word ochre as horizon, turns swiftly on the highway, arrowing his way back to town to sound the alarm. Ally clicks through mile zero, somewhere a calendar has been turned, she falls backwards through the pages of a book.

Ally runs before the hot breath of the fire, from a distance her figure is blurred by the heat, she is dancing. The flames are a little in love with her, they want to join in. At the core of the heatwave in the hottest summer ever, a woman dances on the bare prairies with a fire. Ally, Ally –

After – after, that word that gasp. It is afterwards and the spiders have spun my hair to years, I have prepared all my life to accomplish this death. The garden is behind me, the first garden turned black in my memory, a hangnail. But I have one or two things to say before they fill this mouth with earth. People still visit the stone garden, although the house is gutted and the orchard burnt to the root, the animals remain – the serpents and bears, the dragons, the monkeys. Beyond this page I grow my hair, like everyone, I wait for spring.

There is nothing I can say anymore that would duplicate what you already know. Somewhere beyond the frame a woman dances before fire in the dawn. She tears the paper she is clutching into pieces and throws them over her head into the flames. They are caught on an updraft of wind and flutter about her hair like confetti. She puts up her face to the sun, a bride of the morning. When she comes to the highway she sticks out her thumb. Perhaps the next car that comes by will somehow encompass what it is she has been for all of her life, waiting.

Pier

J. JILL ROBINSON

My sister and I clamber out of the yellow Karman Ghia and run, out of our mother's sight, without looking back, run way, way down to the end of the pier where you must either turn back, jump onto a crab boat, or descend to your swimming lesson. Every day for two months each year we ran – away, far, out – and descended, leapt into the sea. She – our mother – was gone for the day; our life was ours. No weeding of pansy beds here in the salty wind. No pushing wheelbarrows of horse manure on this wet grey beach. No sweeping steps by these chunk piles of granite. No Useless girls, no Heartless, Selfish, Thoughtless girls.

Neither of us with salt in our eyes or our hair now, neither of our mouths gasping to swallow, neither of us fearing to drown. There is no stubbing our toes as we flee our mother. Can you remember us then, Kate? A third our present size? Running the straight long length of the pier, warm wood under our bare feet, the warm beads of spike heads under our toes.

Kate? I say to your answering machine. I wish you were home. I want to tell you I'm pregnant! Call me? Please?

The trestle that crosses the river near my house is like White Rock's pier, but goes across, joins sides, doesn't jut out into endless sea, or make you turn back at a breakwater. But still it makes me think of our summers, of you. If we ran together along this wooden structure, we would run *with* the grain of wood. We would run perpendicular to the water's range of flow, and we could not run side by side – one would *have* to be

behind the other.

tides, planks, sand,

wind, salt, cries.

Along the breakwater, gulls and pigeons cluster.

Geronimo!

Boys jump off the pier on the beach side of the crab boat moorage, swan dive or cannon ball. They bob back to the surface and flick long wet lashes of hair from their eyes and a strong unschooled crawl takes them back to the pier. Don't need no fucking lessons.

Geronimo!

Boys. Those are bad boys, aren't they Kate?

Shut UP, Jessie.

Aren't they, though?

How would I know? Hurry up. We're late.

Of course, this trestle bridge carries its railway tracks alongside, while at White Rock, to reach pier or beach you must cross the tracks on crushed granite, tracks on a T to the pier. And here you cannot descend concrete steps and go underneath, into dark, make-shiver cold and wetness, where crabs and mussels cling to thick black oily posts.

Bad things happen underneath, Jess, you whisper to me ominously after our lessons, as we start slowly back down the pier. Bad things happen below.

Below where? I say. As we walk we can hear the boys underneath, robbing the nests of the gulls. Later on the beach we will see the boys walk cockily by, the baby gulls cradled in their jackets.

You know. The belt.

No, I don't. Belt? I don't get it.

You know.

Kate, I DON'T.

You're so dense, Jess. Shut UP.

We are heading for fish and chips. Wrapped up in our beach towels after our lesson, pale, skinny twelve-year-old me shivers with cold in spite of the sun, while you are a warm, brown, voluptuous thirteen.

A girl sits at the beach end of the pier, legs splayed, menstrual blood staining her white bikini. Whisper:

Kate, LOOK!

Yuck.

Do you think she knows?

Of course she knows. She's showing off.

Showing off what?

You turn doubtful here, and your words come out slow.

How she's a woman, I guess. I don't know. Come on. I'm starving.

You shake so much vinegar onto your fish and chips that they are awash, and the smell gags you on each bite. This is how you like them.

Katharine, our mother said one morning as she dropped us off. Keep Your Sister Out Of The Sun. See She Doesn't Burn.

You are somehow my protector, then, I pondered, puzzled, as we ran (late, always late). Why do I need protecting and you don't? What sets us apart? Is it breasts?

Some days when I walk across the trestle I can feel myself transported, flown. Can forget I'm in Saskatoon, can believe the boards I run along are to our lessons, warm under bare feet, toes tender for slivers and stubbing.

I can see the gasping bullheads lined up on the warm wood of the pier, hunks cut out of them for crab traps. Pinned flailing to the pier with a jackknife. Bullheads. Just fucking bullheads, say those boys. Who fucking cares?

Here, Canada geese, cormorants, huge white pelicans rest and squawk and feed from sandy islands that appear and disappear one day to the next like memories; and like memories, the same ones tend to come back, but according to a dam man's whim, not the planet's revolutions. Gulls the most common denominator. And the sand.

I am not a prairie girl. I ache for the sea, for moisture on all sides, and what I receive is sky and more sky, dry, blue, consistent sky, an ambivalent universe pressed seamlessly to endless undulation of grain-coloured hills.

Follow the stick, make dashes, curlicues; step around hearts made by and for others. Walk to the White Rock and back treading only on wood – jump, from log to log, mince across twigs, lay down a carried stick when you're desperate. Shifting wet pebbles under your feet, bits of dead crabs, broken shells; lacy mustard seaweed, slippery green sheets, and bullwhips yellow and long, slimy tresses, bulbs broken and odoriferous.

Towel and driftwood caves on the beach. Boys kick sand as they chase each other and a woman sits angrily up, topless, as she yells, Fuck Off you little buggers, and, shocked and impressed, we see her breasts – both of her bare-naked breasts.

At home in my bedroom I have peered at what our mother calls my "spots"; they are just that. I have not seen your breasts; I only know they are there, and growing, and with them the distance between us. I long for breasts; long to renarrow the distance between us. Me in my navy blue tank suit; you in your turquoise bikini.

In the distance the Peace Arch, portal to the States, the line, across the line, America, U.S., down South. In the distance where our father's boat is moored. Beyond the white white marble.

Kate? I say to your answering machine. I wish you were home – I called last week and couldn't get you. I'm pregnant! Call me, okay? Please?

What is absent from my life is salt in the air
What is absent is the pull of tides
What is absent is my sister, wherever I am; it is not just

here in Saskatchewan. She has removed herself from my life, consciously; deliberately.

At the end of the afternoon we wait. She is late, late, late, again, still, eternally, our mother, late, her first, middle, and surname, Late, we sit, and stand, and wander, up and down in front of the granite post office, because You Girls Had Better Be There When I Come All That Way To Pick You Up. Up and down, up and down, days in the rain, huddled in the alcove like match girls waiting for our tardy, terse, and always fucking late bitch of a mother.

You will not call me.

There is no lull between lunar-guided waves, no soothe of whoosh, pause, whoosh. The weir's water constantly rushes.

My longing for you is not a constant like this, though a steady current lies below. Its tides tug at the lunar phases of my heart.

Hot chocolate at McBride's, where birds dip towards glasses of water on the shelf, endlessly, rhythmically, dipping to drink. Red licorice shoestrings from the English candy store. Our father saved the husband's life and they always remind us. We walk along the tracks, that smell of oil, of preserved ties, hanging stronger, the hotter the sun.

It's the smell that smacks the places together. The smell that started this sorrow's coursing. Oil on railway ties in the hot sun. Trestle bridge, pier. White Rock, Saskatoon. The smell transcends place. Tracks and beds. Travelling north to south, bank to bank.

Kate? I miscarried.

Vinegar

Coppertone

Hot chocolatet

the sea – salt and sand

The saltwater. Inside me. Pushing. Seeking. Pulling.

Stinky Girl
Hiromi Goto

One is never certain when one becomes a stinky girl. I am almost positive I wasn't stinky when I slid out from between my mother's legs, fresh as blood and just as sweet. What could be stinkier, messier, grosser than that, one might be asked. But I'm certain I must have smelled rich like yeast and liver. Not the stink of I-don't-know-what which pervades me now. Mother has looked over my shoulder to see what I try to cover with my hand and arm, while I meditatively write at the kitchen table.

"Jesus!" she rolls her eyes like a whale. "Jesus Christ!" she yells. "Don't talk about yourself as 'one'! One what, for God's sake? One asshole? One snivelling stinky girl?" She stomps off. Thank goodness. It's very difficult having a mother. It's even more difficult having a loud and coarse mother.

Where was I? Oh yes, I am not troubled by many things. My weight, my mother, my dead father's ghost, and a pet dog that despises me do not bother me very much. On an off day, a few tears might spring to my eyes, but no one notices, a fat stinky mall rat weeping. People believe that fatties secrete all sorts of noxious substances from their bodies. But regardless. The one bane of my life, the one cloud of doom which circumscribes my life, is the odour of myself.

There's no trying to pinpoint it. The usual sniff under the armpits, or cupping my palms in front of my mouth and breathing into them to catch the smell of my breath, is like trying to scoop an iceberg with a goldfish net. And it's not a simple condition of typical body odour. I mean, everybody has some natural scent and even the prettiest covergirls wear deodorant and perfume. And it's not because I am fat that foul odours are trapped in the folds of my body. No, my problem is not a causal phenomenon. There are no simple answers.

Perhaps I am misleading, calling myself a mall rat. It's true, I spend much of my time wandering in the subculture of gross material consumerism. I wander from store to store in the wake of my odour, but I seldom actually purchase anything. Think, if you will, upon the word, rat. Instantly, you'll see a sharp whiskered nose, beady black eyes and an unsavoury disposition. Grubby hands with dirty fingernails, perhaps, and a waxy tail. You never actually think FAT RAT. No, I'm sure, you bring to mind a sneaky, thinner rodent. If I am a rat, think of, perhaps, the queen of all rats. In the sewer of her dreams, being fed with the tenderest morsels of garbage flesh. Think of a well-fed rat with three mighty chins and smooth, smooth skin, pink and fine. No need for a fur covering when all your needs are met. A mighty rodent with more belly than breath, more girth than the diameter of the septic drains. If you think of such a rat, then I am that mighty monstress.

Actually, I always thought of myself more in terms of a vole or perhaps a wise fat toad, or maybe even a manatee, mistaken by superstitious sailors as bewitching mermaids. But no. My mother tells me I was born in the Year of the Rat and that is that. No choice there, I'm afraid, and I can't argue with what I can't remember. Mother isn't one for contemplative discussions. More often than not, all I'll get is a "Jesus Christ!" for all my moral and intellectual efforts. I hope I don't sound judgmental. Mother is a creature upon herself and there are no grounds for arbitrary comparison. Each to their own is a common phrase, but not without a tidbit of truth.

Perhaps I mislead you, calling myself a stinky girl. I am not a girl in the commonly held chronological sense of time. I've existed outside my mother's body for three and thirty years. Some might even go so far as to say that I'm an emotionally crippled and mutually dependent member of a dysfunctional family. Let's not quibble. In the measure of myself, and my sense of who I am, I am definitely a girl. Albeit, a stinky one.

When people see obesity, they are amazed. Fascinated. Attracted and repelled simultaneously. Now if we could harness all those emotions my scale inspires, who knows how many homes it would heat. How many trains it would move. People always think there is a why to being grand. That there is some sort of glandular problem, or an eating disorder, a symptom of childhood trauma. All I can say is, not to my knowledge. I have always been fat, and, if I must say so myself, I eat a lot less than my tiny mother. I wasn't adopted, either. Mother is always bringing up how painful her labour to eject me from her body was. How she had to be tied down, how she pushed and screamed and pushed and cursed for three days running. Perhaps that's the reason for her slightly antagonistic demeanour. She didn't have any more children after I was born, and I must say, this birthing thing sounds like a nasty business. What with all the tying down and screaming.

Oh yes, I do have siblings, but they are much older than I. Three sisters and a brother who became women and men long before their due. Cherry was born in the Year of the Rabbit, Ginger the Year of the Dragon, Sushi the Year of the Horse, and Bonus the Year of the Sheep. Mother was quite tired of the whole affair by the time her second last child was born. Bonus was so named because he came out of her body with such ease she couldn't believe her luck. After a seventeen year stretch with no other pregnancies, she must have thought that her cycles were finished. And what better way to end than on a bonus? But mother wasn't fated to an easy life, or she wasn't going to inhabit the space of the rest of her life without considerable trial and tribulation. At the age of fifty-one, she became pregnant with me. Promptly after, my father died, and she was left in a trailer, huge and growing, her children all moved away. A tragic life, really, but no, I shouldn't romanticize. One is easily led toward a tragic conclusion, and one must fight the natural human tendency to romanticize the conditions of one's life. One must be level-headed. A fat girl especially. When one is fat, one is seldom seen as a stable and steadying force in a chaotic world. Fat people embody disruptive forces in action and this inspires people to lay blame. Where else to point their fingers, but at a fat girl in striped trousers?

Did I mention I am also coloured?

I can't remember my very first memory. No one can, of course. My living father I cannot remember. But his ghost is all too present in my daily life. I wouldn't be one to complain if he were a helpful and cheerful ghost, prone to telling me where to find hidden crocks of gold or if the weather will be fine for the picnic. But no. He is a doleful ghost, following me around the small spaces in our trailer, leaning mournfully on my shoulder and telling me to watch my step after I've stepped in a pile of dog excrement. And such a pitiful apparition! All that there is of him is his sad and sorry face. Just his face, bobbing around in the air, sometimes at the level of a man walking, but most often down around the ankles, weaving heavily around one's steps. It's enough to make one want to kick his head, but I am not one compelled to exhibit unseemly aggressive behaviour.

Mother, on the other hand, is not above a swift "kick in the can," as she calls it, or a sudden cuff to the back of the head. I would not be exaggerating if I said I had no idea how she can reach my buttocks, let alone reach high enough to cuff my head, for I am not only very fat, but big and tall all around. Well, tall might be misleading. It would make one imagine that my length is greater than my girth. Let there be no doubt as to my being rounder than I would ever be considered tall. Only that I am at least two feet taller than my mother, who stands four foot eight. She is not a dwarf, and I am not a giant.

No, my mother is not a dwarf, but she is the centre of the universe. Well, at least the centre of this trailer park, and she leaves no doubt about who "kicks the cabbage around this joint," as she is fond of reminding me. It gives me quite a chuckle on occasion, because father's ghost often looks like a cabbage, rolling around the gritty floor of our trailer, and even though mother cannot see him, she has kicked his head many times, when she punctuates her sayings with savage kicks at what she can only see as empty air. It doesn't hurt him, of course, but it does seem uncomfortable. He rolls his sorry eyes as he is tha-klunked tha-klunked across the kitchen.

"What are you sniggling at, Mall Rat?" Mother snaps at me.

"Nothing," I say, sniggling so hard that my body ripples like tides. Mother kicks me in the can for lying and stomps off to her bedroom to smoke her cigars. I feel sorry for my father and right his head, brush off some ghostly dust.

"See what happens when you inhabit this worldly prison? Why don't you float up to the heavens or at least a waiting room," I scold. "There's nothing left for you here except kicks in the head and a daughter who doesn't want to hear your depressing talk of dog excrement and all the pains you still feel in your phantom body."

"As if I'm here by choice!" he moans. "As if any ghost would choose to remain in this purgatory excuse of a trailer! Finally dead and I get the nice light show, the tunnel thing and a lovely floating body. I think that I might be hearing a chorus of singing mermaids when an unsympathetic voice utters, 'You have not finished doing time,' and I find my head bobbing in a yellow-stained toilet bowl. It takes me a couple of minutes to figure out it's my own toilet bowl, in my old bathroom, because I'd never seen it from that perspective before. Imagine my shock! What's a poor ghost to do? Oh woe, oh woe," he sobs. Because ghosts have ghostly licence to say things like that.

Frankly, his lamenting and woeing is terribly depressing and I have plenty of my own woes without having to deal with his. I might not give in to excessive displays of violence, but I am not above stuffing him in the flour bin to make my escape.

I suppose calling oneself a rat might seem gender specific. Rat, I'll say, and instantly a man or a nasty boy is conjured up. There are female rats as well, don't you know? His and hers rat towels. Rat breasts and rat wombs. Rat washrooms where you squat instead of peeing standing. A girl can grow up to become a doctor or a lawyer, now. Why not become a rat? Albeit a stinky one.

Yes, yes, the odour of my life. It is large as myth and uglier than truth. There are many unpleasant scents as you twiddle twaddle down the gray felt tunnels of life. Actually, smells hinge the past to the clutter of present memory. Nothing is comparable to the olfactory in terms of distorting your life. To jar a missing thought. Or transmute into an obsession. The dog excrement smell that's trapped in the runnels at the bottom of a sneaker, following you around all day no matter how fast you flee. That high-pitched whine of dog shit, pardon my language. Mother is a terrible influence and one must always guard against common usage. Yes, there is nothing like stepping in a pile of doggy dung to ruin your entire day. It is especially bad when the dog is supposedly your own.

Mother found the dog in the trailer park dumpster and as it was close to my "sorry birthday," she brought the dirty-coloured wall-eyed creature as a gift to me. I was touched, really, because she had forgotten to give me a gift for the last twenty-seven years and I always wanted a dog as a devoted friend.

The dog started whining as soon as mother dragged it into the trailer by the scruff of its mangy neck. It cringed to the floor, curling its lip back three times over. It started chasing itself, tried to catch up with its stumpy tail as if to eat itself out of existence. I was concerned.

"Mother, perhaps the dog has rabies."

"Arrghh." (This is the closest I can get to the sound of my Mother's laughter.) "Damn dog's not rabid, it's going crazy from your infernal stink. Look it! It's hyperventilating! Aaaaaarrggghhh!"

The poor beast was frothing, chest heaving, smearing itself into the kitchen linoleum. It gave a sudden convulsive shake, then fainted, the first time I ever saw a dog faint. Needless to say, my "sorry birthday" was ruined. I actually thought the dog would die, or at least flee as soon as it regained consciousness. But surprisingly, the animal stayed. There is no accounting for dog sense. Perhaps it's a puerile addiction to wanting to smell a horrible smell over and over again. Like after one has cut up some slightly-going-off ocean fish, raising one's fishy fingers to one's nostrils day and night until the smell has been totally inhaled. Or sitting down in a chair and crossing an ankle over the knee, clutching the ankle with a hand, twisting so the bottom of the runner is facing upward. The nose descending to sniff, sniff, sniff the high-pitched stench of trapped doggy dung. There is an unborn addict in all of us, and it often reveals itself in the things we choose to smell.

I must admit, I cannot smell myself because I have smelled my scent into normality. I only know that I emanate a tremendous odour because my mother tells me so, I have no friends, and people give me a wide berth when I take my trips to the mall. There is a certain look people cannot control when they smell an awful stink. The lips curl back, the nose wrinkles toward the forehead, trying to close itself. (Actually, if one thinks about it, the nostrils seem more greatly exposed when in this position than at rest, but I needn't linger on that thought just now. Later, to ponder at my leisure.) People cannot control this reaction. I have seen it the whole of my life, can interpret the fine sneer in the corner of an eye, a cheek twitching with the sudden sour bile rising from the bottom of the tongue.

Let me reassure you, I am not some obsessive fecal compulsive who is actually pleasured by excrement and foul odours. I am not in the league of people who get a perverted thrill from the filth of metabolic processes. I bathe twice a day, despite the discomfort of squeezing my body into a tiny shower stall. Not to mention all the commotion mother makes about how much hot water I use. I must say, though, that mother would be wise, what with her cigars and her general disregard for appearance and decorum, to take greater care of her personal hygiene.

In the summer-time, I can bathe in my shower garden.

I planted a hedge of caragana for privacy and I only clip it in width, so it doesn't invade the yard. It stands over ten feet high, and inside the scratchy walls, when it is heady with yellow blossoms, I can stand beneath an icy stream of hose water and feel almost beautiful.

Mother always threatens to burn my beautiful bush to the ground. "It's like a damn scrub prison in here! Get no bloody sunlight in the yard. Nothing grows. Just mud and fungus and you muck it up with water and wallow there like some kind of pig. Burn the thing to the ground," she smacks me with her words. But mother does not reveal her inner spirit to those who are looking: instead, she heaps verbal daggers in order not to be seen. I know she will never burn down my summer shower because sometimes I catch her standing inside the bower of caragana. All summer long. When the days are summer long into night and the heat is unbearable, the humble yellow blossoms turn into brittle brown pods of seeds. The shells crack with tiny explosions that bounce and scatter seeds on the parched ground. They roll to where my mother douses herself with icy water. I catch her when she thinks I'm still at the mall, hosing her scrawny old woman's body, a smile on her scowl face, and a cigar burning between her lips. I never let on I see her in those moments. She is more vulnerable than I am.

The dog decided to remain in the confines of our trailer and it made me realize one can never foretell the life choices that others will enact. Mother called him Rabies, and hosed him off in the caragana shower out back. Rabies came to, shook himself off like dogs do, slunk into the kitchen, and hunkered beneath the table. Mother laughed once, "Aaarrrrgh," and threw him the first thing her hand came in contact with inside the refrigerator. It was father's head. I had tucked him there to keep him from being underfoot, and he must have fallen asleep. The starving dog clamped down on an ear and knawed with stumpy teeth. Father screamed outrage.

"What you say, Stink-O? Speak up. Fat girls shouldn't whisper."

"Nothing, Mother. I think you tossed Rabies a cabbage. I'll just take it back and feed him something more suitable. Perhaps that beef knuckle we used to make soup yesterday."

"Suit yourself. But don't say perhaps." Mother stomped off "to sit on the can."

"A dog. Your mother fed me to a dog. Haven't I been tormented enough? When will this suffering end?" Father started weeping, the dog keening. I sighed. I am not one who gives in easily to the woes of this world. Sighing is an expression of defeat, or at least a sign of weakness which reveals a lack of worldly toughness. But Father is a sorry shade, a cloud of perpetual doom and defeat. I don't even want to know what sort of man he was before he fell to this. It would only make a tragic comedy out of what was probably a pathetic life. I swooped down, scooped father's head from between Rabies' paws and set him on the table, right side up. Dug through the garbage for the dry soup bone and tossed it to the dog. Yes, a fat girl can swoop. I am remarkably light on my feet, I almost float on the tips of my toes. Certainly, one may be fat and stinky, but that doesn't necessitate stumbling awkwardness. I never drag my feet and I never stomp fit to bring down the roof. Mother is the stomper in this house and many a time I have whipped up the ladder to tap new tar paper on the roof. I may be grand, I may stink and be hated by dogs, but I have a dancer's feet and the endurance of a rice-planter's thighs.

Did I mention that I'm also coloured? One is led to say "also" in the long list of things I am that are not commonly perceived as complimentary. One cannot say "I'm coloured," and expect, "You know, I've always wanted to be coloured myself," as a standard reaction. Not that I would rather be a stinky, fat, white girl. Perhaps mauve or plum. Now there's a colour!

A fat coloured rat girl has to look out for herself, never reveal her cards. Lucky for me, I must say I'm blessed with a certain amount of higher intelligence, a certain sensitivity which enables me to more than endure the trials of this existence. On my better days, I can leap and soar above the tarry roof of the trailer house. On my better days, the stars sing closer to my ears. I may be fat, I may stink larger than life, I may be a coloured mall rat in striped trousers, but I am coyly so.

Ah yes, the mall. Now why would a clever girl like myself bother to habit such a gross manifestation of consumer greed? Is it some puerile addiction, a disfunction I cannot control? Ahh, many a time I've pondered on this, but it is not as an active consumer that I return to the mall. My forays there are part of an ongoing study of the plight of human existence in a modern colonized country. A mall is the microcosm, the centrifugal force in a cold country where much of the year is sub-zero in temperature. A mall reveals the dynamics of the surrounding inhabitants; yes, the habits of the masses can be revealed in the Hudson Bay department store. In the vast expanses of Toys 'R Us where hideously greedy children manipulate TV dinner divorcées into making purchases which have the monetary equivalence to feed a small village.

When I fully understand the human mall condition, I will reach a doorway to a higher level of existence. One must understand one's limitations, the shackles of social norms, in order to overcome them. And when I have accomplished this, I will cast aside my mantle of foul odour and float to the outer limits of time and space. Alas, one must always have a care not to steep oneself too deeply in theoretical thought. It will only lead to the sin created by the Greeks and taught in every western educational institution today. Hubris, dreaded hubris.

Lucky for me, my father's pale and pathetic head is confined to the parameters of our trailer lot. Imagine what a hindrance he'd be in my pursuit of higher consciousness! I slip into my gymnast's slippers and dance through my caragana bower and out the tattered gate, Father's head rolling down the walk after me as far as the last concrete slab, then teetering back and forth in what I assume is a head wave. Feeling extra generous, I throw back a kiss. And he levitates a few feet in pleasure. There is no sight nor sound of Rabies, much to my father's relief.

"Arrr! Stink-o! Pick me up a box of cigars. Don't cheap out on me and buy those candy-flavoured Colts, you hear!" Mother snarls from the tiny bathroom window. I blow kisses, five, six, seven, and flutter down the sidewalk, mother or her bowels growling from the dark recesses of our tinny home.

As I walk between the rows of identical rectangular homes, highlighted with large, colourful butterflies and plastic petunias, I hear the slamming of doors and the snap of windows being closed. My odour precedes me and I never need an introduction. My signature prevails. Alas, a thought. If one smells a smell and was never taught to like it, would one not find it distasteful as a result of ignorance? Let me pursue the opposite line of thought. If one is taught as a very small child, into adulthood, that roses are disgusting, that they are vilely noxious and ugly to boot, would one not despise the very thought of their scent? It may be that I smell beautifully beyond the capacity of human recognition. The scent of angels and salamanders. And no one to appreciate the loveliness before their very senses.

The mall. The mall. Saturday, and the mall is a virtual hub of hustle and bustle. Crying infants and old women smoking. Unisex teens sprouting rings from every inch of skin that's revealed and the mind boggles thinking about what's not revealed. Fake and real potato french fries, stand-in-line Chinese food, trendy café au lait and iced coffee. It is crowded but I always have a wide path to myself. A minimum three feet of circumference is the space I am given. No one dares come any closer than that, I'm afraid. Like a diver in a shark cage, no, that's not quite right. Regardless.

I have a daily route I take. Even if my eyes were put out, I could wind my way through the blind corners and dead end halls of this mall. Like the tragic Shakespearean kings, I would prevail with an uncanny sense of despair and enlightenment. The merchants all know me by smell and sometimes a wave or a brief nod of a head is offered. There was a time when most of the merchants convened to try to put an end to my forays. To banish me from my chosen road of human contemplation. But legally there is nothing they can do as long as I buy an item now and again, like mother's cigars, or a soup bone from the butcher. They can't evict me for the way I smell, or how I look in my striped trousers. There was a time when I could have been evicted for being coloured, but at this moment in history and geographical location, I am lawfully tolerated. Alas, no one wants to be merely tolerated, like a whining child or an ugly dog. Such human arrogance. We dare assume that some are meant to be merely tolerated while others are sought out to be idolized, glorified, even to wipe their dainty asses. Have a care! I mustn't fall into my mother's pit of baseness. The utter unfairness of it all is enough to make one want to bite one's own tongue off, a mute supplication to the evils of this world, but that's the other end of the stick. Father's end of misery and woe. It is my chosen path to seek another.

I glide into Holy Smoke to pick out a box of cigars for mother. If I wait until I have done my daily study of the machinations of mall existence, I may very well forget and mother will be sorely vexed. In a manner which will be audible for several square kilometers.

"Good afternoon," Adib nods politely from behind his pastel handkerchief.

"Lovely," I breezily smile. Step up to the marble counter.

"The box of usual for you?" He backs a pace, smiling behind the cover of his handkerchief, to make up for his instinctual retreat.

"Please," I bob and lean my arm against the cool grey rock slab that runs the length of the entire store. Men on stools on either side of me hop off, stuff burning pipes in trouser pockets in their haste to escape me.

Adib sighs, even though he has his back to the exodus. Turns with a box filled with cigars as thick as my thumb, individually wrapped and sealed with a red sticker. He has thrown five extra ones on top so it will take longer before I have to return.

"Your generosity is so greatly appreciated," I bow, clicking my heels like some military personage. Pay him with bills sweating wetly from the pocket of my striped pants.

Adib accepts them as graciously as a man, extending a pair of tweezers, can. No, I am not angered by his reticence to come into direct contact with me. Indeed, I find his manner refreshingly honest. He never hurls abuse.

"My best to your mother," Adib nods, handing me my change via tweezers. "By the way," he adds, "you might want to take in the new children's play area in the west wing of the mall. I heard that it's quite the development."

"Why thank you," I beam. Then frown. "But how is it that I am not acquainted with this wonder of childish bliss?"

Adib just shrugs, breathing shallowly from behind his scented lavender hanky. I thank him again. Glide gracefully through the door, and, toes pointed, leap excitedly to the West wing.

FRIENDZIES

The sign reads, one of those obscure conflations of words that means almost nothing at all. Like a joke with a punchline from another, one realizes there is an attempt at humour but nothing to get. Grand opening balloons and streamers trail limply from painted pillars, curl with dust on the cold floor. A table with free coffee and donuts and Coke-flavoured pop made out of syrup. I walk up to the gate, disheartened, but must enter for study purposes. One must not let first impressions alter one's methodology, one's code of ethics.

"One adult please," I smile courteously.

"Where's your kid?" a girl chews out with an unseemly quantity of gum.

I am amazed. She does not curl her nose in disgust from the stench that permeates my being. Her eyes do not water and she doesn't gape at my size.

"I have no children," I nod. "I just want to see the

newly constructed premises." How is it that she doesn't seem to notice? Perhaps her nose has been decimated from smoking or lines of cocaine.

"Ya can't go in without a kid, because adults go in free but a kid costs eight bucks," The girl tips forward on her stool to rest her chin in her hands, elbows sloppily on the countertop before me.

"My goodness! Eight dollars for a child!" I am shocked. Who can afford to entertain their children here, and is it worth it?

"What if one were to tell you that the child is inside already, that I've only come to join her?"

The young woman kicks a button with her foot and the gate swings open. "Don't forget to take off your shoes and keep valuables on your person," she intones.

And I think, she is from a generation where nothing seems to matter.

Plastic tubing, colours of a diseased mind, runs crazily throughout the room, twisting, turning back on itself to no end, no beginning. Plastic balls fill a pit of doom, three toddlers drowning to their parents' snap-shotting delight, primary reds, blues, and yellows clashing horribly with khaki, lavender and peach. Children, fat children, skinny children, coloured children, children pale with too much TV, run half-heartedly through the spastic pipes, their stockinged feet pad-padding in the tubes above my head. They squeal listlessly. From expectation rather than delight. A playground for children from a culture of decay. There is enough plastic here to make Tupperware for a whole continent. Mother would think that this is a grandiose joke. Would laugh her cigar-breath, her ever-present stogie clenched between her molars in a way to make Clint Eastwood envious. Mother would enjoy this place to no end, but I am stricken. I am an urban rat, but I still recognize the forces of the sun, the moon, the patterns of wind that clothe me. Albeit, through a film of pollution. The children here are encased in an artificial life. What follows is only an artificial death.

I wander, dazed, dismayed, my dancer's feet dragging heavily on the astro-turf. Some of the older anaemic children stop and stare, whisper to each other from behind covered mouths. I take no heed. Wander through the cultural maze of hyperartificiality.

There is no hope, my mind mutters incessantly, there is no hope.

But my diagnostic mood prevails. It is not enough to simply stand on the outside and gape, albeit with a closed mouth.

I must enter the maze.

"Watch your fat can," I can hear my mother's raspy voice breathing cigars all around me. "Don't come crying to me. I'll only say, I told you so, and kick you in the butt."

Mother, oh Mother.

I circle around the strange configuration of man-made maze. Thinking to myself, a woman never would. Circle thrice before I spot a young child scurrying up a hot pink pipe, like a rabbit with a watch. I adjust my mental clipboard and squelch my body into the mouth of the tube. Wishing for a ball of string.

Fat rat in a sewer pipe, the thought bubbles hysterically to the surface of my mind, but I kick the thought in the can in the manner of my mother. What is strangely interesting is that instead of getting stuck like an egg in the throat of an overgreedy snake, my body elongates. Spreads towards the ends with space so that all I need to do is flutter my toes to incorporate a forward motion.

I slide, glide, smooth through the twisting tubing. Except for the large metal heads of bolts used to fasten the portions of pipe together. The friction of clothing against the plastic raising such electricity that I am periodically zapped with great sparks and frazzle. Definitely a design flaw.

Then I notice, for the first time in my life, something which has always been with me, yet never perceived. So completely encased by plastic that it cannot be diluted by outer forces, I can smell myself. But the wonder! Because my odour is not smell, but sound. The unbearable voices of mythic manatees, the cry of the phoenix, the whispers of kappa lovers beside a gurgling stream. The voice of the moon that turns away from our gaze, the song of suns colliding. The sounds which emanate from my skin on such a level of intensity that mortal senses recoil, deflect beauty into ugliness.

And my joy. Such incredible joy. The hairs on my arms stand electric, the static energy and the heat mix smell/sound of such dizzying intensity, the plastic which surrounds me bursts apart, falls away from my being like an artificial cocoon.

I hover, twenty feet in the air.

The surrounding pipes collapse and children begin to tumble to the ground, but the pitch of sound intensifies, like beams of coloured light, and the children bob, rise slowly upward to where I float. I extend my hands and the children grab hold, hold each other's hands, smile with wonder.

"Oh my God!" someone finally gasps, from far beneath us. Another screams. Fathers faint and an enterprising teenager grabs a camera from a fallen man and begins to snap pictures. But none of it matters. This moment. Tears flow from my eyes, and I burst out laughing. And the children laugh too. We float, hover. The plastic pipes shimmer, buckle beneath our voices, then burst into soft confetti.

The Garden of the Medicis
DAVID ARNASON

Joe slowed the Toyota and pulled over to the edge of
the road. They seemed to have been climbing for a very
long time, the Toyota unable to handle the steep grade
in anything higher than third gear. Now steam billowed
from the engine. Carla turned her attention to the children in the back seat.

"It's okay," she told them. "Daddy will get it fixed
in a minute. Just stay still and don't undo your seat
belts."

"Daddy's not going to get us out of this one so
easy," Joe muttered under his breath, but he only said,
"Oh, nothing" when Carla asked what he'd said.

Joe opened the hood of the car and looked at the
motor. Steam was still coming from around the radiator
cap, but it seemed to have slowed down a bit. A Jeep
came from the opposite direction, but it passed without
even slowing down, and Joe realized that they hadn't
seen any other cars for a quite a while.

Water, he thought. I'll have to get some water to
fill up the radiator, then maybe we can limp to a garage.

But there was no water anywhere near, no ditch, no
mountain stream, not even a puddle. There were only
the high banks of the rock cut on both sides and a few
small rocks that had tumbled onto the road.

"Nothing I can do," Joe told Carla. "We've boiled
over. I have to add antifreeze, or at least water, before
we can drive anywhere."

"Didn't we pass a garage a while back?" Carla asked.
"Or a motel or something? Someplace that might at
least have a phone?"

"I don't know," Joe said. "We passed something, but it might have been twenty miles away."

"You can just glide down the hill," Jason said from the back seat. He was eleven and had just recently felt old enough to offer advice to adults. "Just turn around and we'll keep on gliding until we find something."

"Oh, sure," Kerry, his older sister, needled him. "And the brakes will fail and we'll go off the side of a cliff. Besides, we've got power steering and power brakes. Neither of those things works unless the motor is running."

After a half-hour, in which only one vehicle passed, a bus whose passengers apparently thought his appeal for help was simple friendliness and waved at him from the window, Joe was prepared to follow Jason's advice.

"Sure," Kerry said. "Now we'll all die."

"Enough," her mother told her, and that quieted her. Kerry was fifteen and given to unexplained moments of weeping, as if she had suffered some great tragedy but was forbidden to speak of it.

Joe cranked the wheel of the Toyota, and it was much easier to push than he had thought it would be. It also started downhill much faster than he'd expected, and if Carla hadn't pulled on the emergency brake, he would have been left behind watching his family rocket to their fates.

"I'm going to go quite slowly," Joe told the family. "Look for signs. Sometimes there are places that you don't notice until the last second."

And it happened in that way. They had drifted slowly downward for about five minutes when Carla saw a small sign that would have been unreadable to anyone going faster than five miles an hour. It read "Garden of the Medicis" and it marked an almost invisible road that led steeply down. Joe turned without hesitation, and the

Toyota bounced over the uneven gravel path. There were hairpin bends he could hardly negotiate and, before long, the brakes were beginning to smell.

There better be something at the bottom, Joe thought to himself, or we'll never get out of here. All that stood between his family and starvation was a couple of Cokes and a large bag of tortilla chips.

There *was* something at the bottom. A stunning mountain lake that appeared to be half blue and half green with a blur of pink in the centre. They caught glimpses of it through the trees, and, just as they made the final turn, it opened before them in all its glory.

"Wow," Kerry said. "No boats, no cottages, no anything. Just water and sand." The Toyota eased to a final stop just at the very edge of a large sandy beach.

"At least there's water," Joe said. "I can probably get the car started, though I don't know if we'll ever climb out of here without boiling over again."

They all got out to look at the lake, and Jason discovered another sign that said "Garden of the Medicis" with an arrow that pointed down a narrow path along the shore.

"We may as well find out what it is," Carla said, and they walked single file through the ferns and shrubs that surrounded the pathway. After just a minute of walking, they rounded a little headland and came on another bay and sandy beach. Here, a garish pink building with a false front and a high fence proclaimed itself the "Garden of the Medicis" in ornate lettering. A string of coloured lights hung just above the fence, and a gate that was framed with pillars so that it looked ancient and Roman was locked with a padlock. The windows of the main building were boarded over, and though a sign on the door said "Open," the building was locked.

Joe rapped on the door, but there was no answer. He rapped again, and a voice from behind them said, "No use knocking. It's closed."

The voice came from a young man of indeterminate age. He might have been in his early twenties, but he might also have been much younger. He wore shorts and a white T-shirt with a baseball cap turned backwards. He was barefoot.

"What is this place?" Jason asked. He seemed to have decided in favour of the man's youth, and there was nothing of awe or respect in his voice.

The young man didn't answer for a while. His eyes were a startling green. "It's a resort," he said finally. "Or at least it used to be. It's been closed for years. I'm the caretaker." Then, as if he had decided that they posed no threat, he confided, "It's just a summer job. I watch that nobody vandalizes the place or sets it on fire or anything. Apparently it was really popular around the time of the First World War, but it's been closed for about seventy years." Joe turned back to the building. He noticed that what he had first thought a decorative motif on the pillars of the gate was actually real grape leaves.

The young man's name was Tomaso, and he was working his way through university. He didn't really know much about the place. He'd answered an ad in the newspaper, and the next thing he knew, he was here. Once a week, a truck came by and left him supplies, but the rest of the time, he just read the novels he had brought with him. He helped Joe fill up the radiator with water and waved goodbye as they started up the hill.

About a hundred yards further, the steam from the engine made it impossible to see at all. This time Joe noticed the hole in the hose from which the steam issued. Tomaso could think of no solution. He had no phone, and the truck did not come until Thursday, another four days. He had plenty of food, though, and if they wanted to camp, he'd be glad to help out. The kids loved the idea, and even Carla seemed content.

"You wanted something unspoiled," she said. "You're not going to get much better than this."

They set up their tent back on the first little bay near the car. The kids wanted to set up by the Garden of the Medicis where Tomaso had his tent, but Joe had noticed a bit too much eagerness on Kerry's part, and he wasn't prepared to be caught in the middle of the fantasy of a summer's romance. She was certain to fall in love with Tomaso, and then she'd weep all the way to Vancouver when they left.

Tomaso brought over a bunch of wieners and stale buns, and they ate hot dogs. Joe took out a couple of lawn chairs, and he and Carla read in the shade of an old ponderosa pine. Tomaso and the kids went swimming, Kerry in a bikini, which Joe would certainly have banned if he had seen it before that moment. Then the sun slipped behind a mountain, and though it was only four o'clock, the air was suddenly cold.

Tomaso brought cans of ravioli, and they cooked it in a frying pan over an open fire. Everybody agreed it was one of the finest meals they had ever eaten. Finally, Tomaso said good night and disappeared into the path along the edge of the lake. He'd be back with breakfast, he said.

Sometime in the night, Joe awoke to the faint sound of music. When he got out of the tent, he could no longer hear it. The night was starry and clear, and the lake was entirely silver. Joe walked to the edge of the lake, and dipped his toe. To his surprise, the lake was warm. On an impulse, he slipped off his pyjama bottoms and waded in. The water was as soft and pure as silk. It got deep quickly, but it seemed to have more buoyancy than water should have. Joe had never thought of himself as a good swimmer, but now he moved with ease, slicing his way through the water.

He aimed for the point of land that separated the Garden of the Medicis from the campsite. It was a long swim for him, but he wasn't far from shore, and he could always return along the beach. He rolled over and eased into a gentle backstroke. He felt he could go on for hours. When he thought he must be past the point, he rolled over to see the shore brilliantly lit by hanging lanterns. A shape loomed out of the lake in front of him, and as it passed, he realized it was a gondola, a dark figure in a striped shirt poling it, and lovers clasped in each other's arms at the far end. The music was unmistakable now. Figures flitted along the beach, and he could hear the ripple of laughter above the music. He could make out other craft now, and a barge, brightly lit and decorated with flowers, was anchored in the centre of the bay.

Joe swam in to the shore. As soon as he left the water, he was intensely conscious that he was naked, so he kept very close to the line of trees. A couple came down the beach, and he hid behind a tree as they passed. The man was wearing an elegant three-piece suit with a striped tie and a white shirt, but he was barefoot. The tie-pin and cufflinks gleamed against the darkness of the lake. The woman wore a long white gown and a tiara. She, too, was barefoot. They stopped directly in front of Joe, and the man took the woman in his arms.

"It'll be over in three months," the man told the woman. "That's what everybody says. If I don't go, how will I ever live with myself later?"

"Just don't get yourself killed," the woman said. "They say the Ramsay boy got killed in France a couple of weeks ago."

"I won't get killed," the man said. "Three months. That's a promise." And he folded her in his arms and kissed her. Joe thought the woman was the most beautiful person he had ever seen, and he felt embarrassed at witnessing the intimacy before him. He found the path just back of the beach and continued down it to the Garden of the Medicis. The building was ablaze with light, and dozens of teams of horses still hitched to elegant coaches and wagons stamped their fight and whinnied on the night air.

Joe edged his way to the beginning of the fence, then plunged into the undergrowth and followed the line of the fence to a spot where he could climb the lower branches of a tree and see over.

Inside was what seemed the balcony of a ballroom. Through a set of open doors, Joe could see dancers whirling to the music of an orchestra. Women with fans cooled themselves behind the pillars of the balcony. Joe listened intently to hear what they were saying, but all he could make out was "The Count. The Count."

Then a man dressed in an elaborate costume that looked like something from a Shakespearean play appeared, accompanied by a tall elegant woman in a bejewelled gown. The woman looked amazingly like Carla. Her hair was swept up in an elaborate coiffure that showed off the lines of her neck. A small page in a black uniform with ruffled sleeves brought them glasses of wine on a silver tray. The page looked remarkably like Jason. Joe wished he could get closer, but any closer movement would reveal him naked to the dancers.

"Anything you wish, my dear," the Count said. "But it must look like an accident. We shall report him as drowned." These words came sharply and clearly, but it was impossible to hear what the woman answered. The

Count and the woman followed the page back into the ballroom.

For a while there was no one, only the whirl of distant dancers and the music. Then a young couple emerged from a doorway below the balcony. Joe had not noticed it before. They were laughing, and the young man tried to kiss the woman, who twisted away and ran towards the fence where Joe was hiding. In the light from a lantern their faces were clear. The young woman was Kerry and the man was Tomaso. He was dressed entirely in black and she in a wispy white dress. He caught her just below the branches of Joe's tree and this time she did not resist his kiss.

"Kerry," Joe shouted, "what are you doing?"

The lovers looked up at the tree and discovered Joe there in all his nakedness. The woman he had thought was Kerry screamed, and in a moment the lawn in front of the balcony was filled with running figures. Joe slipped out of the tree and made his way back through the undergrowth, not daring to walk either on the path or on the beach. Branches whipped into his eyes, and he stepped on sharp roots and stones. There were cobwebs everywhere.

Finally, he made it back to the campsite. He picked up his pyjama bottoms where he had let them fall by the lake, and he put them on. He checked the kids' tent. Kerry and Jason were both sound asleep in their sleeping bags. Carla snored gently in the larger tent. Joe rummaged through his suitcase and found the half bottle of rye he kept there, and he took a long draw directly from the bottle.

The next morning, Tomaso arrived with breakfast, Aunt Jemima pancake mix and some emergency powdered eggs. Joe asked him if he had heard anything odd last night. Tomaso had. Something, probably a bear, had been crashing around in the underbrush. He'd gone out to check and saw what looked like a naked man, though of course that was impossible. Some trick of the moonlight.

After breakfast, Joe asked Tomaso if they could look inside the Garden of the Medicis.

"I'm not supposed to," Tomaso said. "That's the one rule. I mustn't let anyone in or else I get fired. Besides, there's nothing there to see. Only a few old models in costumes and some ratty furniture. There's a window around the back you can see through if you want, but even I am not allowed to go in there."

By early afternoon, Carla had decided to take a nap, Jason was building a fort, and Tomaso was watching Kerry in her bikini, and not likely to move until she gave up swimming. Joe took a pail from the car and announced he was going to pick huckleberries. Nobody paid any attention to him.

The window around the back was just where Tomaso had said it was. Through the window, Joe could make out tattered furniture and obscure figures in the shadows. The window was locked with a small clasp. Joe took out his Swiss army knife, and twisted the clasp. The wood was rotten, and the clasp came out easily. Joe put it in his pocket and crawled through the window into the shadowy room.

The room was apparently a store room. Old flowered sofas were piled on top of each other, but they were covered with sheets and appeared to be in better shape than the dust and cobwebs would lead you to expect. Chairs were piled haphazardly, and all along one side of the room, costumes hung from hooks on the wall. Like the sofas, the costumes were protected by sheets, and were in much better condition than Joe had expected. He took down a brown three-piece suit that looked like the one the barefoot man on the beach had worn, and tried the jacket on. It fit him perfectly. A batch of parasols stood upside down in an elephant's foot basket. Ornate gilt mirrors and lamps were propped between the other items.

The figures that Tomaso had mentioned were gathered near a staircase that led upwards. They appeared to be made from papier-maché, and much of the paint had chipped from them. There were six figures in all, and they represented the serving classes: a cook, a waiter, two maids, a pageboy, and a butler. It seemed that the garden of the Medicis had once been a museum. The top of the stairway was much brighter than the room below, as if it were lit by electric lights.

It was sunlight that lit the room, Joe discovered when he entered it. The stairway led to the ballroom he had seen from his tree the night before. The ballroom was much larger than seemed possible when you looked at the building from outside. Here, figures were gathered in groups. The musicians, complete with instruments, were frozen in mid-song at the far end of the room. Couples swooped and dipped in an elaborate minuet. These figures were far better made than the ones below. They were exquisitely shaped from some material that Joe could not identify. At first sight it looked like wax, but the surface, when you touched it, had all the softness of skin. There was not a speck of dust or a cobweb anywhere.

The Count and the woman he had seen with her the night before stood in the opening of the balcony. Seen more closely, the female figure's resemblance to Carla was superficial. It was about the same size with the same colour hair, but the eyes were different. The small page who presented them with wine did look like Jason, but only in the way that an army of small boys in uniform would resemble each other. The expression on the Count's face seemed to be rage. His eyes followed Joe in an eerie way as Joe moved about the room.

From the balcony, Joe could see the tree in which he had hidden the night before. His hiding place in daylight was obvious, impossible to miss. On the lawn, the figure he had taken to be Tomaso chased Kerry's double in a parody of young love. In a dimmer light, it might be possible to mistake them for the real thing.

Joe was about to leave when he noticed a door behind the musicians, which led to an alcove. He slipped behind the curtains that separated the musicians from the room, and entered. There the beautiful woman he had seen on the beach leaned in a gesture of mourning and grief over a figure who lay on a hospital bed. The figure was dressed in full military uniform, but his chest was covered with blood, and an open hole showed that he had been shot through the heart.

Joe leaned over to see whether the figure was the one he had seen on the beach, the man who had promised to return in three months. It was like looking into a mirror. The face that stared up at him was clearly his own.

On his way back to the camp, Joe decided to confront Tomaso. Tomaso obviously knew more than he had let on. Someone tended those figures daily. Someone vacuumed the dust and the cobwebs and polished the instruments of the musicians. On an impulse, he turned back and examined the earth in front of the Garden of the Medicis. The prints of horses were everywhere, and the tracks of wagons led up a path into the forest.

Tomaso was not there when Joe arrived. He had told the children that part of his duties included checking on a cabin on the other side of the lake, and he had taken a canoe and paddled off. He had offered to take

Kerry for a ride, but Carla had vetoed that plan, and now Kerry was weeping gently in the tent.

"There are no ripe huckleberries yet," Joe told Carla, but he didn't tell her about his visit to the Garden of the Medicis.

"At nine o'clock tomorrow morning the truck comes with the supplies," Carla told him. "Then we can get away from here. It's beautiful and everything, but there's something very strange about this place. I don't think I like it."

Tomaso did not come back with supper as he had promised, and everyone was a little hungry and a little cranky by dark. Kerry was certain that Tomaso had drowned, and wanted to set out to rescue him. Joe explained that there was no way to rescue him since they had no boat, and Kerry went back to the tent and wept some more.

When the music started that night, Joe vowed to resist it. By nine they next morning they would be gone, and whatever ghosts inhabited the Garden of the Medicis could go on without him. But the image of the woman looking down at his own dead body haunted him, and he couldn't sleep. He rolled over to put his arm around Carla, seeking comfort, but she was gone. Her sleeping bag was empty. He would probably find her, unable to sleep, sitting on a rock near the beach. He would tell her about the Garden of the Medicis.

But she was not on a rock near the beach. She was nowhere to be found. He looked into the kids' tent on the off chance that one of them was sick and she had gone to comfort them and fallen asleep. The kids' tent too was empty. He called their names into the darkness, but no one answered. The distant sound of violins drifted around the point.

Joe put on his bathing suit and walked down to the edge of the water. There was no moonlight, but the stars alone made the lake bright. The water was warm and as smooth as silk. Joe swam steadily until he rounded the point. The scene was nearly identical to what he had seen the other night. Boats flitted back and forth across the water, and people partied on a barge anchored in the centre of the bay. Joe swam to land right at the point and made his way along the beach to the brilliantly lit building at the centre of the bay. He heard the whinney of a horse and knew that the carriages were waiting in front. He crept along the fence until he reached the window he had pried open earlier. It swung open now with only the slightest creak. The light pouring down the staircase from above made the room brighter than it had been during the day. Joe found the three-piece suit he had tried on earlier, and he put it on now. It fit perfectly, and once he had put on the white shirt, the tie, the tie pin, and the cufflinks, he thought he must be indistinguishable from the man he had seen on the beach. He couldn't find any shoes, but he consoled himself that the other man had also been barefoot.

Joe took a deep breath and walked up the stairs into the ballroom. The dancers swirled around so that he had to move back to the wall to avoid being hit. They were dressed in a strange assortment of costumes. Many of the women wore elaborate gowns, but some wore simple pleated white skirts and light sweaters. *Flappers*, Joe thought. That's what the costume was. Some of the men were dressed as courtiers, but most were in suits very much like Joe's own. Several wore army uniforms.

Joe made his way around the ballroom until he came to the balcony. The Count was standing with his back to the railing, talking to a tall blonde woman.

319

"It's settled," the Count told her. "Tonight's the night. And it will be perceived as a drowning."

"But won't there be an investigation?" she asked.

"They may investigate all they want," the Count replied. "There will be nothing here for them to investigate."

Just then a small page brought them each a glass of wine. He handed them the wine on a silver platter, then turned and walked right past Joe into the ballroom. The page was Jason. There was no doubt about it. He looked directly into his father's eyes but gave no hint of recognition.

The Count and the woman turned to go back into the ballroom, and the woman was certainly Carla. In the afternoon, when her features had been frozen it had been difficult to tell, but now there was no doubt. As soon as they had left the balcony, Joe walked to the railing and looked over. A young couple were in a tight embrace under the tree in which he had sat naked the other night. They pulled apart reluctantly, and in the light that poured from a window he identified them positively. Kerry and Tomaso.

Joe thought he should do something, but there didn't seem to be anything he could do. The music surged and the dancers whirled. From one window, he could see the boats on the lake and the lights from the barge. He moved past the musicians to the alcove where he had seen the woman and the representation of himself, but it was empty. From the window, he could see the teams of horses in front, and a little higher up the bank, Tomaso's tent.

Suddenly, a woman was in his arms. The woman from the beach who had mourned him that very day.

"You're alive," she said. "I saw you dead only a few hours ago, but you're alive."

"No," Joe said. "It's all a mistake." But the woman silenced him with her lips, and he kissed her back, a long, slow, delirious kiss. Then she moved back a little so that she was staring into his face.

"Let me look at you," she said.

Joe looked back at her, but over her shoulder he could see Tomaso's tent and the horses and carriages. People were beginning to leave the Garden of the Medicis and climb into the carriages. One by one, they drove off into the darkness.

Then the sun came over the mountain and Tomaso came out of his tent. He stretched languidly and walked out of sight as if to meet someone. In a moment he was back, and a truck towed Joe's Toyota into the clearing. Tomaso and the other man did something under the hood, then Tomaso started the car. Carla appeared then, and from a distance, it looked as if she had been weeping. Jason climbed into the back seat of the car, and Kerry walked over to Tomaso and kissed him a gentle goodbye kiss. Joe could hear their voices, but the only word he could make out was "drowned."

Then a man in a bathing suit rushed into the clearing and Carla flung herself into his arms. Joe couldn't be sure, but it looked like the man he had seen barefoot on the beach. He wished he could move closer to the window, but the woman in his arms was motionless and he didn't dare disturb her. The man in the bathing suit got into the car, and it followed the truck up the pathway the horses had used the night before.

The road up the mountain was even steeper than the road down. The Toyota choked, and the man driving was afraid it might start to boil over again, but after a minute it seemed like the repair was going to work. The children were silent in the back seat.

"You know something?" the man in the driver's seat said, and then he hesitated.

"What?"

"Never mind," he said. He was sure there was something he had to tell her. He felt that something terribly important had happened at the Garden of the Medicis, something that would change everything, but he couldn't quite remember what it was. They rounded a bend and popped out onto the highway. He turned on the radio and the car filled with the sounds of violins.

Long Gone and Mister Lonely
DIANNE WARREN

1. Karma

Shortly after ten o'clock on Saturday morning, just as Sheryl finished stripping the beds, the front door opened and Sean came in and confessed that he and Perry had spent the night in jail.

"It wasn't our fault, hon," he said. "It was that bouncer at Lenny's. You know the one. He has it in for us. We weren't doing anything, at least not anything you would call seriously criminal."

"Umm," said Sheryl, standing in the hall with the dirty sheets in her arms. She already knew about the night in jail, but she didn't say so. Kate had made her promise not to. She wasn't quite sure what to say so she just stood there. She had a burn blister on the ball of her foot and it hurt. She wondered what to do about it.

"I guess I should have called," Sean said, mistaking her silence for anger.

"Never mind," Sheryl said. "You're home now."

"You're not mad then?" Sean said.

"No," Sheryl said. "I'm not mad." She headed for the basement stairs and threw the sheets down. The blister hurt when she walked on it.

"I'm hungover," Sean said. "I feel like shit."

Sheryl had her back to him and she suddenly felt like laughing. She decided to follow the sheets to the basement so she wouldn't have to face Sean for a few minutes.

"They're not going to charge us with anything, if that's what you're wondering," Sean called down the stairs. "I thought for sure we'd get hit with mischief. Perry and I spent most of the night talking about it, what our chances were for this and that. It's surprising how much you know about the law when push comes to shove. We surprised ourselves. Anyway, we got off lucky."

Sheryl buried her face in the dirty sheets, which she'd picked off the bottom step, then she managed to say, "That's good." She dropped the sheets on the floor by the washing machine. When she climbed the stairs again, Sean was still standing in the hall.

"So you were in jail," she said, having regained her composure.

"That's right," Sean said. "I can't exactly say it was a good experience, but I think in the long run I'll be able to look back and see how it was meaningful. I never want to go through it again though. Once was enough for me."

Teddy came into the front hall and wrapped himself around Sheryl's leg. He was five years old, but small for his age, a funny little blond boy with thick glasses that he kept losing. His head was right at the level of her hand and she stroked his fine yellow hair.

"Hey kid," Sean said. "How's my kid? Did you wonder where I was?"

"Me and mom went camping," said Teddy.

"I'm through with Lenny's," Sean said. "At least, until that bouncer is gone. He's not the kind of guy you can take on. He's got too many friends and they're all built like brick shit houses." He looked down at Teddy. "You went camping?"

"Yeah," Teddy said. "Me and mom."

"In the back yard," Sheryl said.

"Oh," said Sean. "I wondered." Then he said, "I don't care about Lenny's anyway. It's a dump. I'm tired of it."

"You look terrible," Sheryl said. His hair was greasy and his eyes were red and swollen.

"Yeah. I guess I'd better take a shower. Make me some scrambled eggs, will you. With cheese and onions. And toast, but don't put the toast on until I'm ready to eat, so it doesn't get cold."

"We stayed up all night," Teddy said.

"No kidding," Sean said. "Me too." Then he said, "Mom stayed up all night?" Sheryl knew what he was thinking. Since she'd started teaching she hadn't made it past ten o'clock on a Friday night. Even in the movie theatre, she'd fall sound asleep. Sean teased her about it, but she knew it irritated him. "Yeah," Teddy said. "We stayed awake all through the stars."

"I feel good," Sheryl said. It sounded lame and inadequate, but she couldn't put into words how she really felt.

"I feel like hell," Sean said. "Physically, at least. Mentally, I'm not sure. I don't have it figured out yet." He went upstairs to the bathroom and turned on the shower. Sheryl remembered that all the towels were on the floor in the basement, dirty. She shouted up the stairs at him.

"What's that, hon?" he shouted back, turning the water off.

"The towels are all dirty," she said. "I haven't done them yet."

"Christ," Sean said.

"Sorry," Sheryl said.

"I just spent the night in jail. I need a towel."

"Check the back of the door," Sheryl said. "I think I left one there."

She heard the shower again, and hoped she hadn't used all the hot water in the washing machine. She leaned against the wall, slipped her foot out of her sandal, and examined the burn. It didn't look bad, she decided. The blister was small and would heal on its own.

"So what's it like," Sheryl asked later, "being in jail."

"I'll tell you one thing," he said, "they have no respect for you." He was eating the scrambled eggs Sheryl had made. "Did you use Velveeta cheese?" he asked.

"Yes," she said.

He took another bite. Sheryl could tell he was trying to figure out what was wrong with the eggs. "They don't let you ask questions in a dignified way," he said. "When you get arrested it's your right to ask questions. They treat you like someone who's there just to give them grief, as though you planned it."

"You were caught red-handed," Sheryl said. "You had the evidence in the back seat of the car, as I understand it."

"We never claimed to be innocent," Sean said. "But it was just a caper. They didn't have to throw us in jail. It's that bouncer. He has it in for us. I wish there was something I could do about him, but I don't see what. I'd like to get him fired but I think he's too well connected."

"He's probably too good at his job," Sheryl said. "That would be the real reason."

"I don't see why you would say that," Sean said. "Perry and I won't be going back there. He's bad for business, the way I see it."

Teddy was playing on the floor under the table. He had his cars and trucks and was imagining roads in the linoleum pattern, a game he played often.

"God damn it," Sean said to Teddy. "Don't do that."

"Your foot is big mountain," Teddy said.

"It's not a mountain," Sean said. "It's my frigging foot. Take your trucks out back to the sandbox."

"The sandbox is all burned up," Teddy said.

"You should go to bed, Teddy," Sheryl said. "You were up all night, remember."

"I'm not tired," Teddy said.

"Well, go out on the deck then. You shouldn't be listening to us talk about this anyway. Don't tell anybody daddy was in jail."

"I'll kick your butt if you do," Sean said.

"Did you kill someone?" Teddy asked Sean, as he came out from under the table with his trucks in a plastic tackle box.

"Jesus, no," Sean said. Then he said to Sheryl, "What's wrong with him anyway? He's always saying weird stuff. And what's he talking about, the sandbox is all burned up. Jesus."

"Just go out to the deck, Teddy," Sheryl said. "I'll be out in a while. I'll bring some Kool-aid."

Sean finished off the scrambled eggs and Sheryl poured him another cup of coffee.

"It feels good to be home," Sean said. "I think that night in jail was good for me. I appreciate things more. A hot shower. Scrambled eggs. I don't mind saying, you get scared when they put you in a cell and lock the door, even if you know they can't keep you there. Even if you know you haven't done anything of any consequence."

"I lied about the cheese," Sheryl said. "It wasn't Velveeta. I bought the store brand because it's cheaper. I didn't think you'd notice."

"Oh," Sean said.

"Is that all?" Sheryl asked. "Oh?"

"Well, I'm not going to have a fit, if that's what you mean," Sean said. Then he asked, "Is the kid going to have a nap or what?"

"Probably not," Sheryl said. "You know him. Why?"

"I think I could do with a conjugal visit," Sean said.

"You can think all you want," Sheryl said. "But I'm in the middle of washing clothes and somebody has to get the groceries." Sheryl took his plate to the sink and rinsed it. As she stood there, she lifted her sore foot. She wished Sean would take a nap. She wished they hadn't let him out of jail so soon.

"I'll tell you why I don't care about the cheese," Sean said. "It's pointless to get worked up about trivialities. That night in jail had an effect on me. Maybe it was like one of those near-death experiences. You come out of it and you can never look at life the same way again."

Sheryl turned and stared at him, her sore foot resting against the calf of her other leg. "What are you talking about?" she said.

"I don't know," Sean said. "Karma, I guess."

She took a glass pitcher from the cupboard and mixed up a package of grape Kool-aid.

"You know," Sean said, "you've been acting strange ever since I came through the door. Before, you were almost smiling. But now there's another look. I don't know what it means."

Sheryl handed him the jug of Kool-aid and a glass. "Take this to Teddy," she said. "And if he spills it, think karma."

"What's that supposed to mean?" Sean asked.

"Figure it out," Sheryl said.

2. The Koenig Brothers

It was Kate that Sean first liked the looks of, not Sheryl. The two girls were staying in a cabin a quarter mile up the hill from the water. Sean drove the bread delivery truck then, and he passed them most mornings as they walked down to the beach in their bikinis. He told Sheryl that at the end of the day, after he'd finished making his deliveries, he would often go looking for them. First he walked up and down the beach, then he checked the café and the hotel bar, but they were never anywhere to be found. A few times he even peeked in the window of the cabin he thought was theirs, but they weren't home. It became a mystery to be solved, what the two girls did, who they did it with, where they went.

Early one Friday afternoon there was a fire at the bakery. It wasn't much but the sprinkler system cut in and made a mess and the boss told everyone to go home for the rest of the day. Sean drove out to the beach and parked his car across the street from the cabin, and at about four o'clock the two girls came walking up the hill. They walked right past his car without looking at him and went inside the cabin. Shortly after that they came out again wearing tight t-shirts and faded jeans and sandals, and got in the old mustard-yellow Toyota that was parked in the drive. It took them a long time to get it started, but they finally did and then they headed for the highway. Sean followed their trail of blue smoke at a distance. He didn't think they'd noticed him, but of course they had.

In the Toyota, Kate said, "That guy who drives the bread delivery truck is following us."

Sheryl wanted to turn around and look, but she didn't want to be obvious. Kate, who was driving, watched him in the rear-view mirror.

"Are you sure he's following us?" Sheryl asked. "It might just be a coincidence."

"He was parked in front of the cabin," Kate said. "I hardly think it's a coincidence. It's pretty weird, if you ask me. I hope he's not a psycho."

"If it's the bread delivery guy, he's not bad looking," Sheryl said. "I wonder which one of us he fancies."

"It better be you," Kate said. "I'm not interested in having any lost dogs follow me around."

"You don't think he's good looking?" Sheryl asked.

"I didn't say that," Kate said. "But right now it's beside the point."

They turned off the highway and headed west toward Morgan. Kate reported that the car following them had driven on past the turnoff, but before long it was behind them again.

"A pea brain could do a better job of following us than that," she said.

They came to an approach to a farmer's field and Kate pulled off. The car behind them went by in a cloud of grid-road dust. Then, minutes later, Kate and Sheryl passed it again, poorly camouflaged in a stand of trees by the road.

"I guess he is a pea brain," Sheryl said.

Kate honked the horn at him as they drove by.

Sheryl started to laugh. Then Kate got the giggles and could hardly drive. She had to slow down. By the time they pulled up in front of the Morgan Hotel they were both laughing so hard their sides hurt. They sat in front of the hotel for a few minutes, watching for the other car to appear, but it was nowhere in sight.

Finally Kate looked at her watch. "God damn it," she said. "It's quarter after five. That asshole made us late for work." "Good thing the boss is your uncle," Sheryl said.

Sean came into the bar with Perry about half an hour before last call. They were already three sheets to the wind. Sheryl was waiting tables and Kate was in the women's washroom cleaning up vomit. It was Sheryl's turn, but Sheryl had a weak stomach so she'd talked Kate into doing it for her. "I'll do anything you ask," Sheryl had promised. "I'll lick your feet if you want, just please, please, don't make me clean up that vomit. I'll get sick, I swear it."

"Why would I want you to lick my feet?" Kate said. "That's weird." But she'd agreed to do it, saying, "Just remember, you owe me."

Sean and Perry sat down at a table and when Sheryl went to wait on them Sean said, "Where's your partner in crime?"

"My partner in crime?" Sheryl said. "I don't know what you mean."

"The other one," Sean said. "The cute one."

Perry gave Sean a clip across the back of the head, knocking his ball cap off.

"Don't mind him," Perry said to Sheryl. "He's an asshole."

"Tell me something I don't already know," Sheryl said. "Now what'll you have? Not that you need anything else, but it's my job to ask."

"Where'd you say your friend is?" Sean asked.

"I didn't say, but if you must know she's mopping up puke in the women's can."

"Oh," Sean said. Then he said, "I wish you hadn't told me that."

"Bring us a couple of Buds," Perry said.

Sheryl went back to the bar and ordered the beers, then Kate came from the washroom.

"Christ," she said. "I'd like to know who made that mess."

"Well, there's not a woman in the house right now except for you and me," Sheryl said, "and I don't think it was either of us." The bar was almost empty. There was a dance at the lake and a dance always cleared the place out early, except for the old men.

"Maybe it was one of the Koenig brothers," Kate said. "They wouldn't know the difference between the men's and the women's can." The Koenig brothers were playing

331

pool. They were both over eighty and spent most of their pension cheques in the Morgan Hotel bar.

Sheryl pointed at Sean. "Look who's here," she said. "And guess who he's got his eye on. I'll give you a hint. It's not me."

"Great," said Kate. She looked at the two Budweisers on Sheryl's tray. "For them?" she asked. Sheryl nodded. Kate took the beers and said, "We'll see how long his dick stays hard after he meets bitch-barmaid from hell."

The bartender, who was Kate's Uncle Steve and the owner of the hotel, heard her. He said, "I don't know where she learned to talk like that. Not from my side of the family."

"You have to talk like that, working in this place," Sheryl said. "No offence intended."

"None taken," Steve said. He came around to Sheryl's side of the bar and sat down on a stool.

"Christ almighty," he said. "My feet hurt."

"Mine too," Sheryl said. She sat on a stool next to Steve and they watched Kate deliver the beers. They couldn't hear what was being said.

"So how's the cabin working out?" Steve asked.

"Great," Sheryl said. The cabin was Steve's too, and he let Sheryl and Kate live there for nothing. They liked living at the lake. They almost always worked the night shift, which meant they got to spend the day on the beach, as long as the sun was shining.

"How's the boyfriend?" Steve asked.

"He dumped me," Sheryl said. "For a girl who plays basketball."

"Is she tall?" Steve asked.

"I don't know," Sheryl said. "I've never seen her. Anyway, I don't care. He was nothing special."

Sheryl didn't think she should moan about the boyfriend to Steve. She hadn't really cared that much about him, and Steve had an ex-wife that he apparently cared about a lot. He referred to her as Long-gone Lucy, even though her name wasn't Lucy, it was Marian.

"Well," said Steve, "I was going to say I was sorry he dumped you, but if he was nothing special I guess I won't bother. Maybe I should congratulate you instead."

"I don't know if I'd go that far," Sheryl said.

Steve looked at his watch and then turned his attention to the Koenig brothers, who were still playing pool. "It's about time for the Two Stooges to go at it," he said. "You can just about set your clock by them."

"They're late tonight," Sheryl said. The words were hardly out of her mouth when the Koenig brothers began waving their pool cues around and shouting at one another. Steve said, "Same damn thing every night. One of these nights someone's going to take it in the eye and I'll be the one who gets sued." He got up, shouting, "Yo, you old buggers cut that out before you hurt somebody." Sheryl watched as he expertly manoeuvred his way between the waving pool cues. He managed to disarm the two brothers, and then he steered them toward a table where several other old men were sitting. Sheryl heard him say, "Last call, boys." The spectre of last call usually made the Koenig brothers forget whatever it was they'd been arguing about.

The old men always ordered the same thing, draft beer, so Sheryl went behind the bar and poured a dozen glasses and took them to the table. She had to make two trips. By the time she got back for the second time Steve had the Koenig brothers shaking hands, first with each other, then with whoever they could reach without getting up. They wanted to shake Sheryl's hand too, but she was sick of them so she left Steve to collect the tab.

She went back to the bar, put her tray down on the counter, and kicked her sandals off. The soles of her feet were burning and she regretted not wearing her running shoes. She looked at Kate, who was now seated at the table with Perry and Sean, and appeared to be deep in conversation with Perry.

Steve came back to the bar with a handful of change and small bills. "It must be true, what they say about old people reverting to childhood," he said. "Look at them. This place is like a daycare centre, only they drink beer instead of Kool-aid." Sheryl laughed. Then she pointed at Kate and said, "Look what's happening over there."

"So much for bitch-barmaid," Steve said.

"They'll probably give her a huge tip," Sheryl said. "That would piss me off."

At twelve-thirty Steve kicked Perry and Sean and the old men out. Usually the bar stayed open until one, but it was so dead Steve decided there was no point. Sheryl and Kate were going to help him clean up, but he told them to leave.

"I'm going home," he said. "I'll clean up in the morning. You girls can still catch the dance. Go have some fun."

On the way to the car, Sheryl said, "Your uncle is a pretty cool guy." She was thinking about how he was alone and still relatively young, younger than her parents anyway, wondering how he would ever find anyone to replace Long-gone Lucy in a town the size of Morgan. "Why don't we go get him and take him to the dance with us?" she asked Kate.

"Don't be stupid," Kate said. "He won't want to come with us."

"Why don't we ask him," Sheryl said. "He can say no if he doesn't want to come."

"You go ask him then," Kate said.

Sheryl went back into the bar. Steve was racking up the balls on the pool table. He looked lonely.

"Oh," she said. "I thought you were going home."

"This is home," he said. That was true, sort of. He lived in a suite in the back of the hotel.

"Why don't you come to the dance with Kate and me," Sheryl said. "Maybe we can find you someone to dance with."

"What makes you think I need someone to dance with?" Steve said. He didn't sound particularly pleased that Sheryl had invited him to come along. There was a definite cool edge to his voice and the way he looked at her. She thought maybe she'd offended him by implying he couldn't find anyone on his own.

"I just thought you might want to come," she said.

"You work for me," Steve said. "That's all."

"Okay," Sheryl said. "Well, good night." She turned to leave and then she figured out that Steve thought she was coming on to him. She felt herself turning beet red and quickly hurried out the door.

"I knew he wouldn't want to come," Kate said as Sheryl got in the car. "He's too old to go to dances at the lake. He'd feel stupid."

"It didn't hurt to ask," Sheryl said. She was glad it was dark so Kate couldn't see her red face. She felt completely humiliated and didn't know how she'd face Steve when she came to work on Monday.

Kate tried to start the car. It wouldn't turn over.

"Maybe it's just flooded," Sheryl said.

They sat there for a few minutes, then Kate tried again. The car still wouldn't start.

"Great," Kate said. "Now I'm going to have to go and ask Steve to drive us back to the lake."

"No," Sheryl said. "We can't ask him to do that. He's tired. He said he was really tired."

"Well, if we're going to ask him, we should do it now,"

Kate said, "not half an hour from now when he's in his pyjamas."

"I don't imagine he wears pyjamas," Sheryl said. "I can't see it."

"You know what I mean."

"We can't ask him to drive us," Sheryl said. "He's pretty good to us already. It would be taking advantage of him." She was afraid Steve might think they'd engineered the car breaking down. He might think it was a ploy, thought up by her, Sheryl.

"Well, what are we going to do then?" Kate wanted to know. "Hitchhike? Like someone trustworthy is going to come along at this time of night."

Sheryl was trying to think of a solution that didn't involve Steve, when Sean and Perry came driving up the street.

They angle parked next to Kate and Sheryl, on Kate's side. Perry rolled down his window and said, "Anything we can do for you ladies?"

"Yeah," Kate said. "You can give us a ride to the lake. This god damned car won't start."

Perry got in the back seat and Kate climbed in next to him. Sheryl got in the front with Sean.

"So this is your car," Sheryl said to him, conversationally.

"You noticed," Sean said. He was obviously sulking. Sheryl supposed that was because she was sitting beside him instead of Kate. She was tempted to tell him to go fuck himself and take her chances hitch-hiking, but she quickly decided that would be excessively dramatic and a major inconvenience. Instead, she said, "You drive the bread delivery truck."

"Tell me something I don't already know," Sean said.

"I guess that's touché," Sheryl said, and gave up.

Kate talked all the way to the lake. She told Perry how

she and Sheryl had taken the jobs at her uncle's bar so they could live at the beach for the summer, and also because they could save money living for free in Steve's cabin. They were both going to university, she said, to get their teaching certificates because teachers worked only ten months of the year and earned a pretty good salary. It wasn't just for the salary though. They both liked kids, they wouldn't do it if they didn't like kids, how could you. In fact, she told Perry, she liked kids so much she was planning to major in handicapped kids. They were challenging to work with, she said, but if you had the talent for it, that's what you should do, not everyone's cut out for it. By the time they got to the lake road, Sheryl wanted to scream at Kate to shut the hell up.

When they reached the town site, Sean drove them straight to the cabin. Sheryl wanted to put him on the spot and ask him how he knew where it was, but she didn't bother. At this point, it seemed like too much trouble. She opened the passenger door to get out and Perry said, "How about we drive over and see if the dance is still going."

Kate said, "I'm up for that, how about you, Sheryl?"

Sheryl said she was too tired.

"Great," said Kate. "Well, I guess I won't go either then."

"You can go," Sheryl said.

"I'm not going without you," Kate said. "Come on. Just for an hour. The band will still be playing."

Perry said, "Come on, Sheryl. Just for an hour."

Sheryl was about to declare her conviction on the matter when Kate said, "Remember, Sheryl, you owe me. Earlier tonight? You said you'd do anything, all I had to do was ask. Well, this is it. I'm asking."

Perry said, "She should come with us, don't you think, Sean."

Sean said nothing.

Sheryl thought, what a prick. Still, it was true that she owed Kate for cleaning up the vomit, so she went to the dance. Sean disappeared as soon as they got inside the door, and Sheryl sat at a table and nursed a beer while Kate and Perry danced. No one paid any attention to her. It was like she was invisible. She hated being there. After what seemed like hours Sean showed up from somewhere and sat down at the table with her.

"So what's your name anyway?" he asked her.

"Sheryl," she answered. "Miss Sheryl to you."

"Well, Miss Sheryl," he said. "Do you want to dance or what?"

"I suppose," she said. "I don't seem to have anything better to do at the moment."

They danced, and by the time he took her home, she knew that she had grown on him. She felt just a bit triumphant, and also relieved, because she'd thought of a way to deal with Steve on Monday. She'd be able to slip into the conversation that she'd found a new boyfriend to replace the one who had left her for the basketball player.

3. Black Water

One warm spring day Sheryl took her grade two class to the country. She wanted the children to see the farmers at work in the fields. She took Teddy, who was three at the time, along on the school bus, and the girls played with him and pretended he was a doll. They loved the way he looked with his thick glasses and his long yellow hair. One little girl braided his hair and tied the braid with a pink elastic. Teddy loved the braid. He wouldn't let Sheryl take it out at bedtime that night. In the morning he took it out himself, and was mystified that his straight hair had gone curly.

The school bus delivered Sheryl's class to a farm, and then went back to the city. The farm wife toured the grade twos around the yard and took them through the barn to show them the animals. She'd kept the animals in, she told the children, so they could get a better look at them. There were cows with new calves, and horses and even a goat, but what really caught the children's attention was a cardboard box placed in the manger of an empty stall. The box held a pair of baby raccoons. The woman explained to the children that her husband had found them when he was working one of his fields. The mother was nowhere to be seen, so the farmer had brought the babies home. He'd carried them in his cap; that's how tiny they'd been. The woman showed the children how the babies were fed, with a bottle. She told them that at first they'd had to feed them with an eye dropper.

One little boy asked, "What will happen to the raccoons when they're grown up?"

"Well," the woman said, "grown-up raccoons are a bit of a problem on a farm. We're not sure what to do with them."

"Couldn't they live in a cage?" the boy asked.

"Maybe that's what we'll do," the woman said. "We'll build a nice cage so children from the city can see raccoons when they visit the farm."

Sheryl had a picture of the farmer and his wife gassing the raccoons with the exhaust from the pick-up truck. That's what she remembered her father doing with unwanted litters of kittens. He'd put them in a gunny sack and then tie the opening around the truck's exhaust pipe.

"They just go to sleep," her father used to tell her, before she was old enough to know better. "When they wake up they're in heaven."

After the class had finished touring the barn and chicken coop and the other outbuildings, the woman suggested to Sheryl that she take the children just west of the farmyard.

"My husband is seeding," the woman said. "The children can watch and when he gets to this side of the field he'll stop and explain how the machinery works."

"Would he mind?" Sheryl asked.

"Oh no," the woman said. "He enjoys the children."

The woman also told Sheryl that they might be able to find a duck's nest if they looked in the grass along the edge of the field. There was an irrigation ditch, she said, and sometimes water birds nested there.

"An irrigation ditch?" Sheryl asked, alarms going off in her head. "Is it safe? I wouldn't want anyone to fall in."

"Wait till you see how much water is in it," the woman laughed. "I don't think you have to worry."

They set out, Sheryl and Teddy, seventeen grade two students, and a couple of volunteer mothers who intimidated Sheryl, but still, she was glad to have them along. The farmer was on the far side of the field when they got there, so Sheryl suggested that the children look for birds' nests in the grass while they waited for him to come around. She had the children look in pairs, and the little girl who had braided Teddy's hair on the bus took him for her partner.

Several things happened. First, Teddy went in the irrigation ditch. Sheryl never knew if he fell or if he went in on purpose. Probably on purpose. The little girl who was his partner screamed to Sheryl at the same time that one of the mothers discovered a nest and began shouting to the children to come and see. In the confusion, Sheryl wasn't sure who to pay attention to, but she quickly realized that the girl was frantic and that her screaming had something to do with Teddy.

Sheryl raced over to the hysterical girl and discovered that Teddy was down in the shallow ditch, standing in mucky black water. It was up over the tops of his running shoes. He had a puzzled look on his face, but it was because of the girl's screaming and not because his feet were muddy and wet. In fact, he liked the ditch and didn't want to come out. Sheryl tried to coax him out so she wouldn't have to go in after him, but he shook his head and then, grinning devilishly, sat down in the water. The girl kept crying, "Oh teacher, I'm sorry, I'm sorry," over and over again, and finally Sheryl decided to leave Teddy where he was for the time being, and she put her arms around the girl and comforted her. She said, "Hush now. Never mind, Teddy likes the water."

"But he might drown," the girl said, sobbing.

"He won't drown," Sheryl said. "There isn't enough water in the ditch to drown."

"You can drown in an inch of water," the girl sobbed. "That's why you never leave a baby in the bath."

"That's true," Sheryl said. "And I can tell you'll make a very good baby sitter when you're a little older. But Teddy won't drown in the ditch. We're right here to see that he doesn't."

Sheryl remembered then that one of the mothers had found something. She saw that the woman had a crowd of children gathered around her. So far, the two mothers and the other children were oblivious to the fact that Teddy was in the water, and Sheryl decided she would try to keep it that way. The last thing Teddy needed was an audience.

"Look," Sheryl said to the girl, pointing at the group of children. "I think they've found a nest over there. Maybe it has eggs in it. Go and see."

The girl stopped crying and said, "How will you get Teddy out of the ditch?"

"You leave that to me," Sheryl said. "Go on. Hurry now."

What Sheryl was planning to do was bribe Teddy out of the ditch and she didn't want the girl to hear. She didn't think bribing was quite what a grade two teacher should be doing, but she was willing to try just about anything so she wouldn't have to take her shoes and socks off and wade into the muck.

The girl ran over to the circle of children. Sheryl said, "Teddy, please get out of that ditch. You'll catch a cold if you stay there." Luckily, she had a change of overalls for him in her backpack. He still had accidents once in a while.

Teddy shook his head and began slapping his hands down against the surface of the water, the way he did in the bathtub at home.

"Don't do that," Sheryl said. "You'll get covered in mud."

She immediately realized her mistake. Covered in mud sounded fine to him.

She was trying to think what treats she had in her bag that she could bribe him with, when she noticed the farmer coming toward them on his tractor. He had been going in a circle around the perimeter of the field, but now he was coming across the field, travelling erratically and leaving a bizarre zigzag trail in the black earth.

Something was wrong. This was not how farmers seeded their fields. It crossed Sheryl's mind that maybe this farmer had a peculiar sense of humour and was doing something odd and amusing for the benefit of the city children, but then she quickly realized how ridiculous that was. It would be equivalent to a fireman doing parking lot wheelies in his fire truck for a visiting school group.

Sheryl shouted to catch one of the mother's attention and pointed at the tractor. Then she turned her own attention back to Teddy, who was still splashing in the ditch. She was beginning to get angry. She was also beginning to wonder what the mothers would think of her as a teacher if they got the idea she couldn't control her own child. There was a parent advisory group at the school made up mostly of mothers who didn't work and walked around with halos of superiority on their heads, and Sheryl could just imagine this story of Teddy's bad behaviour making the rounds. She could think of nothing in her bag that would suffice as a bribe.

"Teddy," she said. "Get out of that water right now. I'm losing my patience."

Teddy deliberately splashed her.

"That's it," she said. "Next time we go on a field trip like this you can't come. You'll have to stay home with the baby sitter." She immediately felt guilty for saying that. It was mean. It was also an idle threat, which she tried not to use.

Just then the farmer's wife came running. She had noticed the tractor's unusual course. She was shouting something as she came across the yard, and when she got close enough, Sheryl realized she was saying, "He's having a seizure."

The children turned their attention to the woman, and when they realized she was shouting about the farmer they all looked out across the field. They rearranged themselves so they could see better and soon they were lined up, watching, as though they were at a parade.

The farmer's wife ran past them and into the field, toward the tractor. Sheryl began to think maybe they should get the children away; it appeared that something terrible was about to happen and she thought the children shouldn't be there to see it, but she was transfixed. She watched the woman approach the tractor, managing to stay out of its unpredictable path, and then run along beside it, still shouting. Sheryl prayed that the woman wouldn't try to climb onto the tractor, as to do so she would have to step into the path of the seed drill the tractor was pulling. What if she fell? She would be run over. Sheryl found herself holding her breath. Her heart was pounding.

The tractor was getting close enough that it became imperative for Sheryl to get the children out of the way. The two mothers realized this too, and began herding them up, pushing them toward the farmyard. The tractor was close enough that Sheryl could see the farmer slumped over the steering wheel. His path had straightened, and he was now heading for the spot where she was standing, straight for Teddy, who was still sitting in the ditch splashing mud all over himself.

Sheryl stepped into the ditch. Immediately, she lost her footing on the soft bottom and fell forward onto her knees. Teddy thought it was funny, Sheryl struggling to get to her feet, grabbing him and leaping out of the ditch, dripping black silty water.

The tractor was very close. Sheryl ran for the farmyard, but when she felt they were out of harm's way she had to stop and see what would happen. With Teddy in her arms, she watched the tractor go nose down and sideways into the ditch. The seed drill jacked up and the hitch broke, tearing the hydraulic hoses. Fluids spewed out onto the ground as the tractor tipped awkwardly, becoming wedged in the ditch, half on its side. The motor continued to roar and the tractor's huge rear tires chewed into the soft earth until the farmer's wife managed to climb inside the cab and turn off the ignition.

She was shouting again and waving at Sheryl. Sheryl put Teddy down and went closer so she could hear what the woman was saying. She had a fear of getting too close. She didn't want to see.

"Call an ambulance," the woman shouted. "Go to the house and call an ambulance."

Sheryl picked up Teddy again and ran to the house, but then she sent one of the mothers inside to make the phone call because she was covered in mud.

"Is it bad?" the other mother wanted to know. She was holding a large spotted egg in her hand.

"I don't know," said Sheryl. "I don't think the tractor could have gone over on him. He's still inside the cab, as far as I could see. I think it must have been a seizure, like she said. Or maybe he had a heart attack."

"One of us should try to help her," the mother said. "Do you know CPR?"

Sheryl shook her head.

The mother said, "I'll go. You have yourself and the little boy to get cleaned up." She handed Sheryl the egg, then went into the house. She came back with a couple of blankets and hurried across the yard toward the ditch.

The egg was still warm. The children were all standing quietly, subdued by the turn of events. Sheryl said to the them, "Does anyone know what kind of egg this is?" No one did. She said, "We should try to keep it warm, shouldn't we. How could we keep it warm?"

A little boy said, "Your hands will keep it warm until we get back to school. Then we can put it under a light bulb."

"That's a good idea," Sheryl said. She wondered why the woman had removed the egg from the nest in the first place, and thought she would have to talk to the children about that the next day when the mothers weren't there.

Teddy said, "I'm cold."

"You shouldn't have gone in the water," Sheryl said. She herself was uncomfortable in her wet jeans. She was thankful it was a warm day. She said to Teddy, "Never mind. I have dry clothes for you in my bag."

Teddy wouldn't change in front of the other children so Sheryl took him behind the house.

"Take those wet pants off," she commanded, putting the egg down in the grass and digging around in her backpack for the dry overalls.

Teddy sat down and took his shoes and socks off. They were covered in mud. When he took his overalls off, he discovered a leech stuck to the side of his leg. Sheryl was horrified, but Teddy was fascinated. He pulled at it, but his fingers couldn't hang on to its slippery body.

"It's brown jelly," he said.

Sheryl thought she was going to be sick. She couldn't bring herself to touch it. She found a stick in the grass and tried to scrape it off, but it stuck like glue.

"Salt," she said to Teddy. "We need some salt. They fall off when you put salt on them."

"Don't want it off," said Teddy.

"Teddy," Sheryl said. "Don't try my patience anymore. You'll get sick if we leave it on. You'll get some terrible disease."

She pulled Teddy's dry overalls on and rolled up the pant legs so the leech was still visible. Then she put the wet clothes, including Teddy's shoes and socks, in the plastic grocery bag she'd brought for just such a purpose. She took her own wet runners and socks off and put them in the bag too, thinking she'd be more comfortable in bare feet. She took Teddy's hand and they walked back to the front of the house. Dry grass pricked the bottoms of her feet. What a disaster of a day, she thought.

Sheryl sent the remaining mother into the house for a salt shaker, while Teddy showed off the leech to the children. They all watched, fascinated, as it shrivelled up under a sprinkling of salt, and then fell off. They were poking at it with a stick when they heard the ambulance coming.

Sheryl ran out to the approach to meet the ambulance and direct it to where the tractor was. The attendants drove as far as they could through the farmyard, then got out and carried a stretcher the rest of the way on foot. Moments later, they returned with the farmer on the stretcher. He was motionless. They put him in the back of the ambulance, his wife got in too, and they sped away. It was all over in what seemed like an instant.

The mother who had taken the blankets to the farmer came walking back slowly. She had the blankets with her. She folded them carefully and took them in the house. When she came out again she said to Sheryl, "I don't think he's going to make it. It didn't look good." She said it quietly, so the children couldn't hear.

The farmer's wife had promised them cookies and a drink as part of the visit, but neither Sheryl nor the mothers felt comfortable helping themselves in her house, so they went back to the barn to see the baby raccoons again while they were waiting for the school bus to collect them. Sheryl stayed outside. She wasn't going into the barn in her bare feet. Teddy insisted he wanted to see the raccoons again so she put his muddy shoes back on him and let him go. She didn't feel like arguing with him.

Finally, the school bus showed up. On the way back to the city one of the children asked where the egg was. Sheryl was embarrassed to admit that she'd laid it in the grass and left it there. The mother who'd collected it in the first place seemed to have forgotten she'd given it to Sheryl, so Sheryl didn't bother explaining. The mother kept saying, "I wonder what could have happened to it." Sheryl felt a little bad about the egg, but she was pretty sure it would have rotted under a light bulb in the classroom anyway.

Over the next few weeks, Sheryl became obsessed with the obituaries in the paper. Sean noticed, and asked her what was up. She didn't tell him about the farmer. She said she was reading them to get ideas for her own, which she was planning to write herself instead of leaving it to him.

"That's considerate," Sean said.

"No it's not," Sheryl said. "I just don't want anything totally dumb."

When several weeks had gone by and Sheryl hadn't seen the farmer listed, she decided to call his wife. The woman thanked Sheryl for calling and apologized for leaving without giving the children their cookies.

"Don't worry about that," Sheryl said. "How is your husband doing?"

"He had a pretty bad concussion," the woman said, "but he seems to be fine now. He's epileptic, you know. I've been thinking for years that he should quit farming and this clinched it. All that machinery is dangerous at the best of times. We're going to try and sell."

"What will you do?" Sheryl asked. She was thinking about her own father, and how he didn't know how to do anything but farm.

"I don't know," the woman answered. "I just know he can't go on. He's had three seizures so far while he's been running machinery. It's a wonder he's still alive."

"Well," Sheryl said, "I'm glad he's recovered. We were all pretty worried."

"I'm sorry the children had to be here," the woman said. "I've thought about that many times in the last few weeks. But these things happen. Life is never simple, is it."

"No," Sheryl said. "Life is not simple. It certainly is not."

She hung up the phone then, and although she wasn't the kind of person to feel sorry for herself, she couldn't help but wonder how she'd been able to agree so quickly and with such certainty that life is not simple. She felt a darkness creeping around her, imagined it filling the house, consuming them all. She felt the beginnings of regret and wondered what would come after that. Despair, she thought. Despair that you couldn't live with.

4. Pig's Heart

It was Friday night. Sean and Perry were out playing pool. Kate had phoned earlier to ask if Sheryl was interested in going to a movie, but Sheryl said she was too tired. She didn't know how Kate could manage to have so much energy after spending the week with her class of emotionally disturbed children, several of whom had serious behaviour problems and hit one another and threw temper tantrums. Sheryl had a class of perfectly normal grade twos and she was so tired at the end of the week she could hardly drag herself upstairs to the bedroom. On Friday night, she and Teddy usually fell asleep on the couch with the TV on. She was glad that Sean went out with Perry on Friday nights. It meant she didn't have to entertain him.

The phone rang at midnight and Sheryl woke with a start just as Teddy picked up the receiver. He listened for a minute and then said, "She's sleeping."

"No, I'm not," Sheryl said. "Who is it?"

"It's Kate," Teddy said. "She says to wake you up."

"You don't have to wake me up," Sheryl said. "I'm already awake."

She dragged herself off the couch and went to the phone.

"Guess what," Kate said.

"I can't imagine," Sheryl said, trying not to sound sleepy.

"They're in jail."

"Who's in jail?"

"Perry and Sean. I'm not supposed to tell you, so when Sean gets out or calls you or whatever, you have to pretend you don't know. Perry called me because he didn't want me to worry when he didn't come home, but Sean's afraid to call you. He knows you'll be really pissed. He told Perry to make me promise I wouldn't call you."

"Did you promise?" Sheryl asked.

"Of course, but you don't think I was going to let you worry all night, do you? What kind of friend would I be then?"

"I doubt if I would have noticed he wasn't here," Sheryl said. "At least not until morning. But anyway, thanks." Then she asked, "What are they doing in jail?"

"It's too stupid," Kate said. "They were at Lenny's, and Perry left ahead of Sean and was waiting for him in the car. Sean comes running out carrying a bar stool and shoves it in the back seat, and they take off and immediately get pulled over by the cops, and now they're in jail. I can't believe what a pair of idiots they are."

It sounded like it was Sean's fault. Sheryl said so. She asked if Perry wanted to kill Sean for getting him thrown in jail.

"I don't think so," Kate said. "He was high as a kite on the phone. I think he's getting off on pretending to be an innocent victim of police harassment."

"Did Perry say when they're going to let them out?" Sheryl asked.

"No," Kate said. "It won't be tonight though. I guess I'll go down there in the morning and see what's up. Maybe I'll get to 'post bail.' That'll be a new experience. Anyway, I thought you'd like to know."

"You're not going down now?"

"No way," Kate said. "I hope they're in the drunk tank with someone really disgusting. Besides, I'm in my bathrobe. I was just on my way upstairs to have a bubble bath."

"I guess I'd better go put Teddy to bed," Sheryl said. "We were sleeping on the couch." Then she added, "Thanks for phoning." It was true that she would have worried if she'd woke up in the morning and Sean wasn't there. She probably would have thought he was in an accident.

She hung up the phone.

"Daddy's in jail," she said to Teddy. After she said it, she thought maybe she shouldn't have. She wasn't sure why she told him.

"For how long?" he asked.

"I don't know," Sheryl said.

"For a long time, probably," Teddy said.

Sheryl looked at him, surprised. "Why do you think he'll have to stay there a long time?" she asked him.

"I don't know," Teddy said. "That's just what I think." Then he said, "We should do something special, like when Nanna died."

"It wasn't Nanna," Sheryl said. "I keep telling you, Nanna didn't die. It was Nanna's sister, Aunt Dorothy, who died. Nanna still lives in Calgary." Six months ago, Sean's Aunt Dorothy had died and his mother asked him to go with her to the funeral in Edmonton. Sheryl couldn't bear the thought of being trapped in a car and then some relative's house in Edmonton with Sean and his mother, so she and Teddy had stayed home alone and gone to the museum and McDonald's for supper.

Sheryl wondered why Teddy kept getting mixed up about who had died. She'd told him half a dozen times it wasn't Nanna. She supposed the problem was that Teddy didn't know the person who had died – Aunt Dorothy – so he filled in the blank with someone he knew. She hoped he wouldn't be too shocked the next time he saw Nanna in person. She imagined him deciding Nanna was a ghost.

"Let's go camping," Teddy said.

"Camping?" Sheryl said, surprised. Where had he heard about camping? They didn't even own a tent.

"In the back yard," Teddy said. "Like the neighbours."

"Oh," Sheryl said. "Marcie and Joelle, you mean."

"Yeah," said Teddy. "Camping like Marcie and Joelle."

One night the previous summer Sheryl and Teddy had looked out his bedroom window and seen the two teen-aged girls next door in the back yard with their father. They had a fire going in the barbecue and were roasting marshmallows.

"What are they doing?" Teddy had wanted to know when he saw the fire.

"I guess they're pretending they're camping," Sheryl had said.

"Who's that man?" Teddy asked.

"That's their father," Sheryl said. She wondered if she was going to have to go into an explanation of divorce. She said, "He doesn't live there, you know."

"I know," said Teddy. "You don't have to tell me that."

"Oh," said Sheryl. "How did you know?"

"Marcie," Teddy said. Marcie baby sat Teddy sometimes. Sheryl and Teddy had watched for a while, from the window. The father and his two daughters were sitting around the barbecue in lawn chairs, talking quietly and roasting their marshmallows. The scene was surprising to Sheryl, the father so relaxed in the mother's yard. She'd wondered, briefly, if there was some kind of reconciliation in progress. Then she remembered that the mother was away on a golf holiday.

"Can we go camping?" Teddy asked again.

Sheryl thought about it. There was a bit of firewood in the garage. She could probably light a small fire in the barbecue, roast some marshmallows, and then send Teddy to bed.

"Get your jacket," she said. "It will be cool outside until we get the fire going."

The wood in the garage was too big for the barbecue and Sheryl couldn't find the axe. She tried to get Teddy to give up on the idea, but he was like a dog with a bone.

"Look some more for the axe," he said.

"I've looked everywhere," Sheryl said. "Daddy must have loaned it to someone. It's probably at Kate and Perry's house."

She looked up at the sky, which was sprinkled with stars, like a clear night sky in the country.

"We could have a campfire in the sandbox," Teddy said.

"I don't think so," Sheryl said. "Someone might call the fire department."

"No one would," Teddy said. He went into the garage and began carrying out blocks of wood and loading them into the sandbox.

"It won't start without kindling," Sheryl said. "We need the axe to make kindling."

Teddy ignored her and went back for more. He carried out all the wood there was. Sheryl decided the only thing she could do was try to light the fire and then Teddy would see it wasn't going to work and they could go to bed. She sent him into the house for newspaper, and he came back with some small pieces of wood from the fireplace. Not enough, Sheryl thought as she stacked the wood, paper first, then kindling, then a tipi of the smallest logs. She gave it an honest effort, and let Teddy hold a match to the newspaper.

To Sheryl's amazement, the fire caught. It flared up into a regular campfire, and she began to worry that someone would indeed call the fire department. She got the garden hose from the garage, just in case she had to put the fire out in a hurry.

Teddy thought they should put all the logs in at once, but Sheryl convinced him they should burn just one at a time.

Sheryl kept listening for a fire truck but none appeared, and she eventually quit worrying and began to imagine that she and Teddy really were camping under the stars somewhere. She tried to get him to help her find the Big Dipper but he was too busy poking sticks from the caragana hedge into the flames and then watching them smoke. After a while, he ran out of sticks and went into a kind of trance staring at the fire, which was now burning over a bed of red-hot embers. She asked him if he wanted to roast marshmallows and he shook his head, so they just sat side by side on lawn chairs, both of them mesmerized by the fire. It was four in the morning when the last log burned down to coals.

"I guess it's bedtime," Sheryl said, but Teddy wouldn't go in. She sighed and wondered why she had such a hard time being firm with him, then she thought he wasn't being unreasonable, he was just taking pleasure in a simple thing, and what was wrong with that. She went into the house for a couple of sleeping bags and convinced Teddy to crawl into one of them.

She thought he was asleep. She was wondering what it was about fire that enticed you to stare at it for hours on end, hardly aware that time was passing, when she remembered a TV program she'd recently seen about a group of new-age Californians who went around the country doing workshops on firewalking. She'd been amused by the queue of spacey-looking people who, one by one, hot-footed it across the bed of coals, so quickly that their feet hardly touched ground. It was no wonder they didn't get burned. To prove a point, or perhaps because she wasn't herself from staying awake all night, she stood up, kicked her sandals off and put her right foot in the fire, thinking she would hop across as quickly as the people in the TV show, but Teddy screamed just then and stalled her, and she burned her foot. She wanted to scream herself, because of the pain, but now she was aware of Teddy and what he had seen, and how bad it must have looked to him, his mother walking into the fire, so she sat down on his sleeping bag and put her arms around him. She could feel his little heart pounding in his chest. She knew she should be running cold water from the hose over her foot, but she didn't want to frighten Teddy, so she pretended she hadn't hurt herself. "Shhhh," she said, trying not to think about her foot. "I'm all right. I was just making sure the coals were out before I went to sleep. They weren't though. Pretty dumb, eh." Then she said, "Boy, your old heart is just a-pounding away in there." She took his hand and placed it on his chest. "Feel that," she said.

His beating heart reminded him of something. "We had science fair today," he said.

"You're kidding," Sheryl said. "You should have told me. We could have done a project."

"Just the big kids," Teddy said.

"Oh," Sheryl said. "That's right, I forgot." It was the same in her school. "So you went to look then," she said. "You got to see the big kids' projects."

"There was a heart," Teddy said. "A pig's heart, and it was still beating."

"It couldn't have been," Sheryl said.

"It was," Teddy said. "I saw it."

"It couldn't have been beating if it wasn't in the pig," Sheryl said. "Was it still in the pig?" She was thinking maybe there was a real pig hooked up to a monitor or something.

"It was in a pie plate," Teddy said.

"Oh," Sheryl said. "Well, it couldn't have been beating then. Maybe someone jiggled the table and you saw the heart move."

"No," Teddy said. "It was beating."

Sheryl said, "What kind of teacher have you got anyway? Didn't she explain to you that a heart can't beat unless the pig is alive?"

"It was dead," Teddy said. "But it was still beating."

Sheryl gave up. Teddy often said things that worried her, but right now she didn't feel like dealing with it. There were so many things to worry about and now there was something else, because he had just seen his mother stick her foot in a fire. How could she explain that? She didn't even try, beyond what she had already said, and they simply sat together until the coals were dead and the stars disappeared. When it was light, Sheryl was struck by how odd everything looked, especially the blackened sandbox. There was a plastic dump truck, now half-melted, that neither of them had noticed in the dark. She didn't mention it.

"Are you tired?" she asked.

"No," Teddy said. Sheryl was wide awake too. They went to McDonald's for breakfast. Sheryl tried to walk without limping so Teddy wouldn't know she'd burned her foot, but eventually she had to tell him that it hurt.

5. Fire

Sean was on the phone all the next afternoon talking to Perry, going over and over what had happened the night before. He'd just get off the phone, when he'd remember some other detail and call Perry back again. Finally Sheryl got sick of it and grabbed the receiver and told Perry to put Kate on the phone.

"Do you guys want to come over for a barbecue?" she asked. "You might as well, if all they're going to do is talk about this on the phone."

Kate agreed. Sheryl went for groceries and picked up beer on the way home. When Kate and Perry showed up at the door at six-thirty, half an hour early, Kate brought up the jail incident right away. Sheryl wished she hadn't. She'd been hoping she and Kate could talk about something else.

"So has this jail thing brought about some kind of spiritual awakening in Sean?" Kate asked. "I'm half expecting Perry to get up and go to church tomorrow, join some born-again movement."

Sheryl got Kate and Perry each a beer from the fridge and then took them out to the back deck. When the barbecue coals were ready, she put Sean in charge of cooking the chicken breasts. Fat from the chicken dripped onto the coals and periodically burst into flames, which Sean sprayed with a plant mister. Teddy wanted to spray the fires, so Sean gave the mister to him, but then Teddy sprayed the barbecue so often it looked like the coals were going to go out.

"Jesus Christ," Sean said, grabbing the mister out of Teddy's hands. "Give me that thing. You're not the fire brigade, for Christ sake." It looked for a minute like Teddy was going to cry, but then Perry pulled him over onto his knee and started to tickle him.

"I can't figure out how he's still awake," Sheryl said. "He was up all night."

"So what did you think when old Sean didn't come home last night?" Perry asked Sheryl.

"I don't know," Sheryl said. "I can't really say."

"Well, did you think he might be in jail? I'll bet it never occurred to you he might be in jail."

"She probably thought I was in an accident," Sean said. "That's the first thing a woman will think of. An accident. She probably called all the hospitals. Jesus. It's embarrassing. 'Hello. Would you mind checking your comatose accident victims in case one of them is my husband?' I wonder how often the hospitals get that call."

Kate snorted. "More likely they get, 'Would you mind checking your comatose accident victims, I'm hoping one of them is my husband,'" she said.

"Very funny," Sean said. "Ha ha."

"What would your first thought be if I didn't come home?" Sheryl said to Sean.

"That's easy," Sean said. "I'd think you were with another man." Then he said, "Well, did you call the hospitals?"

A beeping sound came from inside the house. "That'll be the microwave," Sheryl said. "The potatoes are ready. How are the chicken breasts?"

"They'd be ready if the kid hadn't given them a frigging shower," Sean said.

"Well check," Sheryl said. "They look done to me."

"They're not done," Sean said.

Kate reached over and picked up the long-handled

fork. "I'm starving," she said. "I could just about eat these things raw." She poked the fork into one of the chicken breasts. "This one's done," she said.

"Good," said Sheryl to Kate. She handed her a platter. "Put the chicken on this, will you."

"Who's the cook here anyway?" Sean wanted to know.

Teddy was still on Perry's knee. "Daddy was in jail," he said.

"I know," said Perry. "I was with him."

"You're not supposed to talk about that," Sean said. "Mommy told you not to tell anyone."

"For Christ sake, Sean," Perry said. "It's not like I didn't already know. Leave the little bugger alone."

"Go play in the sandbox," Sean said.

"Can't," said Teddy. "It's burned up."

Sean looked over to the corner of the yard. The sandbox was littered with ashes and blackened bits of wood. "What happened to it?" Sean asked Teddy.

"I told you," Teddy said. "We went camping."

Teddy climbed off Perry's knee and went over to the barbecue. Kate had taken the chicken from the grill and the coals were glowing red. Teddy stood staring at them.

"Get away from that barbecue," Sean said. "You're going to burn yourself." He got up out of his chair and walked over to the sandbox. "What the hell were you doing?" he wanted to know. He picked up the melted dump truck. "Did you do this?" he asked Teddy. Teddy shook his head. "Well, who did then? I suppose you're going to tell me mommy did it."

Teddy looked at Sean, then deliberately lowered his hand toward the grill.

Kate, who was closest to Teddy, pulled his hand away from the barbecue, then Sheryl swooped Teddy up into her arms. She balanced him on one hip and took the plate of chicken from Kate. "Come and get it," she said. She was shaking, but she didn't let on.

"I've had just about enough of that kid tonight," Sean said.

"Let's go in the house and get some potatoes and salad," Sheryl said to Teddy. "Do you want some chicken?"

"I don't want anything," Teddy said. "I'm not hungry."

"Okay then," Sheryl said. "It's bedtime. You're dead on your feet." Sheryl directed the others to the kitchen, where she had the dishes and the food laid out on the counter, all but the chicken. "I'll be back in a few minutes," she said. "Don't wait for me. Help yourself to more beer in the fridge." She carried Teddy upstairs, got him into his pyjamas and tucked him into bed. She found his blue stuffed dog and tucked it under the sheets next to him, then sat on the edge of the bed.

"You could have burned yourself," she said to Teddy. "Remember what happened to my foot." Teddy wanted to see the blister again, so Sheryl showed it to him.

"I can't tell you a story tonight," she said, brushing Teddy's blond hair off his forehead. "We have company. I have to visit with the company."

"Are they staying long?" Teddy asked.

"Not long," Sheryl said.

"When is daddy going back to jail?" Teddy asked.

"I'm not sure," Sheryl said. "Soon, though." She kissed Teddy and when she stood to leave she saw Sean standing in the doorway.

"What's going on?" he asked.

"Nothing much," Sheryl said. She turned out Teddy's light.

"Why did you tell him I'd be going back to jail?"

"Good night, Teddy," Sheryl said, and started down the stairs.

"I don't understand you," Sean said, following behind her. "Why did you tell Teddy that? You'll give him the wrong idea."

"I'm not worried," Sheryl said.

"Were you worried when I didn't come home last night?" Sean said.

"Not really," Sheryl said.

"Even though you thought I was in an accident?"

"I didn't think you were in an accident," Sheryl said. "Where did you get that idea?"

Sean pushed ahead of Sheryl, spreading his arms and blocking her way on the landing at the foot of the stairs.

"What are you doing?" he said. "Just what game are you playing here?"

Sheryl didn't say anything. She started humming, nothing in particular at first, but then an old song popped into her head, something about Mister Lonely, so she hummed that. Not like a sad ballad though, she kept it upbeat.

"The chicken's not done, you know," Sean said. "And the coals are out, because of all the water the little piss ant sprayed on them. We're going to get sick from eating raw chicken."

Perry came from the kitchen and saw Sean blocking Sheryl's way. "What's going on?" Perry wanted to know.

Sheryl stopped humming. Sean let his arms drop to his sides.

"Nothing's going on," Sean said. "I just don't feel wanted around here. Like, I was missing and no one noticed."

"We noticed," Sheryl said.

"Your whining is really starting to get to me," Perry said to Sean. "Last night was enough to last me a lifetime."

"What do you mean by that?" Sean wanted to know.

361

"You mean, I was whining last night? Fuck you. I wasn't whining."

Sheryl stepped past Sean and headed for the kitchen.

"She wants me to eat raw chicken," Sean said. "She doesn't love me anymore."

Sheryl stopped. "That's true," she said. Then she said, "Put your chicken in the microwave for a few minutes if you're that worried about it. I'm sure it's done, though. It's not like I'm planning to poison anybody."

Years later, when Teddy was a grown man and Sheryl was middle-aged, she asked him if he remembered the campfire. He didn't. She said, "Don't you remember me sticking my foot in the fire? I told you it was an accident, but I think you knew I did it on purpose." Teddy couldn't remember.

Sheryl was genuinely surprised. She'd thought that moment had been burned into his psyche. She'd worried about permanent damage for years.

"You really don't remember?" she asked.

Teddy shook his head.

Apparently, the night had been all hers. And then she thought, of course it had, and she wondered why it had taken her so much time to figure that out.

The Shells of the Ocean
RUDY WIEBE

1.   All life comes from the sea. It would seem reasonable
then that all life must return to it. Reasonable. He sits
under the palm trees, or sometimes under one of the tiny
frond-thatched roofs served by the solicitous waiter;
watching the sea; listening. Sometimes he contemplates
the two volcanoes floating high above the bay; or the
sound of bare feet in sand. On the curve of reef paralleling
the shore the swells break, smash down like a continuous
and interrupted rhythm of wall toppling from left to right,
climb up and smash down again and again, both their
beginnings and ends lost beyond edges that he cannot
see. Only the shadows of one or the other volcano
occasionally in the clouds insist on land somewhere; certain
and reasonable there, beyond or above the water.

2.   All seas everywhere are the same sea, so he has come
to this one where they never were together. The creatures
in and on them were always the same. Again and again
the porpoises crossed the wake of their ferry between
Honshu and Hokkaido; she of course saw them first,
playing, as it seemed, beside the ship and together they
watched those dark shapes torpedo into the ship's wake,
back and forth, whiter bellies arching ... why was the word
for that 'wake'? The killer whales off Galiano revealed
their enormous black backs once and then the sea
swallowed them, but the porpoises followed as far as he
could see despite the ship's turbulence – perhaps because
of it? – that left them behind while the several hundred
Japanese high school students aboard in their navy and
white, almost military, uniforms came to crowd around

her, testing their rudimentary English, "what your name?", "what age you?", "where you live?" until her blondness swam above their gleaming black heads. She was a celebrity signing books, bits of paper, diaries, and he was in an eddy beside her with his greying beard, they were begging her to accept the tiny carved key-charms, the bells, the chains they were supposed to be taking back to their parents from their school outing, and the delicate girls reached for her with fingertips like leaves, her unbelievable pale skin and golden hair, the grey porpoises riding unnoticed far away in their wake. Was the sea also asleep? Did ships, like intruding bodies, wake it? Sweetest heaven, what a lifetime he had been asleep! Death itself could not at first jolt him out of that; but now he was most certainly awake. Had he slept a minute since ... would he ever?

Only last summer they had travelled the arched coast of Wales. Among the massive ruins of Edward I's enslavement of the Welsh in the thirteenth century she had seemed no more preoccupied and sad than he: their mutual melancholy a closer companionship than they had been certain of before in their lifetime together. He thought then her occasional singing under her breath made her sound almost happy again, and he certainly could have done with a little happiness; again. "Oh, it's just a folk ballad, it's turning circles in my head, you know, just the tune." But she knew words, at least one verse, and her sudden silence when the three students like medieval musicians laid their instrument cases open in the inner ward of what was left of Aberystwyth Castle and piped the melody she had been humming, and the lean girl haltered in the peasant dress sang with aching sweetness,

"There is a deep valley –"

"Hey!" he had exclaimed, "That's your ... now you'll hear the words."

But her face was wiped blank. Stiff, broken like the wall against which they were leaning, blown apart by Cromwell's self-righteous English cannon destroying the Welsh for the last time. The falling sunlight glanced up off the sea there, lit the tiny particularities of her face he had studied, cared for, adored since he held her in his arms within hours of her birth, o God, God.

3.   Wherever he may be looking makes no difference. There is nothing to see but the inside of eyelids and arid tears. The endless roar of the reef has hardened into moments of crash as the tide falls steadily higher and higher up the beach.

"Another drink, sir?" a soft voice in his ear.

"A mixed juice," not opening his eyes.

If he began with alcohol there would be no stopping. The waiter is gone without a sound, dark feet no doubt bleached in the livid sand. Without opening his eyes he knows her song is floating in his head like the volcanoes, now this one, now that one, so easy on their bed of cloud. He should ask the waiter: which way do you prefer that it come? From the solid flanks of the mountains you know are always there inside that mist, or from the sea which you can never not hear? From the flanks of mountains that sometimes adjust themselves, shrug once or twice every generation and run fire and molten rock over you? Or from frightful shapes coming through the white wash of the sea about which you never had any warning either: a thousand years ago the Hindus from India, then the Chinese, then the Arabs, each bringing in turn slaughter and new overlords and religions; and then the ultimate invasions of unstoppable Christians: the Portuguese and Roman Catholicism, the Dutch and Calvinism, the English and Capitalism, until finally the Japanese turn

the deadly circle back to Asia again with no government
or religion or ideological reason for killing except power.
Each in turn destroying and building, destroying and
building in a millennium of invasion from the sea with
knives and spears and arrows and cannon and machine
guns and grenades and diving planes until now the
incomprehensible and ultimate bomb hangs over them
with all the rest of the world, and he sits here day after
day remembering one single life, fingers through that,
thread by thread. How can you comprehend centuries
and millions when one day, one life overwhelms you?

There are so many ways to be destroyed: sliced,
skewered, smashed, shot, blown to bits, incinerated,
overrun by flowing, molten rock. Or the single irrefutable
needle of longing.

4.   There is only the sound of her voice and the words
she never sang:

> *I never will marry,*
> *Nor be no man's wife.*
> *I expect to live single*
> *All the days of my...*

Never sang word for word; never that he heard. All
she murmured once, it was on the northwest tower of
Harlech Castle, where seven centuries of sand dunes now
separated its massive inner wall and cliff from the white
line of the sea and they were staring in a kind of mutual
resignation across the miniature railway and the golf course
and the campground and the trailer park parked tight
window to wall with holiday tenants, on the tower wall
she murmured something about the Carter Family. Later,
much later, that emerged like flotsam in his memory:
The Carter Family was his sad mother humming in the

log house in Alberta, those peculiar Carter guitars laying a clanging riff on the static of battery radio, turning and turning in melancholy, rhythmic whine until Maybelle alone or Sara alone or together or both joined by A.P. droned their flat voices into ineffable tragedy as if the gentle knives of misery were sliding flat through your gut and you would never really know where all the pain originated, would discover tomorrow you had been disembowelled and filleted yesterday, were already eviscerated, dead, though still so sadly walking about the day after yesterday.

5.   There are beautiful palm trees here, yes, but where can you pray, since the molten mountain or the sea are certain to bring some new and previously unimaginable horror? Ricefields now rest like stamps brushed onto the mountain, the endless fish in the sea ... but there is never any warning and you never want to believe it anyway and always hope, hope, hope, hope until factuality crushes you and to what then, when you are crushed, can you pray? Both oh both, oh bring back, bring back o ... mountain or sea oh fish of the sea come listen to me for my daughter my life the joy of my ... there is no rhyme, only rhythm to this run of words behind his eyelids, he is an old dog circling in the endless curl of his unnamable, unfindable place and there is no circle into forgetting, into painlessness. She has forever drawn her life like a chisel along every trace of feeling and he is hacked down to a skeleton by her disappearance, not even skeletal bone, no, no, nerves only; primordial ganglia.

There are no gulls here over the windy sea; there are none anywhere, he has noticed with amazement, there is nothing thrown out to gobble up, there is no garbage. Their wheeling he has known as a life-long ritual, their voracious appetites like the hunger and thirst for righteousness he has only in despair. Above his father's plow folding back the grey-wooded soil of their homestead, gulls circled in the thousands for an occasional offering of worms, that gentle bush piety becoming for him such a certain quicksand that it must be escaped, fled. And having fled he discovered he could offer her only folk-tales, paintings, classical music, ballet, her small sleeping body in his arms swaying to Brahms and, at best, deep, inarticulate (to him) Russian harmony. The Cossacks singing a discovery so deep he broke the record. But her baby face, her perfect tiny fingers curled against it are caught in newer detail: the buttons down her blouse as they walk through wind in Wales. They do not open, the blouse would have to be pulled over her head. "I expect to stay … all the days of my …" Maybelle Carter sang in her voice like a taut string and his clear mind is avoiding the rest of the song branded onto the clarity of sky like the blue volcanoes, now this one, now the other, in their remorseless bed of cloud. He found the record under the Coca Cola sign at Picadilly Circus, the song she hummed before Aberystwyth but never after. This is always some way to find what you are really looking for if it is something as simple as a man-made thing.

6.   And he has looked, he would certainly always look now into every crowd: so many people, especially in cities, thousands, millions. If he stood at Yonge and Bloor or the overpass on Waseda-dori at the Iidabashi Subway Station or sat at a restaurant window above Leicester Square long enough, it must be inevitable that eventually he see her, again. There were so many people it was utterly impossible to be so indelibly different that somewhere on earth you could never be found again – sometimes he did see her,

even among the black heads of Jakarta and Singapore, the incredible complexions of Lima, Kuala Lumpur, Sao Paulo: bits of her, a profile, a momentary back, a jacketfold or flip of hair and shoulder shift, and his heart lurched because he already knew he must certainly be disappointed; and was. But the first betraying detail always crushed him nevertheless – the walk wasn't quite right, or the length of leg, or nose. The hand too large. Millions had been born on her day, her minute, her second no doubt, and he would have found every one in every country on earth if one were only she. He had since then never actually seen anyone, he realized at some point, except those who in some detail suggested her because the very day after he had been somehow walking in or through a park where young women were suddenly playing something, field hockey perhaps, running and he had to crouch behind a tree holding his ears shut, unable to stand erect leave alone walk past their bodies – why were they all there, running, quick, laughing, he would not have missed or groaned for a single one of them if they had not been there, and yet they were all – and one of them had come and touched him with that terrifying girlish tenderness he knew and he could barely shake his head; trying to cover his eyes then also.

But he had found the words, all of them. The earphones clamped to his head in the store above Picadilly Circus. They had chiselled themselves in the acoustic tile of his mind, connecting the numberless holes like runnels, heard them, mouthed them, hummed them. There was nothing so referential needed, not really, but they were hammered onto the sky wherever he happened to be:

The fish in deep water
Swim over my head.

7.   So he has come to the sea. Again. A sea he has never seen before, where they had never been together. Not Peru and the ocean breaking like mountains after a run across the entire Pacific to slice up the beach faster than her child's or his adult legs could run; not the bath-warm curl of hissing undertow at Copacobana hedged in by extravagant cliffs of buildings; not their flight through the middle of one night and in San Juan she curled into the bed, "I want to sleep, Daddy, sleep," when he threw open the curtains of their hotel window to the night surf crashing just below: not any of those beautiful seas he now remembers with despair.

> *The shells of the ocean*
> *Shall be my deathbed;*
> *The fish in the deep water*
> *Swim over my head*

The musicians at Aberystwyth began, "There is a deep valley…" What were the remainder of their words? Were there any? Had he dreamt them? The prairie where he was born, she too, was always being compared to the sea. Praise be, the first time he had seen the ocean was from a ship after a long summer day moving majestic as a mansion through Quebec down the long throat of the St. Lawrence when ships still carried passengers and there was a boat train waiting in Liverpool, the grey heaving Atlantic still so imprinted on the cochlea of his mind that the green English fields and hedges lifted under him like the breathing sea itself. Somewhere the sea held her.

Milton once wrote: "I cannot praise a fugitive or cloistered virtue, unexercised and unbreathed." Good for him: was the greatest virtue, love, fugitive and cloistered also if unexercised and unbreathed, untested by opposite and contrary? So what is most contrary to being? Nothing.

Exercise that, Mr. Milton: great love is greatest when it is
gone…yes…: breathe that if you philosophically please. Sit
on a tropical beach, paradise by any northern definition,
and discover your thoughts are the same as if you were
stretched on your standard bed at home hearing the
furnace groan and noticing the ceiling turn sometimes.
What a waste, yes waste…where is she? Surely I have been
exercised and breathed enough, I changed her diapers
streaked with babyshit and cradled her around the room
against my chest to Handel and Vivaldi and Cree
drumming and Vivaldi and last summer she led me
through every clean and stinking hall and cranny in
Harlech and Carnarvon and Beaumaris and Conwy and
Rhuddlan and Flint and Beaumaris again because it was
so symmetrical, so well preserved and historically useless,
and ruined Aberystwyth also; as if by necessity, returning
to it again in daylight after we walked there in night rain
and we would never have heard the musicians except for
that three centuries of grass, the sudden sunlight on the
exploded stones. Already then she must have been wearing
her necessity everywhere we went, where were my eyes, my
goddamn eyes? Didn't at least my gut insist? But she was
brilliant and quick and laughing, dearest sweet Jesus how
I had longed for that again, even the faintest trace of it
and there it was at last. Apparently, certain.

8.   Only last summer on the Friesian coast – how often
his thoughts are triggered by 'only'… 'just'… 'if only'… 'if'
… and his mother's unassailable Low German peasant
wisdom, as proper on her gentle tongue as profane on his
own: "If 'if' wasn't if, cowshit would be butter" – only last
summer in Schleswig-Holstein they had seen the sea slowly
making land.

    "The winter storms are so good, they bring ground,"

the young man guiding them said carefully, "the heavy wind piles the muddy water against the coast and –"

"The wind does what?" she interrupted.

"The steady winter wind of course, day after day," the guide said into it, his accented words almost lost with all their hair streaming across their eyes. "It is the friction of wind on water, friction piles the water up against the dikes and slopes of the *watte*, here, we call the whole area outside the dike '*watte*,' and as the wind dies the water has to run back of course and that is why we build these low rows of twisted willows, reeds, across the *watte* because when it runs back the mud in the water sinks down, settles against the rows and builds up, you see, grain by grain here, land."

Like snowdrifts caught on prairie fencing, he thought then, but low, slimy soil drifts creating eventually ridge and ditch growing imperceptibly out of the frothing sea that played over them.

"So after some twenties or thirties of years of course the rotting willows are covered over like over there and then there is land, enough for sea grass, and the grass catches mud out of the high tides and the storm flooding even better and then soon the sheep, you see over there, graze in summer and only the high winter storms, very high, come up here and you see it keeps building. Fresh land then of course, not salt."

She was squinting past the young man's pale hair into the sea light. "The rows are all so ... straight," she said. "Right angles."

"It's easiest to make, straight."

The sea light was relentless, like her voice. "But if the sea is muddy here, it must be tearing down the land somewhere else."

"Well of course, the sea is always tearing down and –"

372

"And since there is more sea than land, eventually there will be nothing but sea everywhere and…"

"Well," he laughed, "there are such very big land, and mountains."

"…the mountains will be levelled, the Himalayas into the Sanda and Philippine Trench and the Andes into the Chile Trench and the whole earth will…"

The pale young man and he were staring at her; it was the hard wind finding water in his eyes.

She said, "When the sea has levelled all the land in the world, the entire globe will be two hundred feet under water."

The young man said very gently, "But it will take a very long time. And here," he was bending down and he might have been taking her arm if she had been the kind of woman a man could easily touch, "…here the land mostly comes up from the sea bottom, you see."

His fingers dug in the muddy silt. They were standing on the buried line of woven willows, the grey slime stretching flatly ridged away to the indistinguishable edge of the grey sea.

"Many shells, bones," he said, spreading mud across his hand. "Ground into bits."

9.   It couldn't have been the marrying, no not that. How many times was she asked, asked herself and then said no, better think a bit more. Marrying itself wasn't all there was in anyone's life, especially a woman's now, she said and she would peer at one of them, her profile like her mother's had been so direct, a Dutch beauty that cut her personal image into any man's core. What was it? Just … never?

"Hello, Central, give me he-aven," she sang that Carter twang in Wales,

"For I know my mother's there;

373

With the angels there a-waiting,
Waiting on the golden stair."

"Please," he said. "I can't stand that."

A kind of gradual, inevitably accumulating never-ness that became its own personality, its own certain aloneness even when they were together.

Across a crowded concert lobby he had seen the back of a friend whose wife he knew was dying of cancer. He had known for months but avoided him, unable to endure even the thought of the words they would have to try to say, his own inevitable evisceration, again, but suddenly he was beside him, touching him and his friend turned instantly and they embraced so hard, so quickly between clusters of concert chatter. "I've been thinking about you," he murmured against his ear, and his friend murmured back, "I know, I know." They could hear violins tuning in the auditorium, some elementary Mozart delicacy – neither of them would have dared a Mendelssohn or full-organ Bach – and his friend was describing something, a sigmoidoscope or something like an eye at the end of a hose with which doctors had seen the enormous cancer, and drew a map with his finger on his own shirt-covered abdomen, tucked right in there and they had cut that all out, every bit of that. But the liver was beyond any scalpel. And they stood together almost easily, they found they could speak this factuality easier than a hockey score and it was only later that he remembered he had kissed his friend beside his ear, that they had held each other's hand while they were talking those facts only, things themselves; that mirrored nothing, presumably, if they talked fast, said words fast enough. But at some point they had both said, "Miracle." Almost together, as he later thought about it. For an instant both of them blurting out such an aberrant, echoing word – as if it had been lurking there all along under their voiceable facts. Stupid. Stupid.

10.   He is standing on the reef. Unbelievable, marvellous coral ebullitions hump out of it, reflect a surface in shimmers about his ankles. What may be his own thonged feet ripple there, and a purple starfish inert as stone. His toe approaches it, nudges close, suddenly flips it over. A skiff of drifting sand, it is certainly upside down now but still motionless: long before this dreadful sudden inversion it must have already been protecting its central mouth like that with itself; probably had done so forever in enduring, hopeless anticipation of this one possible act by a merciless Canadian. It will not move. He stares level over the vacant sea, avoids every faint variety of shore or wave and concentrates on what seems to be the empty line of water and sky. Count slowly. After the third quick glance down he knows that the top left arm is beginning to curl under; at the tenth he sees a tiny ripple of water help bend the second arm. In eleven minutes the starfish has almost folded under three, and then a sea surge opens it upright, over, flat. But once is not enough. Twice.

11.   He lay on a hotel bed in Husum, the Schleswig-Holstein town where Theodor Storm wrote *Der Schimmelreiter*, and he was reading the novel in the new edition which included pictures of the movie. When she came through the connecting door and sat on his bed, she barely nodded at the stupendous grey horse he offered her rearing above a dike ripping through in vicious rain.

"You know I don't like horses," she said; she had not yet cut her hair short for travel.

But his mind was lost in Storm's sonorous language and the great farmsteads on their diked islands they had seen coming like ships from the midst of the sea. And the implacable North Sea wind still roared in his ears so it was some time before he comprehended that they were talking about something quite different from their words.

"What?" he said, suddenly apprehensive.

"We shouldn't have come here, now" she was repeating herself, directly. "We should have gone north first, to Denmark, Esberg, and then all the way down the coast through here right to the Ijssel Meer. We should have seen it all. If only the sea can make land then we should see it all, start in the north and drive along every dike and *watte* and polder right to where our ancestors started."

"We'll get to Harlingen," he said quickly. "I promise."

"I'm sorry," she said then.

"For what?"

And that too was like so many questions he had asked her: never answered. If he found that pale young man again on the *watte*, they would be hunched there together, her fingers accepting the smear of mud he offered, they might have been holding hands. "Within a century," he would be saying, "we'll grow wheat here where there was only the sea. This land will be unbelievably fertile."

And it seems she is holding some specks of mollusks or bone in her hand, is rolling white specks ground roundly into powder between her slim fingers, the wind whipping her hair, long again, across her face.

"That's easiest to do," he says, "to try to build it straight. But the sea is always bending everything, of course."

And she is laughing with him.

12.   He is standing on the reef in the sea. When he bends his head the tip of his chin, his nose, are touched

by it; the columns of his body, legs, feet are there as precise as cut crystal bent among coral, gesturing fronds, creatures perhaps moving though seeming still as sand, a multiplicity of world so brilliant he cannot recognize any of it, though his eyes are open. The sea will reveal everything, of course. He simply must know at what moment to look into it.

Contributors

David Arnason is a professor of literature at the University of Manitoba. His books include *If Pigs Could Fly*, *The Dragon and the Dry Goods Princess* (winner of the Manitoba Booksellers Choice Award), *The Pagan Wall*, *The Happiest Man in the World*, and *The Circus Performers Bar*. He is also co-editor of *The New Icelanders: A North American Community*.

Pamela Banting writes poetry, short fiction, and criticism, and is a member of the editorial advisory board of House of Anansi Press. She is co-author, with Kristjana Gunnars, of *The Papers of Dorothy Livesay: A Research Tool* (1986), and has just published *Body Inc.: A Theory of Translation Poetics* (1995). She teaches in the English Department at the University of Alberta in Edmonton.

Ven Begamudré's work first appeared in Coteau's 1982 anthology *Saskatchewan Gold*. His books include *A Planet of Eccentrics* and *Van de Graaff Days*. He has been writer-in-residence in the University of Calgary's Markin-Flanagan Distinguished Writers Programme and is now the Canada-Scotland Exchange Writer-in-Residence.

David Bergen has been published four times in the *Journey Prize Anthology*. His collection of short stories, *Sitting Opposite My Brother*, was nominated for Manitoba Book of the Year in 1993. A novel, *A Year of Lesser*, will be published by HarperCollins in March of 1996.

Sandra Birdsell is an award-winning author who has published two books of short stories, two novels, radio and film drama. Her short stories have appeared in major national and international anthologies. *The Missing Child* was awarded the SmithBooks/Books in Canada First Novel Award and her most recent novel, *The Chrome Suite*, received the McNally Robinson Book of the Year Award and was nominated for the Governor General's Award in 1992.

Bonnie Bishop is a free-lance writer living in Edmonton, Alberta. Her poetry and prose has appeared in more than thirty-five periodicals, including the *Malahat Review, Grain, Event, Prairie Fire,* and *Dandelion.* Her poetry collection, *Elaborate Beasts*, appeared in 1988. She is currently working on a collection of short stories.

Sharon Butala's most recent book is *Coyote's Morning Cry.* She is the author of five novels, two short story collections and two non-fiction books and is currently working on a novel called *The Garden of Eden.* She lives on a ranch near Eastend, Saskatchewan.

Warren Cariou was raised on a farm near Meadow Lake, Saskatchewan, and he still returns there every summer. He is now a Ph.D. student in English at the University of Toronto, writing a thesis on William Blake.

David Carpenter has written three books of fiction, a collection of essays (*Writing Home*), and an anglers' guide entitled *Fishing in the West.* He writes and fishes out of Saskatoon.

Méira Cook was born in Johannesburg, South Africa, and now lives and writes in Winnipeg. Her first book of poetry, *A Fine Grammar of Bones*, was published by Turnstone Press, and a chapbook, *The Ruby Garrote*, was produced by disOrientations press. She is a poetry editor for *Prairie Fire* magazine.

Hiromi Goto was born in Chiba-ken, Japan, but immigrated to Canada with her family in 1969. She grew up in British Columbia and southern Alberta. She is on the editorial collective of *absinthe* literary magazine. Her first novel, *Chorus of Mushrooms,* was published in NeWest

Press' Nunatak fiction series and was the regional winner of the Canada/Caribbean region of the Best First Book Award for the 1995 Commonwealth Writers Prize. She lives in Calgary.

Linda Holeman lives in Winnipeg and writes for children, young adults, and adults. Her stories have appeared in many journals and anthologies; *Saying Good-bye* is her recent YA collection. Forthcoming in 1996 is *Flying Yellow*, an adult collection from Turnstone Press.

Sadru Jetha was born in Zanzibar, attended Dublin University in Ireland, practiced law in the Kilimanjaro area of Tanzania, taught law in Essex, the United Kingdom, then immigrated to Canada, where he writes and does conciliation and arbitration work in the Ismaili community. He has previously published stories in *Vox, Blue Buffalo, Rungh,* and *CBC Anthology*

Kathie Kolybaba has recently completed her first collection of short fiction, *Private Conversations*, from which "The Dangers of B and E" is taken. She is working on a second collection of stories and a novel. She lives in Winnipeg with her three children.

Shelley A. Leedahl writes for a variety of literary and commercial markets. She frequently reads in Saskatchewan schools, and is the author of *Sky Kickers* and *A Few Words For January*. Shelley lives in Saskatoon with Troy and their two pre-teens.

Cliff Lobe was raised on a farm in Saskatchewan, and for some time made his living driving a semi. He has published short stories in *Grain* and *Boundless Alberta* and currently lives in Edmonton, where he is working on a Ph.D. in English at the University of Alberta in Edmonton.

CONTRIBUTORS

Jake MacDonald has written for all the usual periodicals. He keeps an apartment in Winnipeg and a floating house in Minaki, Ontario. Swim across the river and see him sometime.

Dave Margoshes is a fictionalist and poet living in Regina. His most recent book, *Nine Lives*, is a collection of short stories. Other books include *Small Regrets* (stories), and *Walking at Brighton* and *Northwest Passage* (poetry).

Allison Muri writes essays and short works of fiction. Her novella *The Hystery of the Broker Fether* is forthcoming in 1996. She is presently working on a second novella and a collection of short stories.

Sheldon Oberman, teacher, film maker, playwright, and storyteller has written eight books, as well as songs with Fred Penner. He turned his award-winning children's book, *The Always Prayer Shawl,* into a family play at the MTC Warehouse. His adult work, *This Business with Elijah,* is a collection of interrelated stories set in Winnipeg's North End.

J. Jill Robinson has written three short story collections, the most recent of which is *Eggplant Wife*. Her work has appeared in many Canadian literary journals, and has won *Event*'s non-fiction contest, *Prism International*'s fiction contest, and the Alberta Writers Guild Award for short fiction. She is the editor of *Grain* magazine.

Norm Sacuta's poetry and short stories have appeared in *Edmonton* and *Calgary* magazines, *Grain, Boundless Alberta, Matrix, NeWest Review,* and *Dandelion.* In 1989, *Ismay,* his full-length play about the man who built the *Titanic,* won the Alberta Culture Playwriting Competition, Discovery Category. He is currently pursuing a D. Phil in American Literature and Sexual Dissidence at the University of Sussex in England.

Barbara Scott has worked as a jug hustler on a seismic crew, a singer in a small-town in Alberta, and a teacher. She has published in *Prairie Fire* and *Open Letter*, and she is completing her first collection of short stories. She currently teaches English at the Alberta College of Art in Calgary.

Birk Sproxton teaches Canadian literature and creative writing at Red Deer College. His books include *Headframe, The Hockey Fan Came Riding,* and *Trace: Prairie Writers on Writing*. He is a contributing editor to *NeWest Review*.

Fred Stenson's fiction titles include *Working Without a Laugh Track, Last One Home, Lonesome Hero,* and *Teeth*. His short fiction has appeared in national magazines and literary quarterlies across Canada, and he has written over ninety films and videos. As well, he has edited two anthologies of Alberta writing: *Alberta Bound* and *The Road Home: New Stories by Alberta Writers*.

Sheila Stevenson is a member of Pasqua First Nation, of Touchwood File Hills Treaty Four area. In the visual arts, she recently has been part of a group show, "Indian Humour," at Neutral Ground artist-run gallery. She is a member of Woknegesa, a community writing group. A freelance journalist, this is her first publication of fiction.

Wayne Tefs is a Woodrow Wilson Fellow. His books include the novels *Figures on a Wharf, The Cartier Street Contract, The Canasta Players* and *Dickie*. He has edited two anthologies, *Made in Manitoba* and *Hearts Wild*. Wayne writes the fiction column in *Border Crossings* magazine and lives in Winnipeg.

Geoffrey Ursell is an award-winning editor and writer of fiction, drama, poetry, and songs. A founding member of Coteau Books, he continues to serve on the Board and has recently joined the staff as Publisher.

CONTRIBUTORS

Aritha Van Herk has edited a number of anthologies, including *Boundless Alberta, Alberta Rebound*. She is the author of *Judith, The Tent Peg, No Fixed Address, Places Far From Ellesmere, In Visible Ink,* and *A Frozen Tongue*. She lives and writes in Calgary.

Meeka Walsh is a short story writer and critic, who has published fiction and essays in *Descant, The Malahat Review, Canadian Fiction Magazine,* and *Prairie Fire*. She has been nominated for and received gold awards at the Western and National Magazine Awards for her critical writing. Her book of short fiction will be published in the fall of 1996 by The Porcupine's Quill. She lives in Winnipeg and is the editor of the arts magazine *Border Crossings*.

Dianne Warren is a Regina fiction writer and playwright. Her most recent short fiction collection is *Bad Luck Dog* (Coteau Books), which won the 1993 Saskatchewan Book of the Year Award. She is currently working on a new play (*The Last Journey of Captain Harte*) and a new short story collection.

Armin Wiebe, no relation to that Alberta Wiebe, is the author of three comic novels, *The Salvation of Yasch Siemens, Murder in Gutenthal: A Schneppa Kjnals Mystery,* and *The Second Coming of Yeeat Shpanst*. Living and writing in Winnipeg, Armin tries to expand the lexicon of the Canadian language and believes that if Canadians don't wake up and smell each other's stories our country could easily febeizel itself.

Rudy Wiebe is the author of three short story collections and eight novels. He has twice won the Governor General's Award for fiction, in 1973 for *The Temptations of Big Bear*, and in 1994 for *A Discovery of Strangers*. His latest book is called *River of Stone*. Since 1992 he writes full-time.

Acknowledgements

Some stories in *Due West* have been previously published or broadcast. Bonnie Bishop's "Bottom" was first published in *Event,* and was also by invitation translated in Polish and published in *High Park.* Sharon Butala's "Act of Love" was published in *Story Magazine.* Warren Cariou's "Puerto Escondido" was published in *The Malahat Review.* Shelley Leedahl's "Hollywood Legs" was previously published in *The Fiddlehead.* Dave Margoshes's "A Book of Great Worth" was published in the *Windsor Review.* Barbara Scott's "Minor Alterations" won first prize in the 1995 *Dandelion* Short Story Competition. Birk Sproxton's "The Organized Woman Story" was a winner in the 1995 *Dandelion* Short Story Competition. Dianne Warren's "Long Gone and Mister Lonely" was previously published in *Grain.* Rudy Wiebe's "The Shells of the Ocean" first appeared in *The Malahat Review.*